Legend of the Whispering Wind

By
W. Lee Jones

airleaf.com

© Copyright 2006, W. Lee Jones

All Rights Reserved.

No part of this book may be reproduced, stored in a retrieval system, or transmitted by any means, electronic, mechanical, photocopying, recording, or otherwise, without written permission from the author.

ISBN: 1-60002-061-5

Dedication

My book, "Legend of the Whispering Wind" is dedicated to Dewey F. Jones, my patient and loving husband, who is part Cherokee Indian.

Acknowledgements

A special thank you to my friend and critic, Jean Short, thanks to Barbara Russell and Theo Wellington for their assistance and thanks for the patience, understanding, and encouragement of my family.

This novel is an entire work of fiction; however, there are some authentic names and places. Historical figures in situations are also fictional.

Resource

- Visitation to Cherokee, North Carolina.

- "Myths of the Cherokee and Sacred Formulas of the Cherokee" by James Mooney

- Study of Sam Hall, East Tennessee famous Cherokee hunter, of whom my husband is a direct descendent.

- Additional Cherokee lore and history

Historical Background of the Cherokee
In
Myths of the Cherokee and Sacred Formulas of the Cherokee
by
James Mooney

The Cherokee were the mountaineers of the South, holding the entire Allegheny region from the interlocking head-streams of the Kanawha and Tennessee Southward almost to the site of Atlanta, and from the Blue ridge on the east to the Cumberland range on the west, a territory comprising an area of 40,000 square miles, now including the states of Virginia, Tennessee, North Carolina, South Carolina, Georgia, and Alabama.

Chapter 1

Two Cherokee braves watched from a distant hill as John Brandon, Indian Consultant, put the finishing touches on his stockade fence which surrounded his newly constructed two story log home.

"Another fence to keep the savages and another pale eyes sent here by the big white chief to tame these savages. Ai-eee!" Wild Hawk spat as his black eyes sparked his angry cynicism.

"My Brother, all Cherokee feel this," Spotted Horse, his good friend replied, "but your anger is always fierce. How can we follow our Chief's wishes if we don't learn the white man?"

Wild Hawk scoffed, "No one ever learns a forked-tongued White eyes!" He strode toward his black stallion that whinnied a welcome, and in one lithe movement placed his tall, well-muscled frame astride Night Wind as he yelled to his brother. "Spotted Horse, see if that nag you sit on has ever learned to run - race you to the Big Sink!" Anger depleted, laughter and thundering hooves echoed the wildness of the East Tennessee hills.

John Brandon stepped back to observe his handiwork, breathe in the fresh pine scented air, and cast appreciative eyes on the mountainous beauty surrounding his new home, thinking, "God musta' smiled when he completed this spot. And God musta' had a good reason in this spring of 1828 to uproot me and my family from Boston, Massachusetts and move us to the wilds of Tennessee for a job I'm not at all sure I can handle." Shaking his head, he sighs. "Mary, get out here and view your husband's accomplishment."

As his wife descended the porch steps, John's smile told her she was still the most beautiful woman in the world to him. Her auburn hair was sparingly threaded with gray, and her slender figure rivaled that of a younger woman. "Oh, John!" she exclaimed, "you've done a wonderful job with the fence - I'm very fortunate to have a man with so many talents." She smiled up at him.

"I've told you that for years," he chuckled while patting her back end.

"Stop that!" Swatting at his hand, Mary continued, "What if the children are watching?"

"Let them - don't you think they have some idea of how they got here?" He smiled wickedly, his green eyes twinkling.

"John Brandon, such talk!" she scolded, while determined to shift the subject, she inspected his building project. "I do hope Priscilla is more comfortable with this fenced area - she's having such difficulty adjusting to our move here from Boston."

"Humpf! Our spoiled Priscilla has difficulty with everything, especially with Priscilla," John retorted as he eased his weary frame into a nearby chair and stared into the distance. "I know this Tennessee wilderness won't be easy for any of you, Mary." He emptied his pipe, gouging the last tobacco particles with his knife. "I realize how limited any social activity will be, but I was selected by the Washington Council on Indian Affairs as Consultant between the Cherokee and whites for this area," he said as he continued to look out to the hills. "It is a serious responsibility to try and close the gap between the two that has gradually widened. Hell, I didn't want this appointment -Mary, you know that - but I'm obligated and I'll do my best, which may not be good enough." He stood and began pacing back and forth. "I just found out yesterday during the meeting at Fort Hamilton that my greatest opponent in working this out is one young Cherokee brave, Wild

Hawk, who apparently lives up to his name, is next in line to become Chief of the Wolf Clan. He trusts no whites." He looked again to the mountain peaks. "Seems this hostility stems from his witnessing whites killing his father and raping and killing his mother when he was a young boy."

Taking his arm, Mary struggled, "My goodness, John - I had no idea of the extent and danger of this job. You will be careful, Dear?" She placed her head against his arm as he reached over to kiss her forehead.

"Almost forgot to tell you and the children about an upcoming event," John said, smiling broadly as he prodded his wife. "Call your brood, woman. Don't want to repeat myself four or five times."

Shortly after Mary left to do his bidding, the afternoon's serenity was shattered by a piercing soprano. "Jess-i-ca! Tim-o-thy!"

"Coming, Mama!"

"Me too Mama!" two distant voices quickly reported. John smiled, shaking his head. "That's my wife - a sweet, demure, ladylike warhorse!" he chuckled.

Priscilla and Katherine Brandon, two young ladies in their late teens emerged from the house. Priscilla, a petulant beauty, snapped at her sister, "Kate, you've already stepped on my dress hem once - now, watch out!" She swished her red and white full skirted gingham and fluffed her dark wavy hair as it cascaded to her waist, her dark eyes flashing. "Oh! Papa, you've finished the fence - thank goodness! Maybe that will help keep out the savages," she shuddered as her father glared. "Uh, I mean Indians out - I mean, from becoming too friendly!" She smiled at her dad.

Katherine, not considered a striking beauty, revealed an inner strength, her own attractiveness, accentuated by dark thick fringed green eyes, framed with a mass of long auburn hair. "Prissy, you are utterly ridiculous - and Papa, I know you didn't call us out here to view your handiwork, even though you did a good job," Kate responded, inspecting the fence.

He smiled, hugging them both. "My lovely ladies, you're right - I sent for you, but we'll wait until we're all—"

"Papa!" Jessica, a pretty ten year old minx, exploded around the house, mud spattered dress and face sailing into view. "Papa, Mama said you had a surprise."

"Ahhh, Jesse, you smell like manure - you reek. You're absolutely repulsive!" Prissy moaned as she moved away holding her nose.

Jessica glared daggers at her older sister while retorting, "I do not smell like shit. I ain't been near the barn - only been down by the creek, gettin frogs."

Mary, catching herself after practically swooning, jerked Jesse up by the arm, dragged her to the porch, yelling, "Jessica Ruth, you march yourself inside where I'll tend to you—of all the unladylike—to think a daughter of mine—" *Whack, whack!*

"But, Mama," Jessica wailed, "Rusty Poole says it - n' so does Timmy," *whack.* "I'm sorry, Mama," Jessica sobbed.

Everyone else laughed except Priscilla who glared as Timothy, a chubby, freckle faced eleven year old trotted up, mud spattered and breathless. "Papa, did you want me?"

Tousling his hair, John replied, "Yes, I do have a surprise, everybody sit somewhere." Timmy flopped at his dad's feet on the ground, the others sat. "Mary, we're waiting on you and Jesse," he called.

"Coming." Mary emerged as though nothing had happened, while she firmly escorted red faced, teary eyed Jesse to a stool.

John continued, "I hope you will be pleased. Yesterday, while I was in a meeting at the fort, it was decided we need a festival day held there, one which includes both Indian and white, where we can some way encourage a better understanding between the two. There'll be games and races for all ages, horse racing, skill and strength contests, trading of supplies, stitching displays, knick knacks and plenty of food for all. There'll be roasted pig, beef, venison with additional dishes furnished by the ladies. Should be fun and activities for everyone - if the Cherokee respond. What do you think of the idea?"

"Oh! Boy!" Jesse yelled, completely forgetting her emotional trauma as she jumped up and clapped her hands.

Timmy, flexing his chubby arm for a would-be muscle, asked, "When, Papa, when do we go? I can hardly wait!"

"Will the soldiers, ah, participate in everything too, Papa?" smiled Priscilla.

"Wait a minute - one at a time," interjected John. "If plans go accordingly this will be held in five days - yes, the soldiers will participate."

"Oooh! How exciting." Priscilla dimpled with the thought of meeting a dashing lieutenant.

"Mary and Kate - haven't heard a response from you," John prodded.

"Sounds like a fine idea, and I do believe it will encourage a better relationship. I'd like to know something other than what I've read about the Indians," Kate responded.

"Yes, that's my sentiments exactly, "Mary added. "I also thought I would take my damson preserves, my double wedding ring quilt to display - oh! and plenty of fried berry pies—don't you think, John?"

He smiled lovingly at this woman who was his life - wondering if she had thought for a minute about the reason behind this gathering.

Chapter 2

Chief Lone Eagle's village was nestled between two mountain peaks in a fertile valley surrounded on the east side by the wide Caney Fork Creek, on the west by the mountain peak. Many oak, maple, cedar, elms and spruce trees stood as towering sentinels, dispelling heat in the summertime and protection from icy winter winds. The tranquillity and beauty here encouraged strong communication with "The Great Spirit," Yawa.

Lone Eagle, a tall, erect still handsome Indian male, even though gray touched his long hair, stood in front of the council lodge, a lengthy log structure with a dome roof, as buckskin clad Rusty Poole, an old leathery skinned Army scout and longtime friend of the Cherokee, rode slowly through the village, amid barking dogs and laughing children who playfully accompanied him.

"Welcome, my friend, and what brings such an important Army scout to our humble village?" Eagle smiled, saluting Rusty.

"Ha! You can cut that old stuff with me, Chief - you know I ain't important. But I am your friend," Rusty replied, dismounting. They both laughed as he dispensed the horse's reins to the welcoming hands of a smiling lad. "Little Acorn - brush him down, will you son," Rusty said, patting the lad's shoulder. Little Acorn nodded. Rusty sighed, drinking in the beauty and peacefulness of this setting, wishing as he always did that he could remain here for a spell. "Now, Chief, I might have some news that your council will want to hear. Could you gather 'em in for a short spell?"

"Little Acorn, have Young Calf summon the council, quickly, "the Chief demanded, "and what has my friend, Rusty Poole been up to for the past month?" Chief inquired as they entered the lodge.

"Nuthin' much 'cept gittin' sores on ma' back side. If'n I don't git in to some scountin' soon I'll be lazier than one of them ole hound dogs out thar!" Rusty cackled as council members began to arrive and he shared greetings with them.

After several Cherokee of various ages arrived and found designated seats, Lone Eagle strolled to the center of the group and began. "Council members, you all know Rusty Poole, my long time friend and Army scout at Fort Hamilton, "most nodded in agreement, although Wild Hawk sat stoically. "I don't know the meaning of his message, but he thinks it is important." He twitched a smile at the scout. "Please listen until he explains, then there will be discussion." He sat down as Poole stood up, throwing a plug of tobacco into his mouth as he began.

"Now, you know I ain't much for speakin so I'll just get on with it. Couple of days ago there was a meetin held at the Fort run by the new consultant John Brandon," the Indians eyed each other, "Hit wuz thought out then that we 'orta all have sorta of a get-together, a gathering where we kin all git together an' know somethin' about each other. They want to have games, contests, horse racing, running races, wrestling of all kinds - knife throwing - jest 'bout everything you kin think on. Good vittles - roasted pigs, beef 'n other dishes women might bring - also there will be tradin' - this bein' five <u>moons</u> away, and all you 'ins is invited. Guess thet's about all I know." He sat down and let Lone Eagle take over.

"Discussion is now to begin. What are your feelings on this?"

Swift Antelope stood, a rather handsome muscular brave, and after acknowledging Lone Eagle, spoke, "Swift Antelope wish to wrestle and race against Pale Eyes, he wish to <u>beat</u> them." He sat as many nodded and uttered agreement.

Wild Hawk stood, his deep voice resounding in the building as after acknowledgment he spoke to Rusty, "Old Man, what is the <u>real</u> reason behind this festival or gathering day?"

"So's the Indian 'n the white git a better understanding of each other, so's hit'll help 'em to to git along, "Rusty stated, shifting his cud to the other jaw while gazing steadily at the young brave.

Wild Hawk begrudgingly respected this old scout even though he was white, however he continued, "The Cherokee already have much understanding of the white man, too much."

Rusty, dander ruffled, was determined not to let this young coyote's deep seated anger get the better of him and destroy something that could be of great importance to both Cherokee and white. He strode to the door and spit a gob of tobacco juice into the opening before responding, "Well, I kin understand yore feelin, Wild Hawk, knowin' some bad happenin's back when, but they's good 'n bad in all races 'n they's things to be lurnt both ways. Course, if'n you're scart to be tanglin with them white boys in them matches 'n' games, well, I shore understand that, too." Rusty smiled, knowing that he had hit his mark as Wild Hawk jerked his head up with nostrils flaring and black eyes flashing while his fellow Cherokee laughed, poking and teasing, "Wild Hawk, you scart of them whites eyes?"

"Wild Hawk fears <u>no</u> man!" he thundered, "but he does not wish to be a part of white's trying to change the Cherokee way of life."

"Nobody's trying to do that, son. Give John Brandon a chance. He's a good man - let him try to help both Cherokee and white - he shore don't want to do you no harm." Rusty's honesty swayed the group as one by one voiced his opinion to participate in the outing (at the gathering). Even Wild Hawk finally relented as he anticipated physical contests against the white soldiers.

Chief Eagle stood regally and announced, "Let it be known to John Brandon and members at the Fort that Lone Eagle's Cherokee will participate in games and contests at the gathering. We will also bring trade items and food dishes. Lone Eagle has spoken." He waved dismissal. "Our meeting is ended. Please pass word to all about gathering at Fort in five moons. Rusty Poole, remain here and share food and pipe with Lone Eagle. Much we talk about, m'friend." Rusty clapped Lone Eagle's shoulder, nodding his acceptance while spitting a stream of tobacco juice into the air.

Chapter 3

The big day dawned with excitement permeating the very air at the Brandon's home. All animals fed, cows milked, chores completed, breakfast dishes put away. Mary gathered pies, canned foods, cakes and quilts for the Fort gathering. The girls were busily primping and donning their best sprigged cotton dresses with matching bonnets. They waited impatiently for Papa and Timmy to finish harnessing Toby and Zeke, their faithful horses, to the spring wagon.

"All right, girls, we're ready," John placed food, quilts and trade items and assisted the girls and Mary to their seats. He smiled, "My, what beautiful ladies I'm blessed with!"

Timmy crawled over the back gate while Jessica pealed with laughter. "Oh, Papa, you know I'm no lady!" She smoothed her blue skirt and adjusted her most uncomfortable bonnet, wishing she could wear pants and a cap like Timmy.

The peacefulness, the beauty of the early morning hour worked its magic as mists loosed its fingers revealing the distant blue mountains. The music of a rushing mountain stream and the low dance of evergreens, oaks and maples seemed to accompany the wind as it worked its contentment in whispering God's glory.

The serenity of the trip was suddenly broken as Timmy yelled, "There it is! I see the fort - gee, it's _so_ big"

Jesse, flinging her bonnet aside, squealed her excitement, "Oh! Boy!"

Mouths gaped open as they viewed the high stockade fence surrounding several large log structures which framed an inner parade ground where several soldiers, women, children and Indians of all ages milled around. Others were setting up tables for trade items.

Prissy, while rearranging dark curls around her pink bonnet for the third time and pinching her cheeks, viewed several Indians outside the gate and exclaimed, "What kind of ridiculous garb do those Indians have on?"

As John approached the opened gates, he reprimanded his daughter, "Priscilla, that is not a ridiculous garb to the Cherokee and young lady, you are not to look down your nose at anyone today, do you hear?"

After passing through the gates Prissy, too busy checking out the blue uniforms to hear her father, poked her sister, twinkling a smile. "Kate, did you ever see so-o-o many handsome soldiers? This is simply going to be the most exciting day ever!" she whispered.

Kate smiled and nodded as John halted the team. Soldiers quickly approached the wagon. One tall lieutenant stepped forward, doffing his hat revealing wavy sandy hair and infectiously smiling as his hazel eyes fastened on Prissy as he made introductions. "Mr. Brandon, I'm Lieutenant Keith Anderson." As he shook hands with John, he continued, "This is Lieutenant Tom Cason and Sargent Mathias." The others also stepped up to shake hands. "Could we be of assistance, taking your horses and accompanying the ladies?" He smiled charmingly at Prissy as she preened.

John nodded, "This is my family - my wife Mary, daughters Katherine, Priscilla, Jessica and our son Tim. I'll be obliged if you'd see to the horses and wagon, but I'll escort the family. Thank you, Lieutenant." While John assisted Mary down, Lt. Anderson didn't miss the opportunity to hold the lovely beauty's waist while gentlemanly assisting her down as she fluttered her dark sparkling eyes. Tom Cason offered a hand to Kate as she descended, thinking that he had never seen a woman with such eyes. He smiled as his blue eyes stared, fascinated by her dark fringed expressive green ones.

Kate murmured, "Thank you, Lieutenant."

"Lieutenant Anderson, please see that the food items are taken to the proper place. Each dish is marked and please see that my best double wedding ring quilt is handled with utmost care—I wouldn't have anything happen to that," Mary firmly requested.

"Yes, Ma'm, I certainly will take care of everything. His eyes found Prissy before he turned away smiling, thinking fate was certainly smiling upon him, sending such a beauty his way.

Individuals were caught up in the festive atmosphere, strolling about while savoring the aroma of roasted pork and beef. Children happily laughed and played while adults visited and inspected the many table displays of furs, cured meats, tanned leather, jewelry, baked goods, sewing, quilts, wooden crafts and farm items.

John introduced his family to Col. Roberts and his wife. Beatrice Roberts smiled sweetly revealing a genuine kindness. Her lovely complexion indicated youthfulness until one glimpsed her plump matronly figure. "So nice to meet all of you," she said as she took Mary's arm, "I've been wanting to meet you ever since you arrived, Mary, but felt you were too busy settling in for company. There are several ladies here at the fort that I'll introduce you to today and we certainly must plan another lady get together before you leave."

"I'd like that," Mary smiled, "Of course, today is a treat for our entire family, but I'll look forward to the lady gathering."

Rusty Poole stepped to a platform at the north end of the parade ground evoking a loud whistle designating silence. "Welcome everybody to this here first fine gathering of Cherokee, soldiers, settlers, and our new consultant John Brandon - now, if you'll all find seats which are set up all around the parade area we'll begin." A drum roll sounded as individuals complied, sitting on designated benches.

Before Rusty could continue with introductions, thundering hooves drowned out his speech as several horses entered the gate, skidding to a halt in a cloud of dust. These young Indian braves, in festive regalia, were accompanied by their Chief Lone Eagle who slipped to the ground, in all his splendor of eagle feather intertwined into a plume which emerged from a turquoise turban, swinging a magnificent fur piece to his shoulder. His butter colored knee length doe skin garment was interspersed with rows of turquoise, red and purple beading, with the same design on his breech clout. Doe skin pants were wrapped with knee leggings of the same beading with matching moccasins. He followed regally as a soldier brought him to John Brandon, who stood as though meeting a king. The entire group of people were awestruck by the striking figure in its fine parafinalia. He and John shook hands, as the chief took his seat next to the consultant.

Eyes shifted to the entrance again where one young brave, clad in snug white fur trimmed doe skin britches with matching breech clout, vest and moccasins, hair flowing past his shoulders, powerfully controlled his prancing black stallion as his friends slipped to the ground in amusement. After touching the toe of his right foot to the horse's flank and whispering, the animal reared, pawing the air then walked three or four steps on its' hind legs. Wild Hawk then slipped to the ground, petting his stallion's neck, crooning to him in Cherokee. This beautiful animal then placed its head on Hawk's shoulder and nuzzled his face.

Jesse jumped up, applauding loudly and yelling, "I don't know who you are, but you and your horse are wonderful!" The crowd laughed and joined in the applause. Wild Hawk acknowledged the young lady with a slight nod and smiled.

Prissy hissed, "Who is that half-clothed Indian and why is he making such a spectacle of himself - it's disgusting!"

"That's Wild Hawk," John admiringly smiled.

"I don't know what he was trying to do, but he was certainly doing it well," Kate added, heedless of the questioning look her mother bestowed on her. She was too caught up in admiring Wild Hawk's tall muscular frame, his handsome visage as her eyes traveled to his unclothed chest, she suddenly admonished herself, What am I doing? He is a heathen, a savage. I don't care what he does and I certainly won't pay any attention to him, for apparently that's what he wants. The idea! She turned, facing the opposite direction where several soldiers were gathered. One in particular seemed to be quite upset. Keith Anderson, revealing anger at the Indian's performance, snarled, "What the hell does that red skin think he's doing - guess he's trying to show off for the white gals."

"Anderson," another officer spoke up, "come off it - he hasn't done any harm. I rather enjoyed his horsemanship."

"I'll get a chance at him in some match - I don't like show-offs, especially savage ones" Anderson replied, still bristling.

The horses were led away by proud Indian youths as the braves sat near the entrance, laughing and talking. Wild Hawk saluted Rusty Poole.

Rusty continued, "Well, Wild Hawk, that there was quite a entertaining beginning for this here first gathering," he chuckled. "Now, before we begin the foot races that will be held this morning, there are a few people who wish to say a word or two. First, Colonel Roberts who runs this place."

Colonel Roberts, slightly rotund and middle aged, welcomed all visitors, participants and spectators. His brief speech was followed by John Brandon's introduction, along with his family. He also spoke briefly, as Indians of varying ages, older warriors, squaws, maidens and young children moved in closer to the parade ground awaiting the races. Brandon spoke to both Indian and White of their responsibilities to each other and his commitment to both. Finally, Chief Lone Eagle was presented. He eloquently responded to Brandon's statements, before returning to sit with his Cherokee tribe.

Finally, the time arrived for the races to begin - rules and regulations were explained.

Mary realized that Jessica and Timmy were missing. "Where are Timmy and Jessica? I thought surely they would want to see the races." She looked around, searching the crowd.

"I'm sure they will, Dear. Relax - they're probably with some other children," John assured her.

"I saw them talking with a couple of children a few minutes age," Kate added.

Rusty began, "Now listen up everybody - the first race will have young'uns ages 9-11 running around the entire parade ground. There be 10 young Cherokee and white lads running in this race. Now git in here and cheer 'em on everybody! Line up, young'uns. I'll say on yore mark, git set, ready - then I'll fire into the air." He said it, fired, and they were off among cheers, trilling Indians and a waving crowd. Little Acorn, a Cherokee, was in the lead until they rounded the bend and began the last half of the race home when a young lad wearing a cap picked up speed and overtook the Indian. He continued in the lead, but shortly before he crossed the finish line as the winner, his cap flew from his head, and lo and behold he was not a he but a she as her long wavy hair tumbled down her back.

"Oh! John - oh my goodness - that's Jessica!" Mary screamed, feeling faint.

"Yes!" he yelled, "and by damn she's winning, yi-pee!" he shouted, shaking his fist in the air.

"John, how could you - that's the most unladylike - and now you're laughing, using curse words, and shouting," Mary moaned.

"Oh! Mary," he sat down, consoling her as he pulled her to him continuing smiling happily.

Not only did John Brandon admire his daughter - the Cherokee, especially the chief and young braves admired the young white girl who defied everyone, ran a race against the fastest young Cherokee and white and beat them all. They had never heard of a girl who could win a race against a boy.

The next foot race, run between ages 13-16 was easily won by a fifteen year old brave, Black Bear. The Indians whooped, cheered and trilled.

Races continued while only one young white man outshone the Indians as a winner.

Mary put a damper on Jesse's day with strong reprimanding of her most unladylike behavior and demanded that she sit by her side.

A soldier clanked the dinner bell as Rusty bellowed an invitation for all to line up and get their plates.

Lt. Anderson and Lt. Cason appeared shortly thereafter with plates of food for Priscilla and Katherine. "Mrs. Brandon, with your permission, Lt. Cason and I would like to share the dinner with your daughters." Lt. Anderson smiled charmingly as Prissy fluttered and dimpled.

While Mary hesitated to respond, John arrived with their food. "It's all right, Mary—have seats, Lieutenants."

Katherine smiled, rather embarrassed as Lt. Cason stumbled to the bench and fumbled with his plate. Both found it hard to make conversation, but nothing hindered Prissy, who pealed forth laughter at something Lt. Anderson whispered.

As lunch was completed, the tall Indian Wild Hawk suddenly appeared, standing in front of John, black hair and white fringe swirling around him. "Mr. Brandon, I am Wild Hawk."

"Yes, I recognize you, Wild Hawk." John offered his hand - Wild Hawk hesitated, then shook the hand.

Lt. Anderson stiffened, Prissy glared, and Kate stared as Jesse boomed forth, "Oh! Wild Hawk you are plum purty! but you're almost nekked!" She covered her mouth and snickered.

"Jess-i-ca!" Her mother scolded.

"I'm sorry, but he is purty, ain't he, Kate?" Kate continued to stare, as Wild Hawk shifted his gaze from Kate to Prissy then back to Kate as she held him with sea green eyes as deep as the ocean. His mouth twitched to keep from smiling as Mary again scolded and grabbed Jesse's arm.

"Mr. Brandon, I would ask a permission for our chief to escort your youngest daughter, who raced well, to meet Chief Lone Eagle. He would like very much to talk with the girl who runs better than our fastest boys. The Cherokee young would also like to know this girl." The impressive brave held the father's gaze.

John, impressed, responded to the mannerly request in agreement. "It is an honor for us - for Jessica if she wishes this," he turned to Jesse smiling, as she nodded vigorously smiling, "just bring her back before the afternoon matches begin."

"Oh! Thank you, Papa!" Jesse hugged him then scrambled down as Wild Hawk offered his hand and she accepted it. Before turning he again found green eyes, then nodded to John. "I shall return her safely." Jesse continued to hold Hawk's hand as she marched off, trying to match his stride, looking at her handsome new friend whose long black hair and white fringe swayed as he moved. He smiled down at her with the whitest teeth she had ever seen. "You can call me Jesse - my friends do, and you are my friend." Jesse smiled up at him and he thought what a delightful young girl this is, with no hate in her heart for the Indian, and with a strong winner's heart. He then wondered what type of person her green eyed sister was, but what did he care - she meant nothing to him and she had a heart filled with hate like all the others - he was sure.

"Wild Hawk." Dancing Eyes, a beautiful shapely Indian maiden adorned in a cream colored doe skin shift, matching moccasins with multicolored beading fell into step with them with forced laughter and speaking in Cherokee, "are you picking them young these days?" She eyed Jesse solemnly.

"Don't be ridiculous - this is the child who won the race - our chief wished to talk with her, that is all," he replied in Cherokee. "Are you jealous of a child, Dancing Eyes?" he chuckled, continuing to stride toward the chief as Dancing Eyes stormed off, black eyes flashing fire, the fringe of her garment keeping time with the flashing daggers of her eyes. She thought, there'll be a time when he won't laugh at Dancing Eyes - there'll be a time when Dancing Eyes is the *only* woman he looks at, he has no need to be with any white child or others, she hissed as she remembered watching him looking at this child's sisters - Bah!

Fellow braves sitting around the parade ground laughed at Wild Hawk, speaking in Cherokee of his child woman - white girl woman. He paid them little heed as Jesse remarked, slightly out of breath from trying to keep up, "Why don't they talk where I know what they're saying, and that girl back there don't like me - when she smiled and laughed, I don't think she meant it and I sure hope your Chief don't just talk that way."

"No, he speaks Cherokee and the white tongue too, just like you - here we are." He stopped in front of Chief Eagle as Jesse stared at the elaborately dressed impressively handsome Chief whose slightly wrinkled face revealed strength and honesty. Chief Eagle scrutinized this girl child with a winner's heart, finding strength and courage in her direct gaze. "Chief Lone Eagle, this young lady is Jessica Brandon, daughter of Consultant John Brandon, and winner of race against Cherokee young - her friends call her Jesse." Wild Hawk smiled, stepping to the side.

Chief Eagle responded, smiling, "Will it be Jessica or Jesse with us?"

She looked him over steadily, smiling. She nodded, "I think you may call me Jesse for I believe we can be friends." She crawled up by him and sat.

"Thank you, very much, Jesse my friend." His mouth twitched, repressing a smile thinking how much easier life would be if adults, especially whites, could be as direct and honest as this girl child. Why do they have to hate my people?

"Chief, I'm so glad you talk my talk and not just your other talk - do the Cherokee boys and girls talk English too?" Jessica wondered.

"Some," he responded, motioning for Cherokee children to come nearer. As four approached, shyly smiling, one young lad scuffed his moccasin in the dust, while two small girls giggled. All had long shiny black hair, their attire soft fringed tan doe skin with matching breech clouts and moccasins. "Now," Chief Eagle continued, "Little Acorn," he pointed to each, "Young Calf, Bright Flower and Happy Girl, this is Jessica Brandon - the girl who won the race today, so she must have a new Cherokee name. You may now call her Racing Girl."

Jesse clapped her hands, while squealing, "Oh! Chief Lone Eagle," and jumping up she fiercely hugged his neck. "Thank you, "the startled Chief sputtered, struggling to keep from falling, untangled Jesse's arms and replaced her on the bench, cleared his throat and coughed while rearranging his eagle feather turban.

The Cherokee standing near thouroughly enjoyed the spectacle of their chief put in an embarrassing situation by a young girl child. The boys and girls all laughed merrily as Little Acorn shyly spoke, "Racing Girl, Little Acorn," pointing to himself, "runned race - you win."

"Oh! yes, Little Acorn, I remember now, but," Jesse frowned, sensing his sadness, "you almost won, and you probably could have won if you hadn't had your thoughts on something else." His black eyes weighed what she said before a sad smile gradually played across his countenance.

Happy Girl reached a hand to Jesse trying to use sign language. Jesse took her hand, but couiln't understand. She turned to the Chief and asked, "Do you think the Cherokee children would like to learn more of my talk? I couldn't understand Happy Girl, but my sister is a teacher, "she continued, her eyes wide with excitement, "I bet she would teach if people asked her." Jesse looked up at the Chief, questioning, "Why, she can even teach reading and writing." She hesitated, biting her lower lip. "Please tell Happy Girl and others I would like to talk with them, but I can't understand them."

Chief Lone Eagle stared at this young girl who seemed to figure out things beyond her years. "Jesse, the Cherokee will think on what you speak, but before Wild Hawk returns you to your parents, I wish to ask one question. Tell me how you, a young girl, could win a running race against our fastest runners?"

Jesse frowned, thinking. "I don't really know. I've always liked to run, to feel the wind on my face. When I want something in my heart then I guess I try with all my might. Right now, though, with Little Acorn feeling so sad, I'm not sure if what I wanted today was right." She smiled at the children and waved to them as Wild Hawk approached. She took a couple of steps, then turned, bouncing back to the Chief. He offered her his hand which she pushed aside as she reached up and planted a kiss on his cheek.

Astounded, the Chief harumphed. coughed, and again, straightened his turban of eagle feathers, thoroughly embarrassed by the antics of this slip of a girl. "Goodbye, Chief Lone Eagle, girls and boys. I'd like to meet you again sometime, Chief."

The Chief and children waved. Never in all his years had Lone Eagle encountered a young female such as this one - no inhibitions, no fears, no hates, strength of heart and a shocking imp. He smiled warmly, rubbing his cheek as Jesse skipped along, trying to keep up with Wild Hawk.

After returning "Racing Girl" to her parents, Wild Hawk, determined not to lower himself by so much as a glance at the Brandon family, found himself again sinking into deep green. Breaking away, disgusted with himself, he spun around, white fringe swirling, to leave as Jesse called, "Wild Hawk!" He stopped, turned, and she continued, "Thank you, and you didn't even say goodbye," she hurried to him, motioning with her finger for him to lean down. When he did, she kissed his cheek, then ran back to sit with her family. He smiled rather sadly, saluted her, turned, and left with most disturbing thoughts about his own weakness.

Kate watched the tall handsome Indian, noting the play of muscles as he moved, and as he turned to leave she wondered, what on earth is wrong with me? Why would I even glance at a savage, much less an aggressive one. I must be getting ill - I do feel a bit feverish! But lunch was nice, I felt all right then, the food was delicious and Lt. Cason was enjoyable. He's attractive, his blue eyes,—but somehow as she tried to remember his features, dark eyes and long black hair got in the way.

Mary watched her older daughter as she seemed to struggle with some inner disturbance each time the Indian appeared. The mother frowned, failing to understand.

Spitting a stream of tobacco juice Rusty ambled to the platform. "All right, everybody, git to yore places fer this here enin' contests is gonna' be rough ones - knife throwing, arm wrestling, body wrestling, and fast horse racing. Let's have a big cheer for all those who went at it this morning and those who'll compete this enin'." The crowd roared as Rusty bellowed, "Let's git with it."

Loud applause, shouts and trilling went up as Spotted Horse split the center twig for the third time denoting his superior ability in knife throwing. Wild Hawk smiled and clapped his shoulder as his good friend nodded to the crowd.

The next event, arm wrestling was held in the center of the parade ground with just the right size table and stools. The elimination process was held as each contestant strained, puffed and groaned with muscles straining and sweat streaming, as finally there were amid much yelling and cheering only two contestants remaining: Lt. Keith Anderson and Wild Hawk. Both men approached the center table - the two about the same muscular size, Anderson in an open necked short sleeved shirt, Hawk clad in his vest with no shirt. They ignored each other as they took their positions with right elbows on the table.

Prissy shrieked, "I don't think I could stand it if Keith doesn't win – Oh—wouldn't he have to go against that awful half-clothed Indian!" She twisted her handkerchief, shaking her fist.

Timmy, finally returned after thinking his clothing Jessica for her race was forgotten, retorted, "You better get ready not to stand it 'cause," smiling broadly while poking Prissy, "'cause I bet Wild Hawk will take 'im - wanta' put money on it?" He slipped a glance at his mother who strongly reprimanded him.

"Timothy!"

"I'm just kiddin', Ma!" He laughed, "You know me."

"Yes, I certainly do - and that's just it!"

Prissy smiled smugly, then shifted her gaze to Keith Anderson, thinking, what a handsome man, in that white shirt with the curly hair showing at the open neck. He already likes me a lot. He said so. She sighed.

Wild Hawk assessed his adversary, too, finding in his flushed face not only fierce determination, but seemingly hatred as the cold, hazel eyes glared, accompanied by a slight smirk - a true Indian hater.

Keith Anderson glared at the dark visage in front of him, feeling, I'd like nothing better than to kill this arrogant red bastard - flaunting his half naked body around white women. All these dirty savages ought to be destroyed.

The two firmly gripped hands, weighing each other's strength, then began to seriously press the struggle with muscles bulging, rippling, black eyes penetrated hazel ones, the crowd expectantly quiet, and for several seconds the contestants seemed to be evenly matched, arms locked in an upright position, when slowly Wild Hawk took his opponent's hand down slightly. Groaning with an extra surge of strength, sweat tricking down his face, Anderson rights his arm, thinking now I'll get this heathen. Staring at the closed dark countenance across from his the lieutenant's arm was flattened to the table. Disbelieving this, Keith Anderson abruptly stood, practically knocking over the table, scowling at Wild

Hawk—he wheeled and strode red faced to the side line, in no mood for any conversation and daring anyone to comment. They didn't.

As the crowd burst forth with applause, the Indians trilled above all other sound. Jesse jumped to her feet, applauding, yelling and whistling through her fingers as Prissy firmly pushed her into a sitting position, elbowing her and daring her to continue.

Timmiy inched closer. "Whadda' I tell you?" he whispered to grumpy Prissy who in turn pinched his chubby behind firmly. He jumped as though he had been shot.

"Tim, are you by chance having an attack of some type?" his father inquired, having witnessed the exchange.

"No, sir," Tim drew in a breath as he rubbed his smarting back end.

The afternoon sun descended its downward trek on its Western path, bringing mingled shadows over the gathering and lessening its warming hold, creating a slight chill as the evening Spring breeze playfully joined contestants and audience.

The final, and most talked about contest, the horse race, was getting underway. Excitement grew amid laughter, whoops and tobacco spittin' as bets were placed by whites and Cherokee. LT. Keith Anderson, astride "Shadow," the fastest runner at the fort. Straight Arrow rode "Mustang", Paul Stewart, a settler atop "High Stepper", and Wild Hawk riding Night Wind approached the stands as a small band of fiddler, banjo picker, and mouth organ struck up a familiar jig. Even the mounts seemed to be aware of the excitement, and that they were the center of attention. With necks bowed, ears flicking, they pranced as though they were keeping time to the music. Vividly decorated manes swayed while Indians molded bareback to their mounts and whites erectly sat in squeaky hand tooled saddles; both anticipating victory while ignoring each other. They stepped to the starting line as the Indians stroked and whispered to the mounts. The starting gun fired, three horses lurched while Night Wind reared, dismissing his winning chance, but with his strength, his winners heart and his love for his master his powerful stride lengthened as his large hooves beat into the turf and ate up the distance between the animals.

"John," Colonel Roberts rushed up red faced and breathless with excitement as he yelled over the cheering crowd, "have you ever seen anything like that black stallion? With a late start he's closing the distance between them with one of the most beautiful strides I've ever seen - man! And what a superb rider that Indian is - look - look - by damn he's overtaken the others!" Looking at Mary watching, he apologized, "Sorry, Ma'am, just got carried away." She nodded, shaking her head.

The crowd was ecstatic as the four horses pounded the ground in furious competition. Shortly, two emerged in the lead, the roan and the black stallion were neck and neck as they rounded the halfway curve to start back to the finish. Hooves pounding, dust flying, they regained their tempo and pulled out of the curve when suddenly the roan lurched, stumbled and sprawled left on his rider, the big red body jerking, hooves flailing the air as Wild Hawk immediately neck reined his stallion, skidding to a stop while the remaining two riders sailed through toward the finish line. Hawk quickly slipped to the ground, rushed to the jerking, frightened animal, checking legs, coaxing and crooning in Cherokee as he helped the whinnying animal off its rider and to its feet.

He then bent with gentle but strong hands checking Anderson's leg as the Lt. exploded, "Get your dirty hands off me - whadda' you think you're doing?" as he attempted to rise, but a dark hand pushed him back.

"Shut up," black eyes flashed, "and understand this," Wild Hawk impatiently continued, "I don't care for you, White Man, any more than you do for me! Now, you keep still while I check your legs for any breaks. If you don't I'll flatten you totally."

Realizing the Indian meant it, the lieutenant eyed him coldly, obviously furious to be at the mercy of this savage. He snarled, "Why the hell did you drop out of that race?" Angry that this heathen revealed qualities that he did not have.

"I take no pride in winning a race while my opponent is on the ground," Hawk answered, having completed his examination of legs and ankles he continued, "You have no broken bones but the right ankle is badly sprained and already swelling. You should not walk on it, and your horse can't be ridden." The roan, standing near, whinnied as though to answer his agreement, then moved to a fresher clump of green grass. "He's thrown a shoe and he's lame. Now, you have a choice of two things—one, ride back in sitting behind me and leading your horse, or if you don't want to be that near this dirty savage," black eyes flashed again, accompanied by a slight sneer, "the other choice is this savage will send someone back for you."

Locked in indecision, the lieutenant scowled while brushing dust from his pants. If I don't ride in with this heathen, he thought, it'll make me look bad, the colonel won't understand, and he won't like it. Damn this red skin, anyway, even if he didn't finish the race - he still *won*. He glared at Wild Hawk, wishing he could throttle him as he growled, "I can't get on that horse!"

"But I can get you on him," Hawk stated, as he whistled for Night Wind. The horse whinnied, trotting up as Hawk lifted Anderson to stand. He then vaulted to Night Wind's back, with instructions. "Give me your hand, place your left foot on my foot and I'll swing you up behind me. Keith grudgingly complied, groaning, as a muscular arm swung him to the horse's back. Hawk kneed the stallion close to the roan, speaking softly as the roan lifted his head and nickered while Hawk gathered up the reins as the docile animal followed their slow retreat.

The trio entered the parade ground amid much cheering, questioning, congratulations, as the lieutenant and his horse were deposited with the soldiers, after a slight nod and a meekly uttered, "thanks" from Anderson. Hawk turned slowly, leading Night Wind away.

Colonel Roberts, talking with Brandon, called, "Wild Hawk, wait up a minute please." Hawk stopped, turning as the hefty Colonel approached.

"I want to thank you for what you did today - not many would stop a race when they're winning to help someone else - that shows a great deal about a man."

His steady blue gaze revealed his sincerity as Hawk assessed this Colonel, and he simply replied, "Thank you."

The Colonel continued, as he pulled out a gold pocket watch to glimpse the time, "I spoke with your chief earlier about a brief meeting with John Brandon and a few of your council members and mine before we adjourn. He wished you to he present."

Wild Hawk nodded before turning to approach his chief who revealed in his dark eyes the pride he felt in this young brave, clasped his shoulder, saying, "A job well done today, my son. You gave up what you wanted most, to help a disliked Pale Eyes. Lone Eagle is very proud of you." Wild Hawk loved this chief, this uncle who had become his father when his parents were killed - his being proud was all Hawk needed.

Other pale eyes, green ones, watched this amazing young Indian, not understanding. He's supposed to be a heathen, she thought, yet he showed compassion today that few men would toward a disliked white. He could have won the most coveted race yet...

Her penetrating gaze caused Wild Hawk to sense someone watching. He turned, reveling in the fact that "The Green Eyes" watched him; his mouth twitched as she turned away and he forgot the promises he had made to himself earlier.

Festivities over, horses nickered as they were hitched to spring board wagons. People loaded their cherished displays, food and traded items as they rehashed the contests amid their good byes. One old timer remarked, "I tell ye, that there Indian stole the show," he cackled remembering, "that stallion he rode beat anything I ever seen!" he slapped his leg while shaking his shaggy gray head.

Most of the Indians, in all their regalia slowly exited astride their prancing mounts as one dark eyed maiden scanned the entire area for a tall Indian Brave clad in white doeskin. Her eyes fastened on the Brandon family, especially the pretty girls. She frowned and departed.

As the sun nestled into its Western horizon, painting glorious pastels of golds, pinks and lavender hues, a peacefulness settled over the entire parade ground where only a few soldiers milled around and the Brandon family awaited John. After the excitement throughout the entire day, the let down of the quiet, and thoughts of returning home saddened the heart a little as Jesse explained, "This was the wonderfullest day I've ever had in my whole life—I have new friends, too, but I don't know when I'll ever see them again." She smiled sadly, as she brushed at a tear, "And you know, Indians is not much different from us—they're just darker, but I know one thing, Wild Hawk is the purtiest man I ever seen," she glanced at her Mother, "saw. He's my friend and I might just marry him when I grow up," she finished as she pulled her mouth together and nodded.

They all laughed as Timmy said, "Jess, you are the silliest thing I've ever seen," as he poked her. "Wild Hawk is supposed to marry that pretty Indian "Dancing Eyes." Little Acorn told me this, and besides he's old enough to almost be 'yore Papa and besides that, white girls don't marry Indians."

Jesse stuck her tongue out at him and hissed, "Shut up!" as she struggled over his statement.

"Mama, didn't Beatrice Roberts invite you inside while we waited for Papa," Prissy asked, hoping for another meeting with Keith Anderson as she adjusted her bonnet and rearranged curls.

"Yes, but I met the ladies earlier and I wanted to sit here and enjoy the beautiful sunset - it's so peaceful and your father won't be very long."

"Nice try, Prissy," Kate whispered, laughing as she poked her sister. Prissy glared.

The peacefulness was shattered when Jesse screamed, "Here they come now!" as she jumped from the bench most unladylike and ran, losing her blue bonnet when she dashed up to the men. She zoomed in on Wild Hawk, grabbed his hand smiling impishly up at him and attempted to match his stride. Chief Eagle smiled, shaking his head. Wild Hawk untangled himself from Jesse to retrieve her bonnet and plopped it on her head.

As they approached his family, John turned. "Well, gentlemen, "as he shook hands with each, "I believe our first gathering was successful. What did you think, Wild Hawk?" He waited expectantly.

The wind played havoc with Chief Eagle's tall head plumage - at the same time picking up Hawk's long, black hair, swirling it around his massive shoulders as his dark eyes steadily gazed into

Legend of the Whispering Wind

John Brandon's green ones, reminding him of others, as he replied, "I do not know your meaning of successful."

John, taken aback by this reply, assuming it wasn't hostile, clarified, "I mean that by getting together in our contests, sharing food, laughs, wins and defeats we became closer - with a better understanding of each other."

Rusty, moccasin clad, shuffled up to Hawk, grabbed his arm, and said, "I done told this here young whipper snapper thuh same things. He had a good day like we all did." A smile creased Rusty's blue eyes while letting a stream of tobacco juice fly, "he's jest a young stubborn mule!" He clapped Hawk on the shoulder as he looked at him warmly, chuckling, and in spite of himself, Hawk smiled and nodded.

Prissy, spying Keith Anderson hobbling on crutches accompanied by Lt. Cason murmured, "Look who's coming," to an inattentive Kate. "Hey!" she poked her sister, who was looking elsewhere, too firmly causing Kate to lose her balance from the third row up, catching her toe on the second row and then tumbling to the ground face down.

Conscious of this young lady's action, from the corner of his eye, Hawk rushed before others could respond, without thinking, to her side. Kneeling, with gentle hands he turned her over carefully, assessing the beauty of her features amid waving auburn hair, frightened that she might be hurt.

John knelt with him, taking one of Kate's hands, chafing it and calling, "Katherine - Katherine." As she fluttered her eyes open, her gaze met the concerned dark eyes hovering over her. She struggled, "What - what happened?" as she continued her perusal of the Indian's countenance, shocked that he was bending over her.

Her father answered, "You fell."

Hawk suddenly realized his actions were out of line. He stood, abruptly stating, "I'm sorry—I acted automatically—without thinking."

John nodded, smiling, as Mary bent over Kate, rubbing her forehead. Wild Hawk retreated to his friend Spotted Horse, a distance from the group as Spotted Horse exploded in Cherokee, "Have you lost your mind?" Clenching his fist, Hawk stooped down, arm on his knee, picking a stem of grass, chewed on it, thinking on his actions as his friend continued to berate him. "What business was it of yours to rush to that girl's aid - her whole family was there! You should have seen the way her Mother stared at you, "he rubbed his head, "With such actions, whites won't want you near, much less around young women," he revealed anger and fear for his friend as he paced a few feet then squatted down by his brother, "Why did you do it?"

Hawk, realizing his friend spoke the truth, could not defend his actions. He simply murmured, "I don't know." He hesitated, "I did it without thinking," he continued to chew on the grass stem, thinking that he could not reveal to his brother something he did not understand himself, that for some strange reason he seemed to be drawn to this white girl. He thought, I tried to ignore it for I don't need this, I don't want this - Hawk should think of his people.

"While you didn't think," Spotted Horse continued to reprimand, "I imaging there are several white people doing a lot of thinking about you."

Wild Hawk frowned, shaking his head. "My friend, I am not saying these things to hurt you," Spotted Horse eased up, but continued," there are so many obstacles in the path of the Cherokee today - we can not afford another of this great size, you certainly agree."

Touched, Wild Hawk clasped his friend's shoulder, struggling in his throat, as he murmured, "Thank you, certainly I agree, my brother speaks the truth - Hawk will remember to think before acting."

As the group dispersed Prissy, forgetting she caused Kate's dilemma made sure she and Lt. Anderson had a few moments to gaze at each other, after he approached John about the effrontery of that Indian rushing to help Kate, actually touching her - when John Brandon reminded the lieutenant that the Indian had also rushed to help him, denying himself a race. There was no response as the Lt. stared at John Brandon.

Lt. Cason sat with a revived Kate, inquiring of her health and informing her he would be seeing her soon. Kate nodded and smiled, trying to remember what he said.

Jesse waved and yelled, "Good-bye Wild Hawk, Chief Eagle, my friends. Come to see me - I don't live far away." The Indians turned and waved as Kate watched, failing to understand her feeling within.

With dusk settling over the countryside, purple haze wrapped its arms around the distant mountains accompanied by the pinkish lavender sunset, serenity invaded the Brandon wagon as it exited through the tall Fort gates followed shortly by four Indian braves and a Chief. A prancing black stallion said a spectacular good-bye to the Brandon family.

Chapter 4

Birds chirped good morning to each other as a bushy tailed gray squirrel scampered up an old gnarled oak to its home while a lark trilled its welcome to the warm spring morn.

John Brandon drank in the beauty and peacefulness of his new mountain home, sipped on a mug of coffee while awaiting his daughter. Kate emerged shortly from the house in a crisp yellow cotton dress with matching sash accentuating her small waist. She tied a yellow ribbon in her hair, took a seat near her father and awaited her summons. "Papa, Mama said you wanted to talk with me."

"Yes," he replied, still confused as to how to approach his subject, "Katherine, I don't quite know how to ask you something that is very important."

"Papa, Kate smiled, "I never knew you to be at a want for words - guess the best way is just out with it - now tell me," she leaned toward him, straightening her skirt.

"I need a teacher, Katherine, and I'm asking my daughter to fill the job."

"Teach?" she questioned, "Who? Where?" not really understanding.

He replied with hopeful expression, "children, and you'd teach right here."

"Oh! Papa - I don't know -" frowning, "what children are you referring to?"

Excited, he continued, "There are several white boys and girls at the Fort, settlers who are near and," he hurriedly continued, "Chief Lone Eagle wishes very much for his young Cherokee to learn our language." John stooped down near Kate, his eyes pleading.

"Indians! Why - I can't teach them! How in the world would they understand me." She stood, pacing back and forth. "Papa - you can't mean this!"

"Katherine, some one must do it - you are the only one qualified - and its so important to us, the Indians, and my job." He stood, putting his arm around her. "Honey, just try it for two or three months. If it doesn't work out, then we won't continue." Using his persuasion, he continued, "There are plenty of supplies at the Fort, recently ordered, but the would-be teacher never showed up."

Looking him in the eye, Kate answered, "Papa, I'm certainly not qualified to teach Indians - I don't know anything about them! Who in the world would translate what I say into their language?" she continued protesting, throwing up her hands and pacing again.

"Well, naturally an adult who speaks both languages will bring them and translate for you. Oh! Honey, don't you see how important this is to them and us?"

"Oh! Papa - I don't know," she hesitated, frowning, afraid of such an undertaking.

John sighed, hesitated, then continued his persuasion. "I have a confession to make, Katherine," he couldn't meet her gaze, "I invited the children at the fort and the young Cherokee to visit this afternoon. Now," he hurried on, touching her arm, "it's not the way you think - it's just to get acquainted - they're bringing supplies…"

She exploded, "Papa - you what?" She wheeled around, angry. "You couldn't - you didn't," her green eyes glared at him, so much like his own, "the least you could have done was ask me before you invited all these children to come here. How could you do this to me?" She stomped off around the house, struggling with her emotions, frightened, not believing her father would do this to her.

John, shaking his head, thought, I don't blame her - guess I managed to botch this whole thing - damn. I shouldn't have set up any thing without first consulting her. I had no idea she'd react this way. He ran his fingers through his hair. She's always had such a wonderful disposition, she's kind and a qualified scholar with teaching credentials from Miss Julie's female academy, for what that's worth! Maybe, he sighed, shaking his head, she'll have second thoughts. He sat with his head in his hands when he heard a stirring by his side.

"Papa, I'm sorry," Kate placed her hand on his shoulder. "I'm sorry I became so upset - just thinking of myself, I guess."

"I understand, Katherine," John said, placing his hand over hers, "I shouldn't have invited the children here before consulting you, but I was afraid you might find some way to refuse and, I guess, I thought if they come on - and you were around them, then you would consent. I'm sorry, too, honey. What I did was wrong."

She sat by him, putting her arm through his and leaning her head against his arm. "I was just thinking of myself, afraid of the undertaking not even realizing how important this is to you and your job. I'll do it, Papa - at least, I'll try." She smiled as he patted her hand.

"Thank you, my daughter." He flashed her a smile, leaning up to kiss her forehead. "Well!" He stood up, "We'd better get busy. I'll bring in that other bench, couple of chairs - if that's not enough, we could use these stools," as he helped rearrange the seating. Kate watched, seeing the spark in his eyes. "And I definitely want Jessica and Timothy in your class."

"Oh! Papa - do I have to teach them? They are both so - so - so impossible at times," she bit her lower lip, dreading the thought of dealing with her brother and sister's silly antics as she rearranged a small table.

"We sure don't want to raise two ignoramuses now, do we?" He laughed for the first time this day as he strode toward the barn calling, "Jessica! Timothy!"

Timmy rushed up to his Papa, out of breath. "Yes, sir - want me, Papa?"

"Yes, where is Jessica?" John asked as they approached the barn.

Timmy, striding to keep up, answered, "She's riding her pony all over the pasture trying to be an Indian and wearing that poor animal out trying to get it to stand on its hind legs." Shaking his tousled head, he added, "She's such a child!"

Trying to keep from laughing, John cleared his throat and said, "Tim, you and Jessica need to bathe."

"Bathe?" Tim looked startled, then grief stricken.

"Yes, bathe and get cleaned up, we're having company. Several boys and girls from the fort and Cherokee children will also be here early this afternoon to begin their first class." He observed Tim while lifting one end of a bench.

"Class of what?" Tim anxiously questioned, beginning to worry as he grabbed the other end of the bench.

"Kate will be teaching our language, reading, writing, and anything else she chooses, and, young man, both you and Jessica will be a part of it." He smiled, observing Tim's bewilderment, as they carried the bench toward the house.

"Oh - oh - no, you know I don't need no schooling, Papa. Ah kin talk good!" He knew he'd rather have a hickory limb cutting his behind than go to school - especially with Kate, who could be mean as Satan if she wuz of a mind. "Oh - oh - oh," he continued eyeing Papa, but his father ignored his misery.

"Help me set the bench over here next to the other, then hurry to the pasture and inform Miss Pocahontas to hurry along. Explain what I've told you."

John could hardly refrain from laughing at Tim's woebegone countenance as he started out, eyeing his father and wondering how he could be such a demon and acting as though he hadn't a friend in the world while he dragged himself along, kicking rocks out of the way, muttering to himself about being treated bad.

Kate, pulling sugar cookies from the oven and placing them to cool on the checkered covered kitchen table shared her turmoil. "Mama, I'm frightened of teaching Indians. I haven't the slightest idea what to do with them." Frowning, she picked up a cup towel and began drying dishes as Mary washed.

Her mother smiled, "Katherine I know you worry, "she stared through the window. "I would too, but it will work for you." She nodded, "I've never known any child who didn't respond to you."

"Mama, "Kate hugged her, "you're just prejudiced."

The back screen door banged as Jesse bounced into the kitchen sweaty and filthy, snatching a cookie before Kate could stop her, crammed it into her mouth and expounded, spewing crumbs into the air, "Mama, you'll just have to talk to Papa. I can't take a class, especially with Kate, I don't like her sometimes and besides I'm busy with other things." She reached for another cookie as Kate smacked her hand. She rubbed her hand. "See what I mean?"

Mary turned, removing her white apron, and took two steps toward Jesse, pointing her finger. "Young lady, I'll give you 10 seconds to peel those filthy clothes and get into that zinc tub on the back porch. If you don't and I hear another word against Kate's class, my hair brush is handy and I'll certainly use it. Do I make myself clear?"

"Yes 'um." The little dirt dauber returned to the porch, peeled off her dirty garments and jumped into the tub, knowing full well how Mama could swing that hair brush!

Prissy stuck her head in the kitchen door, sniffing. "Uh-m-m, I thought I smelled something good," waited for Kate to turn her back, then snatched two cookies, hiding them in her pocket. "Kate I can't believe you're starting a school and with those-those Indians-oh! How utterly boring; I'd certainly hate to spend my days doing such as that!"

"I doubt that you could," retorted Kate, glaring at her sister as she finished wiping the last dish.

"Oh! My-my-dear sister's gotten her dander up! I certainly hope your disposition improves before the little dears arrive, and I hope they don't stay all afternoon, for I believe Keith Anderson might drop by." She hummed as she straightened her sash and fluffed her blue ruffled skirt, smiling.

Mary intervened, knowing Kate didn't need this. "Priscilla that's enough."

Prissy blew a kiss to her mother, then danced from the room, accompanying herself in a true soprano, "Soldier, soldier, won't you marry me—"

As the sun climbed to its lofty peak, casting ever-changing shadows through the leafy trees, and began its descent, the lazy peaceful early afternoon quiet was suddenly dispelled by wagon wheels crunching to a halt near the Brandon front gate. "Anybody home?" Rusty bellowed, as John hurried to open it and welcome him and five rosy cheeked children from the Fort. Three little girls dressed in pastel pink gingham dresses with matching bonnets, two boys in knee britches and long sleeved cotton shirts.

"Howdy, John, brought you five of the best young uns we've got!" Rusty cackled, shaking hands.

John welcomed all, explaining, "Boys and girls, just sit anywhere you like while I call my daughter, who will be your teacher."

The children scampered to the benches, boys on one, girls on the other, and sat, a bit self conscious, looking at each other, smiling shyly, peeking at the house and surroundings, waiting expectantly and a little frightened.

As John and Rusty exchanged the latest news from Washington and the fort, Kate and her students were getting acquainted with the boys and girls more relaxed as their new teacher seemed to be genuinely interested in them, and seemed to be a human being. Billy Simmons, aged 10, reddish hair and freckles summed everything up. "Miss Katherine, when we first heard we wuz to go to school, I don't think any of us wanted to come, me and Jamie Alberts wuz even thinking of runnin' away." The girls gasped a breath, covering their mouths. "Oh! Oh." He continued, "but if it's gonna be like you said, I believe it might be all right," others nodded and agreed. "Did you say we'd have recess and have cookies and things?" He rolled his eyes, licking his lips and smiling.

"Yes, I did say that," she smiled as horses' hooves pounded up to the gate and stopped. "Good, that must be the other children."

John opened the gate, welcoming the Cherokee children and their translator, calling from outside, "Tim, come and help with the horses."

Feeling important, Tim exited as John continued, "Glad you could come - just go on in. Katherine's expecting you."

Wild Hawk entered, accompanied by five Cherokee children, with shiny black hair and all dressed in doeskin.

Kate stared, thinking, "I don't believe this, I don't want him here. Why did he come, half clothed, too? He's arrogant and he bothers me." Realizing her rudeness she walked the distance between them and pasted a smile on her face. "Welcome, Wild Hawk and children." As she stooped down to their level, Jesse burst into view, tripped and sprawled at Hawk's moccasined feet, exposing pantaloons and other unmentionables, while the white children went into rollicks of laughter and the Indians poked each other. As Hawk bent to assist Jesse up, he cast a solumn glance at the children whose laughter subsided immediately. Jesse brushed dirt from her dress front with one hand and clasped Howk's arm with the other. Looking at him adoringly, she said, "I'm so glad you came, Wild Hawk. Happy Girl and Bright Flower, it's good to see you, too." The Cherokee children smiled shyly, not really understanding.

"Jess-i-ca," Kate's tone scolded, "sit."

Wild Hawk smothered a smile as he gently unchained himself from Jesse, who returned to her seat still smiling at Hawk as he offered introductions. "Miss Katherine," he wanted to say Green Eyes, "this is Happy Girl, Bright Flower, Brown Otter, Young Calf, and Little Acorn who will be in shortly after he tends the horses. They range between ages 9 and 11 and would like to try and learn." He looked at her steadily.

Kate's heart went out to the children's beautiful almond shaped black eyes, their innocence and shyness, realizing how hard it must be for these little ones to be here to try and learn the difficult white language. Maybe some day the knowledge they learn here would help to tear down the thick wall that's been created between the Cherokee Indian and white.

Wild Hawk watched the interplay of different and interesting emotions crossing Kate's countenance and, at last, was impressed as he viewed the beautiful, sincere misty green eyes and sweet smile, hoping this young white woman might feel some compassion for the Cherokee children. Maybe this woman would make some small difference - maybe, time would tell. But he trusted no white male or female until he or she proved him or herself. He watched, as he settled his tall frame, cross legged on the ground near the fence. He observed how Kate carefully placed Cherokee girls with Jesse and the boys with Tim and became mesmerized as he interspersed translation with her ability to control, and at the same time to have interplay from and with both groups by her encouragement and care rather than scolding and threats as he well remembered from the mission school he attended when he was a young boy. Back then they demanded he cut his hair, wear white clothing and refrain from speaking Cherokee. His knuckles were rapped many times for uttering his own language before he refused to return to the school - he did learn to speak but not read or write the white tongue.

Here today Spotted Horse could have brought the children - he speaks the white tongue, and he could have translated, but no - Hawk had to do it. He had persuaded Chief Lone Eagle that the one who would become chief should learn to read the written white word. Maybe this can be, but within he knew it was not the true reason he came. Why do I continue to defy myself, he asked?

Kate handed out slates, chalk, and presented a part of the alphabet with pictures. She explained all words are based on these letters being put together. Each child attempted to draw an A standing for Apple, B for bird, C for coin, and D for dog. The Indians seemed exuberant to draw and learn these few words with Jesse and Tim's help. Three of the whites knew their ABCs with Jamie Albert's explaining, "Miss Katherine, me and some of the others already know this stuff. ABC's is for little children," he smirked at the Cherokee, "maybe we shouldn't all be in the same class." He continued to stare at the Indians.

Jesse, glaring at him, took it up. "Jamie Alberts, I bet the first time you saw ABC's it wasn't easy and I bet if Little Acorn explained some of the Cherokee letters and language you wouldn't have any idea what it meant. So there!" Jamie looked down, uncomfortably scuffing the toe of his shoe. The Cherokee girls smiled, knowing not what 'Racing Girl' said, but they knew it was right. Little Acorn knew enough white talk to puff out his chest and half twitch a smile as Tim nodded to him.

Kate responded, pleased with Jessica's intervention. "I'm sure we will be able to progress in our studies to meet the needs of every student. Now we will take our recess," the children clapped, smiling, "we have time for two short games - if you're not too loud. Maybe Little Acorn will lead you in one of the Cherokee games and Billy will direct one that children at the fort play. You may begin while I get refreshments, but remember, these games can not be too rough or loud." She hesitated, then asked, "Wild Hawk, would you mind assisting if they need help?" He nodded, watching her exit, seeing the fire in her red hair as the sun touched it.

As Kate gathered sugar cookies, cider glasses, and trays, she wondered, why am I so jittery? It's not the children; they are fine, so responsive, and the little Cherokee are sweet and want to learn but I can't seem to concentrate with that Indian watching me. Every time I look up he's staring and I'll lose my train of thought - why, I forget what I'm doing. Oh! She snatched up the refreshments to return.

John and Rusty joined the excitement as the children competed in their final game of rolling a homemade ball with sticks. The Indians' deficiency in the studies was evened up with their athletic ability.

Jamie breathlessly turned to Little Acorn, said "Little Acorn, I want to be on your team next time." Wild Hawk translated, amused. Little Acorn nodded and smiled as Jamie made sure he sat by his new Indian friend. All the children sat, out of breath but giggling as Kate passed cider and cookies.

Rusty and John approached Wild Hawk, who stood to join them as Kate delivered refreshments.

Rusty, plopping a cookie into his mouth said, "Miss Kate, did you make these?"

"If they are no good - I didn't. If they are good, I did." They laughed as she smiled, exposing a slight dimple near the corner of her mouth.

"Ummm," Rusty continued, "hit shore is nice when a female is purty and 'kin cook, too. Don't you agree, Wild Hawk?" He observed Hawks deep black-eyed penetration of Kate's features, as Kate turned a pink hue, rubbing her hand across her face. Hawk finally struggled an answer.

"Hawk does indeed agree, especially if the person is an able teacher, too."

"You are all saying - this first day of school went all right?" Kate anxiously inquired.

"Yes, more than all right. You made my Cherokee relax and want to learn. They will learn. Thank you for having the games so that my little ones would not feel less than the others in every way."

"Oh! "Kate frowned. "Do all of these Cherokee children belong to you?" she asked, astonished.

He twitched a smile. "All Cherokee children belong to all Cherokee."

"Oh! "She smiled radiantly. "I'm glad you were pleased with the children's participation." She turned and retreated while Hawk watched the graceful movement of this rather tall slender young white woman, who had fire in her hair and the deep sea in her eyes.

As Rusty glimpsed Hawk's countenance he wasn't too sure this translator should be Wild Hawk.

"Now boys and girls, you have your assignment to study for the next class meeting. Those who already know and can recite all of the ABCs to me, will try the first book in reading. Others, please practice saying and writing the letters with words. I'm looking forward to our next class time in three days, which will be longer; two hours in the morning with recess - bring a lunch for a picnic together. I'll furnish something to drink, then two hours in the afternoon with recess." She bade them goodbye, happily smiling as Happy Girl reached up, shyly taking her hand, nodded and smiled. Kate automatically hugged her. Jamie Davidson, a pretty blue eyed black curly head in pink, gently took Kate's other arm, tugged her sleeve and said, "Thank you, Miss Katherine. I had a fun day - you're a good teacher." Kate patted her and waved 'bye' to the others.

Rusty, escorting the retreating white children, shed his tobacco cud before telling Kate, "Seemed to me you had a very successful first school day, Miss Katherine. These here young 'uns act happy to be here and I know their Maw and Paws will be tickled over it. We'll be back on Friday when me 'n John might do some recitin'." He cackled as he slapped John on the back. "Wild Hawk - you take care 'o them young 'uns - they're special," he hesitated, "and so are you." He clasped the muscular shoulder as Hawk stared, sensing the deeper meanings to his words.

"Tim!" John called from outside the gate. "Help us with the horses quickly." Tim's chubby legs rushed to comply with his father's wishes while the remainder of the children followed him through the gate.

Wild Hawk, knowing he had Kate's full attention, took his time strolling to her, his fringed buckskin swaying. "Hawk wishes to thank you for teaching the Cherokee, Miss Katherine. "He offered his hand, she hesitatingly took it, feeling drawn into his penetrating gaze as he whispered "Thank you, Green Eyes."

She sucked in her breath, abruptly retrieving her hand, astounded at his boldness as she watched a slow half smile curve his handsome visage, revealing very white teeth, thinking, "This heathen knows he is handsome," but before she could pull herself together to put him in his place he had departed. She stood glaring, rubbing her hand as horses' hooves faded into the distance.

Chapter 5

A warm spring breeze kissed the mountain green as leafy plants, colorful rhododendron, bluebells and white twinkles nodded their heads in accompaniment to the gurgling song of a rushing stream while it played tag with large boulders and rocks.

A beautiful black eyed Indian maiden sat on a flat stone shelf drinking in Mother Nature's soothing tonic, trying to dispel the heaviness of her heart. "Since I first saw Wild Hawk when he came to our village from the south many years ago, as a pitiful, straggly, frightened boy of eleven, I have loved him, even then as I first looked into his sad fierce dark eyes, but he has never returned this feeling, nor does he seem to feel deeply for any of the other Cherokee maidens, who have made eyes for him. Maybe his heart is too full of hate for the White, leaving no room for anything else, but then why does he not show this hate feeling around that paleface Brandon family? He is a most difficult man to understand. Bah! But Dancing Eyes will never give him up, for he is hers." Her flashing dark eyes teared as her deep emotions played across her countenance, Sensing another's presence, she turned to meet the dark visage of Swift Antelope, clad in buckskin, his average height and physique revealing strength while his rather handsome countenance at times held a touch of cruelty.

Yes, he thought upon seeing Dancing Eyes, the most beautiful maiden of all. She is the one who held his heart, but her feelings were all for that devil Wild Hawk. Why did he even come here? Swift Antelope's black eyes narrowed to slits as he thought of his enemy. He approached his dream maiden. "What is such a lovely maiden doing alone and a distance from our village? Is that a tear on your face? Has someone harmed you?" He scrutinized her lovely features anxiously.

"No - I'm fine - this is a peaceful place. I like to come here when I am in a thoughtful mood," she answered smiling, hoping he'd leave, for at times he frightened her - his feelings for her were too obvious.

"You should not come here alone –harm could come to you from the enemy or some wild animal - come, "he demanded," Swift Antelope will walk you back to village." He offered his hand which she accepted as she gracefully stepped down from the stone shelf.

"Would you be sad if something happened to Dancing Eyes?" Her dark eyes teased.

"Yes - very sad," he answered, revealing his true emotion.

She frowned as she fell into step with the muscular brave and was unaware of the hungry glances he cast her way as her long fringed garment accompanied the swaying of her lithe body. They walked in silence through a dense forest, where the stillness was broken only by birds chattering and squirrels scampering in their game of tag.

As the two Indians neared their village, three riders approached from the south, two in uniform and one buckskin clad. Both Cherokee recognized the soldiers from the Fort, along with the old scout.

Rusty hailed the two, as they reined their horses to a stop. "Howdy, Swift Antelope, Dancing Eyes," the Indians nodded. Keith Anderson, awestruck by the beauty of this Indian maiden, thought, My God! I can't believe this creature - such exquisite beauty hidden in a stinking heathen settlement, and wouldn't he be saddled with these two fools while that Indian buck accompanied her. His lazy smile caressed Dancing Eyes as she absorbed the handsome lieutenant's attention with dark eyed invitation. She thought, as she returned his smile, that this one could certainly make Wild Hawk jealous!

Rusty, aware of the heated glances passed between the two and the angry scowl crossing Swift Antelope's countenance grabbed the attention as his roan pranced. "Dancing Eyes-you know where we kin find Wild Hawk? It's important we speak to him and the chief."

She flared her nostrils, raised her chin and hautily retorted in broken English, "Wild Hawk—hunts—not in the village," as she again shifted her glance to the handsome man in uniform.

"Why you want chief, white man?" Swift Antelope angrily scowled at all three.

"Listen here, Swift Antelope-we have a big message for your chief 'n taint none of yore damn business what it's all about-now git out 'uv the way 'fore ye get hurt." Rusty caused his horse to prance near the irritated warrior's feet while Keith Anderson stole a last glance at the beautiful Indian maiden before all three thundered off toward the village.

"Fellers," the Scout held up his hand to halt, "'this here's the fork-you take the right one to the fort and I'll head on left to Lone Eagle's village. I'll probably stay the night 'n hope to catch Wild Hawk before I go back to the fort tomorrow." The soldiers headed for the fort while the old scout turned left. A short time later he made his way through the entrance leading to Eagle's village, where the chief awaited him, having received his scout's signal of the approach.

As Rusty neared Lone Eagle, several small children clamored around him in the midst of barking dogs. After dismounting and greeting them he reached into his saddlebag and produced several pieces of hard candy. He divided the sweets among the little ones who smiled and nodded their thank yous. Little Acorn proudly took the horse's reins as Chief Eagle nodded his appreciation for the kind act. "Well, what's on your mind, old man?" the chief questioned, as they walked toward his home passing several lodges where hides for tanning were stretched on frames.

One rather plump squaw smiled at Rusty as she stirred her savory meat stew in an old leather looking pouch. The rich aroma of the venison and herb concoction made the old scout's mouth water. He waved. Several braves sat cross leg under a large oak jovially betting on a stick game. They acknowledged the old man before quickly returning to their gambling, while two young dark eyed maidens strolled by, eyeing the braves, vying for attention as they swished their well rounded hips.

Rusty sighed, and as always, gave in to the peacefulness of the village, wishing life for these people could remain this way, but he was afraid it was not to be. Too many whites were always pushing and grasping for more of everything, especially land. He was afraid for his old friend, Lone Eagle, who he'd shared so many pipes, food, hunts, tragedies and celebrations-no better man ever lived than this proud Cherokee chief.

"What has happened to you? Have you reached the age where you don't remember anything?" The Chief shook the buckskin clad arm of his old friend, eyeing him closely as they reached his dwelling.

Easing down to sit on the front stoop, Rusty removed his dusty old beat up leather hat, and wiped his sweaty face with his arm before replying, "'jist get carried away with this here peacefulness every dag nabbed time I come here. Takes a little while fer me to git ma' balance again," he smiled.

Eagle, not fooled by the smile, read a deeper meaning, and eased himself down by his friend while continuing to watch Rusty carefully. "Old man, you are not here to elaborate on our peaceful village," his dark eyes penetrated, "what is it?"

Rusty exhaled loudly. "Well, one 'uv them big shots from Washington, the great white father's second in command of Indian Affairs is on his way down here to the fort to speak to the representatives of yore tribe. Course, that means you Chief, Wild Hawk Chief to be and any others you choose, along with Cherokee Chief Standing Bear with his chosen representatives and I suppose others from the east. We've done been down South and talked to him-just come from there. Them from Washington's to git here in three moons 'n the meetin's to be the next day. They say it's mighty important. Kin y'all be there, Chief?"

Eyeing Rusty steadily, the chief responded, "We can be there, but what is this important meeting about?" The dark eyes continued to penetrate.

"Yore guess is as good as mine-you know they don't confide nothing in me. I'm just to deliver messages." He unleashed a bone handled knife, cut a large tobacco chaw and plopped it in his mouth as he dreamily chewed. Standing, Rusty stretched his tired frame. "Fore I get too comfortable a settin', I've got to get some victuals in this here belly fore I bend double. You don't suppose Busy Bee'd mind given a starving old scout a little of that good smelling stew do you?" He chuckled, "Come on, Big Chief, let's see."

The friendly village, a full belly, sharing the pipe and reminiscing with his old friend wrapped Rusty Poole in the night's peaceful cocoon, despite his unmentioned concern over the upcoming meeting with Washington officials and the Cherokee.

As the sun crawled to the mountain peak and blinked its good morning warmth through the leafy branches of village trees, three braves jovially brought their prancing deer laden mounts to a halt near Lone Eagle's lodge.

They unloaded their bounty amid laughter and joking as several gathered to inspect the fine kill while anticipating the upcoming feast. Dancing Eyes glared daggers at three maidens who strained in effort and manners to attract Hawk's attention. The one who received his undivided attention however, was a chubby three year-old boy who tightly attached his fat little arms around the tall brave's leg, laughing in excitement, before he was scooped up in strong arms and tossed into the air as delightful childish squeals vibrated throughout the area.

Rusty keenly observed this tall brave who was next in line to lead these people. How can one dag nabbed Indian be as complicated as this one-who shows no fear of the whites, in fact, his hatred is might nigh obvious-he's smart, arrogant, Rusty chuckled to himself, remembering Hawk's grand entrance at the Fort gathering, a handsome cuss, with all them thar maidens fallen all over theyselves to git his attention 'n him ignoring hell out of them, but he didn't ignore Miss Katherine Brandon the other day 'n I ain't shore that's a good sign, and lookie thar' at him and Little Cub, showing such gentleness and love. The scout shook his shaggy gray head as Hawk strode over to greet his chief. He acknowledged the old scout. "When I delivered fresh meat to Old Crone, she informed me you wish to speak with Wild Hawk," he squatted near Rusty, awaiting a response while studying the scout with dark inquisitive eyes.

The old scout shifted his tobacco cud, spit and repeated what he had explained earlier to the chief. Upon his completion, Wild Hawk scowled thoughtfully, remembering previous "important" meetings and broken treaties. Finally coming back to the present, he responded, "The only meetings Hawk remembers or has heard about between white eyes and Cherokee have been important only to the whites because they brought only harm to the Cherokee." His black eyes flashed as he turned abruptly and strode to his horse, Night Wind.

Rusty, overcome with mixed emotions, wanting to strike out at this arrogant young brave yet understanding his reaction and the truthfulness of his statement, only stared.

Lone Eagle clasped his friend's shoulder. "My nephew is a good man-he is very abrupt at times, but he's honest and he cares for his people. He'll be at that meeting." They clasped wrists as blood brothers before Rusty mounted his roan to head out.

Chapter 6

"Papa," Kate hesitated while glancing at the Eastern Mountain beauty surrounding them. "Papa, I'm having trouble with my class." She fingered her cotton shirt.

"Whadda you mean? The children love you and all of them seem to be doing so well in their studies. What is it?" He took her hand and studied her seriousness.

She looked away, biting her lower lip. "Well-Papa, it's Wild Hawk. He-well, he bothers me." She looked down at her hands, struggling to say the right words. "He's always staring and it unnerves me and causes me to lose my train of thought and I think it would be best for all if someone else brought the Cherokee children and acted as interpreter." She ended almost in a whisper as she stood, walked to the table and began thumbing through a reading book.

Her father gazed intently at this daughter, not understanding. What is Katherine really trying to say? I thought everything was going so well. He remembered the last teaching session on Monday. Why, Katherine seemed almost radiant at times. The children were reading, even the Cherokee were speaking some English after only six or seven weeks of study. Wild Hawk even joined in their ball game Monday, and the children loved it as he assisted both sides. "Katherine, it would be very difficult to explain to that young brave what you have told me. I don't think he'd understand for I don't," he stood, running his hand through his hair then turned abruptly toward her. "Now, if he has said or done anything that he shouldn't-well, that's different," he stared at his daughter waiting for an answer.

She continued looking through the book, hesitating, "No—no-it's nothing like that. It's-oh! I don't know how to explain-he simply makes me very uncomfortable," her voice rose, "and I feel it would be better if someone else brought the Cherokee children." She snatched up the reading book and rushed into the house as John eased himself onto a bench and pondered his daughter's mystifying news, wondering how his dependable calm Kate could be so disturbed over the presence of one Cherokee brave! Women-would it ever be possible for a man to understand any one of them! Thinking of women, he watched his Mary as she approached with a basket of mending on her arm, and took a seat near him. How could she remain so young and lovely with the rearing of their two hellions, Tim and Jesse, thrust upon her and the complications of two grown daughters to unravel? Lord knows, it was too much for him.

"Why, what devastating situation has caused that thundercloud to cross your countenance, my husband?" Mary smiled as she began threading a needle.

"Women," he moaned.

"Women?" a startled Mary gasped, "John Brandon," her voice rose an octave, "explain yourself. What women?"

"Oh! Don't get your dander up, Mary," he chuckled, shaking his head, "I was thinking of one female-our Katherine."

"Oh, "her voice returned to normal, "what is wrong with Katherine? I thought everything was going well with her teaching."

"So did I., but apparently not all things." He filled his pipe, lit it, and puffed a few times as Mary placed the needle in a sock and waited anxiously for her husband to continue.

"Katherine does not want Wild Hawk bringing the Cherokee children and acting as interpreter. He makes her uncomfortable."

He stared into the distant mountain peaks and puffed his pipe, unaware of his wife's strained facial expression as she remembered the festivities at the fort, Katherine staring at Wild Hawk and her disturbed reactions every time that young brave was near her. Her mouth dropped open. Holy Mary-mother of God!

Wild Hawk entered his friend's lodge, knowing that Spotted Horse, who rested on his sleeping mat, was aware of his entrance. "What is so important in your life that you can't let your brother sleep through the night-it is so late-leave my lodge, Wild Hawk, go back to your own-for I am weary from the hunt." Spotted Horse yawned and then rolled over, turning his back on his friend.

Ignoring Horse's outburst Hawk pressed on. "I must talk to my brother-now. It is most important." He stooped down near his friend but only heard the even breathing of one asleep. "Spotted Horse," Hawk spoke in a loud voice, shaking his friend's shoulder, "Wake up. I must talk with you. This can't wait."

"Go away," Horse growled as Hawk stood and jerked the sleeping robe from his nude friend, causing a cold draft to penetrate. "You miserable horse dung, why can't your important talk wait until sun up?" Horse snatched his robe back, throwing it around himself as he sat up rubbing his eyes. "All right-now that you've ruined my rest-talk!"

Wild Hawk smiled at his brother's misery as he strolled the length of the lodge.

"Hawk has a problem," he began.

"That is nothing unusual," his friend responded, yawning, "you keep problems."

"Well, this involves you too, my friend," Hawk sat down, stretching his long legs before continuing. "I must ask Spotted

Horse to take my place as interpreter for our children's school sessions at the Brandons."

"You-what? "Spotted Horse exclaimed, jumping up. "No, sir," pointing his finger, "brother, you're not getting me into that. I remember Wild Hawk stating that this was the chief to be's responsibility. You've got it and you can keep it! Now, I bid you to leave my lodge so your good friend can rest." Spotted Horse waved him to leave as he again stretched out on his bed of robes.

Exhaling a loud breath, "Thank you friend, I didn't know how understanding you could be!" Hawk sarcastically retorted as he stormed out of the lodge and strode to his special place, leading to the rock, where he sat and let the night's peacefulness embrace him, watching the full moon paint its silvery path along the mountain peaks, while in deep thought. No one could have told me I would be in such inner turmoil over a paleface white eyes! Katherine Brandon is not what others would call beautiful but to me she is. I tell myself she is only another hated pale eyes who also hates the Cherokee, but when she looks at Hawk with those green eyes he sinks within. Why? I can't let this happen and I won't. He slammed his fist into his hand. What a ridiculous thing for Hawk to do. It must be because she looks different and is different from Cherokee maidens. There are too many problems for the Cherokee to face, for me to face, without having this one. Hawk will not be weakened by allowing any white female to possess his thoughts. He will stay away from this Katherine Brandon. Someone else must take the Cherokee children for their lessons, he sighed, as he sensed another's presence, knowing it was his friend. "Well, do come forth, Spotted Horse. You are every bit as quiet as a water buffalo," he chuckled, moving over for his friend to sit beside him.

Sitting, Horse declared "Since you totally ruined this night's rest I figured I'd hear all your important talk and get it over with," Horse teased his friend while awaiting an answer.

Hawk hesitated, continued to stare at the mountain range before answering. "I can't take the Cherokee children to the Brandons for their studies-at least not for a while. I must ask your help with this," he turned, imploring Spotted Horse with black eyes. "There is no other to be trusted with this and our children need their learning." He hesitated, looking down. "Hawk's many responsibilities prevent his continuing this."

Spotted Horse gazed deeply at his friend saying nothing until Hawk felt quite uncomfortable. "Well—say something!" he prodded.

"Hey, this is Spotted Horse you speak to-your friend, who knows you so very well and Horse says Wild Hawk does not speak the truth." He stood, turned to leave, stopped, turned back looking at Hawk, "I will help with the children for a short while and, not because you asked, but because the Cherokee children need me." He turned and strode toward his lodge, long black hair swaying in the night's breeze, as a confused Wild Hawk watched, wanting desperately to confide in his friend, but not knowing what to say or how to say it, for this weakness he could not discuss.

As Spotted Horse walked to his lodge, he struggled with mixed emotions for his friend, and anger that Wild Hawk would allow a damn white wench to become part of his feelings when nothing could come of it but hurt for him and his people-knowing, too, that Hawk was caught up in something that he himself probably did not understand or know what to do about it. So—he is to stay away from this Katherine Brandon. He shook his head, chuckling to himself-how ridiculous never had he ever seen Wild Hawk run from anything, and it was doubtful he'd continue running from this white wench. He entered his lodge knowing there would be no sleep for this brave this night.

Kate sat in the maple rocker near the kitchen table where she nodded off after a big breakfast. Prissy glided into the room looking for a little snack of leftover sausage and biscuit when she spied her sister and simply couldn't resist disturbing such a peaceful nap. She leaned over near Kate's ear and yelled, "Miss Katherine your darlings are here!" Kate jumped and blinked as Prissy stepped back going into gales of laughter after ducking to avoid colliding with the book her sister threw at her. "Why, Kate you are so cranky. What's the matter, dear sister," Prissy smirked, "doesn't that Indian brave pay you enough attention?" She exploded in another fit of laughter and she flew from the room, gingham skirts twirling, to avoid her sister's wrath.

What's wrong with me? Kate thought as she stood and looked out the kitchen window watching the horses grazing. I should be used to Prissy's silly actions by now, but I haven't rested well lately-my sleep is broken making me feel tired and irritable I do hope I have patience with the children today. She thought how well they had all done the past two months they had been coming to class. I'll just try to ignore Wild Hawk today.

"Kate," Jesse called from outside, "come on, your students are here."

Kate hurried to the hall mirror, fluffed her hair, pinched her cheeks, and smoothed her blue cotton skirt before pinning a blue ribbon in her hair for the final touch before exiting through the porch door awaiting her students arrival. She strode to the long table, straightening the books and slates as horses' hooves screeched to a halt outside amid laughter and talking. Kate waited a few minutes, but no one entered the gate, however much yelling and cheering was going on outside when Tim suddenly burst through the gate face flushed, out of breath. "Kate, you better come quick-Jesse's simply terrible, she double dog dared Brown Otter to Indian wrestle and she's wallowing all over the ground and she's got him down and I hate to say it but she's winning too, and that's bad for Brown Otter to lose face."

Kate sailed through the gate followed by a breathless Tim trudging along, failing to keep up. She strode to the wrestling match, yanked a grappling Jesse by the nape of the neck, set her on her feet and admonished her with words that Jesse half understood. "How dare you do such a thing! You apologize to Brown Otter this minute-do you hear me, Jessica Ruth?" Kate's voice rose another octave.

"Yeah-course I hear you. How could anybody keep from it the way you're yelling." Jesse glared at Kate with a red dirt streaked sweaty face, her dirty yellow dress torn at the waist. "But what do I apologize for? Me and Brown otter was just wrestlin'-just having fun." Jesse turned to Brown Otter. "Kate said I'm to say I'm sorry for something," Otter smiled and nodded.

"Oh! Dear Lord," Kate exhaled, "Tim, you escort Jesse into Mama where Miss Jessica will explain, in detail, her wrestling match and young lady," she stated firmly to Jesse, "you will not be attending class with the others today; however, I'm sure you will learn a very important lesson from Mama-hopefully, one you won't forget! Now march!"

Jesse sullenly eyed Kate before starting for the house accompanied by a smug Tim. She turned with a quivering chin. "Spotted Horse, you tell Wild Hawk that it wasn't right for him not to say goodbye and let me know he wasn't coming back."

Kate's head jerked up and she gazed at Horse realizing Hawk had not brought the Cherokee children-anxiously wondering, not understanding.

Spotted Horse smiled, "Horse will tell him."

Jesse turned, sniffed, wiped at a tear trailing down her dirty cheek, mumbling as Tim escorted her into the house that nobody had any fun with witch Kate around anymore. Kate, Cherokee students and Spotted Horse entered the lawn study area. Students selected books and slates, received assignments and took their seats on the benches, while they awaited other students from the fort. Kate walked to the fence where Spotted Horse stood staring at the mountain beauty and asked, "Why didn't Wild Hawk return with the children? Is he ill?" Her concern was obvious.

"No, he is not ill." Spotted Horse gazed at the beauty of this Katherine, beginning to understand how Wild Hawk could respond to this white girl. "He said he had too many responsibilities to continue bringing the Cherokee children here."

"But he never mentioned anything like that-I thought he wanted to bring the students and be here with them, to help-I don't understand." She was upset and fumbling for words. Spotted Horse observed the emotions, the concerned countenance, realizing this white woman was quite disturbed because Hawk was not here. Why should it matter to her who brought the Cherokee and interpreted? Obviously, it did matter.

Kate listened to each Cherokee student read, then assisted with writing lessons. Finally, after recess the white students arrived, having had a wagon breakdown. The morning dragged on for Kate, as she observed reading and writing by all, and realized she missed the tall brave who usually brought the Cherokee, his quick responses and interplay with the students. The answer Spotted Horse gave for Hawk's not being here seemed strange, but she wouldn't worry about that-Wild Hawk meant nothing to her-but it did seem strange.

"Students, you have worked very well today, and I'm proud of your accomplishments." The children looked at each other smiling. "Your reading and writing were very good, receiving top marks." The girls clapped while the boys poked each other, rolling their eyes. "Now we will break for lunch and a picnic under the big oak in the pasture as a special treat. After lunch, you will also have about 30 minutes for a game or two."

"Thank you," several students chorused.

Kate smiled, "Tim, you and Brown Otter bring the food basket and lemonade. Jamie, you and Happy Girl spread the tablecloth and don't forget to place four or five rocks around the edge to keep it smooth."

"Yes 'um," The children scampered to do Kate's bidding.

Hungry appetites were sated with roasted venison, corn cakes, warm baked bread, lemonade and cookies. All of the men took double portions which pleased Kate, who was now busy packing the remainder of the food, as she instructed the students, "Girls, I'll need your help cleaning up-two of you pack dishes, silver and glasses while others take care of the cloth and napkins. Happy Girl, please pass remainder of the cookies to the men who are standing over there near the fence."

Happy Girl nodded "Yes ma'am," smiled, pleased with her chore and her English, as Kate continued, "Couple of you boys need to help Tim return all of these things to the house. When the chores are completed you have time for a couple of games while the girls play on their own," she brushed hair from her face, sighing.

"Oh! Boy!" Tim yelped, "Hurry up!" He motioned to the others, picking up a basket. "Help me Jamie, Little Acorn."

Legend of the Whispering Wind

"Thank you Miss Katherine." Susan Patterson beamed as she threw her blue bonnet down and tumbled into the group of giggling girls.

Kate sat and leaned back against the old oak tree welcoming the cool breeze that caressed her flushed face. *I don't know why I feel so depleted. It is usually enjoyable with the children here, but today I'll just be glad when it's over.* Her thoughts were suddenly interrupted as she watched in awe while Timmy's detailed explanation of his newly made slingshot became a reality when he drew back and let a rock fly just as Rusty Poole suddenly appeared in the line of fire, bent over as though looking for something, offering his back end as a logical target. As rock and target came into contact, Rusty tumbled over, grabbing his bottom. Finally gaining balance he stood, wheeled around shaking his fist while exploding, "Ye gosh darned, dag nabbed crazy little whippersnapper-whadda' ya tryin' to do-destroy a body?" Still rubbing his smarting back side, he strode toward Tim who stood totally shaken.

"I'm sorry—I didn't mean to-honest-I'uz jest showin' how my sling shot worked when," he bit his lower lip, his chin quivering, "suddenly when I let the rock fly, you wuz just there all bent over in the way. I shore didn't see you when I shot it." The other boys tried to contain their smiles as Rusty continued rubbing his buttocks. John and Spotted Horse stayed their distance also having difficulty containing their amusement.

"Well," Rusty spit, shaking a finger in Tim's face, "you be careful, boy. That thing could harm somebody! 'N I ain't so sure I'll be settin' peaceful like any time soon."

"Yes, sir." Tim meekly responded looking down, shifting his weight, obviously uncomfortable while the other children continued to enjoy the episode. Kate flew into the fracus, jerking

Tim around, her voice raised. "Timothy, how could you do such a terrible thing?" she reprimanded, turning toward her father. "Papa, how can you just stand there and allow this-this imp," pointing to Tim, "to do such a horrible act without doing—"

"Miss Katherine," Rusty intervened, "I done done that 'n 'sides Tim didn't aim to do 'hit-didn't you hear what he said?"

"I heard him, but that's not sufficient." She grabbed Tim's arm. "First it's Jessica beginning the day with her ridiculous antics and now this-this-"

"Katherine," John stepped up, placing his hand on her shoulder, "let it go-that's enough."

She nodded, looking down, struggling to control her emotions. "I'm sorry-I don't know what's wrong with me."

John put his arm around his daughter who struggled to keep her composure, while her students wondered what was wrong with their teacher.

"Honey, why don't you go on in the house for a while, you're tired. We'll take care of the children. Don't worry about them."

Katherine nodded, and started toward the back door, straining to control her emotions.

Chapter 7

Ten braves and with their chiefs Lone Eagle and Standing Big Bear exited Eagle's village after participating in a council meeting and religious ceremony seeking knowledge and understanding from Yawa (edoda?) throughout the upcoming meeting at the fort.

As the Cherokee arrived at the compound donned in their finest regalia, they were most impressive as were their mounts, prancing as though sensing the importance of the occasion.

Rusty Poole, John Brandon and soldiers welcomed the Cherokee. As Wild Hawk dismounted, a big mountain of a man, clad in buckskin, shoved him from the back. Hawk wheeled, ready to head into a confrontation when the big sandy haired bearded-faced guy cracked a huge grin while grabbing Hawk's arm. "Wild Hawk, you old coon hound-long time no see-'n ye are a sight for sore eyes in all them white duds with fringe shaking every whar," the big man greeted warmly.

Hawk flashed a broad smile, grabbing his friend's hand. "Well, I'll be-if it is not my brother, Jeb Hawkins, Old Moose Droppings! Where in the world have you been for three months?"

Jeb chuckled, walking with his friend, "I've been scoutin' up north 'n east 'n I guess I don't have to say I am more than a little wore out with it-been lookin' forward to going on a hunt with you 'n just relaxin' like old times." He beat his worn leather hat against his thigh to rid it of some trail dust. "We'll have some time to talk 'fore the day is over, guess right now we'd best amble on in 'fore they send for us."

"Right, we must not hold up this important meeting!" Hawk sarcastically responded, his eyes flashing, which Jeb didn't fail to notice.

They entered through double doors following the others, through a wide hallway into a large meeting room, where other Cherokee clans were represented along with several soldiers. Colonel Roberts was there with three men dressed in fashionable attire.

Colonel Robert stood and welcomed the Cherokee chiefs and their representatives. He then introduced the three dignitaries from Washington, extolling their qualifications.

"And now, gentlemen, I'll turn the meeting over to our distinguished visitors from Washington, Mr. John Murray, William Casey, and James White."

"Thank you Colonel," William Casey stood, a plump medium height individual in his mid-40s, with dark eyes and a smile that came and went quickly. "First I want to thank you," he nodded to the Colonel, "and the soldiers for the hospitality shown us since our arrival. It has been top grade, and I might add the food has been absolutely delicious, too," he flashed a smile," and today what a privilege it is to meet with you and these mighty Cherokee Chiefs and their representatives." He flashed another quick smile as he droned on about Washington, the government's accomplishments, understanding and sincere feelings for the well-being of the American Indian—droning on until finally—"and you, of course, realize many of your brothers have emigrated to the Arkansas country, and are very well settled there and I might add, very pleased with their land. Of course, you realize one of your greatest leaders, Sequoyah, lives in the Arkansas area. I might add, he is a famous man for having accomplished the establishment of your alphabet," he flashed his smile again as he drove his point home.

Lone Eagle stood, a regal figure in his soft knee length doeskin shirt, a turquoise turban with a flowing plume. "Mr. Casey, I am Chief Lone Eagle and I believe I speak for all of the Cherokee in saying that we are aware of who our brother Sequoyah is and of his accomplishment, but I fail to understand what that has to do with this meeting," he sat as the other Cherokee twitched smiles but sat stoically.

"Well-harrump." Casey cleared his throat, picked up a water glass and took a swallow. "Well, of course." James White stood, a slight man of average height and weight with thinning brown hair and cold blue eyes, placing his hand on Casey's arm as he came to the rescue.

"What Mr. Casey was saying before he became carried away with Sequoyah's accomplishment," he chuckled at his wit," was that we're here as government representatives in the cause and concern for the Cherokee. There is vast opportunity and land in the Arkansas territory for additional Cherokee. We have a treaty drawn up, backed by the government, to ensure you fine land in the Arkansas, and much money to pay for the land you now reside on." His cool blue eyes held an icy glitter as his thin lips offered a tense smile.

Wild Hawk leaned up to Eagle, whispered to him, received a nod from his chief then stood, emanating power.

"Yes?" James White acknowledged the tall young brave, continuing to hold a smile.

"I am Wild Hawk of Chief Lone Eagle's clan, and I believe each of us is aware of the great concern the government has for the Cherokee, for which has resulted in many broken treaties throughout many years, the land that has been taken from us, the greed, the way whites hope in some way to rid this entire area of all Cherokee. If you people should make Andrew Jackson your big white chief, he will place his hate along with yours against the American Indian. Junaluska will rue the day he saved the life of that one at the Battle of Horseshoe Bend, and to think the Cherokee fought by the side of such a one. This land, our land that you're trying to take with a worthless treaty. This land we love and it is where we will remain. If you whites like Arkansas territory so much you move there. There will be no treaty signing this day or any day by this Cherokee." He sat amid Cherokee nods and murmurs.

James White, red faced, had difficulty controlling his anger. William Casey, mouth gaping open, stared disbelievingly at this young brave who spoke so powerfully and so knowledgeably of the English language, and spoke so rudely against them while John Murray blinked and squinted his near sighted eyes, appalled at the audacity of this heathen.

James White found his voice at last, struggling with words. "Chief Lone Eagle, does this man speak for you?"

Lone Eagle stood with dignity, black eyes flashing, head held high. "My nephew and chief-to-be Wild Hawk, asked my permission to speak. He had it and he spoke my feelings." He sat.

John Brandon rose to his feet, acknowledged the speaker. "Mr. White, gentleman, I was moved down here from Boston as Indian consultant between the Cherokee and White. I have found these people to be honest, peaceful, and loyal. Granted, Wild Hawk does not mince words-he puts it the way he sees it, and it may be harsh, but I rather admire a man who speaks his beliefs. I will have to go along with the Cherokee. They love this land-they possessed it long before any white man came to these parts, and they should keep it." John Brandon found a thank-you in penetrating black eyed glances.

Jeb Hawkins stood, power emanating from his 6 ft. 3 in. frame. "Mr. White, and others," he refused to add 'gentleman', "I have known these Cherokee," he pointed to Lone Eagle, "and Standing Bear's tribe since I was a young boy. No finer people exist. Trying to take this land from them would be like takin' their heart. They are this land and I will always stand beside them."

He took his seat by his friend, Wild Hawk. As Rusty Poole stood, shifting his tobacco cud, "I ain't so good with words, but I'm purty good at knowin' a man 'n these Cherokee is my people. Like Jeb Hawkins done put it, I stand beside 'um. Sides, I done seed more treaties broke than horses fer ridin'," he sat, sniffed as he wiped his misty blue eyes with a weather roughened hand. His old friend, Lone Eagle, glanced at Rusty with warmth in his countenance.

"Mr. White, gentleman," Lt. Keith Anderson stood, his good looks and well fashioned uniform impressive to the white visitors. "I do feel it is my duty as an officer in the United States military forces to offer my opinion on this matter. I fail to see what is so bad about receiving money for a piece of land and receiving additional land especially where there would be more freedom. Hell, people in the military live in all areas of the country and they're not asked whether they wish to be sent to some Godforsaken fort or not." He looked around but no one seemed to join his smile. "Besides, we cannot stop progress in this country." He sat with flushed face as he eyed Wild Hawk, enjoying the twitching face muscle and flashing dark eyes.

Sergeant Mathias stood. "Mr. White, gentleman, I have a tendency to go along with Lt. Anderson's thinking." He glanced at the lieutenant. "Seems to me, ain't no harm in offerin' money fer land 'n offerin' free land to boot. I've certainly never had such a opportunity." He sat, pleased with his thinking and speaking ability.

Colonel Roberts stood, acknowledging the three visitors. "Mr. White, Mr. Casey, and Murray, I must clarify a statement made by the lieutenant, comparing the life of the Cherokee with a soldier's life who volunteered his service in the U.S. Militia, which is hardly the same thing. When Lt. Anderson completes his stint in the military, no matter where he is sent during his service years, he will return to his home. It is the home and land of the Cherokee in discussion today, not an Army stint, and gentlemen, it is noontime." He checked his gold watch to make sure, "time to take our lunch break. The cooks have provided food outside in the compound, where tables are set up. We will now adjourn for lunch-returning here to complete the meeting at 1:30. Thank you."

They exit-The Indians in regal dignity, the soldiers more boisterous following the dignitaries. Rusty found Lone Eagle as Jeb Hawkins, Wild Hawk and Spotted Horse sat under an elm tree where they had a bit of privacy while the two braves listened attentively to the past year's exploits of big Jeb. It was good to have the tension eased by the colorful anecdotes so adequately woven by the big rugged man.

"Now, my brother, fill me in on your life these past months, what excitement other than John Brandon's move?" Jeb asks.

Spotted Horse described the Fort gathering where Wild Hawk made his spectacular appearance, gave details of the white girl child who won the running race over all males, the other winnings and the horse race. All of them laughed, enjoying the easy camaraderie.

"Oh! Rusty said Brandon also has two beautiful older daughters," Jeb smiled, as he sought an answer from Wild Hawk, whose countenance changed and immediately closed to him. What the hell, he thought, is my friend Hawk interested in one of those white females? My God!

Spotted Horse disrupted Jeb's thoughts. "Yes there are two very beautiful daughters, and one is teaching the Cherokee children to read and write the white language."

"Why that's great," Jeb answered, pulling out a pocket knife, continuing to watch Hawk, "but who interprets for them?"

Spotted Horse answered. "Wild Hawk, but for a while I'll be taking this over, since Hawk has been too busy with many responsibilities." He glared at Hawk, who suddenly announced that food was ready, stood and started for the tables.

The afternoon session was a little less heated as two other Cherokee Chiefs voiced opinions similar to Hawk's but lacking his enthusiasm. Only one other military representative spoke against the Cherokee keeping their land. All in all the day was for the Cherokee people; however, the three government officials did not seem overly deflated by the loss, for they knew there would be another day, another time.

As they exited for home, several individuals were left with deep thoughts about the day's meeting. Most of the Indians, including Lone Eagle and his representatives knew even though today was a success, the pushing had begun, and Wild Hawk was right about Andrew Jackson, the Indian hater. If he should become President, this push would indeed some day somehow become a shove.

When John Brandon hung the final lantern on the fence for the upcoming social gathering, Mary approached him. "Honey, hand me that small hammer, please?" John pointed to tools scattered on a chair.

Handing it to him, Mary stated, "I still can't understand why it was necessary to invite these three men from Washington, since you're against what they presented at the meeting yesterday." She finished placing a cloth on the table and setting an arrangement of flowers in the center.

He turned to face her. "Mary, please understand my position here. Regardless of my like or dislike for those Washington officials and even though I was against what they attempted to do yesterday, I am still a representative of the government on Indian Affairs, and it is my duty to invite them to my home."

"Well, it's not my duty," she added as she placed silver, plates and glasses. He turned and walked to her, turned her around to face him.

"Please, dear, this is hard enough at best for I totally went against those men yesterday in defense of the Cherokee, but please understand my position-, I had to ask them. I had no other choice, and I need your help."

"I know." She sighed and placed her hand on his chest. "I'm sorry-I'll try, but I feel for the Cherokee-they're peaceful, still the government wants to remove them from the land that they've held for years. How sad. You know, John," she added thoughtfully, "I'd almost rather entertain the Indians, than pretend we want these Washington people here."

He rubbed her cheek with his thumb. "You know, wife, I almost agree with you."

As Mary heard horses approaching, she made one final survey of her family to make sure Tim had bathed and Jesse didn't smell of horse manure. The older girls looked pretty in their sprigged cottons and as guests arrived Priscilla was in her zenith as she mingled graciously among them, fluttering and conversing while Kate served refreshments.

The three Washington visitors arrived with Colonel and Beatrice Roberts, followed by Major and Sarah Killingsworth. Lieutenants Anderson and Cason also arrived as did Captain and Margaret Dansom. Mary was the attentive hostess among her guests, noting when Lt. Anderson arrived, Priscilla's attention was focused entirely on him, and she excused herself from the plump William Casey, whose eyes followed the pretty Brandon girl.

Anderson ushered Prissey over near the fence as he whispered, "Hello, beautiful, it's great to feast my eyes on you again." He smiled his lazy smile.

Prissy pulled her chin up, tossing her mane of glorious dark hair and pouted. "Well, you haven't done much feasting lately. Thought you were coming last week." Her dark eyes sparkled fire.

"Honey," he caressed her with his hazel eyes and charming smile, "you know how busy I am. I simply couldn't get here." He squeezed her hand.

She looked away, mouth turned down, chin out, fiddling with her sleeve.

"You know-I want to be with you every minute that I can," he squeezed her arm, "Honey, let's not waste our precious time being upset. Come on, give me that beautiful smile of yours." He knew she'd come around.

She simply couldn't resist her Keith-oh! he's so handsome, she thought, and I know he cares for me. She dimpled prettily for him.

"That's my girl, and I do hope we can find some time to be alone this evening," he whispered and she nodded, noting the gate swinging open as Rusty Poole entered, carrying some type of musical instrument and as raunchy as ever in buckskin, followed by a tall mountain of a man she had never seen before who also wore buckskins.

John said, "Do come on in Rusty and Jeb. Believe you might know most of the people here, but not my family. My three daughters: Priscilla, Katherine, Jessica, son Tim and wife Mary-this is Jeb Hawkins, scout for the fort."

Jeb acknowledged the introduction. "You certainly have a beautiful family Mr. Brandon, "fastening his eyes on Priscilla who looked down her nose at the rough scout who obviously wasn't her type.

"And how does your family like the hills of Tennessee?" He smiled at Prissy.

"Mr. Hawkins, it would take a month for me to tell you what I think of-this desolate place." Prissy smoothed her skirt, smiling at Keith while most of the guests gazed at her in astonishment and Keith wasn't enjoying the attention this damn fool scout was giving her.

"It's a beautiful place." Jesse corrected as she handed Jeb a cup of punch, smiling impishly up at the big scout.

"You are so right, Jessica," he replied walking over toward the table while Rusty tuned up his fiddle and struck up a fast mountain tune, which was to everyone's amazement, very good.

Lieutenant Cason approached the table smiling shyly. "This is my third cup of punch-surely I'm not going to have to do this all night just to be near you." He set his cup down.

Katherine smiled at him. "Hi Tom-its good to see you again, and I won't be serving all evening."

John frowned as he observed Prissy and Keith Anderson slipping through the gate while Rusty struck up another lively tune, and a few couples began to dance. When Prissy hadn't returned in ten minutes John quietly exited, not pleased with this situation, and he couldn't put his finger on it, but something about the lieutenant and Priscilla made him uneasy. This daughter was such a pretty naive individual who wanted people to think she was worldly, but she knew absolutely nothing about a man such as Andersen. He quietly walked toward the barn when he heard a giggle and Priscilla's voice. "No, Keith-we can't do this."

"Priscilla," John called sternly, straining to see as he heard the rustling of garments near the oak tree.

"Papa, we were just getting a breath of air," she breathlessly responded.

Legend of the Whispering Wind

"You also have a responsibility to the guests inside," he struggled with his temper.

"Yes, sir."

"Now." He firmly stated before walking back to join his guests.

"Yes, sir," she added. Shortly after John returned, Prissy entered the gate, followed by Keith Anderson, both seemingly a trifle uncomfortable.

Jeb Hawkins observed this beautiful girl who he was sure was too innocent to understand the motives of such a one as Anderson who felt he was God's gift to women. He ambled over as Rusty began another tune. "May I have this dance, Miss Priscilly?" And before she had time to refuse, she was wheeled out with the others in strong arms to begin a high stepping hoe-down. Watching her dark eyes flash fire, Jeb smiled, thinking here is a spoiled young lady who certainly needs taming. "What's the matter, Miss Priscilly-ain't you enjoying thu' dancin'?"

"I think I'd rather plow," she snapped, as he swung her around, making her full skirt billow and much to her dismay, he was very light and smooth on his feet. She raised her voice, "I'll remind you my name is Priscilla," she jerked her head up, looking down her nose.

Keith Anderson watched the two, seething with anger that this back woods hick would interfere when he was visiting with a gal.

"Thank ye, Miss Priscilly for a lovely dance." Jeb's eyes twinkled as the music stopped. He was sure she'd like to smack his face, but before she could respond, he turned and walked to the table for a refill of punch, leaving Priscilla staring after him.

As Jeb held up his cup for more punch, Kate, who was serving, suddenly stared into the distant hills with much emotion crossing her countenance, obviously lost in her thoughts while she poured punch on the table instead of in his cup. Jeb followed her gaze, seeing on a nearby hill the still silhouette of an Indian astride his horse.

Coming back to life, she exclaimed, "Oh! Goodness-what have I done? I'm so sorry for being sloppy," her face flushed as she brushed her hair back. "Did I spill this on you, Mr. Hawkins?" Kate, obviously flustered, tried to cover her embarrassment with small talk.

"No-just call me Jeb-and now if you'll just fill my cup instead of the table-" He smiled at her embarrassment, thinking my friend Hawk you can't stay away can you, and it's obvious she is very disturbed. But Hawk, you've bitten off more than you can chew this time, Brother!

Kate stole a glance at the hill again-he was gone. Before, she thought, it was so strange, when Rusty stopped playing the fiddle and the talking subsided, I became aware of the wind as though it were whispering to me. That's when I glanced at the near hill and there he sat on his horse. Oh! What am I doing-I must get this mess cleaned up before Mama sees it. She glanced at her mother who was watching her intently Oh! My goodness! she thought as she removed the cloth and wiped up.

"Can I help?" It was Tom Cason, who she had ignored all evening without intending to. She'd forgotten him.

"Oh, Tom-it seems I became very busy here, then I made such a big mess spilling. As soon as I finish cleaning up we'll sit over there in the corner where we can talk," she smiled her sweetest and he melted. He's so nice she thought, and to think I forgot all about him. He's so sweet, thoughtful, and boring, bless his heart.

The evening seemed to be quite a success with Rusty's music, the jovial atmosphere and visitation. Even the Washington visitors relaxed and danced. All seemed reluctant to leave, especially Keith Anderson and Tom Cason, but after John Brandon cast several penetrating glances at Lieutenant Anderson, Keith thought it best he depart, for he didn't want to jeopardize his future with this little filly who was always so willing to fall into his arms.

"Honey," he squeezed Prissy's hand, "I'd better go-I don't think your father was pleased with our going outside tonight. I'll come back next week." He didn't like the way Brandon looked at him.

"Keith, don't worry about Papa-I can handle him." She glanced at her father and had second thoughts about her statement. She didn't like the way he stared at her. "Maybe you're right, but do come next week-I'll be waiting."

He nodded, smiled, and squeezed her hand again and she smiled her good-bye.

After everyone had departed, the table cleared and chairs put away, John announced, "Mary, you and Priscilla wait here-Tim, you, Jessica and Katherine go on to bed." John sat on the edge of the table, took out his pipe, filled it and lit it, and puffed away. Mary sat and Prissy nervously eased down onto a bench.

Why didn't he say something? Prissy thought. What's he waiting for? She smoothed her skirt.

Suddenly, John thundered, "Young lady, do you know you acted like a trollop tonight? Running out into the dark with that man?" He glared at her.

"Oh! No, sir I mean yes, sir, I mean I don't know, sir." She squirmed. What was the matter with Papa?

"Well! *I* know-and I'm not sure how I feel about any man who would encourage a young lady to leave a gathering and slip into the darkness, and you don't have sense enough to know that when you act like a loose woman a man will take advantage of you." His breathing was loud. He stood, pacing back and forth.

Prissy's eyes teared as her chin quivered. Papa had never talked to her like this and Mama was saying nothing-just looking at her.

"I'm-I'm sorry-guess I just didn't think," she sniffed. "I like Keith a lot," she smoothed her skirt, "and at the time I didn't think it was wrong to walk outside with him, but I guess it was. Do you suppose he thinks I'm bad, Papa? You know I'm not, Mama," She looked at her father then her mother with tears in her eyes. "You know I'm not a bad girl." Prissy broke into a sob.

"No, Priscilla, we don't think you're a bad girl," her father answered as he puffed his pipe, looking at her, "but you are a naive girl where men are concerned. How many times have you been with this lieutenant?"

"Four."

"Well, I don't like what he did this evening." John stopped pacing, looking into the distance. "His not caring about your reputation and you hardly know this man." He turned toward her. "Priscilla, I'll have to think long and hard about this happening tonight, and you will do a lot of thinking about the do's and don'ts of a young lady staying a lady." He crammed the pipe into his mouth. "I'm not sure this lieutenant will be welcome here again."

"Oh! Papa, please don't do this-I'll do a lot of thinking about my actions. You know I don't want to do something wrong, and I do care for Keith," she twisted her skirt, trying not to cry.

"Don't you think it has been a long day, John?" Mary stood. "I know Priscilla will do what is right for she is a good girl," she patted Prissy's shoulder.

"We'll see," he responded, continuing to stare into the distance. "Go on in, I'll be there shortly."

Mary pulled Prissy up and walked her into the house as John continued to stare into the distance, tapping tobacco from his pipe, still in disturbed thoughts about his daughter.

Chapter 8

The next day dawned with the sun rising over the misty lavender mountains, caressing her golden fingers over the lofty peaks. The hush of beginning day prompted John Brandon's thoughts toward his wife, spending time alone with her at a breathtaking spot he'd only found a few days ago-and after last night he needed a reprieve from the children.

Women! Why must they always keep men waiting! After explaining the day's agenda, the walk and the picnic, Mary seemed as excited as he. Course, he didn't reveal the secret place he was taking her to: That was a surprise. They hurried with breakfast, chores, then packed their lunch and she was ready 30 minutes ago. Whew. He threw himself into a chair.

"Mary," John yelled from the front lawn, as he gazed at his pocket watch for the third time. "C'mon, woman, what's keeping you? If you're not out here in five minutes, I am dragging you out!" He smiled with excitement, thinking of spending a day with his wife and away from the children!

The two younger Brandons boisterously spilled out of the house followed by Kate and Prissy.

"What's up, Papa?" Tim bounded over to his father, cramming a biscuit into his mouth.

"Well," John draped an arm around his son's shoulder, "your mother and I are taking the day off. We're going on a picnic."

"Oh! Boy!" Jesse screamed, "I'll be ready in just a minute. All I have to do is put my shoes on," she spurted toward the house, skirts flying.

"Jessica, you, Tim, Priscilla and Katherine are not going. I'm taking your mother on a picnic alone." John was tiring.

"How come?" Tim inquired, squinting his face.

"What for," Jesse scowled in wonderment.

"Mary," John was losing it. "if you don't get out here now, I'm leaving," he bellowed as he picked up a picnic basket from the porch. The children stared at him. Jess and Tim in bewildered awe, Kate smiling, Prissy with a raised eyebrow. She didn't dare say anything after the strong reprimanding last night.

Mary exited the house and approached them, wearing a blue cotton dress with matching bonnet, and John thought, she was still the same beautiful young girl he married. He reached for her hand. "Come on honey," he assisted her down the steps, loving her with his smile as Jesse pouted.

"I don't want to stay with mean Prissy and hateful Kate-'sides they don't do nuthin' but give orders to work 'n that ain't no fun. Prissy is always lookin' in the mirror, trying to be purty 'n Kate just acts ugly." She snubbed and rushed up the steps. "I'd never treat my children this way!" She turned, chin quivering.

"Jessica, you stop this action immediately," her father roared. "If you are still a baby and continue, then you may go to bed and stay there," her father meant it, she could tell. When his green eyes got smoky-lookin', he was mad!

Jess sank down on the steps, put her chin on her knees and seethed.

"There's stew keeping warm over the fire. Katherine, you are in charge of the meal and Priscilla cleaning up," Mama explained as Papa ushered her through the gate and called, "We'll be back sometime this afternoon-be good to each other while we're gone." They left, hand in hand.

John and Mary strolled across the meadow toward the misty blue green mountain peaks, caressed by the warm sunshine and mountain breeze. As they walked toward John's secret destination, they thoroughly appreciated the late spring flowering canopy of the bluebells, white twinkles, and yellow daisies, smiling their colorful faces at the two strollers. The beginning mountain trail wound itself around boulders laden with a glory of flesh colored to deeper pink rhododendron. A chattering chipmunk flashed its tail in angry protests at the two intruders who dared enter his domain, sailed around a boulder, while a warbler announced the beautiful day's warmth.

Oh! Mary caught her breath, it's so wonderful to be part of God's great glory, she thought. "John," she whispered, for to voice a sound would somehow intrude on this splendor, "Thank you," she whispered while touching his arm. "This beauty makes my heart sing." She smiled at him, her lovely hazel eyes misty. He squeezed her hand, understanding.

They traveled on up the winding pine scented trail, finding conversation unnecessary, simply letting themselves become a part of their surroundings, where squirrels frolicked, birds chirped and trilled, and Mother Nature complemented the entirety with her radiant color of floral displays, shrubs and trees.

They climbed higher when suddenly, around a large boulder God had placed, a vivid green sanctuary banked by mountain laurel intermingled with rhododendron. Mary stopped, awestruck, drinking in the total splendor as John watched her reaction. Where a large boulder rose as a sentinel, a mountain spring gurgled its way down the side to find its resting place in a small blue green pool. A majestic oak offered its leafy arms in a protective canopy. Mary was totally spellbound by the wonderment of the place and moment. Her eyes were teared as John put his arms around her and whispered, "Welcome home-this is my secret to you, and our home away from home!"

"Oh! John-I can't believe this," she clung to him, "the beauty, the glory here-" she looked around, "and your wanting to share it with me-how romantic!" She teased, "How many years has it been since we went on a picnic alone and never to such a place as this. It's as though the hands of time have turned back and we're 20 again, when God said we were right for each other."

He smiled, hugged her tighter, both feeling the beauty of the moment and place, where words were not needed.

Finally, hunger prevailed, and they feasted on the delicious basket contents, washing it down with cider and cold mountain spring water. Both laughed aloud as a disgruntled blue jay squawked his angry protest at the two trespassing on his special area.

From an overhang, Mary viewed the panoramic beauty of the valley below, and turned to find John spreading a quilt under the oak.

"John Brandon, what in the world are you doing, and why the quilt?" Mary laughingly inquired as she strolled toward her husband.

"Well," his eyes crinkled mischievously, "thought after the long walk and filling lunch we might need a nap before returning-or at least a rest. Come on over here and sit by me. He stretched out his long legs, leaning back on an elbow as he watched his lovely wife acting so prim and proper. She eased down next to him, placing her skirt just so and sitting with her back ramrod straight.

"Mary, for goodness sakes-relax-you look every bit as stiff and unrelenting as an old maid school teacher-not someone who's been wed to a wonderful, handsome man for 20 years." He pulled her back against his shoulder as she tried to contain her laughter while uttering,

"You're terrible," but she became serious.

"I was thinking of something we need to discuss. It's been bothering me for some time, John, and" -she turned her head toward him as he placed his finger against her lips, explaining, "not here, Mary-we're not going to bring the outside conflicts to this place," as he eased her onto her back while hovering very near, touching her face gently and brushing her lips with his.

"John, what are you doing?" she blushed.

"Woman, after 20 years, you are asking this?" He brushed their lips together again as he began removing pins from her hair.

"Oh! John-no, we mustn't-not here, we—" the remainder of her words were smothered as his lips found hers in a deeper kiss, while he gathered her to him. Protests simmered to slight moans as her arms crawled up around his neck.

The world was back in focus as John and Mary approached their home, finding Jesse bounding toward them. "What's wrong,? Your hair is hanging all over the place, and your face is pink. Are you sick?" She squinted.

Looking at Mary, John smiled. "Your mother isn't sick-she was warmed today-ah-by the sun-and her head simply got tired of pins!" They strolled on as Tim gave them his warm greeting.

"Mama, you sure look awful! I didn't know old people like you put their hair hangin' like that," his freckles stood out strong as he gazed at his mother.

"Home sweet home," John commented. "Tim, your mother is still in her '30's," he scolded firmly, "she's a young lovely woman and if she wants to wear her hair hanging to her knees, she would still be pretty." Mary smiled at him.

Priscilla and Katherine had entered the porch just-in-time for Tim's warm greeting to his parents, noting their mother's appearance and their fathers quick response. With eyebrows lifted they looked at each other, smiling. Both thinking how pretty their mother actually looked, and how much in love their parents were. As the Brandons neared their entrance, two mounted Indians approached. Both stopped as John Brandon greeted Spotted Horse and Bear Claw, who slipped from their mounts to the ground, tying them.

Jesse exploded toward the Cherokee. "Spotted Horse, why didn't Wild Hawk come with you, too? Don't he care for me anymore?" Bear Claw could hardly contain his laughter at this girl child.

"He couldn't come this time," Horse glanced at Katherine who observed him carefully, obviously interested in his response.

"Do come on in and have seats-I'll send lemonade and cookies out." Mary welcomed the Indians who agreed. "Come children, and give your father a chance to visit with the Cherokee." Jesse took a seat by Spotted Horse.

"But I want to stay and listen 'n sides, I have a message for Wild Hawk." The Indians barely contained their amusement.

"Jess-i-ca, I won't tell you again." Mama's eyes were flashing and when that happened Jess knew better than to push any further. She immediately followed into the house mumbling.

John lit his pipe while asking, "How may I help you?" Spotted Horse nodded to Bear Claw who was pleased that he had a part in delivering this invitation to John Brandon who had sided with the Cherokee against the whites at the big meeting. He began, "Each year village celebrates 'Green Corn' with feast-dance-big thing-last long." John nodded, trying his best to stay with the broken English without questions. Spotted Horse took over.

"This celebration is very important to Cherokee. Our chief sends special invitation to John Brandon and family to join in this. Chief wish to shake hand of friendship and special thanks to Katherine Brandon for her help to teach Cherokee children." They awaited John's reply as he rather emotionally responded, "Thank you and Chief Lone Eagle for such a gracious gesture. The Brandons will be honored to accept this invitation." He knew what a big step the chief was taking.

"Will smoke Brandon's pipe now," and as Bear Claw reached for John's pipe, took it, to John's dismay, gestured in four directions, puffed it, handed it to Spotted Horse who first received John's nod, then repeated the procedure, before returning it to its owner who also repeated the gesture because the Indians were watching. They nodded approvingly.

As they completed the ceremony Katherine approached with lemonade. Jesse followed with cookies and in a harsh whisper for all to hear, "Kate, did you see that? Our Papa is actin' kind of crazy like-he's pointin' that pipe up and down and around ah! Umm I'm gonna tell Mama!"

"Hush your mouth," her older sister reprimanded as John glared at Jessica.

Spotted Horse continued, "in two moons two braves will escort you to village-a lodge will be prepared for you and family for night's stay. Celebration last long time-you would not have time to return to your home same night."

"Oh! Boy! I can't wait," Jesse yelled.

Katherine passed lemonade and cookies while glaring at Jessica. The Indians nodded their thanks and smiled happily as they enjoyed the white man's refreshments.

John explained the invitation to Katherine that the Cherokee wished to thank her for teaching, which pleased but embarrassed her. As John explained, Spotted Horse opened a leather pouch and handed to Katherine a slate with written words on it; "Come and be with us at Green Corn-we love!" Signed by each Cherokee student, Katherine read the inscription aloud, looked down holding the slate to her chest while she struggled with her emotion as she replied, misty eyed, "Tell my students their writing to me is one of the greatest gifts I've ever received, and I will be honored to attend their Green Corn."

Spotted Horse was impressed with the sincerity of the young white woman who obviously cared for the Cherokee children. She was certainly different from most white females he had encountered or even heard about, who usually cringed at the sight of an Indian.

After the Cherokee had departed, John gathered his family together to explain the special invitation to Lone Eagle's village. Tim and Jess were exuberant. Kate was quiet, not voicing an opinion but obviously in deep thought. Mary knew this was a big step for the chief to invite the Brandons in friendship and this was exactly what John's job needed. She eyed the children, aware by Priscilla's flashing eyes and nervous hands picking at her skirt that she was about to explode. Well, they would go, of course. To do otherwise would be a great effrontery to the Cherokee, but spending the night was another thought.

Priscilla ripped, "Papa, you can't be serious-this is the most ridiculous thing I have ever heard." Her dark eyes flashed fire as she strode to the fence, having trouble breathing, and she turned abruptly. "I'm not staying in a dirty Indian village with a bunch of savages! All of you go, but I'm staying here!"

"Priscilla," her father thundered, "you get yourself over here immediately," as he pointed to a chair. She complied, rushing, skirts flying, afraid not to. "Sit and listen carefully for I'll only say it once." The others stared in disbelief not having heard their father use such a tone. "Don't you ever," pointing a finger, "ever again tell me or your mother what you will or won't do, as long as you're a member of this household. You will do as I say, make no mistake about it, and you will accompany this family to Lone Eagle's village, and with a decent attitude. If at any time you act otherwise, the consequences will be most difficult for you to face. I'm sick and tired of your selfishness and it's high time you thought of someone else other than yourself. Go on to your room-two altercations with you in two days is simply too much!"

The entire family left John to smoke his pipe and hopefully cool his temper.

Chapter 9

Jeb Hawkins and Wild Hawk pranced their horses, laden with fresh meat into Lone Eagle's village, where several dark eyed maidens smiled seductive glances toward them amid their chattering and laughter. The amused males responded with their own banter and smiles, Jeb speaking Cherokee as well as the Cherokee himself. At the Old Crone's lodge they were aware of the total activity of the village, the excitement throughout, realizing the Green Corn was a great celebration but the action here seemed to be more than that. The children were ecstatic, running and laughing all over the place, even the dogs joined in, barking and playfully running in circles. Everyone was busy cleaning lodges, brushing the ground around their entrances, cooking with mouth watering aromas permeating the air.

"I wonder what the great excitement is-it's more than the Green Corn celebration," Wild Hawk puzzled as he slid down from his horse at Crone's dwelling and pulled two rabbits down as Old Crone shuffled her wiry frame toward him, cackling with only three teeth visible in the walnut colored leathery skin, creased with a multitude of crisscrossed wrinkles folding in around her still very alert black eyes. She nodded her thanks, taking the game, squinting a glance toward Jeb before shuffling back toward her entrance. Hawk stopped her. "What's all the excitement about, old woman?" he inquired in Cherokee.

As she swung around, she cackled, excitement brimming from her small black eyes. "Them pale eyes is coming-ones that teaches Cherokee children and whole family." She waved her arms as if there were a thousand. "Spotted Horse, Bear Claw, ride with them here. They stay in Spotted Horse's lodge the night." At this news

Legend of the Whispering Wind

Hawk took a step back, nostrils flared, eyes shuttered. Old Crone observed this, young brave, her favorite who was like a son to her.

"You no want pale eyes here?" She wiped her mouth on her soiled sleeve as she observed sadness in his eyes.

"No, I don't want them here," he wheeled, took Night Wind's reins and walked purposefully toward his chief's lodge, accompanied by his friend, who also observed this braves reaction, thinking he reveals fear of seeing one white girl. He had never known Wild Hawk to be afraid of anything. Shaking his head, he ambled over to the large area where Rusty Poole was showing his skill at roasting meat and where he would deposit his fresh kill.

Chief met his nephew at his front stoop, wondering why the scowl and flashing eyes. "My son, what bothers you so? Sit-you look most disturbed," the old chief sat indicating Hawk to do the same.

"Why did you invite the Brandons here?" He squatted, seriously, questioning his chief as he picked up a small stick.

"Why? I invited them because they deserve to be invited. A gesture of friendship to a white man who stood up against the whites for the Cherokee, and a thank-you to the young white woman who has given herself to help educate Cherokee children. I can't believe you're against this gesture. Why?" The black penetrating gaze of the chief observed his nephew carefully.

Wild Hawk shifted his gaze to the ground where he drew circles with the stick, unable to look at his chief. Why did he come here and approach this man with such a ridiculous question? It seemed to be a constant thing, lately-acting without thinking-but how could he, explain to this man that he simply couldn't be around Katherine Brandon, not now. Of course, it wasn't right to allow his personal feelings to overshadow things of importance to his people, which he was doing.

His turmoil was obvious to the chief. "You haven't answered, my son, but you certainly reveal a great disturbance over this gesture."

"I'm sorry," Hawk replied, "I can't explain my reaction, but it was wrong for me to have come here and questioned this. Don't be angry with me." He stood to leave, uncomfortable, as he tossed the stick aside.

Chief nodded, knowing that this young man would reveal nothing until he was ready, realizing, too, he was quite disturbed over something. "Take the meat on over where the celebration will be held. Women are there who will take it."

Hawk nodded and left.

Wild Hawk, leaning against a distant tree as the Brandon wagon approached Lone Eagle's lodge caught his breath as Katherine Brandon's mane of auburn hair caught the sun, and she smiled gloriously for the excited Cherokee children who scampered around the wagon. He watched as her lithe yellow clad figure vaulted from the buckboard, and her arms were suddenly filled with laughing Cherokee children waiting for hugs. His heart thumped and he cursed himself with every derogatory term in the Cherokee language as he strode from the scene.

Not only was Wild Hawk watching the Brandon's arrival, Dancing Eyes watched Hawk, observing his reaction to the pale eyes dressed in yellow, his emotion, his turmoil. She seethed, black eyes flashing with envy and jealousy, vowing to herself that she would do what ever it took to keep her man from this pale eyes.

As John assisted his ladies from their wagon, Lone Eagle approached, donned in a beautifully designed long doeskin shirt.

"Welcome, John Brandon and family, to my village. Thank you for accepting the invitation to our celebration." Chief Eagle offered his hand, greeting the Brandons warmly, smiling broadly as Jesse spied him, galloped up and grabbed his arm in both hands.

"Chief Lone Eagle, it's so good to see you again," She squinted a smile up at him as she squeezed his arm, "but-" she suddenly drew back, looking around. "Where is Wild Hawk-I thought he'd be here to greet me." She looked dejected.

"He's around-somewhere-I'm sure you will see him soon." He patted her as he unhinged himself from the child, who nodded then bounded off to find the Cherokee children.

Lone Eagle ushered the Brandons to seats near his log lodge, as two young maidens, staring at the Brandon girls and their clothes, served refreshing drinks from gourd cups. Even Prissy accepted hers, and enjoyed the apple flavored juice.

Shortly, Eagle spoke to one of the maidens in Cherokee who left immediately.

"Chief," John inquired, looking around the village, "tell us something about your Green Corn celebration."

"You will hear this soon, and also will be taken on a tour of our village if you like. Now if you will excuse me there are some matters I must take care of before we begin the celebration. You will be placed in good hands with someone you already know." He turned, smiling as Wild Hawk quietly approached, buckskin fringe swaying with his stride, trying his best not to show any emotion as he bowed slightly.

"Mr. Brandon and family, welcome to our village." He looked at John steadily, shook hands as he nodded to other family members-hesitated before capturing green eyes for a moment. "Excuse me while I speak with my chief," he strode to Lone Eagle who watched his nephew intently as he attempted a closed countenance, but his chief knew he was very tense, uncomfortable with these people-why? he wondered. Hawk spoke softly in Cherokee, "You sent for me to help with the Brandons, I realize because there are so few of us that speak the white tongue, but I cannot accompany these people around the village. Please find someone else. I'm sorry-" he shifted his weight, looking away, unable to meet the penetrating gaze of his chief. "I suppose I could explain the celebration to them if you wish."

Chief nodded. "I do not know what your problem is, but it must be a big one that I am sure you will explain when you are ready." His black eyes crinkled with humor. "I will send for Spotted Horse, even though he is tired from the journey today, I am sure he is not too tired to escort these lovely young maidens around the village." He smiled as Hawk's black eyes flashed, and his gaze swiftly shifted to the young lady in yellow. Ah! The chief sighed to himself.

A muscle twitched in Hawks face as he responded. "Since Spotted Horse is so weary, we wouldn't want him to be worn out for the contests," he sarcastically retorted, "I guess I can accompany the Brandons after all."

The chief could hardly contain his amusement at this big strapping nephew of his. He shook his head, smiling as he exited while Hawk walked back to the Brandons, entered the circle, stooped down, crossing an arm over one knee attempting to remain casual, but a tenseness continued to prevail. He smiled, "I will explain the Green Corn celebration as it was a few years ago and today." Kate hung onto his deep mellow voice, wondering why this man acted so strange as though he didn't even want them here or that he didn't know them. He seemed so different from the person who had previously brought the Cherokee children for lessons. Then, she thought they were friends.

He continued trying his best not to glance in Katherine's direction, but cussed himself for being unable to avoid looking at her.

"Many years ago our people had very elaborate celebrations for a basic food-corn. They had celebrations for the planting, the first roasting ear and another for the full ripe time. Each of these lasted for days. There were strenuous contests with some quite vicious where arms and legs were broken." Again, he stole a glance at the green eyes who was listening intently and watching him, her mouth slightly open which completely mesmerized him, causing him to forget what he was saying as he drank in her beauty with firelight sparking her hair. Suddenly realizing his dilemma as all stared at him, he offered some foolish explanation that he was sure no one believed. Again, cussing to himself, finding words he didn't even know he knew.

"Our celebration today lasts only one afternoon and evening with skill contests, contests of strength, races, feasting, the blessing of the corn for fertility and ending with dancing."

"Will you participate in the contests, Wild Hawk?" John asked, intrigued by the storytelling and its history.

"I always participate in as many as possible."

Mary, looked at her husband and could have screamed at him. She thought, can't you see anything John Brandon? This young brave can't keep his eyes off Katherine and she watches him, hanging on to every word he says. Why don't you do something instead of discussing celebrations. We never should have come here!

"Mama, is something wrong?" Katherine was concerned, watching the different emotions cross her mother's face as it contained a pinkish hue.

"I'm all right." Her mother wanted to say- everything's wrong. She fidgeted, her hands twisting in her lap as Hawk immediately brought her a gourd of fresh spring water, stooping down near her.

"Thank you," She looked at his handsome concerned face feeling ashamed of her thoughts when these people were trying so hard to welcome them. Too bad this young man was an Indian. He seemed to have good qualities.

"Are you sure you feel well enough to walk around the village? We could postpone it until tomorrow." Hawk revealed his concern as he reached for the gourd.

Mary nodded, "Yes, I'm all right, thank you."

He stood. "Earlier, my chief asked me to explain our celebration, and to escort you on a tour of our village if you wish."

"Yes, we would like that." John stood and answered for all not aware or caring that Prissy looked pained and would have liked just to sit where she was. She wasn't slightly interested in seeing this Indian village or anyone in it.

"We must leave now since the contests will begin soon." They stood as he led the way through a variety of trees with log lodges spaced throughout, where numerous Cherokee of all ages milled around, casting glances at the whites-some smiling, others staring with no emotion. Katherine watched the graceful stride of this tall brave, wondering how many Indian maidens were trying to capture his wild heart.

Suddenly, there was a high pitched piercing yell for Wild Hawk as Jesse bounced up, attacking him around the waist, embarrassing her entire family.

"Jess-i-ca, mind your manners!" her mother hammered as Jessica unhinged herself and grabbed his hand, looking up and thinking he is thu' purtiest man I ever seen.

"You didn't even tell me good-bye and that you wouldn't be back to bring the Cherokee students! That wasn't nice!"

"No, it wasn't-but I didn't know I wouldn't be back when I was at your home," he smiled at this lovely girl child who wore her feelings on her sleeve. "We must hurry now, Jesse-I'm taking your family around the village before the celebration begins."

"But-will I see you again?" She squinted up at him, squeezing his hand.

"Of course," he retrieved his hand as she nodded, smiled, waved and then ran off to catch her friends.

A few braves readying themselves for the competition jibed and yelled to Hawk in Cherokee, "You leading a grand parade, Hawk," they laughed, poking each other.

Hawk retorted in Cherokee, "I'll show you a parade in the contests." He smiled as the braves continued to watch the beautiful pale eyed girls.

The family members were impressed with the village. Prissy couldn't get over the cleanliness of the area and that the people seemed to take pride in their own appearance. She'd always thought Indians were filthy. Several of the maidens were absolutely lovely. Mary was a little overwhelmed by the natural beauty of the area, and the friendliness of many Cherokee.

As they passed near a lodge, a little chubby boy streaked out to meet them, dressed only in a breech clout with his fat tummy hanging over. His plump little arms latched onto Wild Hawk's leg as he pealed forth excited laughter, before the big Indian scooped "Little Cub" up for a toss in the air as the little boy shrieked with childish delight. Hawk laughed with the small pudgy lad as he hugged him before putting him down with a pat on the bottom. The Brandons were shocked by the interplay of this big arrogant brave, showing such gentleness and affection toward the child. They didn't know Indians had such emotions, much less displayed them somehow.

Katherine stared at the two, not quite understanding her reaction, but suddenly she had to know. "Is he your son?" She watched him intently as he turned, smiling slightly, thoroughly amused.

"No, that's Little Cub who belongs to my cousin, but we are good buddies," she smiled crinkling a small dimple near her mouth.

"Yes, I can tell." He continued to stare at her intently, drawn to her, hoping to see her smile again as she began to blush under his scrutiny. He came back to the present, reprimanding himself, what the hell am I doing?

Mary intervened, drawing his attention, "Do you have any children, Wild Hawk?" Hoping he had a wife and children.

"No, I have never been wed."

Oh! My goodness, how revolting, Mary thought, as they strolled on where three maidens watched, one an outstanding beauty in long fringed white doeskin, who called in Cherokee to Wild Hawk while she flashed him a radiant smile. He answered, continuing to move on while she turned and looked daggers of hatred at Katherine, who was baffled at the obvious show of dislike. What in the world have I done to cause such hostility, Kate asked herself.

They completed their tour at the river, which meandered beautifully around the village, bordered by overhanging elms and oaks interspersed with large boulders. The area, it's peacefulness, friendly people, with exception of a few, and the cleanliness impressed the entire family.

Shortly they were ushered to Spotted Horse's lodge where they were to remain the night. Wild Hawk excused himself, "I hope you enjoy the celebration. Rusty Poole and Jeb Hawkins will escort you there. Little Acorn will bring Jesse and Tim." He turned quickly and left. Katherine watched, not understanding such abruptness.

The games and contests turned out to be exciting and interesting, held in a large cleared area with the delightful aroma of roasting venison and wild boar filling the air.

The children's running races varied, by ages with only Indian males participating. They were allowed no contests of strength. Little Cub put on a delightful solo exhibition of trotting half way around, donned only in his breech clout. Upon reaching the halfway turn he sat down, then stretched out to rest as the crowd went wild, trilling and hooting their excitement. The Brandons, seated with Jeb and Rusty found it equally amusing.

Wild Hawk won in two events, arm wrestling and body wrestling, tying with his good friend Spotted Horse in his third event, knife throwing. Both were jibing and teasing the other about cheating; however, it was not the same camaraderie when Wild Hawk bested Swift Antelope in body wrestling. Afterwards, Hawk grasped Antelope's shoulder in friendship to have Antelope jerk away in anger. Hawk stared after him, not understanding.

Katherine, rooting for Hawk all the way, didn't even understand why-what difference did it make who won, but it seemed to make a difference.

The Cherokee children, accompanied by Tim, Jess and Little Cub sat with the Brandons for a while. Jeb could not resist snatching Little Cub up on his knee as he played horse with the chubby cherub. The outbreak of childish delight was infectious to all, including Miss prim Priscilla. Finally, Little Cub reached for Prissy to take him, which she was reluctant to do because he was dirty, but he prevailed and jumped squarely onto her lap, reached up and gave her neck a hug before bounding over and plopping in Kate's lap, who grabbed him up and gave him a loud bussing kiss on his fat tummy while he grabbed her hair in childish glee. She then taught the darling imp patty-cake, and spoke in English to him, pointing to him, "Cub," then pointing to herself, "Kate."

The intelligent tyke picked it up quickly, pointing to self, "Cub," then to Kate, "Kate". Katherine was unaware of the tall black eyed brave who watched her interplay with Little Cub, and who was totally taken in by the scene.

The little brave jumped down, taking Kate's hand, and pulled on her saying, "Kate". She stood as the little guy held her hand, leading her down the side of the field where spectators sat, finally stopping in front of a lovely young Cherokee woman with a beautiful smile.

He pointed to his mother who said, "Little Sparrow," pointing to herself.

Cub pointed to himself, "Cub," then to Kate, "Kate." She smiled at the pretty Sparrow as she was pulled again by the small lad who held her hand, leading her somewhere. Their destination wound up at a tall brave who leaned against an oak tree, smiling. Little Cub latched his pudgy arms around Hawk's buckskin leg and squealed in his childish delight, as he was hoisted up in strong arms, but the small boy decided his buddy wasn't paying attention to him, only the girl. With two fat hands he turned Hawk's face toward him, pointing to himself, "Cub," then pointed to Kate saying, "Kate."

"Yes," Hawk whispered, watching Kate intently. "Kate, but to me-Green Eyes." Kate found herself unable to speak, she was so drawn into the smile and the gaze that seemed to caress her. Finally, she became aware of her surroundings, blushed at her reaction, stammered,

"You were very impressive in your contests today."

He nodded, amused at her embarrassment. She turned abruptly to leave as Little Cub again grabbed her hand to lead her away.

Legend of the Whispering Wind

Wild Hawk watched the graceful girl in yellow, with firelight playing in her hair as she held the hand of a small Cherokee boy.

The food was surprisingly delicious, roasted venison, wild boar, squash, a type of hominy from corn, beans, a fried bread of corn, a small sweet patty of honey and berries, served in clay bowls.

Children's dancing followed the festive feast. Young boys, fully decorated but clad in only breech clouts and moccasins performed an impressive shuffle dance. The young girls followed, clad in long fringed doeskin shifts which swayed effectively in accompaniment to the rhythm of the drum beat and dance steps as they portrayed harvesting the corn crop.

Shortly thereafter, Little Cub ran to the center field, clad in full war bonnet tail feathers, bells and breech clout, jumping and gyrating as though he were plunging a lance into the enemy before he lost total balance and sprawled flatly on his face and tummy. The crowd roared with approval as the little boy stood, rubbed his fat tummy, blinked his black eyes, trying his best to control his tears as he streaked from the field to his amused father, Bear Claw, who stooped to check his son carefully for any bodily harm. Finding none, he sent the wee warrior on his way with a pat, smiling as he watched this tiny replica of himself with a father's pride.

The ritual blesser was magnificent in his green as he took the center of the field, depicting a full grown cornstalk with head of yellow spike indicating corn tassels, his total body painted green, clothed only in a green breech clout, wrists and hands painted yellow offering the full harvest ears of corn. His dance began with the planting of the seed, intricate steps pantomimed the sprouting, his graceful movements and footwork portrayed the growth and a final surge of difficult steps indicated the full growth of the corn as his stature reached for the sky.

He then ran to the nearby corn field, where he asked for Yawa and etsi eli hi no, Mother Earth, the blessing of fertility for the growing stalks, pointing to each.

Following, the braves gave a spectacular hunt dance, stalking, chasing, leaping and gyrating gracefully into intricate steps as they pantomimed the final kill. The crowd roared with approval; the Brandons also joined in the applause. Mary didn't fail to observe the excitement in Katherine's eyes.

All eyes shifted to Chief Lone Eagle as he paraded regally to the center area, clothed in a beautifully beaded designed knee length doeskin shirt, his plumed turban swaying with each step. Little Acorn followed his chief as he proudly acted as interpreter.

"Cherokee and other friends, we wish to extend the hand of friendship before we participate in our final Friendship Dance. Most of you know our <u>old</u> friend," he stressed, "Rusty Poole," he twinkled as Rusty stood. "Jeb Hawkins, the scout who has practically lived with us for years," he motioned Jeb to stand. "John Brandon, consultant and family." All stood as many Cherokee nodded, smiled and applauded for all knew of John's backing the Cherokee over the white at the late fort meeting.

He turned, nodded to Little Acorn as the young brave proudly stepped forward, trying his best to emulate his chief in stance and stature.

"Miss Katherine Brandon, if you will please come." He flashed a smile toward his teacher as Brown Otter suddenly appeared at Katherine's side to escort her to the center area. They were soon joined by the other students as Happy Girl approached her teacher, speaking in her best white tongue. "Miss Katherine, we present gifties-ah-gifts," she corrected, "to you very much good teacher." She hugged Katherine's waist as she handed her a many colored beaded spirit bag. Kate's eyes teared as she accepted beads, moccasins, and a multi colored beaded belt-all made by these children and presented with their broken English "Thank you." Kate was overwhelmed with these giving people, and these children she had learned to love. Suddenly, she had arms filled with happy, smiling girl students. Of course, the young braves were entirely too fierce to hug their teacher before others. They nodded and smiled.

Kate struggled with her speaking. "Chief Eagle, my students and all the Cherokee, thank you so very much, for including me and my family in this great celebration. It has indeed been a privilege to be here." Little Acorn translated as Brown Otter went with a message for Tim who brought Kate's gifts to the children. Each was happy to receive a book, something he or she had never owned.

The Cherokee applauded and trilled as Katherine returned to her seat. There were dark eyes revealing special interest in this young lady; however, one black eyed Indian maiden in white long fringed doeskin stood near, clenching and unclenching her fists, black eyes shooting angry sparks at Kate as she hissed, "Bitch!"

Chief Eagle commanded attention again as he explained the last and final event of the evening, the important Friendship Dance.

Soon the pulsating rhythms caressed the entire group, pulling them into and wrapping them in the mood of the moment.

Wild Hawk and Spotted Horse stood near the sideline, laughing and joking over a private matter when Jesse appeared, breathless, accompanied by Happy Girl.

"Wild Hawk," Jesse exploded as she zoomed in on him pulling at his arm and smiling, "this is so excitin' and it'll have to be our dance," her eyes sparkled, "because it's the last one and we're best of friends," she excitedly grinned up at her idol. As he stooped down to explain to Jesse that children were not allowed to participate, suddenly a flash of white fringe sailed into view.

Dancing Eyes glared at Jessica as though she were a contagious disease, then snapped her black visage to Hawk, sidled over to him, caressing him with her most charming smile, touched his arm, saying in her sultry broken English for the pale eyes benefit, "Hawk dance friendship with Dancing Eyes," she patted her chest. The brave nodded, knowing a refusal was not tolerated. The maiden also knew no one refused a dance invitation.

Hawk explained to Jesse why he wouldn't be dancing with her who again exploded, "That's not fair," she pouted, "I haven't spent any time with you."

Spotted Horse had to turn away to keep from laughing at his friend's dilemma as Dancing Eyes stormed up to Jesse. "Pale eyes-leave-go!" she pointed her finger, eyes flashing anger.

Hawk halted her in stern chastisement, telling her in Cherokee to back off-that this young girl was his friend, and he would not tolerate any abuse from her. The lovely maiden tucked her head, backed up, not wanting to upset this man further, but she still hated all these pale eyes. They had no business coming here.

Jesse turned back to Hawk, pointing to Dancing Eyes. "I don't know why you are around that bad woman-she ain't nice at all and you are the purtiest and nicest man I know except," she looked down, "when you didn't tell me good-bye." She smiled, scuffed her toe as she wiped her nose on her sleeve.

"Jesse," he stooped down where he could look her in the eye, and took her hand. "I will visit with you before you leave. There are special rules about our dances so don't be sad over this." She nodded. He stood, glancing at his friend as Spotted Horse strolled by, thoroughly amused with the situation. Hawk shot daggers at him.

A loud disturbance drew attention near the Brandons, as Old Crone and her friend Crooked Toe flung every derogatory term they could think of at each other, she dog, viper fang, horse dung-before Crone finally tromped purposely on her friends crooked toe, and sent the furious woman away howling. Spotted Horse exploded with laughter as he arrived to unravel the strong altercation, finding Rusty Poole at the bottom of the whole thing.

The old scout had just explained to Jeb and the Brandons how it was very impolite in the eyes of the Cherokee to reject an invitation as a dance partner. This must never be done, he just thought he'd warn them in case one of the Cherokee should ask, so he'd simply mosey on down and around where, "I'll find me one of them young shapely black eyed maidens and me 'n her'll kick up our heels in that thar friendship dance that'll knock yore eyes out." He poked Jeb, slapped his leg as he cackled and stood just as Spotted Horse arrived on the scene with Old Crone, who cackled her own snaggletooth excitement as she asked Rusty to be her dance partner. Horse was more than delighted to fill in as interpreter while Rusty's face fell to his toes and his dreams of a beautiful maiden turned to the long nights struggle with an ancient toothless dried up hag. He turned back toward his friends, who waved, smiled, and nodded knowingly.

"C'mon, Miss Priscilly-we can't let them drums and chantin' go to waste," Jeb pulled Prissy up, hardly able to contain himself when he glanced toward Rusty.

"But I don't know anything about this ridiculous dance. I can't and I won't-quit pulling on me." Prissy jerked away, looking down her nose, flipping her chin up.

"Look, don't pull this high and mighty stuff with me. You're dancin', Miss Priscilly, whether you want to or not. These are good people and they don't need hurt or rudeness from anybody." He took her in hand and pulled her toward the group.

"Well, of all the nerve," she screeched and was ready to continue her tirade when she stumbled and was jerked forward without sympathy. She finally realized her squawking was doing no good.

John escorted Mary toward the dancing group, as Spotted Horse approached Kate and bowed slightly. "May I escort you as your dance partner, Miss Katherine?" She stood and said "Why yes, I'd be glad to be your partner," as dark penetrating eyes watched in angry agony as his friend assisted Kate to the line and placed her by Dancing Eyes directly across from Hawk, then took his place by his friend, mouth twitching a slight smile at Hawk who was in total bewilderment, and nodded to Dancing Eyes flashing anger.

What is going on here, Kate wondered, for Spotted Horse asked me to be his partner, then placed me by this girl who hates me. Hawk seems to be angry most of the time, ignoring me, what's wrong? I thought we were friends. What have I done to him to be treated this way? She glanced at this brave who filled her thoughts, caught him staring at her, but he quickly shifted his gaze to the pretty maid across from him, smiling broadly.

How dare Spotted Horse put that she-dog next to me, where Hawk can stare at her, Dancing Eyes furiously wondered, and she turned, glaring at Katherine, not understanding why any handsome brave would want to look at this ugly pale eyed pale skinned thing. And look at that Spotted Horse with his grinning face, enjoying all this, but maybe he cares for this pale thing, could it be-she smiled to herself.

Hawk glared at his so called friend, observing Spotted Horse's twitching smile and amused twinkle. Right now, he'd like nothing better than to flatten him and wipe that amusement off his face. Of all the guts, escorting Katherine Brandon and placing her here. Why would he ask her to dance anyway? Surely his friend wasn't interested in this white girl! Was he? This thought hit him in the stomach as though a fist had rammed into him.

The frenzied drumbeat and chanting pulled the dance lines into action as the outer line of men shuffled to the left while the inside line of females danced to the right. Each participant was caught up in the rhythm, the movement, and his own thoughts while he moved step slide step slide as the lines moved facing each other.

The hour was late, as the last revelers retired to their lodges for a few hours of rest; however, one young lady wasn't weary or sleepy. Katherine listened to her family's familiar heavy breathing of sleep while she twisted and turned before quietly rising and exiting the log lodge to find a quiet place to sit and let the warm spring night embrace and soothe her runaway thoughts.

She walked a short distance, drinking in the night's beauty and its quietness, when she spied a large leaning rock with a ledge. Kate climbed and sat, sighing, breathing in the soothing peacefulness as the moon sat high in the sky and caressed the tall mountain peak in silvery arms.

For the first time, Katherine actually looked into her own heart and was appalled at what she saw-it couldn't be and it wouldn't be. Surely she couldn't care for an Indian-this didn't happen. No white girl in her right mind would. As she was deep in thought reprimanding herself, she sensed a presence.

"Miss Katherine, you should not be here alone and at such a late hour. It isn't safe." Spotted Horse had seen the young teacher walking and feared for her safety, whether it be wild animal or wild anger.

She stuttered, "Hello Spotted Horse-I don't understand." He stepped to her side. "I can't leave you here alone. Come, I'll walk you back to the lodge."

"No I'm not sleepy. Come and sit if you'd like." She patted the spot beside her. "I'm afraid I won't be very good company, but I need to sit here for a while in this peacefulness tonight-my thoughts seem so jumbled. I don't suppose you could sleep either."

He sat near her, staring into the night's beauty. "No-Wild Hawk and I had a run in. I left his lodge for a breath of fresh air."

"Oh!" Before she could continue, a large frame loomed up near them and spewed forth his angry venom in Cherokee. Wild Hawk's eyes blazed in black fury as he lashed out at his friend in the Cherokee tongue. "What do you think you are doing, you bastard? Are you running after this white girl, even sneaking around to lure her out to this spot at such a late hour?" Horse stood calmly, letting the tirade run its course. "I will not tolerate such treatment of this innocent young girl-huh!" he sneered. "I suppose you will tell me you care for her!" Hawk feared the answer, struggling to get his breath.

"Do you?" Spotted Horse read his friend loud and clear, and it was time this man owned up to his inner feelings.

"Yes!" Hawk almost yelled, startling himself with his answer, staring into the distant moonlit mountain, his anger spent. "My God Yawa, yes, I care for her." He looked at his friend, ashamed of his outburst, seeing the amused smile as Spotted Horse grasped his shoulder in understanding.

"I'm sorry, my friend," Hawk continued in Cherokee, "I was hurting so-afraid you had feelings for this girl who has captured my heart." He glanced at Kate, "I guess I was wild with jealousy-how long have you known my feelings for her?"

Horse sighed and responded, "Longer than you have known-and I saw her walking alone tonight-I only had fear for her safety-That's why I sat with her, she wouldn't go to her lodge and she seemed disturbed."

Kate couldn't understand any of this conversation, since they spoke in Cherokee, but she did know Wild Hawk had fierce anger at his friend, who didn't seem to mind and now they seemed to be friends again. How ridiculous!

"Thank you." Hawk looked down, scuffing the toe of his moccasin and shaking his head. "I've been in such turmoil over her, not really admitting my feelings to myself, but the sad thing is," as his dark eyes reflected his words when he again looked at his friend, "nothing can come of it. We'll talk later-and thank you again, my friend."

Horse nodded and left quietly, as Wild Hawk stood staring at Katherine-wanting to pull her up and crush her against him, bury his face in her firelit hair and feel her body next to his, but knowing all he could do was look, drinking in her beauty, but not touch.

She glanced up at him, obviously worried, not understanding the strong anger that had just passed between the two friends, and now he only stared at her, a great warmth in his eyes. Maybe he didn't dislike her after all. "Wild Hawk, is something wrong? You seemed so angry at Spotted Horse." He sat next to her, continuing to look at her.

"Yes there is much that is wrong, but I can do nothing to change any of it." He shifted his gaze to the distant mountains, wishing with all his heart that there were no such thing as white and Indian, that there were only man and woman-where people were judged by their worth and not by their skin color.

"I'm so sorry-for a while I thought you were angry with me."

He turned toward her smiling sadly. "No, I could never be angry with you."

"But," she continued, looking at her lap, "you quit bringing the children for their lessons, and today-you acted as though you didn't want us here-almost as though you didn't know us." She continued looking at her lap, folding and unfolding her skirt.

"Did that bother you?" he asked, quietly drinking in her moonlit beauty.

"Yes, it bothered me very much." She continued to look down, not able to face him. "I thought we were friends."

He quietly responded, "Katherine Brandon, you and Wild Hawk can never be friends." He looked away, sadness etched on his face and she jerked her head up and around to stare at him.

"And why not?" She questioned, disbelieving what she had heard.

"Because you are white and I am Indian. Put your arm next to mine." She did so, and felt the warmth of his skin next to hers. "See the difference?"

"Of course there is a difference-you are darker than I-so what? That doesn't mean we can't be friends." She searched his countenance, wondering why he looked so sad.

"Oh! But it does, Miss Katherine. I would never be the cause of your being shunned by other whites because you befriended an Indian."

"That is ridiculous! And I will never never adhere to such warped, hate filled beliefs," her mouth set firmly with eyes blazing.

He smiled at this stubborn young woman who claimed his heart. Wondering why she had not sensed his feeling for her, praying to Yawa she would not, and it was impossible for him to remain sitting here by her with the moonlight caressing her beauty while the night breeze played tag with her tumbling hair, when all he wanted to do was hold her in his arms. They must return to their lodges.

"You never answered why you quit bringing the students and why the treatment today," she tried again to understand this man as she watched him carefully.

He struggled with emotions. "I cannot explain those actions to you at this time, Miss Katherine. Maybe someday."

"Do not call me that-it's so formal-I'm just Katherine or Kate-please." She smiled, crinkling that small dimple at the corner of her mouth that took his breath away.

He thought, I must get away from here-away from her. "So be it-ah-Katherine, and we must stay here no longer. Your father would not approve of our being here alone so late at night," he quietly stated.

"You are right, of course, but do you realize this is the first time," she again looked down at her lap, smoothing her skirt, unable to meet his dark gaze, "we have been together alone to discuss anything-and I," she hesitated, "have enjoyed talking with you." She hurried on, "another thing, Wild Hawk I am your friend. It matters not whether you are Indian or white." She raised her head and met his eyes that seemed to hold such sadness. "It is the custom with white people to seal a bargain with a handshake-shall we?" She offered her slender hand as he enclosed it with both of his.

"Thank you-my friend," he murmured while captivating her with his smile. "Come-I will walk you back to the lodge."

They returned to her lodge in silence, each engulfed in his own thoughts. Why is he so quiet, she thought. He has really shared very little with me this evening, he seems withdrawn, so very sad at times. It couldn't be wrong for me to befriend him, and for once I'll go along with Jesse's thinking-he is one of the handsomest men anywhere. The thing that bothered me most, though, is that I didn't want to return to the lodge. I wanted to stay there on the ledge with him, and I wanted him to hold my hand. What is happening to me?

This beautiful green eyed white girl wishes to be my friend-Yowa forbid, for she doesn't know the hate filled white world as I do, Hawk thought. How will I ever handle this situation? Do I stay away from her? That hasn't worked, but I must not be alone with her again at night. Why oh why did I have to care for someone I can never, never have, and a white who is the enemy of my people? How hopeless and sad, for this young girl is no enemy to Hawk. She makes his heart sing and ache. He looked at her, smiled, thinking how great it had been just being near her this evening. Something he had dreamed of, but never thought to happen. He could hug his chief for inviting the Brandons and his friend for getting Green Eyes and him together.

As they arrived at the lodge, he looked deeply into her eyes. "Thank you my friend for this evening. I, too, enjoyed it."

"Good night-Wild Hawk," she murmured, as she watched his tall form vanish into the night.

The following morning as the Brandon wagon prepared to leave Lone Eagle's village, the chief was presented with a beautiful multicolored handmade quilt, with a variety of canned preserves. Several Cherokee bid the Brandons a cordial good-bye, including Old Crone who handed John a leather pouch of dried corn. Little Cub scampered to the wagon calling, "Kate", who immediately jumped down from the buckboard gathering the tiny warrior into her arms, struggling to swallow the lump in her throat. The child pushed back, lip quivering as he pointed to himself, "Cub," then pointed to Kate saying, "Kate." Suddenly he threw his fat little arms around her neck, squeezing hard. Kate was teary eyed as she finally climbed into the wagon, wondering why Wild Hawk hadn't come to say good-bye. A sadness engulfed her as she also wondered what the future held for these beautiful friendly people.

John clucked to the horses, the wagon began moving as many Cherokee trilled their good-byes. Katherine heard a faint little voice, echoing "Kate," which triggered her already sad heart into quiet sobbing, oblivious to the raw hatred worn on the countenance of Dancing Eyes, who watched with a pleased smirk as the pale eyes left. She hoped she'd never be around the green eyed bitch again.

"Get a hold of yourself, for heaven's sakes," Prissy hissed to Kate. "You act like an idiot. Me, I'm thrilled to be going home-I can't believe you actually enjoyed being here! How could any white person want to spend time here?"

"You wouldn't understand, Prissy!"

"No, and I don't want to-I will have to admit if it hadn't been for Jeb Hawkins I would have been more than miserable. But of course, Jeb is certainly no Keith," she continued, wondering when she would see her handsome lieutenant.

Jesse screamed, pointing to the two braves on horses who closed in on either side of them. "Look, it's Wild Hawk and Spotted Horse. Oh! Boy-I guess Wild Hawk wanted to see me home. Did I tell you Kate and Prissy," she used her best grown-up expression, "that I might marry Wild Hawk when I grow big!" She smugly lifted her chin before Tim blew the wind from her sails.

"Oh! Shut up Jess-I've already told you how dumb and childish you are." Tim volunteered his eleven year-old adult wisdom while watching Jess stick her tongue out.

"John Brandon," Wild Hawk smiled as Night Wind pranced near the wagon. "Spotted Horse and Wild Hawk will travel with you and your family to your home." He and Horse nodded to the family as his gaze lingered on Katherine, who smiled, causing his heart to skip a beat. Mary didn't fail to note how quickly her older daughter's countenance changed from rain to sunshine. Why couldn't Bear Claw have accompanied them home?

"Thank you both very much," John was pleased as he clucked to the horses.

The steady clip clop rhythm of horses' hooves, the warm cloak of the late spring sunshine, pine and evergreen scented air accented with the floral carpet of rhododendron, laurel and trailing arbutus, lulled the passengers into a lethargic peacefulness after a filling lunch.

Hawk suddenly approached the wagon. "John Brandon, we will not make it to your home before a storm hits us," he pointed to the cloud formation, aware also of the heavy atmosphere.

John craned his neck, looking at the clouds, seeing nothing out of the ordinary. "I believe you're wrong, Wild Hawk. I will go on."

"No, I am not wrong," he drew his horse near the wagon. "You will be offering your family to the elements if you continue this journey. There is a cave not too far where you should seek shelter for your family." He was steadily pleading with this stubborn man who didn't seem to have knowledge of weather changes.

"He is right. Do you not feel the heaviness of the air?" Spotted Horse added.

"Well, I appreciate the concern from both of you," he looked from one Indian to the other, "but I believe I'll take my chances." He smiled at the two braves, thinking how ridiculous they were with such nonsense when the sky still contained billowy clouds, and the day was clear and sunny. "Git up," he commanded the faithful animals as they again plodded on while the two Indians looked at each other, both worried over the stubbornness of this man who was placing his family in danger. They could do nothing but follow along, and hope to help some way when the force hit. Hawk glanced at Kate with concern. Nothing must happen to this young girl or her family.

Legend of the Whispering Wind

Another hour or so passed, before the sun was completely hidden by dark clouds, while the wind picked up, tossing small debris, swaying leafy branches and plants. John became concerned as Wild Hawk quickly rode out, scouting for a ledge or any place for partial cover, as he thought damn stupid man who wouldn't listen to the truth. He ran his mount back quickly after viewing the sky, and feeling the tenseness of the air, yelling, "quickly, the wagon over to the foot of the peak," he pointed. Lightning flashed as rain began pounding. "Katherine," he yelled louder, "quickly get down and bring Jesse-give me your hand, you are riding with me. Priscilla and Tim go with Spotted Horse. Hurry - there's no time." They complied as he swung Kate up behind him, Jesse in front. For once she was too scared to talk. Hawk galloped Night Wind as Kate's arms tightly clung to his waist while rain slashed them and lightning struck nearby, exploding an old gnarled tree. Hawk deposited Kate and Jess with strict orders for them to stay in the gully under the stone outcropping, after handing her his buckskin shirt for cover. Even amid this turmoil, as she donned his shirt his body warmth lingering as though his arms wrapped around her-its smell of leather, wood smoke and sage, it was him. Horse brought Prissy and Tim shortly after with the same orders as both braves left again to help John with the wagon. Hawk instructed Mary to take his hand and he also swung her up behind him and quickly deposited her with the others, after giving her, too, strict orders as rain splashed even harder while wind picked up with visibility very difficult; however, John with both braves helping managed to place the wagon by the gully as the Indians calmed the nervous animals.

"Get in there with your wife," Hawk yelled to John as he and Horse spoke calmly in Cherokee as they coaxed the nervous animals into the gully near the wagon's slight protection. The sky darkened even more, lightning snapped, the wind and rain picked up to a thunderous roar, revealing the outline of a funnel cloud.

Hawk dashed to Kate's side, covering her and Jess with his body as Horse tried to protect Prissy and Tim. Debris sailed through the air near them, crashing against uprooted trees and boulders, as the funnel tipped down near them, then bounded back up, veered, looking for another target. Shortly the giant villain had paid his destructive call and was on his way. Fortunately, due to the fast thinking Indians, no one or animal was harmed, only frightened and weather beaten.

Kate, in sodden clothes and plastered hair, drew in her breath as she watched Hawk, clad only in buckskin pants and moccasins, long black hair plastered, brown torso rippling with muscle, coaxing and crooning in soft-spoken Cherokee as he persuaded each animal to do his bidding. Everything about this tall man accentuated his savage heritage, which brought a warm feeling and a frown to her face.

John Brandon, ashamed and embarrassed, knowing he had jeopardized the lives of his family, felt sick at heart. How could he have been foolish enough to disbelieve the Indian people who had lived with the elements from their beginning time? What must they think of him? What must his family think of him? He thanked the good Lord for their safety, even though he was a fool. He and Horse restationed the wagon in order to harness the horses as Hawk brought the two animals up, already rubbed down.

"I really don't know what to say-" John stumbled over words as he began harnessing the two horses, water dripping from his leather hat. "You tried to tell me, but I wouldn't believe you, and I took a chance on actually allowing my family to be killed." How could I have been so foolish and so stupid, he thought. Dear Lord, please forgive me and may my family forgive me. "Without your quick thinking, even after my stubbornness, we could have been killed." He stopped, and looked up at both young men. "Thank you," he was misty eyed, "I shall always be indebted to you both for saving our lives and teaching me a great lesson." He shook his head, totally disgusted with himself.

"You owe us nothing," Horse responded as Hawk nodded while adding, "Forgive yourself-we all make mistakes." He strode back for the other horses, as the women and Tim gradually climbed from their safety, Mary, absolutely astonished by Wild Hawk's nakedness, brushing at their clothing, attempting to repair their appearance, especially Prissy who was beside herself over the dirt spots and tear of her sodden blue calico. "Just look at this mess," she hissed, "if that Indian hadn't wallowed me down, this filth and tear wouldn't be here-of all the nerve!" Her dark eyes sparkled fire as she brushed debris from her skirt.

"Prissy how could you be so ungrateful?" Kate snapped at her foolish sister. "If it weren't for those Indians we would all probably be dead, and it wouldn't make any difference whether you even wore a dress. I feel extremely grateful and thankful." Prissy glared at her, continuing to brush the dirt spots as Kate walked over to Hawk who was rubbing down Night Wind. She patted and caressed the horse's neck as the stallion turned and nuzzled her shoulder. She was overjoyed. "He likes me." Hawk moved closer to her, black eyes dancing, remembering the feel of her body against him, and thanking Yawa that this young girl was safe.

"Yes, he does-put your hand over his muzzle-remove it, then place your lips near his nostrils and let him breathe in your breath as you talk to him quietly. After that, he will always know you." She followed his directions, afterwards stroking the black beauty's neck. The animal again nudged her shoulder, resting his head on it. She laughed with delight, green eyes sparkling, totally captivating the young brave beside her. Sobering, she became aware of the penetrating gaze that held her own.

"Thank you and Horse with all my heart for saving our lives today. Without you we wouldn't have made it, and its pitiful to think how stupid my father acted."

"Don't blame him-let it go. He is already down on himself-hurting for what could have happened. Everyone makes mistakes and this has been a big lesson for him."

She nodded. "All right-oh! I almost forgot-here is your shirt, and thank you again for everything."

Taking the shirt he chuckled, "your mother is probably half out of her mind seeing my bare body!"

"Probably," she laughed as he slipped his shirt on, walking toward John.

"If you are ready we should move on-it will be slower going, avoiding the tornado destruction." John nodded. "Here," Hawk handed him a dry shirt from a leather pouch. "Your wife might need this around her." Horse secured two dry blankets for the others to huddle under.

"Thank you so much, my friends," John Brandon was moved by the thoughtfulness of these so-called savages. If they are savages, what in the world does that make the white man!

The wagon progress after the tornado was at a much slower pace, with frequent stops for debris removal while John was thanking the good Lord that these braves were accompanying him with their extra strong backs, even Tim tried his best to display muscular strength in removing a large limb from their path, but his chubby body failed to cooperate. Finally, realizing he was more in the way than helping, he pulled his faithful slingshot, wanting the Indians to see his ability with it. Suddenly, a rabbit scurried nearby, which would be a good supper. He drew back, slowly glancing at Hawk to make sure he was watching, before letting the rock fly, missing the supper dish by a mile.

Jess hooted while slapping her leg with laughter. "Timmy, you couldn't hit the side of a barn-the only good shot you ever made was when Rusty Poole bent over that time and you shot him in the ass."

"Jessica Ruth! How dare you use such crude and ridiculous terms for the-ah-anatomy "Mary admonished.

"and," Jess continued, not paying enough attention to her mother, "when you did pound his ass, it was an accident." She exploded again with laughter, remembering. Her mother jerked her around, "Young lady," Mary was too exhausted with the day and damp clothes and she was more than a little out of sorts with her husband's dumb stubbornness to put up with Jesse's crude antics. She more than sternly reprimanded, "If you utter another unladylike term, I'll do more than wash your mouth with soap." Mary promised her additional punishment that she would never forget.

Jess nodded, "Yes'um," knowing Mama was bad mad 'n she would mind her. Yes sir, she'd try very hard and only say a few things when Mama wasn't around.

The two Cherokee had to turn from the group, pretending work, to keep from bursting forth with laughter. Finally, they contained themselves to twitching smiles, while Prissy and Kate covered their laughter under the blanket.

"Well, that about does it," Horse stated as the braves moved a large pine from their path. "We should be able to move on now."

"Where is Timothy?" Mary asked, concerned, looking around the area strewn with much debris.

"I guess he wandered off," John stated, calling, "Tim- son-we're ready to go!" They waited a few minutes but there was no response as John called again. "Tim!" in a stronger voice, walking a short distance, searching, his green eyes anxious.

"I will find him," Wild Hawk started walking toward a group of evergreen and pines-slowly picking his way as he carefully checked the signs left by the boy between fallen limbs and debris.

"Do not worry about your son," Spotted Horse supplied. "Hawk can track anyone-anywhere-he will find him."

Why didn't this young boy have better sense than to wander so far from his parents, who were already worn out from today's turmoil and were anxious to get home, Hawk wondered, as he hurried on through strewn debris and boulders, soon picking up the sound of childish laughter. Following the gaiety he soundlessly approached a small clearing where he found Tim rolling over and over with his arms full of a small black bear cub-both in total delight as Hawks immediate fear became reality when a thrashing through bushes and trees produced Bigfoot, the gigantic black female bear that apparently had found her lost cub in the arms of Tim Brandon, who was not yet aware of his danger, and who continued to tumble with his furry friend in childish delight. With one loud roar Big Foot reached her seven and a half foot height a few feet from the boy. The brave knew there was not enough distance between the two of them for him to fight this big animal without being hurt. He had no choice if he were to save the boy. He must be quick and sure of his knife or they could both die. He spoke quietly to the startled lad who had released his playful pal upon hearing the angry roar. "Tim-don't move-Ai Yee!" the Indian yelled as he jumped between the huge black beast and the boy, knife in hand, as Big Foot's attention changed and focused on this disturbing force. With another roar she swiped at this creature, catching him in the chest as he twisted, pivoted and rammed the knife to the hilt into the animal's vital life organ, twisting, and ramming it again as the huge beast tottered backward a few steps before gradually sagging and sinking to the ground with the man's blood staining her belly. Hawk sank to his knees, the bloody knife still grasped in his hand. "Tim-get Spotted Horse." He sank down on his back, his eyes closed as blood flowed steadily from his chest.

"I can't believe Tim would simply walk away like this," John's worry was obvious, as he again checked his pocket watch, realizing it had already been 30 minutes. He paced back and forth. How could anything else happen today-knowing something was wrong. As he was ready to take off in the direction Hawk had gone, he heard a noise in the brush. Someone or something was coming-Tim burst forth, out of breath, eyes large as saucers, struggling to speak.

"Horse-come-quick- Wild Hawk's been hurt-bad."

The Cherokee responded, grabbing Tim's shoulder immediately. "How?"

"A-big-bear," Tim gasped. The Brandons looked at each other. Anxiously John wanted to help, but he knew he must stay with his family. Horse grabbed a pouch from his horse, scooped Tim up on his shoulders.

"Show me the way, Tim." He knew the boy couldn't keep up with him as he trotted through the countryside, following the boy's direction. How in the world could this have happened-he must hurry if his friend were bleeding. At last, they entered a small clearing where a huge black bear lay sprawled in death, Hawk not far away, bleeding steadily from a chest wound. He knelt by his friend. "Hawk, can you hear me?" Wild Hawk opened his eyes, nodding.

"Listen to me-you've lost a lot of blood-I must clean your ripped chest and use the powder to help keep the evil heat out-it will be very painful, but I must hurry and try to stop the bleeding. We'll try closing by binding, hoping it will work." Hawk nodded as his friend worked deftly and quickly, knowing the pain he was creating. The wounded man made no noise other than sucking in his breath. During this procedure, Tim struggled with emotions, looking away to keep from throwing up.

"Tim, Go fetch your father quickly-I need his help-hurry." Horse commanded as the young lad immediately took off toward the wagon, thinking, it's all my fault-he saved my life and now he's hurt bad. What if he dies, then it'll all be my fault-oh! Dear God, please don't let him die. Breathlessly, he arrived back at the wagon, chin quivering and eyes misty. "Papa, Horse wants you to come quick and help with Wild Hawk-'n-'n-I caused it all to happen," tears slid down his plump jaws accompanying his quivering chin. "Papa, don't let him die," the young boy sobbed.

John patted Tim. "Shh-we'll talk about it later. Now-tell me where to find them quickly." John prodded as Tim struggled through emotions to describe where the braves were.

"I'll go and help-" Kate quickly jumped from the wagon as her mother emphatically stopped her.

"You'll do nothing of the sort!"

"But, he may need-" Kate persisted.

"Katherine-I have spoken." Mary's hazel eyes told Kate more than words could say, as the mother felt too tired for controversy, and had much concern over her daughter's reaction to this Indian.

Jess jumped from the wagon. "If Kate can't go and help then I will." She started streaking after her father as her mother bellowed.

"Jessica Ruth., you get back here immediately. I've had all I'm going to take today, and I'm sure your father can handle the situation." Her mother was certainly acting like a damn old bat and Tim sniveling like a girl-she plopped down on the ground as Kate strolled over to Night Wind while he nickkered a welcome.

John soon reached the wounded man, appalled at the sight of blood loss. Horse described the wound, his treatment of it, his fear of infection. "I don't understand how this could have happened-I've seen him fight too many times, and there is no one I'd rather have protect me. Here, we will get on either side and practically carry him." Horse began lifting one shoulder.

"No," Hawk dazedly attempted to rise. "I will walk," he struggled, too weak to rise.

"Stop it," Horse thundered. "You will do as I say, damn you. You are too weak to walk." He raised the shoulder again, nodded for John to lift the other as the two struggled, finally getting him up, arms around their shoulders as they slowly started the return trek, practically carrying the large brave back to the wagon, and finally placing him on a bed of quilts as the Brandon family watched with concern. Kate observed the blood soaked binding, and his loss of color. Anxiously, she inquired, "Have you given him any water?"

"Yes, but he needs more-he has lost a lot of blood," Horse replied as he grabbed the water pouch, reaching his friend's side.

Kate grabbed the pouch. "Give it to me-I'll take care of him." She scooted back to the brave, putting her arm gently under his neck, lifting his head. "Hawk, Hawk," she leaned down, watching for any reaction near him. The Brandons observed the intimate scene and Horse observed them with a slight smile, thinking this mother is in great turmoil over her daughter's reaction to my Cherokee friend. Hawks eyes fluttered open-he smiled slightly before his eyes gradually began to close.

"No-open your eyes, And look at me. You must drink more water-don't you dare pass out on me-open your eyes-please," she whispered the last word very near his face. He nodded, as she placed the pouch to his mouth. He drank, placed his hand on hers to gently push the water pouch away, while opening his eyes slightly and murmuring, "Thank you." Kate swallowed the lump in her throat, and handed the pouch to Horse as she gently placed the brave's head in her lap, afraid of what might be. Oh! God-don't let anything happen to him. He can't die-he's too young. Then something must be done to stop this awful bleeding! She looked up, misty eyed. "What are you staring at-can't you see this man might die if this bleeding isn't stopped?" Kate's voice raised in concern, "Mama," she called, pleading, as Mary was helped into the wagon and to her daughter's side, observing the prostrate form and blood soaked binding. She'd do what she could to help.

"John, get the whiskey jug and my sewing box-hurry."

His mouth dropped open as she mentioned both, surely his wife wasn't going to take a slug of liquor, but he didn't question her. Mary knew what she was about in time of crisis. He crawled back across from her with her requests.

"Pour some liquor into a cup-Priscilla, hand him a cup from the box under the seat. We'll get as much liquor as possible into this man before caring for his wound." Mary spilled forth her orders as John let out a sigh of relief as she explained the procedure while Kate and John struggled to lace the big brave with whiskey to dull the pain. It wasn't easy, but with Kate's pleading and her soothing voice they finally managed while Mary doused scissors and a very large needle with the same pain killer. Horse observed all this in skeptical wonderment, never having seen anyone stitched before, as Mary doused the wound with the liquor while he straddled Hawks legs, who jerked but made no noise. She then threaded the large needle with a thick cord after sprinkling the wound with some kind of healing powder, and proceeded to sew the wound together. She was quick and deft with her work, and to Horse the stitching was a miracle. Quickly, a clean white cloth was torn into strips, and wound tightly around the Indian's chest to prevent any pulling apart. Horse observed this attractive and skilled wife of John Brandon, sensing she was aware of a growing feeling between this wounded Cherokee and her daughter, also sensing she was bitterly against it, but she helped the man anyway-and she knew what to do. This is much woman.

Kate looked at her mother with emotion filled green eyes so like her father's. "Thank you, Mama-you just saved his life," as she wiped his wet forehead.

Mary nodded, smiling at her daughter with a sad heart, knowing she had had to help, but not sure it was the right thing for everyone. "He isn't out of danger yet."

Jess observed the entire procedure in awe, so anxious for Hawk she was lulled into silence for which Mary sent up a 'thank-you, Lord'. Prissy couldn't stand the sight of blood, which encouraged her to walk several yards from the scene. She was thoroughly upset that her entire family was falling all over themselves, and taking all of this time piddling and hovering over one Indian with a scratched chest. She was worn out with this entire mess.

Tim observed all that he could stand of Hawks ordeal, thinking it was his duty because he caused it all, but when his mother actually began stitching the Indian's flesh with needle and thread he had to leave and throw up.

It was time to go home. Mary suggested a pillow under Hawk's head would be more comfortable to him than Kate's lap, as her daughter blushed and followed her mother's suggestion. But she and Horse remained by the wounded man's side, ready to respond to any need as the wagon pulled out, horses tied to the back, and they started the few remaining miles.

They arrived home without additional mishps shortly after dark to find the Brandon homestead intact. Apparently, the monster tornado only tipped his hat here or possibly it gave out of breath. Which ever, the family was thankful.

John suggested the wounded man be placed in Tim's bedroom where care could be given him. He again thought how much these two had given of themselves to the Brandons. The least they could do in turn was to care for this wounded man, but Horse refused the offer, knowing Hawk would not want to be beholden to anyone.

"This is ridiculous," Kate disapproved emphatically. "We can't give him adequate care when he's in the barn!" her eyes snapped.

"But I can, and it is what my friend would want." The Indian was adamant while Kate glared at him, thinking how stubborn and crazy this Indian was. A wounded man needed a decent bed rather than a straw palate in a stable, and nursing was a woman's job. He could certainly grow very ill even with proper care, but this Indian's dark gaze kept Kate from protesting further.

After, Mary and Priscilla started for the house to prepare supper, Prissy feeling anything would be better than staying in that wagon in filthy clothes and listening to all the silly commotion about a wounded Indian. Lord, she hoped he got better soon so he could just leave. John drove the wagon on to the barn.

Jess and Kate prepared a bed of fresh straw covered with a quilt in the unused stable while Kate continued to seethe inside over such a ridiculous and senseless choice of sleeping quarters, and that Spotted Horse was not capable of taking care of his friend, as she heard him say:

"I'll try to rouse him, but if I cannot, we must carry him." John nodded, as Horse began shaking his friend's shoulder, calling to him, "Hawk, wake up-open your eyes." He continued shaking the shoulder.

The wounded brave stirred, struggling to rise. "Can you hear me?" Horse continued.

Hawk nodded, murmuring weekly, "Yes-must return to village." He struggled to raise himself, Horse attempting to assist him when he was roughly pushed aside, losing his balance.

"Wild Hawk-listen to me-you've been hurt," but his wild eyed friend burst forth,

"Get out of my way-I must leave immediately." Hawk's eyes wildly searched for something as he sat up, struggling to stand while the Brandons looked on in astonishment, realizing this man didn't know what he was saying or where he was. Suddenly, Spotted Horse rose, slammed a fist into Hawk's face and caught him before he hit the wagon, knowing the brave was out of his mind and he had to stop him before he harmed himself.

"Great day, did you have to hit him so hard?" Kate's green eyes flashed at Horse as the men carried the inert form to his straw bed, and Jess added her angry echo, grumbling,

"That's what I say!"

Spotted Horse glanced at Kate as though her question was too stupid to answer.

"Yes, I had to give him a solid punch in the jaw before he harmed himself, before he tore the stitching out." He gazed at Kate, thinking what a stupid question this smart young woman asked, and this was just the beginning. How he wished they were at their village where someone else could help take care of this stubborn male, and where people didn't ask ridiculous questions all the time. He knew when Hawk realized where he was all hell would break loose. In the meantime he had the problem of making sure the fever was kept down and the wound didn't get infected.

"Tim, would you bring a bucket of water-he will need it throughout the night." The young boy left immediately, glad to be needed. While waiting for the water, Horse explained to Kate and

John the Cherokee medication for fever that he always carried in his leather pouch.

"I'm staying out here tonight with Wild Hawk," Tim piped up after Horse explained that the Brandons were no longer needed. However, before they left, the lad stopped them, looking most disturbed. "I've gotta tell you about today. I can't stand to think about it all by myself any more." Tim looked down, kicking at nothing in particular with the toe of his shoe.

"What is it?" John walked over to him, placing a hand on his son's shoulder, his gaze questioning.

"I didn't want Wild Hawk to get hurt," he pleaded with his eyes, snubbing, trying hard not to cry-he knew he was too big to cry, but he sure felt like it, "but I caused the whole thing." He looked down again, unable to make eye contact with his father.

"How?" His tired father steadily probed.

"When I walked today on the way home, I found the cutest little black bear, 'n we wuz jes playin' rollin' over and over when I heard the awfullest roar that ever wuz." His eyes became big as saucers, as Jesse's matched them, "and there stood the biggest black bear three or 4 ft. from me mad as a hornet. That's when Wild Hawk jumped out between us yelling, with no room to fight. How he killed that bear, I don't know, but he saved my life." His voice became quieter. "And now," he looked at his father with tear filled eyes, "he-he might die because of me." He broke down, sobbing, as his father gathered the boy to him.

"We won't let him die, Tim-he'll be all right." John smoothed his son's hair while soothing his raw emotions, hoping he was not lying to the lad, and wondering how he could ever ever thank this Indian for saving his son's life. He cringed to think what might have been.

"Yes," Horse added, feeling his comment was necessary as he observed both Kate and Tim, "he is too ornery to die and believe me, I know this man, and no bear I am acquainted with could destroy a Cherokee as tough as this one." Tim nodded, sniffed, but felt better that he had shared his ordeal of guilt, and thinking this man who risked his life would be all right.

Kate wasn't so sure, and she certainly wasn't taken in by Horse's comments. She knew they were made to soothe her brother's feelings. Kate returned to the stable one more time to look in on the wounded brave before going to the house. She must check the water supply and leave extra blankets.

She stood, staring at this strong man who was brought to his knees, then knelt down, assessing the strength of this Indian's countenance, smiling as she observed the long thick sooty lashes that dusted his high cheekbones-lashes too long for a man, especially a wild Indian-and her mind traveled back over the horrid day's events, wondering where and how the Brandons would be without this man with the long lashes and his friend. She hesitated, then gently touched his forehead, checking the fever, knowing it would probably rage higher before it lessened. Dear Lord, please take care of this very special man. She stood, knowing she must leave also, knowing she was still against placing this wounded man in a stable where it was much easier for his wound to become infected. She walked out of the barn without another word as Jesse trailed behind her.

With little sleep, struggling fiercely at times with his patient while using many colorful expletives, Horse was able to get the medication into his friend.

Chapter 10

The next two days were passed in and out of consciousness for the wounded man, who was not totally aware of his surroundings; however, he had the constant care and concern from his friend and the Brandons, with the exception of Prissy who thought the entire thing was a great infringement. What if Keith came, what in the world would he think of all this carrying on over a savage. She doubted they would give her all this attention if she were the one hurt. Well, they'd better not call on her to assist. Horse was spelled by Kate and John, who continued to spoon rich beef broth into the patient. Mary checked the wound, changing the bandage after adding healing ointment, finding no severe infection evident.

During this rather dramatic period, Tim had a most disturbing dream of a small black cub bawling for its mother, running, trying to follow the Brandon wagon. This disturbing force dealt such a blow to the boy that his father had no choice but to take his son to find the small, lonely, helpless creature, and sure enough, not too many miles from home Tim grabbed his father's arm, screeching, "Look, Papa!" as John's gaze fastened on the direction of the pointed finger. A tiny furry ball was scooting along the trail, occasionally taking time out to bawl it's lonely hungry cry. Before the wagon stopped completely, Tim tumbled out, sprawling, but he was so ecstatic over finding his new pal, a scratched knee didn't matter. He jumped up, closed the distance as he scooped the live cuddly fur piece into his arms, hugging him as the furry animal licked the boy's face in warm welcome. On the journey home, with his little belly full of warm milk from a leathered nippled bottle, the cub lay its head back against Tim's shoulder and went sound asleep. The boy, looking at his father, smiled warmly. "Thank you, Papa." John nodded, smiled, wondering if this were such a good idea. He could foresee as this animal grew in size the chaotic turmoil awaiting him. He would talk with his son and some way convince him that they must rid themselves of this bear before he rid the family of its members.

The third day after the tragic happening, amid birds chirping and squirrels chattering during their frolicking games in the warm sunshine, Wild Hawk blinked his black eyes open, void of fever. He scrutinized the area, realizing he was in a barn, but whose? Pushing himself up on an elbow, he questioned his friend who appeared in the stable door opening. Hawks anxious eyes searched the barn interior.

"Where am I? What happened?"

"This is the Brandon's barn." Horse waited for the explosion.

"What? Oh! Why am I here?" He flung the quilt aside, "My Yawa!" He attempted to rise, but found he was too weak and settled for pushing himself to a sitting position. Slightly dizzy, and rubbing his head, "What happened?" A pained expression crossed his face as though he hated to hear the answer.

"You remember the tornado?" Hawk nodded as his friend continued, "later on as we had stopped to remove a fallen tree, and Tim wandered off and found a bear cub."

"Yes—" Hawk stared into space, remembering. "Big Foot came for her cub, and I had to kill her before she killed-" he suddenly remembered the claws opening his chest, and looked down at his neatly wrapped body.

"Your wound was bad-you had lost much blood-Mary Brandon stitched you up-she actually sewed the skin together, and we had no choice but to bring you here since it was the nearest place, and it has been hell convincing Katherine Brandon that you would be fine here in the stable where I could look after you rather than in a soft bed where she could nurse you."

"I'm not so sure you were correct in your thinking," Hawk sighed, a half smile lifting the corner of his mouth as he visualized Katherine's ministering healing services.

"Why-you ungrateful piece of horse dung! I have not had sleep these two nights for waiting on you." He paced back and forth. "Giving you water, medicine, helping you to the bush-"

"Speaking of that-help me out-before I go here." His friend pulled him up, noticing he staggered slightly.

Horse grabbed Hawks arms to steady him. "You all right?"

"I will make it," and he stood for a few seconds, getting his bearings and strength before taking a few steps, stopping, holding on to the barn door, hearing voices and laughter coming from the front lawn. He listened, peering around the door at the exact moment Tom Cason became so enamored with Kate's smile that he forgot his shyness and planted a kiss on her cheek while squeezing her hand. She smiled and backed away, Hawk wished he were some other place. His heart slammed into his chest as he took in this scene, only seeing the kiss and her smile, feeling sick inside. What did he expect? That she would have feelings for an Indian-of course not. Sure, some pale eyed pale face would have feelings for this girl, and she for him, and there was nothing a Cherokee Indian could or would do about it, but there was one thing-he would not stay around here to watch that skinny paleface pawing and slobbering over this girl. He cautiously slipped around the barn, relieved himself, and returned to state he was leaving.

"But you are not well enough to travel," his friend interrupted.

"Maybe not-but Hawk must leave-he can no longer remain here." He was adamant as he slowly strode to Night Wind to ready his horse for travel, determined to ignore his weakness, resting his head against Night Wind's side as the stallion nickered, not offering an explanation for his sudden decision. Horse took this time to step outside. As he saw Katherine and the lieutenant he was immediately aware of the reasoning behind his friend's sudden departure. He, too, prepared his mount for leaving, knowing Hawk couldn't travel alone, and knowing he was more than ready to return to his village, his lodge, and turn the nursing of this stubborn man over to someone else if he remained ill.

The Brandons were shocked when the two Indians stopped by their back door to thank them for their help and care. Both John and Mary realized Wild Hawk was in no condition to travel, but their persuasion had no effect-his mind was made up. After filling their water pouches and at Mary's insistence the saddle bag with roasted meat, biscuits and cookies, they led their mounts slowly toward the front, Hawk in the lead, hoping he would not be too weak to mount up, and also hoping he could avoid Katherine Brandon.

"What the hell is he doing here," Keith Anderson exploded abruptly, standing when he viewed Wild Hawk, as though he would do something about it. "Excuse my language ladies, I didn't expect to see that savage," looking daggers at the Indian who ignored him.

"Mr. Anderson, I don't believe that Cherokee is any more savage than we are." Kate sternly put the lieutenant in his place.

"Kate," Prissy scolded as she stood, taking Keith's arm, soothing him as he gazed at Kate with fury in his cold hazel eyes.

"Excuse me." Kate left the three staring after her as she hurriedly exited through the gate, her green skirts twirling as she rushed to Hawk.

"Where in the world to you think you are going?" Her concern was obvious.

"I am leaving," he kept walking slowly, beads of sweat covering his forehead, avoiding her eyes.

"You can't-you're not well," she pleaded.

He stopped, turned, and raised his eyes to meet her disturbed ones.

"No, I am not well, but I will travel and I won't remain here," he shifted his gaze to the pale faced lieutenant who had kissed this girl.

Katherine followed his gaze, beginning to understand his thoughts that prompted his leaving. "Oh," her face became flush, and she pointed to the lieutenant, "Tom Cason is only a friend."

He stared at her, his eyes hypnotic in their black deaths as he tried to contain his jealousy, knowing this was not for him to change, as hard as it might be, then it must mean nothing to him. "Of course, he is your friend."

"I don't want you to go," she persisted, hesitating, touching his arm that sent a disturbing feeling through her. "After all you've done for us-surely you can let us care for you."

He turned slowly, making himself walk away as Night Wind nickered to Kate, the Indian struggling to avoid looking at her, feeling his heart on the ground as she caressed the black stallion. "Thank you and your family for your care- say good-bye to Tim and Jesse for me."

"Katherine," Lt. Cason firmly called, taking a few steps near the fence, "is there a problem?" He eyed the big Indian with open hostility. Wild Hawk slowly assessed this weakling paleface, knowing he could totally destroy this one with a few punches, sick or well, and he would like nothing better than to do it right now, but that would prove nothing except to make Green Eyes dislike him. He strode on, slowly wondering when or if he would ever see this lovely girl again. Knowing it would be better if he did not.

Mustering all his strength, he mounted up slowly, feeling as though he might topple over, but righting himself, and rode off without a backward glance, leaving part of his heart at the Brandons while Kate stood watching, wanting to race after him, but suddenly feeling cold and lonely.

The sturdy two-story log structure of the Brandons was no longer just a house they moved to from sophisticated Boston, but it had become their home, nestled in its mountainous wonderment. Birds continued their early-morning wake-up trills amid the constant chattering and scampering of gray squirrels and chipmunks, while the spring days easily slipped into lazy summer warmth.

The children continued to come for their lessons, knowing they would not be able to travel often in deep winter; however, students came only twice a week rather than three times. Wild Hawk never accompanied the Cherokee, to Kate's disappointment. It was always Spotted Horse, who arrived with them, but he wasn't needed as interpreter very often, since the Cherokee students were doing extremely well in all their studies. Kate often wondered about Wild Hawk, thinking of the time they were together at the Green Corn, his being wounded, and leaving so abruptly when he was too ill to travel, and never returning. She didn't understand. Maybe some black eyed Indian maiden had made her claim on him. Thinking about this almost stifled Kate-what in the world was wrong with her? Of course, that's the way it would and should be, but the thought was very upsetting.

Rusty and Jeb rode up one late day in June with invitations from the Fort. The Brandons spilled out of the house as they heard horses' hooves approaching. Prissy was totally disappointed it wasn't Keith, as Rusty and Jeb walked to the gate. "Howdy

Brandons," Rusty bellowed as John maneuvered the guest along to seats.

"It's good to see you two. What's been going on?" John pulled out his pipe, stuffed it, lit it and puffed.

Mary inserted, "Katherine, you and Priscilla fix lemonade and cookies. I'm sure the men are tired and hot."

As the girls complied with their mother's wishes, Jeb fastened his appreciative gaze on Priscilla's beauty, and the enticing sway of her hips in her blue calico, hoping she would soon get her fill of the smooth Keith Anderson.

"Well," Rusty spit, "We got us a big to do come up in July at the fort. Yes sir, a two day affair this time."

As Kate and Prissy emerged with the refreshments, the old scout continued while chomping on a cookie. "There's to be two days of activity-the third of July women's quilting 'n gossip-'cuse me, ladies, know that wouldn't apply to you-the men, horseshoes 'n checker contest-then that 'evin a big blowout dance. The hour'll be late so arrangements are made for you to spend the night."

"Oh! Boy-" Jesse exploded, "I can't wait!" her face flashed excitement, then sobered, "But what about the Indians?"

"They're coming the next day for the fourth of July, the barbecue and races. There will be running races and horse racing. No strength contests, and no girls allowed to run against boys."

"Shucks," Jesse growled, knowing she could beat them all, but she sure hoped Timmy didn't get out there and making a fool of himself. With all his fat rolls hanging around, he couldn't do nothing.

"Rusty or Jeb," Kate's green eyes were filled with concern, as she picked at her skirt. "We haven't seen or heard from Wild Hawk in two months since he was wounded by the bear and left here before he was well enough to travel. Is he all right?"

"Um-oh! My yes!" Rusty took over as Jeb's concerned gaze studied this green eyed girl while plopping another cookie in his mouth. "Hit's hard to hurt a big bull moose like that 'un-and he's got a passel of them pretty black eyed maidens trying their best to latch on to him, but so far ain't none done it. My bet's that Dancing Eyes'll be sly 'nuff to nab him, tho." He chuckled, hoping he had put a point across to John Brandon's daughter. Kate excused herself, feeling as though someone had slammed a fist into her stomach-it must have been something she ate. Jeb observed this girl, knowing she cared for his friend Hawk and knowing his friend also had feelings for her. What a pitiful situation, both knowing that they must not let this happen. He wished there wuz some way he could help, but how?

Tim yelled from the side of the house as he walked into view leading a black cub by a rope. "Look what I got, Rusty 'n Jeb." He proudly displayed his pet as Prissy sternly vented her dislike.

"Don't you dare get that thing near me, Tim. He smells to high heaven and makes such horrid noises!"

"I ain't noticed no odor," Tim complemented his possession, patting him.

"Of course you wouldn't-wallowing with him, you smell as bad as he does."

"Priscilla! "her mother reprimanded.

"Well, let me tek a good look at this here cub," Rusty rose, sauntering over to inspect the cub as Tim explained Wild Hawk's killing the mother, leaving the cub alone. Just as Rusty reached to pat the bear-being of small stature, the animal thought he was another child for a game and immediately bounded on the old scout, clasped him in his furry arms, tumbled onto the ground, rolling over and over while the cub licked Rusty's face amid his bellowing. "Get this damn varmint offen me 'fore ah kill him and get the dag nabbed stinking hot breath out of my face!" he shouted.

Jess and Tim hooted with laughter at Rusty's misery, as John jerked the wild creature away from Rusty, hardly able to contain his own laughter. John ordered Tim to take the bear to the barn.

"I'm sorry," Tim apologized, "I guess he thought you 'uz another boy, and wanted to play." Rusty eyed him as though he'd like to wallop him.

"My God-such pets," the old scout moaned as he hobbled on over to a chair, plopped down, his heart thumping from all the activity as he mumbled, "a body might nigh needs one of them coats 'uv armor to visit this here place." He absent mindedly stuffed in an another cookie while glaring at Tim and the bear's retreating forms.

"We'd be glad for you to stay and eat lunch with us." Mary invited the two men as she stood to return to the kitchen.

Jeb rose, "We'd like nothing better, Ma'm," he gazed at Priscilla, involving her in his lazy half smile as he fingered his dusty leather hat, "but we're due at Lone Eagle's village, then back at the Fort, but we'll sure look forward to seein' yawl at the celebration soon." He again fastened his blue gaze on Priscilla's loveliness as she fidgeted, a trifle disturbed under his bold scrutiny.

Chapter 11

Verdant mountain peaks, leafy arms reaching for the sky, multicolored rhododendron with trailing arbutis, the rushing water of Blue Creek whispering its tune to the boulders and rocks, wrapped the Brandons in nature's glory as they wound their springboard over the last few remaining miles to the fort for the celebration.

The Brandon wagon was hardly through the gate before Lieutenants Anderson and Cason converged on it, assisting the girls to their feet, aware of their beauty in their pastel cottons. Prissy's dark eyes flashed with excitement at her tall lieutenant as he caressed her with his handsomeness as he coaxed a lazy smile. "Hello, Beautiful." Tom was his usual shy self as he whispered, "How are you, Katherine?" She replied with a smile as he assisted her down.

Jess interrupted the mooning. "Well, ain't you gonna help the rest of us?" She glared at the soldiers, hands on her hips.

"Certainly Madam," Lt. Anderson teased as he strolled over, bowed, Jess tittered when he offered his hand and she jumped down most unladylike while Tim hooted with laughter, hoping she'd fall. John and Mary looked at each other, shaking their heads, hoping there might be some planned activity for the young ones, away from them.

The visitation lasted only a few minutes before the ladies were whisked away by a sergeant to join Beatrice Roberts' luncheon and quilting bee. Jess and Tim were ushered to Jamie Albert's home, where the children gathered for chaperoned activities, thank goodness-Mary breathed a sigh of relief while the men gathered in the compound for lunch, horseshoes and a checkers tournament.

The ladies from the fort and surroundings settlement filed into the main paneled dining hall for lunch and quilting, the only place large enough for the quilting frames which were already in place.

The Brandons were greeted warmly by Beatrice Roberts, her rotund floral draped figure gliding around to all guests, making sure each one felt at ease, while she was in her zenith qualifying as the perfect hostess.

"Ladies," she tapped on a glass, "if you will take seats I believe our lunch is ready-just sit anywhere you like." She ushered them to two long tables, set with multicolored floral arrangements on each, encouraging Mary to sit next to her while she introduced and placed the Brandon girls by two young ladies about their age, who had recently moved to the fort, Evelyn Hollins and Janice Cooper. Kate immediately responded to the sweet countenance of Janice, with her soft brown eyes and shy smile, while Prissy and Evelyn were sizing each other up-each a little disturbed by the other's beauty.

After lunch of creamed chicken on egg bread, a combination of vegetables, spiced pudding and tea, the ladies adjourned to work on the quilts.

"Ladies," Beatrice crooned, "we have four quilts already on the frames as you can see. I believe that will give each of us a space to work-and this is definitely for a very good cause, don't you know." She smiled sweetly, shifting her weight from one foot to the other, her oversized ankles spilling over each shoe which were a size too small for her plump feet. Hopefully she'd be able to sit soon and stay seated. "We make the quilts for those in need, if we have a surplus, then we present one as a wedding gift, don't you know," she tittered, "now let's find seats and begin." She almost fell into a nearby straight chair with a sigh of relief, hoping her dress was full enough to cover her bare feet. Beatrice wiggled her fat toes amid blessed contentment.

Sewing essentials were passed around while Prissy was hoping there wouldn't be an opening for her to sew-if there were anything she hated, it was sewing and all the silly chatter that accompanied it, knots' and stitches and strands and needles. She'd be worn out with all that and here she was sitting next to that new girl, Evelyn, of all people.

Kate and Janice were placed at the frame with Beatrice, Mary, Sarah Killingsworth and Margaret Dawson, ladies who had visited the Brandon home. Most of the conversation was involved with happenings at the fort until Sarah Killingsworth broached her favorite topic. "And how are your classes going, Katherine-are those Indians actually-learning anything?" She gazed at Kate with a slight smirk, as she poked her needle viciously into the fabric.

"All of my students are doing very well, including the Cherokee." Kate did not like this woman who was trying so hard to belittle the Indians.

"Oh!" continued Sarah, enthusiastically, with her pale frosty eyes glistening, "I heard about that Indian-that ah! ah! what's he called-wild-something or another-Wild Bird I think-oh! That one who tried to put on such a show-you know-to draw attention to himself at the other gathering-well, I heard," she zoomed in not wanting anyone to miss her stressed inflection, "I heard he was hurt in some kind of fight, and he and another one stayed at your house, Mary, for goodness sakes! Oh! I would have been petrified with those savages near me, weren't you, Mary?" She pretended to shudder. "Oh!"

"Not in the least, Sarah-in fact I have found qualities in both of those Cherokee who stayed there, that I would wish more whites had." Mary's hazel eyes dared this woman to keep pushing.

"Well, do tell!" Sarah began easing off, not liking the flash of Mary's hazel eyes.

Kate could have kissed her mother as Beatrice edged in with her comments. "I thought Wild Hawk was spectacular at the last gathering and when he stopped his horse from winning the race to help a white, well," she squinted her eyes at Sarah, "not many white or Indian would have done that, don't you know. Colonel Roberts was certainly impressed." She eyed each one with her emphatic statement. Sarah didn't dare go up against both of them.

What a relief to get away from pins and needles talk and those stuffy women discussing babies, Prissy thought. She simply couldn't have stood another minute, and the damn needle had stuck her finger twice, making it bleed. As she walked out with the new girl she inquired, "How long have you been here?"

"Only three weeks. My father was sent here from the Washington area." Evelyn responded, assessing this dark eyed companion.

"Well, you really haven't had time to get acquainted, have you?" Prissy wasn't really interested, but it was something to say as she smoothed her skirt.

"Janice is the only other girl my age around here but I have met a very nice lieutenant," the blonde headed blue eyed girl dimpled prettily, "that I've been seeing, Keith Anderson."

Prissy, dumbfounded, practically swallowed her tongue and she abruptly left Evelyn standing inside the door while she bounded through it. That two timing bastard-wait until he begins all his sweet talk-just wait. She seethed as she thought of that blond, talking about the nice lieutenant-nice-my rear end! A damn dog, but why would he be interested in that pale eyed, mealy mouthed girl who thought she was pretty? Well, she'd take care of the nice lieutenant. She was still seething when she reached Kate and Mary, and they retired to their quarters before the evening festivities. Shortly thereafter, as Prissy paced back and forth, the explosion rocked the walls as she described Keith's two-timing episode. Mary and Kate looked at each other as she spewed.

"That will be enough, Priscilla," Mary firmly reprimanded her ranting daughter who subsided, plopped into a nearby chair, eyes flashing, while she dreamed up her attack on the nice lieutenant.

The buffet banquet was held in the main dining room amid lavish multi-floral and green plant decorations throughout. Ladies glided in their many colorful satins, taffetas, and sheers with laces and ruffles accentuating their movements. Soldiers milled around in their blue dress uniforms, while settlers were spruced in their best, amid chattering and lovely musical tunes by the music makers consisting of banjo, flute, bass, fiddles and accordion.

The Brandons entered and were immediately waylaid by the Roberts. Both daughters radiant in pink and green satins with sheer overlays commanded the attention of both males and females who were gathered in small groups. Lieutenants Anderson and Cason proudly appeared at their sides while offering their arms as Prissy ignored Keith. Not to be deterred, he leaned near her and whispered, "You look ravishing, darlin'," caressing her with his smile while she continued ignoring him. Not understanding her coolness and not about to tolerate it, for never had any female ever ignored Keith Anderson, and he certainly wouldn't allow this snit of a girl to do so. He suddenly squeezed her arm, turning her abruptly to face him, pulling her away from the others. "What the hell is wrong with you?" His hazel eyes were not smiling, they were shooting sparks.

She lifted her head, chin up, glanced toward the milling people and adjusted her long gloves.

"I asked you a question, and dammit," he leaned close, his face inches from hers, "I'm going to get an answer if I have to drag you out of here," his voice lowered, hardened as he squeezed her arm until it hurt, his eyes snapping.

She squirmed, pulling her mouth down, lifting her chin, flashing her dark eyes at him before she retorted, "I thought you would probably be with Miss Cinderella over there in the yellow," his eyes followed the nod of her head as he immediately picked up on her dilemma, realizing she had heard about his being with Evelyn Hollins. Damn!

"Have you lost your mind? Why would I want to be with her?" She eyed him closely, realizing he sounded very sincere.

"That's what I would like to know-she told me you'd been with her," She looked away, eyes flashing. He was taken aback, wondering what else the blonde had told her-if she had mentioned the number of times they had "accidently" met and talked, and that they had plans for another date. Easy does it, old boy-this little flower is worth the plucking.

"Yes, I have been with her, but it was because Colonel Roberts asked me to escort her to a function, and I couldn't get out of it. Please understand. And, honey, she certainly isn't my type." He squeezed her with his eyes, "and why would I be interested in anyone else when I have you?" He smiled his lazy charm. "Please, let's forget this ridiculous thing and have a good evening." He slipped his arm around her waist. "I've missed you, darlin'."

She pouted, "I'm sorry I jumped at conclusions-and you know it's hard for me to stay away from you for long," she teased and smiled, "and you can tell the Colonel next time to find some other lieutenant." He chuckled while ushering her over to Kate and Tom as they found seats for the ladies while the men went to fill their plates.

"I can tell you really let him have it-didn't you?" Kate teased with a smile.

"Shut up," Prissy snapped, eyes flashing. "He had to escort her-the Colonel insisted." Prissy's eyes traveled to the girl in yellow, wondering—

"I bet!" Kate retorted, knowing she wouldn't trust Keith Anderson as far as she could throw him.

The food was delicious, the music compelling the steppers to move out as a tall scout tapped Keith Anderson on the shoulder. Jeb Hawkins smiled, bowed slightly before swinging Prissy into his arms. She'd like to tromp on his foot for taking her away from Keith, but she did enjoy dancing with this big galoot.

Kate's feet had only been stepped on three times during three dances, and if this evening didn't end soon she thought she'd scream! Tom Cason was sweet, thoughtful, attentive, not bad looking, nice, attentive, nice and she stifled a yawn and she waited for attentive Tom to bring her a cup of lemonade.

Jeb eased into a seat next to Kate and burst out laughing as she stifled her yawn, blue eyes twinkling. "My, my-is the evening that bad?" His gaze was warm.

"Yes-" Kate smiled, "and I shouldn't say that-the food is excellent, but my feet are sore from being stepped on and Tom Cason is nice-oh! He's just too nice, attentive and boring-that's what's wrong! Excuse me, Jeb-that was rude of me," she stated wearily as he eyed her keenly.

"You are too lovely to be sitting here bored to death-would you like to take a stroll with me, find a bench, sit down and just talk?" He eyed her, understanding, as the music makers struck up a lively jig.

"Oh! I'd love that-I've wanted to talk with you." She looked down, sighing. "But what about Tom Cason?" She looked around, hoping she wouldn't see him returning so soon.

"You wait right here-I'll take care of Cason." He smiled, then strolled toward the refreshment table. Returning soon, "C'mon, lovely lady, the evening is ours," he bowed, offering his arm as he escorted Kate outside where they strolled, drinking in the evening's quiet and beauty. Finding a bench beneath an oak a short distance off the compound, they rested as the night's breeze caressed them, whispering quietly through the leafy branches.

"I'm all mixed up, Jeb, and I've needed to talk with someone. I can't talk with my family," Kate looked down, fingering her skirt. "You and Wild Hawk are close, aren't you?"

"Yes-we are brothers-if we wuz' born of the same woman we couldn't be closer." He waited, not pushing, gazing at her steadily.

Kate continued, "I don't understand." Picking at her skirt, she rushed on before she lost her nerve, "but I care for Wild Hawk-I also realize nothing can ever come of it, but Jeb," She looked at him, her green eyes full of sadness, "I can't help myself-I've been miserable these past two months-he was hurt-he left, and I—what am I to do?" Her eyes pled with him, the moonlight reflecting the sadness.

His heart went out to this girl and his good friend. "I can't give you the answer, but why do you think Wild Hawk has stayed away from you?" The breeze picked up and caressed her warm flushed face, playing with her auburn hair.

She searched his steady gaze, hoping, wondering - "you mean it?" Struggling with her thought.

"Yes-I mean he also cares for you, and probably realizes as you do about your future."

"But-he has never mentioned or let me know-" thinking of the night they sat together in his village, remembering, wondering—

"No, he wouldn't." Jeb sighed, leaning up, resting his elbows on his knees. "He is the most honorable man I know and he would do what he feels is right to keep you from any harm or white ridicule." He realized he had said more than he should have. Wild Hawk would throttle him if he knew. "It's getting late, Miss Kate-I'll walk you to your place." He felt sad for this young girl with the big heart, for she was bound to get hurt one way or the other.

"Yes." Kate stood, feeling better that she had a friend she could confide in. "Thank you, so much, my friend for listening-for sharing. Keep us in your prayers." He looked at her steadily, nodding.

Kate was still awake-hearing the even breathing of her family's sleep-her father's steady low snoring, as she reviewed her conversation with Jeb, feeling warm with the thought of Wild Hawk's caring for her, thinking again of her visit to the Indian village. She saw Hawk in many situations, his dark penetrating gaze, his smile, his accompanying them home, protecting her from the storm, his nearness-her thoughts were quickly interrupted as she heard a faint scratching sound coming from outside. Suddenly, Prissy tiptoed, shoes in hand through the room and quietly exited through the door. Kate immediately scrambled out of bed, ran barefoot to the front window, peering out as her sister met a tall soldier, both turned and walked away, arm in arm.

Kate couldn't believe her eyes that Prissy would have so little sense as to slip out and meet a man at this hour. Nothing good would come of it, she bit her lower lip frowning, and any man who would encourage a girl to do this-well, his intentions were far from what they should be, nor did he have any respect for the girl. How could Prissy be so stupid!

Kate returned to bed worried, knowing she would not tell her parents, also knowing sleep probably wouldn't come. Apparently, she was too tired to remain awake, but became instantly alert hours later as her sister crept through the door and began her quiet return, but Kate stood in her path before she could reach the sleeping area.

Prissy sucked in her breath, "What do you think you are doing? Get outta my way, Kate," she hissed, but the older sister did not budge as she retorted in angry whisper.

"How could you do such a thing? Meet a man and spend the night with him? You weren't reared to be a hussy. How dare you treat Mama and Papa this way-if they only knew-you'd never lay eyes on that Keith Anderson again!—and he is no gentleman to encourage such actions!"

"Shut up!" Prissy hissed her angry frustration. "How would a goody good like you know anything about love, you'll end up an old maid." Prissy felt that was the most horrible thing that could ever happen to a human being, "but not me! Keith and I plan to be married, so what I did simply showed my love for him and it's not wrong when you love someone and plan to be married-so quit your goody preaching to me, but you'd better not tell Mama and Papa," she hissed.

Wanting to get away from her foolish sister, "Prissy, don't threaten me with anything. I won't have to tell Mama and Papa. You will do that." Kate retreated to her bed, hoping there might be a couple of hours' sleep if she could untangle her emotions.

Roasting meat permeated the air as the visitors and soldiers gathered in the compound the following morning, celebrating the fourth with flags and music, and waiting for races to begin. Just as a fiddler, banjo picker and harmonica player struck up a lively tune, the Cherokee entered. The chief, leading his mounted parade of festively clad Cherokee astride painted pintos, roans and blacks was donned in plumed and fringed festival regalia. Wild Hawk followed, spectacular in his white fringed attire as Night Wind arched his neck and pranced to the music. Jess, spotting Wild Hawk, screamed and whistled through her teeth a welcoming above all other noise, to her mother's total embarrassment. The Indian turned, long black hair swaying in the breeze, nodded, smiled, then fastened his dark gaze on the girl who had touched his heart and caught his breath as Kate smiled, her beauty even enhanced by the hat and the ribbon that so matched those green eyes. Earlier he was so afraid he would not see her, and also afraid he would. Kate viewed the magnificence of man and animal as though they were one, the wild, handsome virility of this Indian causing her heart to thump wildly. Their eyes locked and held until he had to move on.

Kate supposed Tom Cason's feelings were hurt since he hadn't been around today. Actually, it was almost a relief. Jeb and Rusty strolled over to the Brandons, with plates of food as Jess and Tim, with permission, excitedly left to join their Indian friends for lunch. Prissy sat with her lieutenant halfway around the compound, explaining to her parents they'd like to sit away from the entire family for once, which Mary thought was reasonable.

"Rusty Poole-you old coot-where were you last night?" John had missed the old scout, who was always jovial, but full of vinegar too.

"Wall-been gone fer a couple of days-scoutin' round-didn't git back till late evin-'n I tell ye I'm pert nigh worn to a frazzle." He eased his still tired frame onto a bench by Kate. "My," glancing around at her, "if 'n you don't take the rag off'n the bush 'n prettier than a picher with that there green ribbon tied 'neath yore chin matchin' up with them eyes of your'n." He chuckled as Jeb arrived with more food in time to see Kate blush prettily. He handed her a plate, taking a seat by her and commenting.

"I must have scared that shave tail Cason off completely." He smiled as he attacked his roasted venison.

"I've simply wept all morning over it!" Kate's eyes twinkled and her lips twitched to keep from smiling. "Ah-have you visited with the Cherokee yet?" Her gaze steadily probed his.

"Yes, I have-everyone seems well. They were asking about you-especially someone, I've forgot who it was, but someone who called you Green Eyes. Course, I thought that wuz a little bit out of place," He twitched his mouth to keep from smiling as he crammed in another large bite of meat, eyeing her flushed face.

"Yes-it certainly was out of place." She smiled warmly, staring thoughtfully.

Mary observed this little confab, not slightly amused by any of it and well aware who would be impudent enough to call her daughter Green Eyes. Oh! Something must be done about this situation-she had hoped Wild Hawk's not being around for the past two months would take care of things, but apparently Katherine was still enamored with the Indian-which showed so little sense on her part. She glared at her demented daughter.

After the first race where Little Acorn swept out in front of all 10 Indians and whites to be the winner, Kate's Cherokee students, with Jess and Tim, paid the Brandons an exuberant visit-all chatting at once over Little Acorn's win, while the little Indian pumped his chest out. Finally, they remembered to invite Kate to visit Little Cub who had been asking for her, and was not allowed to leave the Cherokee group. Kate explained to her family and with excitement left with the children, while Mary didn't like it one bit. She knew her daughter would some way meet up with that Indian. The students continued jabbering their excitement until they reached the Cherokee. Suddenly, the name "Kate" penetrated over the din of noise as one chubby little Indian, clad only in breech clout and moccasins, exploded into view, rushing as fast as his chunky little body allowed. A delighted Kate open her arms and scooped the small chubby warrior up for a big hug, both girl and child happily hugging and laughing. Cub pushed back, pointing to the girl holding him saying, "Kate," he then looked around, saw his friend and pointed to him, "Hawk." Kate suddenly felt too warm as she stared into those penetrating black eyes. Putting the Indian child down, they slowly walked over to the big brave. Cub latched onto his leg, pointing, saying "Kate," but his friend didn't seem to hear him.

"Why didn't you come back?" She searched his warm gaze. "It's been two months."

"Did you miss me, Green Eyes?" His dark eyes and half smile teased her.

"Yes," she whispered, a little out of breath as Hawk picked up the little brave who was struggling for attention.

"Why would this be when you had your soldier hovering over you?" He smiled, but it didn't reach his eyes.

What's with him? Her mind raced back to the last time she saw Hawk.

"You mean Tom Cason? Why, he doesn't mean anything to me- he's only an acquaintance." He must be referring to the day he left. Tom was there. She frowned, trying to remember. Little Cub pulled Wild Hawk's face around, determined to get his attention, but his friend kept staring at the girl.

"That is very strange," Hawk's eyes were no longer warm, they were disturbed. "You allow men to kiss you who mean nothing to you?"

Kate's mind traveled back, and suddenly focused on that day when Hawk left. The lieutenant, without warning had kissed her cheek. In embarrassment she smiled. Of course, Hawk saw that and took it the wrong way-who wouldn't.

"No, I don't allow it to happen. Tom Cason startled me that day and I guess himself too by suddenly kissing my cheek. I didn't want this, and I suppose I felt sorry for him, he is so very shy. Instead of slapping or reprimanding him, I just smiled and backed away," She looked down as she completed her thought, "I don't even enjoy his company-do you believe me?" She looked up, pleading with him.

He placed the squirming lad on the ground, stooped down speaking softly in Cherokee, patted the little brave's back end as the child waved, saying, "Kate," and scampered away. "Come-I wish to speak with you away from many prying eyes and ears." She followed him away from the crowd, her heart thumping loudly, behind a large elm where he turned facing her. "Yes, I believe you, Katherine Brandon, but why was it so important that you tell me this?" He smiled warmly at this girl who meant so much to him, knowing her answer, but also knowing it was a must that he hear it from her lips.

"Because," she looked down-hesitating not able to look him in the eye as she revealed her emotions, "because-I care for you." She slowly raised her misty green eyes as Hawk struggled with his breathing, trying his best to control his emotions. Oh! How he wanted to pull her to him, crush her in his arms, and reveal his love for her, but instead he knew what he had to do-he must do it now. He must stop this now-his feeling and hers.

"Oh! I am sure the lieutenant means well," he gave a hollow chuckle, "and I am sure he considers himself a good friend-someone you can depend on-" He looked away, not able to trust himself with his lies while looking into her eyes.

"Stop it!" Her eyes were near tears at the feelings she had revealed and he was ignoring her. "Didn't you hear what I said or don't you care?"

He turned away-staring into space-not able to answer or look at her. Yawa help me, he pleaded within.

"I see," she whispered, turning to leave.

"Wait," he couldn't let her leave this way.

She turned as he took a step toward her.

"I would like for you to have this." He handed her a beautifully beaded bracelet. "And I will ride the race for you today."

Her eyes slowly left the lovely piece of jewelry, climbing to fasten on his disturbed gaze. "No-you give this gift and ride your race for someone you truly care for." She handed the bracelet back which he refused to take. She dropped it on the ground, turned and left, her vision blurred.

A beautiful dark eyed Indian maiden observed the gift passing. Her black eyes filled with jealousy and hate, her fists clenched until the nails bit into her palms-someday, her turn would come. She wheeled away, long fringe whipping against her body.

Wild Hawk sank behind the elm, leaned against it and wanted to cry his lonely heart out as a small boy might do, but he had no heart-she took it.

The running races were completed with most of them being won by the Cherokee. Colonel Roberts had taken the checkers tournament the day before, however Rusty assured him it was only because he was absent. Burt Lambert, a settler, had wiped them all out in horseshoes.

The big event, the horse race, was getting under way with the excitement explosive. Bets were placed on the ten riders: four soldiers, two settlers and four Indians. The horses pranced their beauty to the lively music as the riders readied them for the start, the Indians crooning to their mounts. They were off as hooves churned the turf while riders and mounts performed a magnificent race; however, on the backstretch a charging black stallion left the pack as he and his rider moved as one and crossed the finish line first.

The Indians went wild with their yelling and trilling as their favorite emerged the winner.

Wild Hawk walked Night Wind to the compound's center for his award, as he talked to his friend, petting the animal as it nudged him. He then fastened his gaze on Katherine Brandon, telling her with his eyes that he rode this race for her. She turned her head away, saying something to Jeb, which hurt this Cherokee deeply. He wondered if life would always be this cruel, as he turned and walked slowly back to the Cherokee.

He and Spotted Horse were helping to round up the children for returning to their village when they spotted two soldiers standing away from the people, half concealed by a a cedar tree. Hawk recognized Keith Anderson as he seemed to be in animated conversation with Dancing Eyes-the brave frowned-it was certainly not the usual that soldiers intermingled with the Cherokee, especially one who hated Indians! He didn't like it. The lieutenant flashed the maiden a charming smile as he turned to leave, followed by a sergeant. The Indians cleared a path for the soldiers as they strolled arrogantly through the group. Before they cleared the area, though, Sergeant Mathias stopped abruptly, turned, grabbing his right hip as he latched onto a leather pouch with a broken strap. "What the hell?" he exploded with small beady brown eyes darting all-around, shooting sparks—"Who stole it?" he thundered.

A Cherokee lad, Brown Beaver saw the money fall, picked it up to return it, walked forward to the soldiers as the sergeant grabbed him, shaking him viciously before knocking him to the ground while the lieutenant looked on with a slight smirk. Mathias continued his attack. "Why, you dirty thieving little savage-I'll teach you-" but before the soldier could continue the beating and angry tirade, strong brown hands jerked him around, slamming a vicious fist into his jaw that flattened the chunky sergeant. As he blinked his close-set eyes to get his bearings while struggling to regain his breath, a moccasined foot was placed on his ample middle. Keith Anderson immediately rushed up.

"What's going on here?" trying to throw his authority around, but was totally ignored by Hawk who spoke firmly to the sergeant as he continued to pin the man with his foot.

"Get this straight, you cowardly squint eyes-if you ever touch a Cherokee boy again I will personally destroy you. You remember this. Brown Beaver did not steal your money-he would have no use for it, you stupid man. He saw it fall, as I did, from your broken pouch and was returning it to you. If you wish to fight, try a man. Wild Hawk would welcome it-any time. Now get up and go back where you belong." Hawk strode over to Brown Beaver, checking him for any harm-ignoring the angry glare that Anderson gave him.

The lieutenant commanded, "Come on, Mathias-let's get out of here. This place stinks." He flashed his anger at Wild Hawk. The sergeant struggled to rise, glancing at the big Indian, eager to get away from this Cherokee. He grabbed his painful jaw, thinking it might be broken. God! What a punch. He'd sure make it a point never to tie in with that one again.

Most of the Cherokee were jubilant over Wild Hawk's action. The young braves looked at their hero worshipfully; however, Hawk, Spotted Horse, the Chief and a few others realized the whites would retaliate some way. They certainly wouldn't allow a heathen to best a white, no matter the reason. The Indians readied their mounts for departure as Hawk sent Little Acorn to bring Jeb Hawkins to him.

Jeb found his brother talking to Night Wind while the horse responded with a whinny and a nudge. "What's on your mind, my brother?" The scout stroked the stallion's neck.

"Katherine Brandon-you know my feelings for her?" he continued, rubbing his horse.

"Yes, I know," Jeb studied his friend, seeing the sadness as he caressed his stallion.

"I hurt her today, Jeb," he lifted his pain filled eyes, "she revealed her feeling for me and I ignored her and did what ever I had to do to stop this emotion. It tore at my insides. I've fought many fierce battles during my life," the black eyes stared sadly into the distance, "but making a lie, for her sake, of my feelings was the most difficult thing I have ever had to do." He reached into his leather pouch as Jeb clasped his shoulder, struggling with his own hurt for this friend and the white girl. Hawk pulled out the beautifully beaded bracelet that he had previously offered to Katherine, staring at it, rubbing his thumb over the beads. "My mother made this many moons ago," he smiled, "it was to have been my bride's gift. If Katherine can't fill that position, and in this world there is no way or place for an Indian and white together, then in Hawk's life there shall be no other bride." He looked deeply into the scouts' eyes, struggling in his throat. "Make sure she takes this special gift. Earlier, she left it on the ground, saying I should give it to someone I truly cared for."

Jeb nodded, so touched by his friend's sadness and his confidence, knowing what an honest and good man this Indian was and yet by the white world he was shunned and despised. He was so much more of a man than those who judged, shunned, and dubbed him savage.

"I'll see you soon, my brother." They clasped wrists. As he strolled toward the Brandons, Jeb thought, what a hell of a life some people live.

Chapter 12

A few days later the sun beat down with its August fury as Jeb reined in at Lone Eagle's village. What a welcome relief this shady place was. He removed his leather hat, wiping his sweaty face with his arm.

Several black eyed children gathered round the big scout, chattering and giggling, a couple of hounds thumped their tails, but it was too hot for them to be overly energetic. Little Acorn reached for the horse's reins as Brown Otter neared the big scout's side.

"Where will I find Wild Hawk, Brown Otter?"

"You find Hawk with Chief." Smiling broadly, Otter was proud to give instructions in the white tongue. Miss Kate done teach-ed him good.

After passing the time of day with two pretty giggling maidens, Jeb strolled up to Chief Eagle's lodge where he found his Indian brother.

"Wonder what this big galoot wants, Chief," Hawk welcomed his friend, smiling.

The Chief was more hospitable. "Come, my son-sit with us, and I am seeing in your face you have a message, too," the chief inquired seriously.

"Yes." Jeb squatted down near them, pulling a blade of grass. Hawk sobered immediately-sensing the seriousness of his friends visit. "The day of the celebration I overheard only bits and pieces of a conversation between Keith Anderson," Hawk stiffened at the mention of this name, "and three white no-goods, who are not above any criminal act. Anderson mentioned something about dirty savage beating up a sergeant-then he said something about killing some dirty heathens. He had no idea that I was near. Later,

I was told about you, Hawk, and the sergeant. I praise you for your action, but I'm sure Anderson was planning some dirty retaliation. You must be careful." Jeb's concern was obvious.

Chief sighed, "We expected some type of retaliation, but not so soon." Chief and Hawk exchanged disturbed glances.

"What is it?" Jeb inquired, sensing alarm, looking from one to the other.

"Three of our young warriors took Brown Beaver hunting early this morning. Green Turtle, Sly Fox and Black Crow. I now worry for their safety," Wild Hawk explained to Jeb, frowning.

"Oh! My God," the big scout whispered, standing. The brave quickly inserted,

"Let us leave now and find them." Jeb nodded; the chief agreed with them, the three standing while the chief gripped their arms.

"Be careful, my sons."

"We will take Spotted Horse with us," Hawk explained as they hurriedly left to ready their mounts and summon their friend.

The two braves and scout left their mounts ground tied under a wide spreading oak as they cautiously made their way through the thick green foliage, when suddenly running feet were pounding near them. Almost instantaneously Brown Beaver burst into their path with wild horror etched on his countenance. They feared what they expected was true; however, they were too stunned to question. Finally, after trying to console the boy, Hawk was able to ease him into a sitting position and Horse contained himself enough to question softly in Cherokee. After gulping and struggling with sobs and breathing Brown Beaver related in jerked sentences the brutal murders of his friends.

Half sobbing, he explained, "My-brothers—let-me go alone to—hunt-deer tracks-we had—found—I-lost—deer-and was-returning—when-I-heard white tongue—I-hid—and watched," he struggled to continue with voice breath and tears, "some way-those-pale eyes surprised—my brothers—knocked them out—then stabbed—each many—times—oh!" The young brave broke down as he covered his face.

"My God-" Jeb breathed.

It was as though the men had been slammed in their middles—breathing was very difficult and the horror of the act was also transferred to their facial countenance. Hawk finally stooped down by Beaver, putting an arm around his shoulder, his eyes also tearing, looking up at his friend as he struggled to speak. "Horse, would you please take Beaver back to the village-he can't stay here alone and he must not return to the scene."

"Yes- we will walk back-you may need the horse." He thought anything would be better than facing those poor murdered victims right now. He hated that his friends had to do the difficult job. "Come on Beaver," the boy went with him as Horse placed an arm across the youths shoulder and spoke softly to him in Cherokee while they quietly walked through the forest.

"Let us go, Brother-the longer we put this off, the harder it will be," Hawk urged Jeb as they led the horses slowly through the dense forest, checking for any signs and dreading each step that took them closer to their destination. They soon rounded a turn that opened into a small clearing where they found the three young warriors sprawled grotesquely in death, each lathered in his own blood. Both men fell to their knees, so overcome with grief that they were unable to function adequately - Jeb with bowed head, Hawk with head thrown back, arms outstretched, reaching toward heaven, pleading to Yawa, eyes misty. Jeb finally pulled Hawk to his feet, both realizing they must function. Trying to bring their emotions under control, they began checking the surrounding area, finding shod hoof prints, one with a split in it. They checked the trail briefly where the three left-knowing they would pick it up later. Right now, they had a very grim but important tasks to accomplish.

It was with great heaviness of heart, and one of the most difficult jobs either man had ever attempted as they wrapped the young Cherokee in blankets and strapped them to the horses. Such young handsome braves to have their lives snuffed out and for no reason at all except hate. Hawk was crying inside for these young men who never really tasted life. They headed back to the village, each man engulfed in his own grief. This was the time for grief-soon they would have to put it away and drag up their anger to find and take care of the killers.

The entire village awaited them with the sad death keening and wailing, shorn hair and garments torn. The bodies were deposited at the young braves' lodges while Jeb and Hawk continued to be engulfed in grief.

They met with their Chief, where Spotted Horse joined them.

"We will first talk with Brown Beaver, when he is able to speak, then leave to track the killers. We must avenge the deaths of our young braves who had no chance for life. We wish your backing, Chief, as we find and take care of these murderers." Hawk implored the older man.

Lone Eagle looked into the distance sighing. "Yes," his long hair swayed in the breeze, "we cannot turn our backs on this killing. It is with a great heavy heart that I give my consent," his sad eyes connected with each brave, "for killing breeds killing, but such a heinous crime cannot be passed over. May Yawa give you strength." The chief slowly walked into his lodge, his countenance reflecting the sadness of his heart, as the sad keening and wailing continued.

Brown Beaver struggled through a detailed description of the killers, wanting in some way to help avenge the horrible deaths of his friends. "They were all filthy pale eyes-one was tall, skinny, had long brown stringy hair, chin and face hair-he shifted his eyes a lot like he was scared. Another one was not so short, wide built with flaming hair and face hair. The other one was dark, medium-size with stringy hair and he giggled all the while he stabbed Black Crow." The boy turned away, closing his eyes, trying hard to forget the scene which would even follow him into his dream world. He stumbled away, his head down, tears streaming.

The three men left quietly, after gathering supplies, leaving their grief with the mourners at the village, bringing with them their war paint and letting their festering anger surface. These three brothers, two Indians and a white, knew their destination and their intent. Silence prevailed as they carefully scrutinized the area where the bodies had been found, where the killers had hid in waiting behind a large thicket after tying their horses a distance away, well concealed behind a thick grouping of cedars. They picked up the trail where the three whites had entered the area from the Northeast, and left going South. Apparently, the killers were convinced the bodies wouldn't be found for some time. Indians stayed for days when they hunted and by the time they were found the tracks would be washed away or blown away. Maybe they were too dense to cover tracks or split up, which made the tracking child's play for the Cherokee and Scout. The split hoof print was obvious.

Shortly, the three Indian ponies were spotted, grazing near a small branch that had trickled beneath out spreading oaks and elms. The ponies whinnied a welcome to their guests and without much ado they were in tow. "Guess it was a good thing Beaver didn't ride his own horse. I thought it foolish for him not to borrow one since his was lame-he rode double with Crow-guess it was a good thing or he would be gone, too." Horse sighed, shaking his head. The other two nodded as they continued their trek, following the trail with the split hoof as it veered East, closing in around a rather wide creek where apparently the pursued had stopped for water in the cool of shade trees surrounding the creek. Quietly, Jeb motioned for the others to dismount.

"It's my belief those three are holed up in that old shack two or three miles from here that's up against the mountainside 'n hard to spot with all the trees and brush surrounding it. We've been traveling four to five hours 'n we're a long way from your village."

The other two nodded, thinking he might be right. Hawk inserted, "We will ride for a short distance, stop-let the horses drink, secure them and walk from there."

When they found fresh horse droppings, the pursuers finalized their plans, left their mounts and went the remaining distance on foot. Finally the old shack was spotted and sure enough Jeb was right, the trail was leading directly to it. It was true this old ramshackle place was thoroughly enclosed in trees and bushes. A perfect place for anyone to overlook.

The trackers had previously decided to wait until dark. When the moon began her climb and sprinkled silvery shadows over the mountainous beauty, dotting the landscape with her charm, it was time. This peaceful beauty seemed totally incongruous with the night's happening. The three trackers stealthily emerged, creeping in three directions toward their one destination. Their silent travel went undetected due to years of practice for moccasined silence. One window at the side of the hovel, covered with cobwebs and filth left a visible crack where the dim lantern light filtered through, revealing to Jeb's keen eyes the same three villains described by Brown Beaver, and the same three Keith Anderson had talked with. Jeb reported by sign as Spotted Horse reported no back door and only one room.

From inside one rather high pitched male voice pealed forth, "Well, I'll be damned, Jake, you din' have no ace-air you cheatin' me? Ah don' take to nobody a cheatin' me."

A deep bass bellowed, "Aw! Shut yore chickenshit mouth-ah ain't cheatin' 'n if'n ah wuz ain't no damn thing you could do 'bout hit. Why you chicken livered you even tried to back outta' that job today." He bellowed with a harsh laugh.

A third raspy voice chimed in, "I'm wore out 'n I'd like ta git me some sleep," his voice grew louder, "before them red bastards start on the warpath!"

Just as Jed Gibbons completed his last loud word the decrepit door burst open as three large frames rushed into the room, spreading out evenly, two Indians, both with red and black war paint streaked across their faces, dressed only in breech clouts and moccasins, a scout stripped to the waist accompanied them, each carrying weapons.

The three criminals all jumped up, knocking over two chairs. Skinny high voice reacted first with his prominent Adam's apple jerking up and down, eyes bulging with fear. "Oh! My Gawd-they're here already-" his voice squeaking on the last word as he spurted pee all over himself. Fierce black eyes and cold blue ones watched carefully, assessing the killers as Red Beard inched his hand closer to a rifle butt.

"I wouldn't," cracked like a whip from the big scout, causing Skinny's Adam's apple to convulse harder while Red Beard knocked whiskey and cards all over the floor as he jerked his hand back. Dark Hair who giggled when he stabbed Black Crow was the total unconscionable killer. Nothing bothered him.

One nod from Hawk, and all guns and knives were confiscated by Horse. Frisking was unnecessary since they were only clad in underwear.

"On the floor," Hawk thundered, as he and Horse quickly and securely tied hands behind each and feet together, each secured to a piece of furniture.

Hawk continued in his deep voice, "We will place things in the open now." Eyeing each other steadily, they were shocked that this heathen could speak their language so good.

"We know you killed our three Cherokee brothers. To deny it will only go against you." The three suspects looked at each other-afraid to admit and afraid not to when giggling Dark Hair shook his head slightly for the others to say nothing. This slight movement was detected by all three pursuers.

"Then suppose you, Dark Hair, fill us in since you instruct the others not to speak." The Dark Hair only stared at Hawk-the others shifting their gaze. "That is fine with me-either way-but if you think Keith Anderson gives two hoots in hell what happens to any one of you, you are crazy!"

The criminals looked at each other amazed that this Indian knew-how?

Hawk turned his back on the men, speaking to Horse and Jeb, mainly to impress the killers with the knowledge that he really did not care one way or the other what they said and to make plans for their destruction.

Skinny yelled out, "You two," he looked around at his buddies, "kin lay here with yore traps shut, but I ain't-that there lieutenant don't mean a damn tu' me-he jus got us ta do his dirty work. Them Injuns didn't do no harm to us 'n ah don't blame these hear fer killin' us fer whut we done, but-me-ah wished 'hit hadn't a been." He looked down and quietly finished, "I'm mighty sorry fer any part I had in it-that young boy's face stays in my mind, all the time." He looked up slowly with tears in his eyes as one slipped down his grimy face.

The other two villains eyed the skinny one as though they could tear him limb from limb if they were free.

Regardless of what he had done, the skinny guy had made a small impression on the three men who had come to kill the murderers. He did have some human quality after all. The three made their plans. Jeb and Horse immediately untied Red Beard and Dark Hair's feet and the ropes securing them to the furniture, yanked them up amid curses, and shoved them through the door, ushering the two a short distance from the shack.

The two trackers could smell the fear of these villains, but that made little difference. Horse's fierce black eyes commanded Red Beard's half crazed countenance as the killer pled. "Please-for God's sake-have mercy," his voice broke into a sob.

The Indian replied quietly, "Yes, the same kind of mercy you showed our Cherokee brothers-Red Beard, if you have a death chant, you best find your tune." He hesitated while Red Beard continued to sob-then in one swift motion, Horse slipped a wicked blade from his moccasin, ramming into Red Beard's heart and again as the man grunted and a startled expression froze on the bearded countenance while his life's blood streamed to the ground as the body collapsed.

"And now, giggling boy," Jeb spoke to Dark Hair.

"I don't wanta' die," Dark Hair yelled, shaking all over, his eyes darting, wild.

"Neither did Black Crow as you drove your knife into him and giggled while you killed him-let's see if you get any fun out of the use of this blade-" Jeb held up a fierce looking bone handled blade that gleamed in the moonlight. When cool Dark Hair saw it, he fainted from fright. Jeb completed the hated deed that was his to do. There would be no more joy this one would receive from killing.

Within 30 minutes Jeb and Horse returned to the shack with no indication of any outside happening-nor would anyone walking near the dilapidated hovel be aware of any outside action.

Hawk looked down at the skinny one. "What are you called?" the man's eyes still frightened by the Indian.

"Ah-Clyde-ah-Clyde-Jenkins." The Adam's apple began working again.

"Listen to me carefully, Clyde Jenkins," Hawk continued, pulling up a rickety split bottomed chair, straddling it, leaning his arms on the back, "if you do as we say-your life just might be spared." He steadily watched the man as did the other two.

"I sure will do what ever you say." Clyde struggled to push himself to a sitting position.

"If you do not cooperate," Hawk continued, "we won't hesitate killing you." Clyde got the point, Adam's apple working more vigorously.

Horse stepped up, easing his frame to the dirty floor against his better judgment, but he was weary. The trauma of the entire situation, his brothers' deaths, the long ride, the hated unnecessary killing that he and Jeb had to perform! They had all drawn sticks-he and Jeb had received the honors, but it had all taken its toll. He injected, "Clyde, we need some information." Clyde shifted his uncomfortable gaze to the other formidable Indian, trying to scratch his legs after Jeb slit the rope securing his feet together and bed attachments. "Was someone to meet you here? If so-when and who?" Horse continued.

Clyde nodded, shifting his eyes from one to the other, "Lt. Anderson-he was a payin' us $200 fer killing Indians 'n bringin' a squaw gal here. We snuck 'round yore village three days watchin' hits comin' 'n goin' 'n couldn't git to no squaw Dancing Eyes-them young Indians come huntin'." He looked down, disturbed, "Ha had to do whut they said or be kilt maself." He looked up, pleading.

"When is Anderson supposed to be here?" Jeb put in as he sank on to the edge of the table.

"Don't rightly know, but Ah'm a thinkin' he said he'd be here 'n three to four days 'n this here is the third."

"If he asks you where the other two white men are?" Horse reminded Clyde.

"Ha will say ah don't know-they jest got scairt 'n left," he nodded, smiling, "'cause that's whut done happened."

"He will not ask that-it would only involve him," Hawk pointed out, "and please," speaking to Clyde, "change those pissed clothes-you smell stronger than a dead warthog."

Clyde guffawed as he was rushed outside where Hawk doused him several times with pouches of water.

The next day, weary from little sleep, after eating their noon meal of jerked beef washed down with water, Horse's shrill bird call from outside told the other two the lieutenant was on his way. They made sure the door was locked, requiring Anderson to knock. They heard a horse nicker, steps brushing through the tall grass-finally boots on the rickety porch, before the rapping on the door.

Hawk nodded to Clyde as the skinny man asked, "Who is it?"

"It's me, Lt. Anderson-who'd you think it'd be-hurry up and open up."

"Keep your shirt on, lieutenant-Ah'm a comin'." Hawk nodded to Jeb as the scout unlatched the door, opening it a crack as Keith Anderson pushed it completely open, taking a step inside, not pleased with the rudeness of this trash, to keep him waiting. "What the hell-" as he spotted Clyde sitting on the filthy floor, his hands tied behind him, a sneer marking his narrow face.

Before Anderson knew what was happening, he was totally divested of all weapons by Hawk. "Do come in, lieutenant," the Indians sarcastically invited, "we have been expecting you. Do have a seat." He roughly shoved Anderson into a straight backed chair as the lieutenant growled,

"You."

"None other, "as he tied the lieutenant's hands behind.

"What do you think you are doing?" The arrogant Anderson hissed angrily, but fear was revealed in his hazel eyes.

"I might ask you the same thing," the brave answered complacently. "I already know the answer," Hawk nodded to Jeb as the big scout took the lieutenant's money pouch, flipped it open to find it contained $200. He nodded to Hawk.

"What the hell are you doing with my money?" Anderson exploded.

"Why, I'm keeping it. You don't need it for a while," the big scout smiled smugly as he strapped the leather pouch to his own body, easing his frame to rest on the table corner.

"Listen carefully for I won't repeat," Hawk explained. "Within one hour we travel to the fort," he observed the sudden startled expression in Andersen's eyes before the lieutenant realized and quickly looked away. "We are only waiting to rest your horse, Anderson." He waited until the lieutenant looked at him, amused by the fear he saw. Clyde nodded, anxious to please this big Indian who he had come to respect.

Travel to the fort was long, hot, dusty and sweaty; however the five arrived around dusk and set up camp near the compound, while Wild Hawk rode in to speak with Colonel Roberts.

The Colonel was rather astonished when he opened his door to the big Cherokee. "Well, Wild Hawk-this is a surprise-come on in," he motioned for the buckskin clad brave to enter. "Have a seat," he motioned to the floral designed couch across from the fireplace which the Indian declined.

"I will rest here." He eased his body onto a straight maple chair. "I am dusty from traveling." The Colonel observed the brave's disturbed countenance.

"What's bothering you, Wild Hawk?" The Colonel probed, easing his heavy frame onto an overstuffed chair near the Indian.

Hawk revealed in detail the happening, beginning with his fight with the sergeant, Keith Anderson's talking with the villains, through the three Indians killed, tracking of the killers, Andersen's arriving at the shack and the return to the fort with the lieutenant and Jenkins in tow.

The colonel's face blanched as he drank in the horrendous crime, unable to fathom any man being a part of such hate and horror. He rose, pacing back and forth, picking up his pipe from the mantel, stuffing it, lightning and puffing. "My God! Wild Hawk-this is too horrible to speak of. My heart goes out to you, Lone Eagle, and your people. How any man could do such a vile act is inconceivable," he continued pacing and puffing. His voice suddenly rose, "Where is this scalawag now?"

"We are camped near the gate, and Colonel," Hawk stood, "I would like nothing better than to destroy," he ground the word out, "Keith Anderson, and I could easily do it, but I am turning him over to you for your justice. Let us hope it is justice. We also brought one of the killers, Clyde Jenkins, who will gladly verify my story." Hawk was ready to sink his weary frame onto a bear robe and sleep. The two days had been long.

"Son, I'll get a military trial going as quickly as possible-in a couple of days at the latest. In the meantime, both the Lieutenant and Jenkins will be under military arrest. Both will be confined to the fort and under guard." The Colonel clasped Hawk's shoulder-wishing there were something he could do to erase the horrible happening and sadness. "I'm so very sorry, I wish there were more I could do," He shook his head, moving his bulk through the door as he followed the Indian out. "Oh! I won't ask what happened to the other two murderers." The Colonel turned on his heel with a twinkle in his eye.

"Take me to your camp-we'll bring those two in now." He sent his aide for the officer of the day and his choice of one other, as Hawk watched this man who seemed to care. Shortly, a captain and a lieutenant appeared with snappy salutes as they mounted up and followed their Colonel and the Indian through the gate, as the early evening fading sun cast her pinkish hue over the countryside while misty blue mountain peaks reached for the sky. How could something so peaceful and beautiful, God's handiwork, have to witness the vile crimes of mankind's hatred, the Colonel thought.

A mile from the fort, the four approached a low burning camp fire near an over shadowing elm where four men were gathered. Keith Anderson managed to stand, his hands still tied. "Colonel, I can explain this ridiculous mistake," he turned an angry gaze on those who had brought him in. "Please have these fools release me immediately."

The Colonel barked quick orders to the captain and lieutenant who immediately took Anderson and Jenkins into custody as he totally ignored Keith Anderson. The two were marched off, Anderson glaring at the Colonel as the commander turned to the remaining men, "You are welcome to stay inside the fort and take your meals there if you wish. Jeb, you have room in your quarters." The scout nodded.

"Thank you, Colonel but I wish to rest here under the stars." Horse responded, his weary body ready to turn in. Hawk agreed as Jeb left the two, looking forward to resting his big frame in a real bed. The Colonel assured them the hearing would be held the day after the next and they would be needed as witnesses.

The peacefulness of the star-studded night, the gentle breeze caressing their bodies and the crickets' lullaby were enough to lull the two braves to sleep, but one, even though weary of body, was wide awake. His black eyes searched the heavens as he spoke in silence, asking Yawa to guide his brother's, those who lost their lives, on their spirit path. For the girl who held his heart, Yawa keep her safe and may she find happiness. Thinking of her finding happiness with another man tore at his insides, even though he knew it was to be. Thinking of her and the nearness of her had such a pull on him he knew tomorrow he would ride to the hill overlooking the Brandon farm. With this settled, his mind relaxed, the inner turmoil smoothed, and sleep found Hawk as he thought of green eyes and a smile that caused a tiny dimple to crease.

Chapter 13

As Night Wind picked his way to the familiar hill overlooking the Brandon farm, Katherine, clad in a green cotton, emerged from the house, stopped abruptly and caught her breath as she stared into the distance, recognizing the all too familiar figure astride the black stallion. She didn't remember when or how she went through the gate, but suddenly she was running through the field toward the Indian.

As Hawk watched her running toward him it was all he could do not to run and meet her. He should ride off now, but he couldn't. He watched the bonnet fly from her head and the sun fire her hair. *Yawa give me strength to do what is right.*

Suddenly she stopped running, as though coming to her senses. *What am I doing? I mustn't throw myself at him.* She stared at this magnificent man who had walked right into her heart without asking.

The brave watched the change of expressions, the turmoil of her countenance realizing her inner feelings as he slid from Night Wind and walked toward her, the fringe on his buckskin pants and vest swaying with his body movements. He smiled that charming lopsided smile that took her breath.

"Katherine Brandon," his deep voice caressed her," the sun lights a fire in your hair, and I want to know that you are well."

She smiled, thinking he'd rather say something else, crinkling a dimple, making it difficult for him to think. "I've been well-and I wish to thank you for the lovely bracelet."

He searched her arms, her eyes, "but you do not wear it-," he looked sad, "I suppose I understand."

"No, you don't-I wear it on a chain around my neck-why I wear it and why you gave it to me is no one else's business." He nodded and again she was captivated by the white teeth and smile.

"Our parting at the celebration," he stared into the distance uncomfortable, "I made statements that I thought I should say but I was not honest with you nor myself. I am sorry, Green Eyes." He pled with his eyes for understanding.

"I know," she smiled, "you're forgiven. Come on-it's too hot here in the sun. I'll fix some cool lemonade and Jess will never forgive either of us if she doesn't see you."

"I never meant to stay—only to—only—," he looked distressed.

"Come on, "she smiled, pulling at his arm, her touch filling him with warmth through and through. He whistled for Night Wind. As the stallion trotted up, Kate spoke softly while patting him and was rewarded with a shoulder nudge. Her delighted laughter and beauty filled the Cherokee as he watched mesmerized, knowing he should leave. He picked up her bonnet, plopping it on her head as they strolled toward the house.

All too soon, Jess spied them. With a whoop and skirts flying, she screeched to a halt grabbing Hawk's arm. "Oh! Wild Hawk-I'm so glad you came to visit me-you haven't been here in a coon's age-why not?" Hawk smiled at this young girl who had no inhibitions.

"I have not been able to-Jesse-," He glanced at Kate, sadness revealed in his dark eyes as they strolled on.

Kate wondered why she couldn't be as open with feelings as Jess-why adults had to say things they didn't mean or just avoid the truth. She knew her parents would have a fit if she told them she cared for this Indian, especially her mother, and yet he was the finest man she knew. Her father highly respected Wild Hawk, but not as someone for his daughter.

As they entered the gate, Jess pulled Hawk beneath the big shady oak, where she pushed him down on a bench, plopping beside him, looking at him, devouring him with her smile. She was so taken with this handsome man that she completely forgot Kate-as her sister cleared her throat. Jess turned, "Oh! Kate-ah-you can run on and get us something cool to drink." Hawk shrugged his shoulders, flashing a helpless smile at Kate as she shook her head, wanting to pull Jess up by one of her dirty ears, but on second thought she'd rather not touch the little pig.

"Come on, young lady, you can help-I'm sure Wild Hawk can spare you for a few minutes!" she teased, scowling.

Jess moved reluctantly, mumbling about hateful old sisters, as the Indian fastened his gaze on Katherine's retreating form.

The kitchen was hot while Mary finished peeling potatoes for the evening meal when Kate and Jess entered, preparing to pour cider. The mother knew something was amiss when she observed Katherine's rosy cheeks and sparkling eyes. It had to be that Indian.

Jess burst forth, "We have comp'ny for supper, Mama," she exuberantly clapped her hands, "Wild Hawk is visiting me, n' he's even purtier than ever," she dreamily sighed as she grabbed a glass.

Mary steadily watched Katherine as her older daughter added, "I do think it would be a nice gesture since the Cherokee were so gracious to us." Mary dumped flour into a bowl from the bin-why John Brandon had to have hot biscuits all the time she didn't understand-one would think he was reared in the South!

"That's fine," she didn't really mean it, didn't want that Indian here, but what could she do or say?

"Oh! Thank you, Mama." Jess grabbed her mother around the waist, causing her to do a spinning dance with the flour bowl.

"Jessica! Stop it!" Mary bellowed as Kate grabbed the cider and headed for the door before her mother exploded. She was sure

Mama didn't want Wild Hawk here, but she did and she'd see that he stayed.

He watched the swish of her hips as she walked toward him, wondering if he had lost his mind coming here, knowing the mother did not welcome him, knowing it would probably cause more hurt than anything else.

She handed him a glass of cider, brushing his hand in the process, blushing, knowing she was acting like a silly young girl. Sitting next to him, she broke the silence, "You are invited to eat with us this evening," as she sipped her drink.

"Who invited?" he questioned, watching this girl who suddenly seemed ill at ease.

"Well, Jess and I, and my mother approved." She looked at the glass as she turned it round and round.

"I should leave, Katherine-I had no intent of visiting here, and your mother does not want this," he held her with his warm dark gaze.

"But I do-please stay," she pled with those green eyes that drew him into their deaths. How could he refuse her? He sighed, a weak man where this green eyed girl was concerned.

She gazed at him steadily. "Why don't I know anything about you?"

"What do you wish to know?"

"Anything-your family-what you do-why you are you?" She smiled her little dimple, "I don't know anything about you."

He looked into the distant mountains, the breeze stirring his long hair as he drank in the picturesque beauty of the surroundings. He sighed, "My home was many miles south of here, down by the big water. When I was a young boy I was sent to a mission school where my hair was cut, I was dressed in white man's clothes, and taught the white tongue, and forbidden to speak my language," his dark eyes flashed angrily in memory. "I could not stand this life, even though my father wished me to learn. I ran away, returning home. Shortly after, my father was murdered, my mother raped and murdered by white renegades. At age eleven I ran and hid, starving and afraid until I reached my uncle Lone Eagle's village." He smiled warmly. "Since then, he is my father and I would give my life for him at any time. I have lived 24 summers. I am strong, believe in Yawa, have never wed," he glanced at her smiling, "and I fear no man. My close brothers are Spotted Horse and Jeb Hawkins-do you know me a little now?" He held her with his dark eyes as her misty green ones looked up at him with sadness.

"Yes," she whispered, "Thank you."

A loud bellowing voice penetrated this conversation when Jess and Tim bounded into view leading a sizable bellowing black bear cub around the house and into view. Ecstatically Jess and Tim galloped up, so very proud of their pet, and wanting Hawk's approval.

"This is our surprise," Jess burst forth, "this is Stink Bear-Rusty Poole named him and Prissy agreed it suited him." The big Indian walked up, petting the animal when Stink Bear grabbed him around the waist with both front paws. Hawk threw his head back with a hearty laugh, exposing his even white teeth. Stink realized this one was no child to wallow so he just held on and loved the big critter. Kate's heart thumped, watching the two wild creatures playing together.

The evening meal was served outside, where there was a cooling breeze and lanterns lit. John was more than receptive to this young brave, whom he greatly respected. Mary's cheeks were splashed with high color, her movements quick and decisive, seemingly with pent-up feelings that might erupt. Prissy wasn't feeling well enough to join them, while Jess and Tim, seated on either side of

Hawk were elated to be near their guest, Jess smiling and chewing at the same time gazing at him.

As John passed the green beans to the brave, he inquired, "What's been going on in your village lately, Wild Hawk?"

Hawk took a helping of the vegetables, and hesitated. "Sadness-three of our young braves were killed," he looked down, staring at his plate.

"What?" An astonished John Brandon held a spoon in mid-air as all stared at the Indian in disbelief.

"It is true," Hawk took a bite of a biscuit as the family continued to stare.

"Well, for goodness sakes," John sputtered, "what happened" Genuine concern evident, everyone else stared.

"Three killers were hired to kill Indians," it was difficult for him to remember and discuss the sadness. "Three of our young braves were hunting and were killed. This happened five moon's past. We tracked the killers, found them, and I do not wish to go into any more explanation at this time." The Brandons began picking at their food.

John nodded, understanding thoroughly. "I'm so very very sorry-please offer our condolences to your chief and other Cherokee," John responded, completely torn by such a vile act. Mary admonished herself for her hostility toward this young man who had already lived such a harsh life. He had always been a gentleman and had even saved their lives-she was again very ashamed as she gently touched his shoulder.

"I'm so very sorry."

He nodded, looking steadily at Mary. "Thank you."

Kate and Jess helped to clear the table, the two younger bidding Hawk, "Goodnight," Jess making him promise he'd return to visit her again as she grabbed and hugged his neck.

Kate slipped through the back screen door, carefully and quietly walking around the outside of the fence to where Night Wind grazed.

The brave wondered why Green Eyes didn't return. Disappointed, he bid John good night. As he exited the gate he heard John climb the porch steps and enter the house.

Moccasined feet quietly approached his stallion while a lush full moon crept slowly on its upward path casting its silvery sheen over a beautiful apparition as she strolled toward him. "I wanted to tell you good night alone," Kate whispered softly, her eyes glistening in the moonlight as she took another step closer. He smelled the flower scent of her hair, wanting to take her in his arms and never let her go. "I want," she whispered, moving closer until he felt her breath on his chest, "I want you to kiss me good night."

He stiffened, catching his breath. "You don't know what you are saying, Green Eyes," unable to look at her standing this near, not trusting his own actions-his breathing became irregular.

"I know exactly what I'm saying. You have never even touched me-never even held my hand-" her eyes never left his face as she inched closer, slowly placing her hands on his chest which totally broke the stand off; moaning, he gathered her into his arms, crushing her to him as her arms slipped around his neck and his lips captured hers, telling her in the depth of the kiss the many things that should but could never be. Before he carried her away with him, he struggled-and took her upper arms and with great difficulty pushed her away slightly.

"Oh! Green Eyes," he struggled to speak having trouble breathing, "you don't know what you are doing to yourself and to me! I only wish I could take you with me and never let you go." He fiercely stated, his eyes sad, "This can not be-what we did tonight cannot happen again."

"Is it wrong for me to want to be kissed by you, and I guess I'd have to say I loved it and wanted only to stay in your arms and your kiss also told me how you care for me," her eyes filled with tears. "Is that so wrong?" She struggled with her voice.

"<u>No</u>-it is not wrong and <u>yes</u>, it is wrong for us-for you and me because we have no future, no life together!" His voice broke, "Do you think I could ever pull you into the harsh Cherokee existence with a future for us that looks so bleak, so grim? I could never do that to you. I will never hurt you." His own hurt caused harshness to enter his voice.

"Then-you don't care enough!" A tear slipped down her cheek, shining in the silvery moonlight, ripping his heart. "And if you run from this, from us and our feeling for each other-then-then you are not the man I thought you were," she turned quickly striding back toward the house, tears streaming down her cheeks, blurring her vision, hating herself for loving a man she couldn't have. Wild Hawk watched his life walking away from him as his heart yelled to stop her, to take her away, to make her his. He stood staring until she was completely out of sight as shiny moisture slipped slowly down his own cheeks.

The Board Room was set with an air of tenseness as the 10:00 a.m. preliminary hearing of Keith Anderson and Clyde Jenkins was ready to begin with three officers in judgment. The two Cherokee accompanied by Jeb Hawkins sat opposite Anderson, as they awaited the arrival of Clyde Jenkins who was to be escorted in. Several minutes passed, Colonel Roberts gazed at his gold pocket watch for the second time before Lieutenant Thompson entered, walking quickly to the Colonel for a confrontation. Roberts stood abruptly, totally disturbed, pacing a few steps, again turning back to Thompson who nodded firmly.

Colonel Roberts, face flushed, frowning, strode to the front of the group. "Gentlemen of the court, I have very disturbing news- Clyde Jenkins is not in the compound. Apparently he disappeared sometime during the night. When, how or why we do not know at this time."

Hawk, Jeb and Horse knew what had happened to Clyde. Keith Anderson had had him silenced permanently-he couldn't afford to let him testify. They looked at each other, knowing this move by Anderson had won him his freedom.

The testimonies were given to the court by the Indians and Jeb, omitting the vanishing of two killers; however, they were not eye witnesses, and without the key witness, Clyde Jenkins, there was no actual evidence against Keith Anderson other than talking with three villains and arriving at the shack which Anderson smoothed over nicely, smiling his charm.

"I had seen a lovely little Indian maiden," he smiled, "that I had spoken with and agreed to pay Jenkins, and a couple of others to 'persuade' her," a few chuckled at the word persuade, "to meet me at the shack." He knew he had a few sympathetic ears.

Colonel Roberts was deeply disturbed over the outcome of the hearing, feeling Keith Anderson was indeed guilty of instigating the entire act, but it would never be known because he had some way, some how prevented Clyde Jenkins from testifying. He frowned, shifting his bulk on the uncomfortable hard oak chair. He looked at the Indians, his heart going out to them, but wasn't this the typical? It made little difference what happened to them. He had thought of bringing the little Indian boy who saw the killing, but that had nothing to do with Keith Anderson and besides, he was only an Indian boy.

The Colonel stood scowling. "This may end today's hearing, but there will be a total military investigation of Jenkins' disappearance and the entire case." He glanced at Anderson, "Thank you gentlemen, we are adjourned."

He walked over to the Indians and Jeb, offering his deepest sorrow, regrets and apologies for the court outcome, promising to do his best to get to the bottom of this entire evil mess.

Lt. Anderson smugly sauntered from the court room, a slight sneer on his handsome face as he glimpsed the red heathens, wishing it had been these two bastards who had gotten it, and if they thought they could best him at anything they had another thought coming! He chuckled to himself, thinking how easy it had been to explain the procedure to Mathias and hire him to 'take care' of Clyde Jenkins, the sniveling son of a bitch, and hell would freeze over before anybody ever found out what really happened to him. He had nothing to worry about.

Jeb and the Cherokee were standing together near the gate opening before the Indians left for their village-each with his own thoughts of the evil ordeal, knowing Anderson was guilty, but reluctant to continue hashing it over since there was nothing they could do about it. They would bide their time and continue to stay alert and stay in touch with Jeb.

As the big scout clasped the shoulders of his Cherokee brothers, bidding them farewell, two pretty girls approached clad in pastel cottons with matching bonnets. Evelyn Hollins, the aggressor, thrust her hand to Jeb, "Well Mr. Hawkins, I haven't seen you around in simply ages," as he took her hand, she shifted her blue eyed gaze to Wild Hawk, assessing and devouring him as she crinkled a smile, "and this must be the man who won that great horse race at the celebration. You were marvelous." Hawk nodded, "Thank you." She was shocked at his English while he also assessed this very forward young white girl, the type to stay away from.

"Evelyn Hollins and Janice Cooper, this is Wild Hawk and Spotted Horse." The Indians nodded as Evelyn took a step forward. "Wild Hawk, could you teach me to ride?" She placed her hand on his arm. "I've always wanted to learn," she fluttered her lashes and dimpled prettily as Jeb rolled his eyes. Startled by her aggressiveness, Hawk replied,

"No, I do not teach." Evelyn pouted while Janice was startled speechless at this most forward behavior of her friend.

"Excuse us," Hawk turned, making it a point to leave as quickly as possible, for this blue eyed white girl could be big trouble. Horse followed as they exited the gate. Evelyn Hollins continued to stare blatantly at the handsome Indian.

"My! He is some man!" the blonde whispered as Jeb excused himself, strolling away, concern over the obvious actions of the blue-eyed blond which could cause problems for his friend.

As they walked on, Janice's irritation was obvious. "I can't believe the way you acted back there toward that Indian."

"Isn't he magnificent?" Evelyn giggled. "He could place his moccasins under my bed any time." Sighing, Evelyn turned to watch the retreating figure of Wild Hawk, his fringed buckskin swaying with each step.

"But he's an Indian!" Janice reprimanded.

"Oh! He certainly is!" Janice couldn't believe this girl, and had never in her life witnessed such a brazen performance. She would not be a party to such a display again. No wonder the Indian left in such a hurry.

"My brother," Horse's smile twitched as the two walked toward their campsite where their horses were secured. "Seems you have again found a wee bit of trouble." Hawk's black eyes snapped at his friend.

"Don't remind me!"

Horse threw his head back rumbling with deep laughter while his friend glared at him, then shifted his gaze to the hazy mountain range that cast its bluish hue over the countryside. Why, Hawk wondered, did he continually attract trouble or turmoil? The three young braves killed and he could do nothing to avenge their death on the one responsible, a girl who held his heart and he could do nothing about it, he was afraid to be around her, after kissing her he didn't trust himself, and now this loose wench who could very well cause an Indian trouble with lies or actions, he had seen this kind before, ready and willing to slip around with a savage and do anything in the dark, but not with this savage she would not.

"That slut is hardly amusing, Spotted Horse!" Hawk saw no humor in any of this-he continued packing his gear.

"No, but you are-Problem Hawk adds another to his list," Horse smiled warmly at his friend. "What in the world would your Green Eyed Kate do if she observed this blond in action around you?" he chuckled.

Hawk thought what a turbulent storm might be-Horse called her "his Kate"—remembering the taste of her lips as a weakness overtook him. He had to stop this-thinking of her, seeing her running toward him, her small dimpled smile, holding her in his arms, kissing her, tears glistening on her cheeks. His breathing became shallow. He could not continue this torture, letting her possess him-if he did he would cease to function as a man. He knew what he must do-return to his village, woo a black eyed, dark haired maiden, wed her and have children, but as he thought of Cherokee maidens and his future, green eyes framed with lustrous auburn hair erased any other female image. "Damn-damn her!" He muttered, turmoil written on his countenance.

"I am sorry-my friend," Horse became serious as he grasped Hawk's shoulder. "I did not realize the trouble you're going through."

Hawk nodded, vaulting onto Night Wind's back. "Let's ride, friend, our people need us."

Chapter 14

Kate couldn't believe her lazy sister was up and wanting to talk with her at this hour while the sun was just beginning to peek over the mountain range and the birds hadn't finished their good morning chirping. "What is so secretive, Prissy, that we have to come outside to talk? You have certainly acted strange of late." Kate descended the porch steps, wiping her hands on her apron as she walked to the bench where her sister sat, and plopped down. "Umm! That bacon smells simply wonderful-doesn't it?" Kate twitched her nose in delight as she looked at her sister who had turned a greenish shade before grabbing her mouth and running through the gate.

Frowning and quite disturbed, Kate jumped up and followed. "Prissy, what in the world is wrong?" she questioned as she watched her sister bending over, holding her head.

Prissy straightened, turned slowly, eyes watering, face drawn as Kate observed the dark circles beneath her sisters lovely dark eyes. Prissy groaned, "Every morning I puke my head off-so guess what my problem is?" The sarcasm was obvious. "Yes, dear sister, I'm pregnant," her dark eyes flashed as her voice snapped.

The two stared at each other. "Well, quit staring at me!" Prissy retorted, wheeling around, skirts twirling and striding back through the gate where she leaned against the table drumming her fingers as she watched Kate return to the bench under the oak. "For goodness sakes-say something-you look at me as though I have a contagious disease."

Kate thought I'd hate to say what I'm really thinking. She gazed at her sister steadily. "What can I say, Prissy-that I'm sorry-that I told you so-that I'd like to kill Keith Anderson? All of these things matter not—now, but are you sure about this pregnancy?" She whispered the last word.

"Yes," Prissy turned away, her chin quivering. "I'm sure," she turned back, her eyes filled with tears. "Oh! Kate, I need you."

Kate's heart went out to this sister who was so lovely, so foolish so weak and silly, seemingly only interested in herself, and if Kate's thinking were right, Keith Anderson would never marry Prissy, in fact he never intended to. "I'll do what ever I can to help you, Prissy, you know that."

She nodded, wiping at her eyes, "You know I don't want this baby," she spat, "it's not me-being fat and swollen, then a mother with all those dirty smelly diapers-ooh-the thought of it makes me sick, but I mustn't dwell on that now." Her countenance took on a determined gleam. "The important thing is to get to the fort and talk with Keith." She stood, pacing back and forth, as though to convince herself. "We'll just have to move the wedding date up." She smiled for the first time.

The porch screen door closed, both girls looked up as their father approached, coffee mug in hand as he took a seat by Kate. "You two are up and about at an early hour-what's so important?" He eyed Priscilla.

"Well, Papa, you are right," Prissy flashed her charming smile as she shifted her position to a lawn chair. "Kate and I want to visit our new friends at the fort, Evelyn Hollins and Janice Cooper-it's been such a long time since we've been anywhere and fall is almost here-there'll be even less visitation then."

John turned toward Kate, "Is this your wish too, Katherine?" He scowled, thinking Priscilla may have invented this to see that lieutenant.

"Yes, it certainly is-the quilting fourth celebration was the last time we were there," she pled in her sister's behalf.

"Well," he sipped his coffee, "if your mother can do without you-I do have business with Colonel Roberts and had planned to ride over there today. Check with your mother first, though." He stuffed his pipe, lit it and puffed away hoping his daughters would leave him to the peacefulness of the early morning, which was his time to relax alone.

When John delivered his daughters at the Cooper residence at the fort, they were greeted by an excited Janice who looked quite pretty in a yellow cotton full skirted dress accented with a yellow hair ribbon.

"Oh! Do come in-it's so good to see you both again," she squeezed their hands, "and I'm so glad you came. Mr. Brandon, they will have lunch with me if it's all right. Please, have seats. I was so excited to see you I lost my manners," she smiled rather embarrassed.

The girls sat as John excused himself. "I mustn't be late for a meeting with the Colonel. Lunch is fine, but be ready to leave at 4:00. I'll pick you up here. Nice to see you Miss Janice," he turned to depart as soldiers waited to escort him and take the spring board.

"We'll be here, Papa," Prissy followed and smiled him away, turning back, she sat with the other two in a pretty crimson Victorian side chair.

"Well, tell me what you've been doing all summer?" Janice probed, smiling at both.

"Before we do that, we thought you might ask Evelyn Hollins to join us since we met her, too, at the celebration-course, it's up to you." Kate suggested as she removed her bonnet.

Janice looked down at her lap, pleating her skirt, hardly knowing how to answer. Her guests waited, watching her-all seemingly a little uncomfortable-she finally looked up. "I don't see much of her anymore."

"I thought you two were friends," Prissy injected, sensing a little gossip and certainly not wanting to miss out on anything, but uneasy about hearing the answer-remembering the blue eyed blond had dated Keith.

"We-were," Janice continued to look down, folding a pleat in her skirt.

"Then if something is wrong, Janice, we should know, too," Kate explained as she leaned up, expecting an answer.

"I suppose so," Janice continued fingering her yellow skirt as she proceeded. "Not too long ago, two weeks or so, there was a hearing here at the post. I don't know the details, but it had something to do with Lt. Anderson, two Indians and Jeb Hawkins" Prissy's attention was now focused on every word. "Anyway, after the thing was over, Evelyn and I were walking around the compound when she spied Jeb and the Indians-nothing would do her but she must go over and speak to them. Well, I have seen a few females in action, and maybe I am shy, but I've never been around anyone like her. She totally swooned over Wild Hawk and I believe would have offered herself to him if others hadn't been around-she acted like one of those women, so forward," Janice blushed, thinking over her expressive terminology. "She even said, "he could put his moccasins under her bed any time"! And she's even tried to get me to accompany her to his village." Janice's eyes sparked, shaking her head and looking at each of her guests, finding Kate very pale, obviously very shaken or maybe sick. "Kate, are you ill-why don't you lie down here on the couch," Janice suggested, quite concerned.

"No-no-I'm all right," Kate wiped her face with her handkerchief, "must have been something I ate for breakfast." Kate attempted covering her faintness as she glanced at her knowing sister who wore a rather interested half smirk as she stared back at her.

"There is something you can do for me Janice," Prissy smiled her charms as she strolled to the stone fireplace. "It is very important that I speak with Lt. Anderson, now if possible-ah!- without my father's knowledge-you understand," she smiled pleadingly.

"Sure-I'll send one of the soldiers immediately, and emphasize discreteness." Smiling, she excused herself and exited the room.

"Well-well, sister dear-so your heart throb is a savage-I can't believe this, but on second thought, you have been rather-ah!- attentive to that Indian," she giggled. "Yes-sweet-demure Kate-wouldn't Mama and Papa have a dying off duck fit! Who knows," she kept her dark eyed gaze on Kate as she paced the room in thought, "I might just slip and tell," her eyes flashed as she laughed swishing across the room.

Kate eyed her sister steadily. "I don't think so! Not in your condition."

Prissy's face straightened and became flushed as she comprehended her sister's meaning.

Shortly, Keith Anderson appeared at the door, neatly and handsomely attired in his snug fitting blue uniform. He was ushered inside and upon seeing who the guests were, he smiled charmingly at the girls, especially Prissy. "What a wonderful surprise." He walked over and took Prissy's hand.

"You two won't be disturbed-my mother is at a sewing circle. Kate and I will be in the kitchen if you need us." The two nodded, continuing to stare at each other as Kate followed her hostess from the room.

Keith pulled Prissy up and into his arms, kissing her deeply. "Oh! Sugar-I've missed you something terrible-and I know its only been two or three weeks since we were together, but it seems like a year. He pushed a curl from her forehead. "You get prettier each time I see you. How have you been, darling?"

She walked to the couch, and sat as he followed, sitting by her, taking her hand, leaning up to look at her. "I haven't been too well of late," she responded quietly, looking down.

"What's wrong?" he questioned, disturbed. "Look at me, Priscilla," she did and as always melted under his hazel scrutiny. "What is wrong, honey?" His brow furrowed.

"I'm pregnant," she whispered, seeking with her dark eyes his understanding. Instead, his gaze was shuttered. As he stood pacing back and forth, his mind racing, wanting to say the right thing not to cause an altercation with her at this time, but if she thought he'd fall into this trap-pregnant, for God's sake! If this little chit thought she was going to snare him to give her brat a name-well, she had another thought coming! He turned back and sat by her, again taking her hand, deciding for the time being to play along with her.

Prissy wanted to see love and warmth but somehow this was not revealed in his countenance. Maybe it was the shock of being a father. She continued, "Since we were going to be married anyway, I thought we could up the wedding date." She smiled her prettiest for him, love shining in her features.

He hesitated before answering, smiling, "You are right, darling, of course. Guess I was a little shocked finding out I was to be a husband and father, but honey, our wedding can't take place for at least four weeks. I have a reconnaissance patrol coming up-don't know exactly how long it will last-should be over within a month, then we can make our plans."

"Oh! Keith! I'm so happy," she nestled her head against his muscular shoulder, squeezing his arm as she thought of this handsome man being hers alone and spending the rest of her life as Mrs. Keith Anderson. Even having this baby didn't seem so bad now.

"I do think we should keep our wedding a secret, a surprise, don't you honey?" He warmed her with his smile as he put his arm around her, pulling her close.

"Yes, I suppose you are right."

He leaned down and kissed her before whispering, "and the month will pass quickly if we stay busy and think of all we have to look forward to. You are not that far along that it will make a difference are you?" He revealed his concern for her.

"No," she smiled up at him, glorying in his concern for her, "I'm only about seven or eight weeks now." She remembered how she had hated the day they moved to Tennessee from Boston, thinking this was the most godforsaken place in the world until she met this beautiful man by her side. Her features softened and took on a rosy glow as she scrutinized this magnificent male who had made these Tennessee hills become such a beautiful world.

As she snuggled even closer, Keith made sure she kept their surprise. "Dear, just as soon as I return from my patrol, I'll come to you. We'll make all of the final wedding arrangements and then explain our marriage plans together to all of the family and friends- if this is what you wish, too," he pled with his crooked smile.

"Of course, dear-they will all be shocked and pleased," she squeezed his arm again, smiling broadly, thinking how envious Kate would be, who was doomed to be an old maid.

As the Brandon wagon traveled homeward, Kate was oblivious to the slight nip of autumn in the air which promised to soon dress these stately mountain peaks in their colorful fall cloaks. The day had been miserable for her, as Janice chattered continually while preparing lunch of cold meat, salad, and home baked bread. It was all Kate could do while she sat at the checkered covered kitchen table staring out of the window, to utter a sensible response. Since that special night when Wild Hawk had kissed her, it was difficult for her to keep her mind on other things. Now, it was thrown in her face that another white girl who, apparently a fast female, was throwing herself at him, and if this girl continued, Kate bit her lip, frowning-no man would run forever! Oh! The thought of his being with that girl made her ill. This Indian had stolen her heart, whether she liked it or not, and remembering how it felt to be in his arms-she couldn't stand the thought of someone else being there, especially a wayward woman-but what could she do? He didn't belong to her, and apparently never would. She hadn't even seen him since that night two months ago. She sighed, eyes misting as she wondered why life had to be so very cruel!

Mary observed her daughters at the evening dinner table as she passed the biscuits. Priscilla sparkled with happiness, chattering incessantly while stuffing her face as Katherine picked at her food, obviously her thoughts some other place. Something happened today to both of these girls-guess she'd never know what it was. She passed John his favorite bread.

Her husband finally intervened between Prissy's ranting about Janice's lace trimmed yellow dress and the luncheon dessert. "Excuse me, Priscilla, but I need to discuss a point with the family." She subsided as she chewed her venison, which had never tasted so good.

"Well, it's 'bout time somebody shut her up-she ain't stopped her mouth since we sat down to eat," Jess scooped a mouth full of potatoes, "it's plain nerve wrackin'!" Jesse sighed.

"Jessica, watch your manners and your English!" Mary snapped. However, she couldn't be too harsh, for this was one of the few times Jessica was right!

John cleared his throat to keep from laughing. "In a few days I will accompany Jeb and Rusty to where all of the Southeastern

Cherokee clans will convene. This is an annual affair and by far the largest and most important meeting of the year. Hundreds will group there to formulate future business, decisions, leadership changes, elect delegates, and participate in social activities. This will last three or four days." All stopped eating to stare at him.

"And I feel very fortunate to be included in the group attending."

"Oh! Boy-I can't wait," Jesse exploded as Tim interrupted,

"I'll be glad to go with you, Papa," his big eyes grew bigger as he realized this was men's business and he would shoulder his part. He'd be glad to go and visit his Cherokee friends.

Placing his hand on his son's shoulder, John explained. "I'm sorry, Tim, only adults are invited and few of those other than Cherokee will be present." Tim nodded as he crammed in another biscuit with blackberry jam while Jesse looked disgusted. He continued, "This is a difficult time for the Cherokee-they fear for their future if Jackson is elected president, and I can't say that I blame them."

Kate stared at her father realizing he was worried for these people who had become his friends, and those who had become—dear to her.

Chapter 15

At New Echota, the Cherokee capital in the Georgia area where the different clans gathered for their annual fall social and business meet, Wild Hawk and Spotted Horse strolled along the pathway that snaked through the many long lodges, counsel buildings, and temporary skin dwellings.

Autumn had also made her debut at this important spot with her nippy air, chilly nights and painted hues of red, yellow, russets and browns that she had artistically brushed across the tops of surroundings maples, oaks, elms and sycamores.

Both braves were caught up in the excitement of the event where Cherokee had gathered together to socialize and participate with their leaders in discussing the future.

Many of these Indians milled around laughing, talking, renewing acquaintances, women cooking, children playing games as two pretty young maidens dressed in soft butter colored doeskin shifts adorned in beautiful multicolored beading made it quite obvious they were not adverse to attention from these two young men. One sidled over to Wild Hawk, black eyes snapping.

"This one cannot believe a wild brave is so high and mighty he fails to speak to the sister of his friend," the maiden teasingly smiled as she tossed her long black hair.

Hawk wheeled around, fringe swishing as he questioned, "Little Bird? But it cannot be!" He flashed a brilliant smile at this maiden as he took in her entire beauty. "The Little Bird I remember was a skinny, whimpering, stringy haired girl trying to follow Raven and me everywhere we went!"

Little Bird threw her head back, laughing heartily, then shifted her gaze to the other brave as her long lustrous hair swayed below her hips. "Who is he?"

Spotted Horse couldn't remember when he had seen such beauty. He was spellbound.

"This is Spotted Horse of the Wolf Clan-but really an old bull moose," as Hawk clasped his friend's shoulder, chuckling. Little Bird felt a warmth as she looked into the deep dark eyes of this handsome friend. Forgetting her manners, she stared openly as Horse smiled appealingly.

"Oh!" remembering her friend, "Gentle One," she turned, tugging at her friends sleeve as a rather tall well endowed doeskin clad not pretty, but very attractive maiden with a direct gaze appeared by Bird's side.

Wild Hawk found this Gentle One appealing in a strange way, although her gaze made him slightly uncomfortable. He would wager she rarely smiled or teased. Horse's attention was totally captured by the vivacious Little Bird as his friend inquired, "Where will I find that lazy no good coyote of a brother of yours?"

"Um-" she continued glancing at Spotted Horse, her dark eyes sparkling, "chasing some skirt or betting on a game of chance-he could be anywhere." Hawk laughed, knowing she spoke the truth-and what is this with young Bird, he wondered. Why can't she keep her eyes off his friend-more power to her if she can turn the head of this cranky Horse!

The two braves watched with interest as the maidens departed, hips and fringe swaying after Little Bird received a commitment from Horse that they would get together later.

In the cool of the evening many Cherokee gathered at the contest field, amid the panoramic setting of autumn's surrounding multi colors that were vividly tinted with the late afternoon's pinkish glow.

John Ross, Guwisquwi, Rare Bird, the young mixed blood and principal chief of the Cherokee Nation, climbed the wooden platform and stood before the large gathering in his white man's attire, but he was no white. He was a full blood in beliefs, work, leadership and heart, and the people knew it. He gathered each one into his hand as he emphatically stressed the necessity of the entire nation being strongly bound together united, not one Cherokee would be permitted to sign any type of treaty with any white, sell or deed any tract of land. The whites had already confiscated many tracts of Cherokee land with a greed that could never never be sated.

Complaints were brought up of whites over running Cherokee boundaries since gold was found on the branch of the Chestatee near Dahlonega. This was voiced with great concern, also, if Jackson were elected the Big Chief of the white nation in their soon-to-be election. How would this affect the Cherokee future?

Ross revealed no fear in responding, but with concern for all of his people stating, "We will face what ever problems there are wherever and whenever they arrive."

Many Cherokee, both leaders and followers, highly respected this young principal chief who led and at all times revealed his sincerity, loyalty and lack of fear in his leadership. Life had been bleak at times for them and might be again, if Jackson were chosen the big white chief, but their Cherokee Chief Ross was educated, could and would handle himself well against any adversary for the Cherokee cause. This belief had its calming effect on the people where they could enjoy the feasting, skill and strength contests, and friendship.

The following day Wild Hawk made his mark in strength and fitness by capturing the coveted title in body wrestling as he in the final round finally bested his longstanding friend Raven. The two walked from the field laughing and joking as Hawk cuffed his buddy. "Old Coyote, if you didn't chase around after so many maidens, your strength wouldn't be so easily sapped!"

The grin even broadened on Raven's handsome countenance, revealing why many young maidens were attentive to this tall muscular brave. "Ai Yu, mongrel dog, you lucked out on one hold or you would never have taken this title from Raven!" The cameraderie was evident between these two as they strolled to the sideline. Many eyes watched along with Rusty, Jeff, and John Brandon who were exuberant with whistles and yells while a rather tall slender maiden fastened her gaze on the spectacular brave who had just captured the wrestling title, and she hated to admit it, but from the way she felt when around him she was afraid he might just capture her heart, too, if he tried.

As Spotted Horse took the title in knife throwing, several of the chiefs chuckled while wondering aloud what Lone Eagle fed his braves for two of them to take the titles from so many. Chief Big Bear thundered, "Eagle, you old horse dung-cut out some of that corn fodder you feed these braves."

"Old Moose Droppings," Eagle retorted laughing, his turban plumes and fur piece shaking with his exuberance, "my braves could take yours if they had no food." The other leaders laughed heartily, thoroughly enjoying the banter while pretty Little Bird spanked her hands to a stinging red, yipped and trilled until she turned and found many of her clan members staring as she made a spectacle of herself. Let them wonder, she thought as she strolled toward the brave who had just taken the knife throwing title and caused her foolish action anyway.

The day had been long-too long with the physical contests, additional speeches and discussions from tribal leaders. Regardless of the Cherokee belief in their principal chief, there still seemed to be an undercurrent of concern and uncertainty.

It was late as the two title holder's wove their way toward their lodging while their thoughts were elsewhere when suddenly their peacefulness was shattered by two playful females who accosted them. Little Bird pulled Horse into a clearing surrounded by trees as he laughed heartily, more than a willing captive. Gentle One twisted Hawks arm behind him, using great strength for a woman. He wheeled, catching her in his arms as she laughed openly, her eyes shining with warmth. She broke free, running in the opposite direction toward an overhanging elm as the brave caught up. He gazed into her eyes long and steadily as he brushed her cheek with the back of his hand. Maybe, he thought, this one will imprint upon me her beauty helping me to forget another. Slowly, he leaned down and captured her lips, pulling her to him as her arms wrapped around his neck and her body molded to his, telling him with every movement that she wanted him. What is wrong with me? The kiss is pleasant, but I feel nothing for this maiden. Slowly, he drew back, removing her arms from his neck, holding her away from him and sadly stared into her beautiful eyes. "I'm sorry, Gentle One"

She struggled with her emotions as the crickets performed an unusually loud cacophony while she gazed into his dark eyes, knowing this feeling was entirely one-sided. For the first time she cared for someone but the feeling was not returned. "Another claims your heart," she whispered the statement.

He turned, looking down, raking the toe of his moccasin against a tree root. "Yes - I thought when I saw you that maybe you could change things, but there seems to be no room in this heart for another. I am sorry-I did not intend to deceive you," his countenance revealed his disturbed emotions.

"Is she Cherokee?" Somehow this seemed important to her.

"No."

"Does she feel the same love for you?"

"Yes," his thoughts drifted to that special night several moons ago when he had held her in his arms and kissed her. A warmth crept throughout his body as he smiled sadly.

"I wish I could be that maiden," she whispered as she turned and walked slowly toward her lodging.

Wild Hawk sank to the ground, leaning against the sturdy elm as the wind whispered softly through the leafy branches. He stared into the star-sprinkled night thinking, again of the young girl with firelit hair as she ran to meet him. "Oh! Green Eyes-what have you done to me?"

During the night Horse continued twisting and turning, not able to sleep, his mind laced with the beauty of Little Bird who had marched straight into his heart in a very short time. Never had he felt this way about any maiden. As he attempted to sort out his future and where she might fit into it, he was pulled back to the present by Hawk's moaning and groaning, lashing back and forth on his bear robe obviously in great turmoil while living in his dream world. After his yelling and slashing continued back and forth, Horse shook his friend's shoulder vigorously. "Wake up-wake-up!"

Hawk shot up to a sitting position, eyes wild-until he realized it was his brother calling to him. He tried to control his ragged breathing as he stared into the low burning fire, vividly remembering his disturbed dream.

Horse returned to his fur pallet not pushing for talk, knowing his friend would speak whenever he was ready. Finally, while staring into the weak flame, Hawk uttered, "I tried to care for Gentle One-I like her, the way she looks, her mind, but when it was put to a test this evening, there was nothing-I felt nothing for her!" Exasperated, he gazed across at his friend. "I was hoping she would be the one to make a difference."

Frowning, Horse questioned, "Surely that didn't throw you into such a bad dream world where you were moaning and yelling."

"No," Hawk drew the vivid picture from his memory as he kicked the fire embers to a brighter glow. "In my dream world-my people were crying, moaning while walking slowly in the direction of the setting sun." He stared as though hypnotized by the flame. "I saw and heard this, but I turned and slowly rode Night Wind in the opposite direction where I stopped, reached my hand out, clasping the hand of a maiden, pulling her up in front of me, holding her close as we continued slowly on our path while I heard the echo of my people's cries and moans but I could not turn back," he continued staring sadly into the fire.

"—and the maiden that was with you was Katherine Green Eyes!" Horse smiled the statement.

"Yes," Hawk picked up a stick to stoke the meager flames, "This dream has nothing to do with our real world. You and I have never believed in such the way our shaman does, and never would I leave our people." Horse stared at his friend wondering about the validity of dreams.

The final day brought a bright sun to glorify autumn's already vivid multicolors surrounding the contest field where people gathered, socializing and enjoying roasted pork and venison with all trimmings. The last get together was for food and friendship with business announcements of any council changes and newly chosen delegates to visit Washington.

John Brandon, Jeb Hawkins and Rusty Poole were gathered with Lone Eagle and clan members who attended as Rusty admitted, "Ah'll tell ye, old friend, this here's might nigh the best vittles ah ever tasted - why don't you ever have eatin's tastin' this good when I visit you?" his blue eyes crinkled as he plopped a huge bite of sweet potato followed by a big slab of pork into his mouth which was already too full to catch the excess grease that slipped down his chin.

"Oh! Wipe your mouth," Eagle inserted, "and I have never noticed the many times that you stuffed yourself at our feasts that there was ever a wee morsel left in your bowl. Of course, the last feast when you danced with Old Crone you were probably so enamored by her good looks that your appetite completely failed you." Lone Eagle chuckled, his black eyes twinkling as he bested his friend. The others joined in the laughter while Rusty sputtered, spewing crumbs from a too full mouth and wiping his greasy lips on his sleeve while he shot daggers at the chief.

"Now, you kin jest shut yore trap 'bout that thar' old snaggle toothed heifer that I had to dance with at the Green Corn-Well you probably sicked her on me n' ah'll never fergit hit, you old coon dog!"

Eagle threw his head back, plume and fur piece swishing as he guffawed, remembering Rusty's misery with old snaggle tooth Crone. The others thoroughly enjoyed the quips and banter between the two; however, their laughter eased as Rusty glared at each one.

Last announcements were stated by a council leader before adjournment. Three names were given for counsel seat replacements. A listing of delegates to attend Washington after election of the new white chief included Raven of the Bird Clan and Wild Hawk of the Wolf clan. All delegates were required to read and write the white tongue. As murmurs were heard throughout, John Brandon spoke to Eagle, while Chief Big Bear responded, "some of our braves mentioned as delegates do not read and write the white tongue."

"Then they must learn-surely there are those who can teach." He searched the crowd for responses.

After receiving permission to speak, Lone Eagle climbed the platform steps. "I am Lone Eagle of the Wolf clan."

"We know you, Moose," Big Bear interrupted as several chuckled while Eagle continued.

"We are fortunate in my area of the Southern Smokies to have consultant John Brandon, a friend, and his daughter Katherine, who has taught the white tongue reading and writing to my Cherokee young. John Brandon is with us today," he smiled, pointing to John, who held up his hand amid Cherokee applause. Eagle held up his hand for quiet. "He has also offered his daughter's service to help teach the delegates near my area."

Raven had strolled up to confer with Hawk upon hearing their names as delegates, knowing neither could read nor write the white tongue even though they spoke the language well. When Lone Eagle made his announcement Hawk suddenly stiffened noticeably, nostrils flaring while a severe frown creased his forehead.

Raven was concerned at his friend's reaction. "What is wrong with you-or maybe I should ask what is wrong with this white woman who teaches?" Raven questioned while staring.

"Nothing."

"From the way you were acting I thought she might have two heads! Ah!" he stared, "I understand-you always have had much hate for all whites, but it won't matter that much, if she can teach us."

"Us?" Hawk gazed at his friend, thinking of spending hours studying with Green Eyes, listening to her, watching her. It would be impossible. "What did you say?" He knew his friend was rattling on.

"I said-what is wrong with you?" Hawk simply stared at him "can't you hear? I said I would be living in your village while I am studying with this white woman who must be some sort of dog." Disgusted, he ambled off, thinking his friend was about as interesting as a ground rat and he certainly was not looking forward to learning anything under some dog faced white! Knowing no one declined when chosen as delegate, Raven kicked his frustration against a rock that was deeply imbedded in the soil. Grabbing his moccasined foot, he howled every Cherokee expletive he could drum up.

Chapter 16

Kate was leery when her father called her to come outside for a talk. He always had a shocking surprise and tried to smooth things over, but leaving no way for anyone to answer "no". She snatched up her old blue shawl, for autumn was here in all her glory, nippy air and beauty but too cool without a wrap.

Smoothing her checkered skirt, she settled on the bench by her father awaiting her sentence. "You sent for me, Papa?"

He continued sipping his coffee doing a superb job of concentrating on his coffee mug wondering how in the world to approach this daughter for the second time about teaching Indians. He had overstepped himself again, but there was nothing else he could have done. The Cherokee needed teachers, and someone had to volunteer! "Well," he continued to stare at his coffee mug. "I've done it again."

Kate stared at the sky, wanting to scream at him, realizing he had again volunteered her services some way or he wouldn't be here hemming and hawing so much! How could her own father treat her this way, with absolutely no concern for her feelings? "What is it this time, Papa?"

"Katherine," he finally unglued his eyes from the mug, touching her arm gently, "please understand, honey."

She angrily glanced at him, her mouth firmly placed as she jumped up striding to the table, leaning against it. She crossed her arms, continuing to gaze angrily at this man. "I'd like to understand!"

John put his empty coffee mug on the ground looking at his daughter pleadingly. "At the Cherokee gathering in Echota, there were delegates elected to visit Washington after the presidential election. This is very important to these people. However, the delegates are required to read and write the English language. Many of them cannot." He looked down, running his fingers through his hair.

"What does that have to do with me?" Kate inquired, still glaring at her father, auburn hair whipping around her shoulders.

He looked up, green eyes meeting green eyes. "Someone must teach them. I told Lone Eagle that you would teach those in this area." His voice softened as he again stared at the ground. "He made the announcement. Believe me, Katherine, these people are desperate-there were only two other volunteers, both Cherokee who obviously won't be able to do the job as well as you."

Kate strode to the gate, leaning on it, not believing he'd stoop to flattery to get his way. She spoke softly as she gazed into the distance. "I can't believe this, Papa, that you would do the same thing a second time and offering for me to teach adults yet." She wheeled around. "Well, I can't do it!" She strode toward the porch, avoiding eye contact with him, her long skirt whipping around her legs.

"Katherine." She hesitated, her back to him. "These people have no one else. There will only be four or five to teach, and it will only last a few weeks. It's not as though you don't know any of them. Wild Hawk is a delegate!" She stiffened, sucking in her breath. "Please," he continued-" think about it." She nodded as she stumbled up the steps, entering the house.

And think about it she did as she returned to her bedroom, plopped into her favorite old rocker and rocked away, thinking only of one Cherokee brave, wondering how she could possibly teach him.

Kate's privacy, though, was suddenly shattered as Prissy swished into the room, sprawling on her own bed while she exuberantly and incessantly chattered about her upcoming marriage—"and there is no way I'll have such odious creatures as Tim and Jess in my wedding, and I must know now today whether you want to wear green or blue." She leaned up on an elbow demanding a response.

Kate rocked and thought of a lopsided smile, the warmth revealed in his dark eyes that were framed with those too-long thick lashes, the strength of his arms around her-she smiled.

"Have you lost your mind?" Prissy screeched. "Here I am trying to discuss a very important subject with you-my wedding," she bolted up, pounding her pillow, "and you sit there rocking like some blooming dumb ass with your eyes closed and that inane smile on your face."

Kate blinked, "Huh?" But before Priscilla could continue her tirade, a piercing scream from below shattered any thoughts, conversation or peacefulness there might have been. That's Mama both girls thought as they tumbled from their bedroom, gingham skirts flying, and galloped down the stairs where they screeched to a halt. Mama was swinging a broom as a club like a natural, catching big Stink Bear on the head as he bellowed madly, loping toward the kitchen where he crashed a large bowl of mashed potatoes and gravy all over the floor before clawing into a fresh baked apple pie, stuffing it into his mouth. Mama caught him another blow upside the head while continuing her frantic screech with a few choice unmentionable expletives that no lady would ever utter. The furry monster made for the open doorway as dead eye Mary walloped him again, her wild eyes flashing, causing a continued bellow while John, Jess and Tim rounded the corner of the house in time to witness Stink Bear, holding his head, loping and bellowing with bits of apple pie dripping from his mouth.

John was enjoying his woman in action, knowing she wasn't really harming the bear. It was all he could do to contain his laughter-if he didn't, she'd probably use the broom on him!

Jess ran up to her mother. "Surely you didn't hit Stink Bear - why, you'll hurt his feelings!"

Mary spun around, breathless, "I hurt more than that beast's feelings and if you say anything else about that varmint I-," her hazel eyes continued to shoot sparks, "I might just use this broom on you!" Jess and Tim's mouths dropped open, not believing their mother. She was supposed to be nice!

"Mary," John walked toward her, attempting to soothe, "what happened in there?"

"What happened?" she thundered, "That - that horrible smelly creature was loaded up on our bed asleep-he was even on my pillow! Ooh!" She shuddered, still clutching the broom. Prissy and Kate's giggles finally pealed forth for all ears to hear. Both girls were unable to contain their laughter any longer.

Mary wheeled, glaring through the door. "If you two girls think this little episode was so funny you will clean the kitchen where your dinner was spilled all over the floor and you will also wash my bed covers! Maybe that won't be so amusing!" Her dark eyes continued to flash as she commanded the giggles to cease. They did.

John motioned for Tim and Jess to leave, as he again approached his wife. "Honey, don't be too harsh-"

"John Brandon," she spewed, "don't you dare tell me what I should do or should not do-I've never been so upset-mad as a wet hen, and it's all your fault." She flung her back to him.

"My fault?"

"Of course, you brought that horrible creature here," she flung over her shoulder.

Legend of the Whispering Wind

John knew his Mary and this was more than a bear, he realized as he eased up behind her, putting his arm around her waist, pulling her close.

"John Brandon, you needn't try your charm to smooth things over."

"Can you think of something better?" he murmured, nuzzling her neck. He turned her around to face him, still holding her. "What is it, honey? A bear being in the house shouldn't cause you to snap like that."

She looked up into his eyes, hers misty. "I don't really know-." He eased her to sit on the steps, pulling her head to his shoulder.

"Seems things have been building up of late-we rarely go to church. I miss that, John, and that's a good reason why our two young ones are such heathens," she emphatically stated.

"Guess you thought you needed church when you so handily flung those choice cuss words today," he teased, chuckling.

She ignored him. "I've been worried about Priscilla lately, too," she leaned up, arms around her knees. "Something isn't right. She rarely eats breakfast, and I know of twice that she was sick to her stomach." She turned, searching his eyes. "Oh, John, you don't suppose—"

"Shhh - you are letting your imagination run wild, Mary and that's not like you. Now what else bothers my pretty woman?" He wrapped a loose tendril of her hair around his finger.

"Katherine, and that Indian."

"What? What Indian?"

"Wild Hawk."

"Oh! Mary, for goodness sakes-it looks as though you dream up things to worry about. Honey, you'll have to stop this for you are being utterly ridiculous!"

She looked down, smoothing her skirt over her knees. "Maybe-we'll see, but there's one thing I'm certain of-that bear must go. Imagine that thing being lolled back on our bed-oh! My goodness!" She pushed back against his hand as he massaged her back and shoulders, feeling the tension leaving.

"I'm sure you did a good job of running him off-if not, I'll take care of things." He continued rubbing her back.

"I'm sorry I exploded the way I did, and used certain language," she became embarrassed, thinking of her terminology. "Oh! I forgot," she jumped up, "that monster ruined our dinner," She started for the door.

"Don't worry about it-the girls and I will take care of the kitchen and the changing of the bed.—Come on, I want you to find a good book and a comfortable chair and that is an order young lady."

"Yes, sir," she smiled lovingly at her special man.

As he ushered her inside, he whispered, "It's about time I took my best girl back to our mountain retreat before it turns too cold." He smiled wickedly, kissing the tip of her nose. "Have I told you lately how much I love you, my fiery cussing wife?" he teased, squeezing her arm.

It was the autumn and final Fall Festival at the fort before winter set in where settlers from the distances of Knoxville and Chattanooga areas joined with Indians and soldiers to gather winter supplies, exchange foods, buy necessary equipment, visit and socialize. All turned out well for this festivity, knowing there wouldn't be another gathering before spring time, and sometimes these mountain winters could be very harsh and drawn out.

The Brandons were exuberant, especially Jessica and Timothy as their buckboard crawled through the picturesque countryside on this bright late October day. Never had Mary witnessed such panoramic glory as these mountains, attired in their vivid fall cloaks, and never had she seen Priscilla with so much bobbling excitement. It was almost unnatural. Katherine, though, was just the opposite as she sat, seemingly oblivious to the surrounding beauty, lost in her own thoughts.

As Kate mused over her future commitment to teach the Cherokee delegates, she almost smiled thinking how cleverly her father manipulated people to his own thinking and whims! He should have been a politician! She knew she could not say no to Lone Eagle when the Indians needed her help, but her father pounded this point in to her over and over again. Of course, she wanted to see Wild Hawk, and be near him, which was probably the worst thing she could do.

After chomping a bite of apple Jess, disturbed her thoughts. "Kate, you're like some old woman who ate too many persimmons 'fore they wuz ripe-why didn't you just stay home 'cause you ain't gonna be no fun to nobody!" She took another resounding bite of apple.

Prissy and Tim joined in with a roar of laughter. Her brother agreeing, "Tell her, Jess-nobody wants to be around an old sour apple like her. This is supposed to be a fun time!" he bellowed.

"That will be enough!" Mary admonished, while Kate remained quiet, eyes misting as she stared into the colorful mountains.

Lone Eagle's entourage was no less excited, adorned in decorated buckskin and doeskin, anticipating the upcoming gathering for many did not make the long journey to Echota and were looking forward to visiting with members of Big Bear's clan. Several squaws and maidens walked for companionship including Old Crone and Crooked Toe, who captured a female audience with their spiced up tales of long ago. Dancing Eyes also had her followers as the maidens giggled, tittered, and ogled the braves, but only one brave caught the dark flashing gaze of Dancing Eyes who couldn't understand why Wild Hawk was so solemn on this special occasion. Usually, he was laughing and joking with his friends.

As the Brandon wagon neared the fort gates, Prissy again pinched her cheeks, readjusted her most becoming pink bonnet, rearranged the dark curl over her shoulder and gazed with sparkling dark eyes, hardly able to contain her excitement. She couldn't wait to be with Keith, feel his strong arms around her and make their final wedding plans which would take place next week. She giggled to herself. Of course, she already had everything worked out, but she'd let him think part of it was his idea!

"Oh! Look," Jesse bellowed, "There's Lone Eagle!" As she leaped from the wagon, sprawling in the dirt, feet and pantaloons gracing the air before she uprighted herself, sprinting toward her goal, losing her blue bonnet along with any girlish dignity a young female might have. Tripping on a tree root, she exploded into the back side of the chief who was unaware of the approaching danger, and found himself suddenly upended with Jesse draped over him. The surrounding clan members suddenly turned their backs and became extremely busy with nothing chores to suppress their laughter. Seeing this dignified chief upended, turban askew, long legs pawing the air, was the most fun they had had in ages.

Jess untangled herself and reached for Lone Eagle's hand. "I'm so sorry chief. I wouldn't have knocked you down for anything! But I tripped and I just couldn't stop in time. Let me help you." She offered her hand.

Standing, Lone Eagle glared at Jesse while he adjusted his crooked turban and dusted his doeskins, black eyes shooting sparks, wanting so to reprimand this young impetuous scamp who had caused him so much embarrassment, but upon searching her sad countenance his face finely crinkled into a smile. "My friend Jesse, that is without a doubt the strongest greeting I have ever had!" He continued to brush dirt from his shirt.

John approached, noting several hide shelters already erected outside the entrance. "Lone Eagle," he shook hands with the chief, "I apologize for the uncalled for actions of my daughter. Please forgive her rudeness." He glared at his daughter, "-Jessica Ruth, you go to your mother immediately." Jess left, scuffing the toe of her shoe, mumbling to herself,

"I'z only sayin' hello"

"Don't be too harsh on her, John Brandon, she meant no harm- regardless of how exuberant she is at times, and I might add, she was powerfully exuberant this time." He rubbed his back end as they both chuckled. "Would that other whites were as sincere and void of hate, regardless of her vitality, as my friend Jesse is."

After discussing the two day's festivities and a scheduled meeting to introduce Katherine to her new students, John left to check on his family who were impatiently awaiting him just inside the entrance while Mary expounded on unladylike behavior and what her youngest daughter would and would not do! Jess was wilting now under Mama's tirade, but they all knew it wouldn't make much difference in the long run 'cause Jess was Jess and she simply did things without thinking.

Thank goodness, Prissy sighed, as Papa climbed up to pull the wagon on inside and pull Mama into a conversation to stop her sermonizing. Her gaze shifted around the compound, seeing soldiers of various ranks milling all over the place, but where was her soldier? He usually met them, but guess he was busy with some post duty. Anyway, it wouldn't hurt for her to freshen up before seeing him.

As John drew his team to a halt, two soldiers assisted the ladies and helped unload the wagon of trade items, food, and Mary's crafts for competition which were placed in designated areas. Before John could usher his family to their lodging, they were accosted by two buckskin clad scouts.

"Wall hit's 'bout time you brought yore good lookin' family out of hibernation John. Howdy, ma'am, children," Rusty cuffed Tim on the shoulder.

Jeb drank in Priscilla's beauty while Rusty picked up the valise to assist the family inside. Prissy grabbed Jeb's arm, whispering, "Wait up, Jeb-let them go on inside." Her dark eyes flashing with excitement, when the family was out of earshot, "Jeb, do me a big favor, please," she smiled prettily, warming the big scout's heart. "Find Lt. Keith Anderson-he probably has some kind of post duty, and tell him I'm here, that I'll meet him by the display tables in an hour." She smiled again as a frown creased Jeb's forehead, and he stared questioningly at her. "Well, don't just stand there-this is important!" She turned slightly but realized he continued to stare at her. "What is it? Why are you staring at me?" Her dark eyes questioned, thinking he must be stupid or something.

"Priscilla, I—ah! I thought you knew-ah! Lt. Anderson hasn't been at this post for a month-he asked for a transfer to another post, I don't know where." He watched her startled expression.

She struggled to breathe, clutching his arm frantically, whispering "Wh—at-did-you-say?"

"He ain't here-he left a month ago," he replied, watching her closely as her eyes rolled back, her face paling to a deathly white, but before she fainted, he swept her up into his arms, fearing for this young girl who had become so special to him, but who cared for that damn snake. Following the family he kicked the door open, walked to the couch where he gently placed the limp form of Priscilla.

"What-the?" John sputtered, rushing to her side.

"Oh! My goodness," Mary joined him at her unconscious daughter's side. "What in the world happened?" Mary shouted as the family gathered around, staring at Priscilla's paleness. Mary lifted her head. "John—do something-for heaven's sake"

"Get a damp cloth, Katherine," he commanded, "Jeb what happened?" John stared at his daughter as he questioned.

"She stopped me as you wuz goin' inside, and asked me to find Keith Anderson and tell him she was here and to meet her in an hour," he continued watching the unconscious girl, wanting to destroy the bastard who had done this to her. "I thought of all people she would have known he was gone, but when I told her Anderson transferred out of here a month ago she could barely speak, paled like death-then fainted-I caught her before she went down." John and Mary's gaze held.

Kate overheard the conversation as she bathed Prissy's face with a cool cloth while Mary chafed her hand, thinking that disgusting lying mongrel dog! I knew he'd never marry her, but I didn't think he'd run!—and poor Prissy, believing everything he told her. What in the world will she do now? Soon she'll begin showing!

Priscilla moaned, fluttered her eyelashes and opened her eyes, trying to focus and get her bearing. Seeing all of the people hovering around, she remembered the message Jeb had handed her. It couldn't be true-surely, he was mistaken for her Keith couldn't do this to her. "Well," she snapped, "What are all of you hovering over me for? And-staring? Haven't you ever seen anybody faint before? Just leave me alone!" she flung out as she turned her head away.

"Honey," her mother soothed, still holding her hand, "we were all concerned," she stroked her daughter's forehead.

"Just leave me be-I'm all right and I can't stand all of you staring at me. Kate, you stay," she muttered. Kate nodded.

"Well, don't just stand there-go!" Prissy screeched, her eyes flashing.

Jess retorted as they filed through the door, "She's sure back to normal, as hateful as ever!" Her parents scowled as they abided by their daughter's wish and left.

Prissy hissed, clutching Kate's arm, "Did Jeb share his message?" Kate nodded. "Well, there's simply some mistake-there has to be-he'd never do this to me-he loves me!" She again screeched and she broke down on a sob,.

"Prissy, don't - you'll only cause harm to yourself-and the baby!"

"The baby-for God's sake," she shrieked, "I hope something does happen to it!"

"Prissy, you can't mean that and I won't stay here and listen to such talk." She turned to leave, disgusted with her sister.

"Kate," Prissy struggled to speak, tears filling her eyes, "please go and find out from Colonel Roberts-Jeb Hawkins must be mistaken, and don't let the family or anybody back in here. Please, keep them out." She closed her eyes as tears streamed down her face while she sank to the depths of misery, fearing truth in the scout's message.

But keeping Mama out was a battle in itself, and Kate by no means won. Later, answering the rapping at the door, she was delighted for any escape from the Brandon chaos; Prissy yelling as Mama finally ushered the belligerent miss to a bedroom where she would indeed be left alone, Papa bellowing at Jess and Tim who were fussing over the biggest piece of apple pie.

"Hi, Jeb," Kate grabbed her shawl, closing the door behind with a sigh. "It's good to have a breather from the Brandon turmoil inside." As she eased onto a bench she asked, "What did the Colonel say about Keith?"

"The same thing I reported earlier. Anderson asked to be transferred to some place in the Arkansas territory. He left a month ago-an' I could have cared less the reason." He eased his frame down on the bench by Kate, who looked extremely worried. "I'd say it wuz good riddance-a bastard like that!" He observed Kate's expression carefully. "What is it, Kate? What's wrong with Priscilla? It has to be more than jes' feeling for that no-good!" his penetrating blue gaze held.

Kate looked at her lap, fingering the checkered skirt wondering if she should confide in this man who was her friend-knowing she had to talk with someone-the turmoil of Prissy's entanglement, the secrecy from the parents-it was all getting to her. "Jeb," she raised her eyes to meet his, "Priscilla is with child."

He stared into space, warring with his own emotions. "My God-that low crawlin' bastard!" He leaned up resting his elbows on his knees, twirling his dusty leather hat as his mind reeled, thinking I've loved that spoiled stupid beautiful girl from the first time I saw her, but she only had eyes for that low down cur who had only one thing on his mind, to lure an innocent girl into his bed. How could a man be low enough to do that and leave her with child? "Did he know she was carrying his child?" he probed.

She hesitated. "Oh! Yes-she told him over a month ago. They were supposed to make wedding plans as soon as he returned from a reconnaissance patrol which would take a month. He wanted the wedding to be their secret." She continued staring at her lap.

"I bet!" He barked a sarcastic laugh. "He reconnaissanced all right-by skedaddling as fast as his worthless hide could across the Mississippi. I'd like nothing better than to strangle the good for nothing with my own hands." He plopped his hat on his head and stared at this sister.

"Kate, do your parents know about Priscilla's condition?" Kate shook her head. "Well, don't tell them yet-for I'd like to marry Priscilla and give the baby a name. I'd care for the little 'un like it wuz my own-'n maybe you don't know, but I've loved yore sister since the first time I saw her." He sighed, shaking his head.

"I've known," Kate looked at this big gentle man who cared enough for her sister to take another man's leavings, to care for and cherish this unborn child. Her eyes teared. Why couldn't her flighty sister have loved this good decent man? "You and Prissy will have to work that out-keep in mind, Jeb, she thinks she is overcome with love for that no good."

"I understand-I'll wait and talk with her after she is home," he stood to leave. "See you Brandons later, the eatin' should be good tonight. I've smelled that pork all afternoon. Don't forget, you're ma' partner fer the reel!" He strode off.

Chapter 17

Kate was as nervous and excited as a young girl going to her first party while bathing and dressing for her upcoming meeting with the Cherokee. She dreaded the whole thing, but couldn't wait to see Wild Hawk. It had been such a long while. Did he have another girlfriend? Did he really care for her? Suddenly, she was entirely too warm as she tied the sash on her green and tan dress, aware of the sobbing that continued in the next room.

"Come on, Katherine-it's time for the meeting," Papa was impatient as he rapped on her door and strode through the hall.

"Coming." She gave her cheek a final pinch, tying the green taffeta bonnet streamers underneath her chin, satisfied it was the right shade for her eyes.

As John opened the door to the meeting room where she would hold her classes, Kate's heart pounded so loud she knew her father could hear it and for a moment she wanted to turn and run back to the safety of her lodge. Instead she entered, walking sedately to the long table in the center of the paneled room, where a low burning fire cast its warmth and glow on five braves who lounged near a window. Three pairs of dark eyes observed this lovely pale eyes with the auburn hair, wondering who she was. Others knew-especially one whose gaze fastened on those green eyes. For several moments, no one else was in the room as their eyes spoke volumes. Kate was suddenly entirely too warm, and Wild Hawk swore to himself that he couldn't go through with this torture.

"I'm John Brandon and this is my daughter," John pointed to Kate as he smiled, "Wild Hawk! Spotted Horse, it's good to see you again." They nodded.

"Mr. Brandon," as three braves inched closer to the table, each dressed in fringed buckskin, Raven, the tall handsome brave questioned, "we thought to meet our teacher today," he looked toward the door, "-when does she arrive?"

"Hello, Raven," John smiled, "you just met her-this is your new teacher, Katherine Brandon," he motioned toward his daughter.

"Her? Oh," he practically swooned, "what a pleasant surprise," his smile was infectious as his dark gaze drank in this pleasant surprise.

"Hi," Kate smiled, "it's good to see you again, Spotted Horse, Wild Hawk," she finally pulled her gaze away, her heart thumping as she removed her bonnet, hoping they did not detect her shaking hands. "Why don't we gather around the table-I would like to know your names, something about each of you and I'm sure you are wondering about these classes. Please come and sit at the table with me."

John sat next to Kate, across were the three braves from other clans including Raven, whose black eyes sparkled with admiration while Wild Hawk pulled the chair at the end of the table next to Kate. Suddenly, the teacher was again entirely too warm, her face flushed and she was aware of only his scent of leather, wood smoke and sage. Oh! I should never have agreed to this, she thought.

"I am called Running Elk and a member of Big Bear clan. My village is south of here near the big water." A well built medium height Indian with intelligent black eyes spoke.

"Thank you for joining us, Running Elk." Kate's gaze assessed the brave before observing the next one. If her face would only cool off and she'd stop shaking, she thought, things would be easier.

"I am Raven of the same clan," his black eyes sparkled with humor. "Somehow I was under the impression," he gazed at Hawk, leaning up near Kate, "that our teacher would be some older uh!

dogfaced pale eyes, but meeting you, Miss Katherine, has told me what a pleasure this class will be." This handsome brave smiled his charm as Kate observed the attractive rogue who was well aware of his good looks. She was amused by his glib tongue and smiled in spite of herself.

"Thank you, Raven-let's hope I won't soon sink to the title of Dog Face!"

He threw his head back rumbling with deep laughter; however, the Cherokee at the end of the table saw no humor in this unnecessary exchange as he stared at his friend, Laughing Boy!

"My name is Thunder," a deep voice explained, "of Old Turtles clan. My village is located south, but also toward where the sun sleeps." This slender brave of medium height twitched a shy smile at Kate, as though he could think of other places he'd much rather be.

"Hello, Thunder-it is nice to meet each of you," she welcomed the three, "I have known Spotted Horse and Wild Hawk since teaching the young Cherokee many months ago." She could only afford a glance at those hypnotic dark eyes.

While the new teacher explained class procedure, study of reading and writing five days, morning and afternoon with weekends off, Wild Hawk drank in her beauty, observing her nervousness, flushed face, shaking hands, and was amused knowing this was also difficult for her. How could he continue day in and day out being around her, listening to her, watching her, wanting her. He had tried staying away-had not seen her in over two months, but that did not help-she was always with him, even, he smiled to himself, keeping him from wanting to be with other females. What a fool he was!

As Kate finalized her meeting, dismissing the students until their first class session after the festivities, she watched Wild Hawk ease from his chair with panther grace and walk to the window, his back to everyone while others milled around, one or two in embarrassment as John Brandon conversed with them, trying to put them at ease.

Raven again sought Kate's attention, asking, "May I help with some of these supplies, Miss Katherine?" He smiled at the lovely teacher who seemed to draw him to her.

Kate realized someone had spoken. "Oh! Raven-yes," she began gathering her papers and stacking books. "Most of my things will be kept in the oak cabinet there against the wall," she pointed to the object as he picked up books and slates, taking his time placing them neatly on a shelf, hoping the others would leave. He would like to know his teacher better. Discussing upcoming classes would be a good beginning-he smiled to himself.

"Thank you, Raven," he heard when he turned to continue his thoughts verbally, and he watched her retreating figure walk over to Wild Hawk who stood staring out the window not bothering to turn until she spoke. He would let this Hawk know of such rudeness.

As John gathered others in easy conversation, dispelling some of their tenseness, Kate observed the profile she had seen many times in her dreams. He continued staring at nothing until she spoke. "You haven't said a word today," she prattled on despising herself for her inane chatter, "it's been so long since I've seen you."

He turned and held her with his dark gaze, a slight smile twitching his mouth.

"What is there to say, Katherine Brandon? That it is most difficult being here and having you as my teacher-that I am well-

and, yes, it has been over two very long months since we were together." His mind drifted back to that night as he again stared out of the window.

"I have missed you," she whispered softly.

"Don't do this," he moaned, barely audible as he continued staring through the window at nothing. "I am not made of stone, Green Eyes, and it will be hard enough just to get through this foolish class requirement." He turned abruptly. "Excuse me." He could no longer stand there with her looking so beautiful in that pert little hat with the green ribbon matching her eyes. Maybe it was seeing her again after such a long while. No matter, he did not trust himself, but before he moved away, her voice interrupted his thoughts.

"How can you continue this running game when we will see each other every day?" she teased smiling, "Good luck," as she moved toward the others.

Before the Cherokee could exit, John halted them. "It seems I was so caught up in listening to Katherine's explanation of your study class and visiting with you, I forgot something that's important to me." He smiled, glancing at his daughter. "She will be coming home weekends, but this Friday I must be in the Knoxville area. Ah- I was wondering if one of you could escort her home. She'll be riding," he picked up his leather hat, looking at Hawk and Horse.

"I'll be glad to escort her, Mr. Brandon," Raven spoke up, taking a few steps nearer, smiling at Kate. Hawk's black eyes flashed as he also stepped near, emphatically intervening. "Raven, you know nothing of this area, while I know every foot of it and the location of the Brandon property. I will escort Miss Katherine," black eyes shot sparks to black eyes as Wild Hawk bested his friend who glared but said nothing more. In Hawks estimation, this brave was entirely too familiar with this girl he had just met, and he was also well aware of Raven's confidence in his ability to charm the maidens. If he valued his well-being, he'd save his charm for the next one.

"Ah," John stammered, hardly able to contain a smile, but bothered at the same time by Hawk's rushing in and answering so emphatically, almost daring the other to question his decision, "I appreciate your offer, Raven, but Hawk did make a point about knowing this area well." Raven nodded, facial muscles flexing as he gazed at his so called friend before exiting while Kate busied herself wiping the table with her handkerchief, her eyes dancing with joy.

As John closed the meeting room door, he and Kate following the Indians outside, a pretty blonde donned in a becoming blue outfit with matching bonnet hailed Katherine. "Why Katherine Brandon, it's so nice to see you again-Mr. Brandon." John nodded as she smiled prettily, shifting her gaze to the Indians, "I heard you were here and that you were going to teach the Cherokee," she tittered again, glancing at the Indians. "Why I could hardly believe my ears!"

"Hello, Evelyn-yes, that's right."

"Well," Evelyn took a few steps toward the braves, the plumes on her bonnet catching the breeze, raising her voice, "these must be your students!" She strolled nearer the men.

The Indians turned, wondering who this pretty white girl was and why she was being obvious in seeking attention. Wild Hawk cringed, wanting to flee as quickly as possible; however, Raven openly admired the blond beauty.

"Yes, these are the Cherokee I'll be teaching," perturbed, Kate watched in awe as Evelyn approached the Indians, zooming in on Wild Hawk.

"Well—," she strolled near her target until she reached his side. He glared with cold dark eyes. "Wild Hawk, I didn't know you were one of the students!" she exclaimed, smiling her dimples.

"Yes." He stated flatly, turning away, bumping into Horse who was more than a little amused at his friend's dilemma.

"Don't forget, I'm still waiting for those riding lessons," she outmaneuvered him, reaching his side again, tapping his arm with her gloved hand, "and I won't take no for an answer!" She dimpled prettily, eyes inviting.

His dark eyes glanced at the hand on his arm as she removed it. "I am afraid you will have to wait, for I do not teach riding lessons," he adamantly retorted, his cold gaze warming when he glanced at Kate before turning to leave.

"We'll see," Evelyn shifted her blue eyed gaze to the other tall handsome Indian, thinking he might just do in a pinch, and that Wild Hawk had better not try this uppity business with her or she'd have to take him down a notch or two. The smile suddenly ceased as her eyes became icy.

Kate could hardly contain her anger at this girls obvious overtures toward Wild Hawk-The brazen hussy! She was disgusting and a little frightening, too. No telling how far one like this would go to get her way.

"Well, Katherine and Mr. Brandon," Evelyn strolled up to them, pulling a curl over her shoulder, "I must run on." She adjusted her gloves, "but I'll probably see you this evening at the dance," she cut her eyes again at the Indians as Hawk murmured in Cherokee.

"Not if I can help it," the other Cherokee laughed their amusement at Hawk's murmured response as they walked toward their encampment wondering about the brazen actions of the white girl, feeling one like that spells trouble. Even Raven was leery of such actions.

The brilliant autumn sun cast her glory on the colorful mountains before resting her head on her nightly bed as festivities reached their peak. The overflowing tables laden with roasted pig, beef and venison accompanied by all the savory trimmings, beckoned to all with it's mouth watering aroma.

Following the feasting, the Indians would perform a dance before the whites ended the festivities with a reel.

As Kate finished her apple pie, she was aghast as she watched Evelyn Hollins performance, the blonde sitting three rows down, maneuvering, gyrating, jumping up and down and with a loud voice punctuated with giggles managed to attain her goal-attracting male attention. How disgusting!

"Katherine," John touched his daughter's arm as he stood. "I'm going to accompany your mother back here. She enjoys the dances so much. I'll stay with Priscilla while you ladies enjoy the evening."

"No, Papa," Kate held his arm, stopping him before he turned away. "You need to be here for the Indian dance. They expect that. I'll stay with Prissy," as much as she hated to miss seeing the colorful paraphernalia worn and graceful footwork of the Cherokee, especially one male in white. Kate wondered if the pretty Indian maiden, the one who hated her, would again work her magic on the tall Indian. Her father was staring and she gathered her thoughts to the present. She took his arm while stepping down. "Just walk with me to the lodging."

As Kate and John turned to leave the bleachers, a tall brave in a cream colored outfit, splashed with an intricate color design approached. "Miss Katherine," a deep voice delayed her. She turned as Raven smiled warmly. "I would like for you to have this." He handed her a most unusual and lovely small beaded pouch. "I will also ride for you tomorrow, and I wish to apologize for ever thinking you could be a dog face." His charming smile exposed beautiful white teeth.

"Oh! Raven, thank you so much," she couldn't believe he was actually presenting her with a gift, and such a beautiful pouch, she thought as she ran her fingers over the beaded design. "I can't accept this-this pouch is entirely too lovely for me to accept." She attempted handing it back.

"No-you keep," he held up his hand, refusing to take it.

"But I might just become an old dog face before this teaching session is over. Who knows—" she cast him a mischievous glance, "-what you students may cause."

He threw his head back rumbling with deep laughter before staring at this green eyed girl with pale skin. He realized his infatuation for this white girl was definitely showing. He also knew nothing could come of it, and he was probably acting childish. He chuckled to himself, thinking he could have his pick of any Indian maiden, but at present, all of them seemed to have faded into the background.

"Thank you, Raven," she fingered the beautiful bag and she smiled, a tiny dimple for his dark appreciation. She turned to leave, finding herself drawn to Hawk's dark penetrating scowl, knowing he had witnessed this unusual gift transaction, which she didn't understand herself, nor could she expect him to. To have refused the gift would have been an insult, but she realized she must be careful around this handsome Indian.

The days with classes sped by rather quickly, despite Kate's remaining ill at ease with the brooding dark countenance observing everything she did and said while Raven vied for her individual attention; however, she found her students very intelligent, soaking up everything she handed out, progressing much faster than she had anticipated. Even the shy one actually seemed to relax and enjoy his learning.

Finally, Friday arrived-her excitement obvious in her sparkling eyes as she anticipated traveling alone with Wild Hawk. She was also anxious to see Prissy, concerned about her sister's depression and threats of doing away with her baby, but she'd face that situation when she got home. She hummed a tune as she packed a few items before donning her most becoming bonnet with the green trim that matched her riding habit. Soon Rusty would be here to escort her just beyond the gate where Hawk would be waiting. She was disgusted with herself for being as excited as a young girl with a first date. She commanded her heart to quit thumping as she opened the door to Rusty's knock.

"Well, now, if'n you ain't a sight for these tired old eyes in that there perky outfit," the old scout boomed forth, eyes twinkling. Before entering, he divested himself of a sizable tobacco cud. Picking up her small valise, he wheezed, "we 'uns best git along fore that there young whippersnapper 'cides we ain't a comin'." He ambled through the door while Kate caught up and they headed toward the gate.

Coming into view, the vision in green caused the Indian's heart to jump wildly. Damn! He ridiculed his silliness and suddenly busied himself saddling her mare. Females-sidesaddles. With this ridiculous contraption it's a wonder white women don't break their necks! He jerked on the girth.

Kate crooned to Night Wind, petting him while receiving her usual nickker and shoulder nudge before strolling to the mare with a greeting.

Rusty's amusement mounted as he watched these two trying desperately to ignore each other, but not being very successful as they cast shy glances like two sick young 'uns. He shook his shaggy head as he stuffed a fresh chaw in his mouth. Whadda shame, he thought. "Wall, Wild Hawk, you 'bout ready t' ride?" He shuffled over to his horse.

"Yes, as soon as I make sure this terrible contraption is as sturdy as possible." He gave a final jerk to the belly girth, delaying the whole procedure, wondering and knowing at the same time why he had volunteered to escort her home. He must be insane but he certainly could not allow that woman chasing Raven to accompany this girl.

Observing the old scout's horse, Kate's excitement wavered upon questioning, "Rusty, where are you heading? I see your horse saddled over there." She glanced at Hawk, who continued to busy himself checking and rechecking her gear.

"Wall," Rusty twinkled, "I'm jest gonna' tag along with you 'ns-this here young brave wanted ma compny' 'n hits such a purty day," he chuckled as he observed the girl's green eyed gaze flash fully on the Cherokee.

"I suppose you felt we needed a chaperone!" she fired, adjusting her gloves.

"Possibly," he twitched a half smile as he stepped back, drinking in her beauty which was enhanced by the spark in her eyes. He motioned for her to mount up. With jutting chin she approached her mare. Instead of giving her a hand up, he lifted her by the waist as though she were no larger than a child, hesitating when her face was even with his. After warming her with his dark gaze he placed her on the mare.

Rusty shook his gray head again while mounting up, wondering what this world had to offer these two fine young people-feeling mighty sorry for both. He heard the brave murmur, handing her the reins, "Be careful-is dangerous for you to ride sitting on a thing like that, wrapped in so many layers of clothing." He shook his head as though disgusted.

She saucily replied, "I've always ridden sidesaddle except," she hesitated as though remembering, "when I rode with you on Night Wind during the storm." He nodded as their eyes met, both remembering all too well the closeness of their bodies as she held tightly around his waiste, her body pasted to his while the rain slashed its fury at them.

Hawk motioned for Rusty to take the lead as he vaulted onto Night Wind's back, walking his horse next to Kate's as they headed for home.

The vividness of the late autumn day, the bright sunshine, dispelling the crisp coolness, colorful mountains surrounding them accompanied by the rhythm of the nearby rushing stream enfolded Kate with a peacefulness, a total contentment as she rode by the side of this man who was so much a part of this wonderment. They rode side by side quietly-words weren't necessary. Occasionally, a leg brushed the other, a glance spoke many words, both attuned to the completeness of the moment and both wishing life could always be where they rode together in their own world.

After stopping to water the horses near a peaceful meadow and partaking of a meager lunch of ham and biscuits, Rusty entertained the two with a colorful tale of Jeb Hawkins scurrying up an oak tree from an enraged Mama Bear before he chuckled, reliving Jeb's dilemma, and departed into the trees. Hell, the old scout thought, they deserve a few minutes alone.

After several moments of silence other than the gurgling stream and the horses blowing and moving, Kate looked at the Indian, who was close enough to touch. What a handsome countenance-one knee drawn up while an arm rested on it as he leaned his back against the oak tree trunk, his long dark hair swirling gently around his shoulders. He stared into the distance, his mind in a turmoil over his destiny, knowing this girl who held his heart had no place in his future.

"Wild Hawk." She scooted near, leaning up to get his full attention.

He turned, smiling at the picture she created in her saucy little hat, green outfit and depth of emotion revealed in her vivid eyes, but the smile faded as she murmured, "What are we going to do?" He then became mesmerized by the tear filled eyes and quivering mouth that underlined the sadness he felt over their situation-a sadness he tried to keep dormant.

A tear slipped down the side of her face, pulling at his heart-he wiped it gently with his thumb. "I don't know what to do," she struggled in her throat—"I love you, but what do we do about it? I rarely see you, except at those classes. I need to feel your arms around me, but that doesn't happen. You practically ignore me!" She brokenly continued, "Do I live the rest of my life with one and only one memory, one brief moment in your arms and one kiss. I don't believe God would be that cruel." She was like a small child who was lost. Her eyes were streaming while his heart was being ripped open. He could struggle with himself no longer as he scooped her up into his lap, enclosing her in his arms while removing her hat, placing her head on his shoulder.

Rusty's timing, he felt, was not exactly right as he viewed the two young people so wrapped up in each other. Thinking he should break it up, but knowing he wouldn't, he turned on his heels, giving the two lovers a little more time alone.

"Oh! My beautiful Green Eyes-I cannot stand to see your tears, to feel your hurt-it tears me apart. Don't you know the first time I looked into your eyes, something happened to me," he smoothed her hair, his large hand very gentle as she snuggled closer, breathing in his clean woodsy scent. "By the time I stopped bringing the Cherokee children for your classes, I knew I had lost my heart to the white schoolteacher, but I wouldn't admit it even to myself." He smiled sadly as he continued smoothing her hair. "Oh! Katherine Green Eyes, you hold this brave's heart-he feels great love for you whether he is with you or not, that does not change." He held her up to look into her magnetic eyes. "Know this, Green Eyes, a man cannot be less than he is. Of course, I want to hold you, kiss you, make you my woman." He shook her shoulders slightly. "I dream of this until I have no interest for another female. See what you have done to me," he smiled, "but this man can not and will not sneak around like a skulking cur dog in the dark for a stolen kiss or embrace that would only lead to more-which is wrong. No!" he adamantly injected, "I could never harm you that way no matter how my body cries out for yours." He pulled her head back to his shoulder, rubbing her back and neck, drinking in the flower scent of her hair.

"Hawk, we could get married, then I would be your woman," she nuzzled in a little closer. "I don't care how harsh the Cherokee life is, I just want to be with you."

"Katherine, stop that! It is not only the harsh life which would be very difficult for you, I have genuine fear for my people and their future, something I would never never place you in the middle of."

Pulling back, she looked into his dark eyes. "Don't you know I'd rather die at your side than live without you and die a little every day-you big stubborn Indian!" She hooked her arm around his neck, pulling his face to hers while murmuring, "It isn't dark now," as he captured her lips, ravaging them while crushing her to him. Groaning, he set her away from him, noticing the slight puffiness of her lips which beckoned to him. Helping her up before things got out of control, he brushed dried grass from her skirt as he handed her the hat. Anything to keep busy.

"And that, my Green Eyes, is the reason this Cherokee stays away from Katherine Brandon." He squeezed her hand, gazing deeply into her eyes, feeling overpowered by life's unfairness and swearing never to be alone with this girl again.

Rusty made as much noise as possible, tramping through leaves and humming a mountain jig, announcing his approach while cleaning his tobacco stained teeth with a teaberry stick brush. "Wall, yawl 'bout rested so's we kin git a goin'? "He waited, but there was no response. He chuckled to himself, aware that neither had heard him, or if'n they did they paid no never mind, but followed anyhow 'n mounted up. Lordy, hit'd be a sight shore 'nuff if'n them Brandons got wind of these two 'n their feelings. Specially if'n Miz Mary did. Lord have mercy, hell's fire would shore break loose! Poor young un's-ain't got no chance.

Approaching the Brandon spread, the three riders were shaken out of their lethargy, the afternoon peacefulness totally shattered by Jesse's high pitched screech as she spotted the trio. With a flurry of petticoat and pantaloons, she zoomed in on her favorite target, grabbing his moccasined foot, causing Night Wind to shy, while squealing "Wild Hawk! It's 'bout time you came back to visit me!" She tried batting her eyes at him the way she had seen Prissy do when she was around that soldier.

"Jesse, what is wrong with your eye?" Hawk revealed deep concern while he tried desperately to conceal a twitching smile as he leaned toward her.

"What an insufferable imp!" Kate murmured, despite her amusement. "Jessica Ruth, I'm the one who has been away!"

"Aw-hullo Kate 'n Rusty-uh- I didn't see you-just guess something got into my eyes," she rubbed the mentioned subject to emphasize her truthfulness.

"Howdy, Miss Jesse," Rusty tipped his old dusty leather hat, smiling knowingly.

Forgetting her eyes, Jesse held her hand up. "Wild Hawk, please let me ride in with you." He hesitated, then swung the child up behind him, shrugging his shoulders and smiling helplessly at Katherine as Jess wrapped her arms tightly around his waist, sighing contentedly before cutting her eyes at Kate beginning to laugh uproariously. "Kate, if you ain't the silliest lookin' thing perched up there on that side saddle-bet that's the uncomfortablest thing that ever was 'n you'd really like to be where I am on Night Wind." She smiled smugly, sticking out her tongue at Kate.

The older sister glared at the young female demon wondering how she could be so blessed with this impossible creature for a sister. Her thoughts were interrupted by a low rumbling laugh from Hawk and, reminding her how truthful Jesse's words really were.

Kate stood by the fence, pulling her cape closer to avoid the afternoon chill that had begun to penetrate. She watched her escorts depart, feeling lonely after having spent the afternoon with him. As she watched, the two crested a hill where her Indian stopped, turned on his prancing black stallion and signaled to her. Oh! Dear Lord, she thought, wondering if and when she'd ever be alone with him again. What will happen to us? It's ironic that my sister flaunted herself with a man who cared nothing for her, but one who left her pregnant. The public would have deemed that one a worthy mate. I love a man who in turn loves me; one who would never harm or shame me, yet he, although the finest man I know, would be an impossible mate-one to be shunned because he is an

Indian. Why, my mother and father, especially my mother would be totally destroyed if she thought a daughter of hers held any feelings for an Indian-Mama, if you only knew!

"Katherine! I thought I heard someone ride up." Mary barged through the door and down the steps, welcoming her daughter with a smile and wiping her hands on her apron. "We've missed you," she hugged her daughter. "Who brought you home that was in such a hurry to leave?" They strolled toward the porch while Mary watched this daughter who she hoped would some way help Priscilla.

Kate brushed an imaginary fleck from her skirt while she contained her emotions. "Uh---Rusty Poole and Wild Hawk escorted me home. Papa," she rushed on, "Papa arranged this before leaving me at the fort."

Mary continued to stare at her daughter, observing the flushed face and lack of eye contact. Worrying and wondering why this particular Indian seemed to some way be around or with her daughter frequently.

"How is Prissy, Mama?" Kate hoped to steer the subject from herself for the time being as she stopped on the porch to inquire.

Mary shook her head, obviously disturbed. "I simply don't know-she stays mainly in her room, seems lifeless when she does stir, eats practically nothing and avoids the family as much as possible." She looked down. "It's worrying us to death not knowing what to do," she tugged at her apron, "maybe you can help some way, Katherine." Mary placed a hand on her daughter's arm, pleading with her lovely hazel eyes that were etched with dark circles.

"I'll try, Mama." They entered the cheerful, log paneled living area where the big stone fireplace offered a cheery greeting, helping to dispel some of the gloomy conversation as bright flames greedily licked around a large log. Kate was mesmerized as she sank into Grandma's old walnut rocker while staring intently into the bluish flames, her mind drifting back over every detail of the day's journey from the fort. Dear God! She had fallen in love and in such a short time, with a man who knew not his own destiny much less one that included her. Well, she would make herself find another; maybe a soldier, a good man and she would make herself love him.   He would be dashing and handsome in a blue uniform and-and when she tried to dream up facial features, she only saw a lopsided half smile, revealing beautiful white teeth, dark penetrating eyes with too long lashes, handsome chiseled features while long dark hair gently swirling-oh! Dear Lord—

The noise of a crunching apple broke the peacefulness and her dream world. Kate turned to observe the source of the sound; finding her brother busily enjoying mammoth bites of a red apple while he deposited bits of fresh mud onto her mother's fine braided rug. Oh! Yes-she was definitely home. Tim flung the apple core into the fireplace before sprawling in front of the warmth and for the first time noticing someone in the rocker.

"Oh! Hullo, Kate-whadda you doin' here?" he screwed up his freckles as he questioned.

"I happen to live here," why was it that she and her young brother and sister usually got off on the wrong foot? Seemed they tried her patience whenever possible.

"Well, whadda' you come back for?" Freckled face seemed perturbed.

Rather than scream her frustration at this little self-centered dirt ball, she sugar coated her response, avoiding any additional turmoil.

"Tim," she made herself smile, "I happen to love my family and I want to be here. I'm only away at the fort during the week because I have a class to teach-an important one." She continued rocking.

He looked down, fumbling with a bit of apple that had dropped on the rug. "Well, all I know's with you gone 'n Prissy no 'count stayin' in her room all the time, well me 'n Jess been havin' a good time 'cause there'z only one boss-Mama, but one thing's bad though," he looked down, his chin quivering. "We've searched everywhere, but Stink Bear is really gone," he looked down trying hard not to tear up. "He's gone for good 'cause Mama beat him with the broom."

It pulled at Kate's heart as she watched her pudgy freckled faced brother trying valiantly not to shed tears over a pet bear. She knew life was not always easy for him when his younger sister could best him at most anything plus having three or four bosses would add misery to anyone's life. She felt ashamed!

"Tim," she leaned down smiling, touching his shoulder, "I know how much you loved Stink Bear, but it was only a matter of time until he left on his own anyway. He needs to live with his own kind. Mama's whipping didn't keep him away."

"Maybe you're right," he looked down pulling a bit of loose fabric from one of the braids in the rug, not wanting his sister to see his misty eyes, "but I miss him cause I raised him from a baby."

"I'm sure you do," she tousled his hair as she rose, exiting the room, drumming up courage as she climbed the stairs to approach her sister and jump into what she was sure would be a heated confrontation.

What she saw when she entered her bedroom to unpack the valise was shocking; she couldn't believe that in a week's time, her pretty vivacious sister could change to this pallid dark circle eyed languid creature resting against pillows.

"Oh! Kate," yawning, Prissy muttered, "I thought I heard your voice," pulling the afghan over her body, she resumed her rest with closed eyes, dismissing additional conversation.

"My, my! Prissy-what a rousing welcome," Kate retorted while she hung her dress in the wardrobe. "I've really looked forward to this cheerful get-together with my sister and I can see you felt the same." Sarcasm dripped as Kate rocked in her favorite chair, glaring at her sister intently.

"That's enough, Kate," she flung her hair out of her eyes, "Can't you see I'm trying to rest?" Prissy's voice rose, delighting Kate that she had ignited a spark.

"Of course, I can see what you are trying to do, but what you are really doing is wallowing in disgusting self pity. Go ahead and wallow making your entire family miserable-but guess who the big loser is-you!" Kate emphatically let each word hit home as she rocked steadily.

"How dare you come in here and start preaching to me?" She flung herself up to a sitting position, pounding her pillow. "Get out of here-I won't listen to any more!"

"You'll listen, too!" Kate yelled, abruptly jumping up, and jerking up a hand mirror and shoving it up in her sister's face. "Take a good look at what you are doing to one of the prettiest girls anywhere. Do you recognize her?"

Prissy stared at features that seemed to belong to someone else. How could this be her face? She stared long and hard at the deep dark circles surrounding dark dull eyes in a pale lifeless face before she finally burst forth in heart rending sobs, throwing herself into her pillow, continuing her loud outburst.

Kate sank down on the edge of her sister's bed, hating the deep sobbing, but feeling any emotion was better than the lethargy she found earlier. Finally, the ragged sobs subsided to sniffs. Prissy turned onto her back. "Kate," she put her hand on her sister's arm, "I'm so miserable," her own statement reflected in the dark circled eyes. "I don't know what to do," the miserable eyes beginning to fill with tears again. Kate took her sister's hand.

"I know," her heart going out to this sister who had always been so impetuous and careless, totally ignorant of the trap that the lying cur of a lieutenant laid for her.

Prissy looked down, struggling with words and thoughts while frantically picking at a loose strand of yarn from the Afghan. "I've got to get rid of this baby, but I don't know how-I don't know what to do, but you could find out from some body at the fort." She pulled at Kate's arm frantically, "I know you can-I can't let Mama and Papa know I'm pregnant and if something isn't done soon-oh! My God, I'll be showing!" She pled with Kate, "please help me."

"Prissy, I could never help you to miscarry this baby-never, but I will stand by your side and be there for you as long as you quit this morbid self pity and take care of yourself. I know, and you must realize you were tricked by a scoundrel professing love and marriage-it's happened before and it'll happen again. You can't continue putting all of this blame on yourself. Life is not over-you're still young."

"That's well and good for you to sit there and tell me what to do, Miss Goody," some of the old Prissy flaring in her eyes, "all pious and sweet with your sermon, but dammit, it's not your belly thats swelling with a baby-its mine." Jumping up, she threw the afghan on the floor and began pacing. "And if I can't rid myself of this baby I might as well end my own life," her pain filled eyes darting back and forth.

Kate watched her sister, wondering if she were deranged, going from one extreme to another, flying off the handle then sobbing deep grief, to conniving and wheedling her way. "Listen to me," she stood, grabbing her sister's shoulders, shaking them. "If you continue this self abuse and thoughts of destruction, then you are playing right into that lying no good lieutenant's hands. Do you want that scalawag who planted his seed in you, professing his love then skipping out to leave you facing your problem, to win? Do you want him to win? What a laugh he'd get out of this, to learn you destroyed yourself. It would indeed inflate his already large ego to know you couldn't live without him. Is that what you want?" Kate raised her voice, her green eyes steadily holding the dark circled ones until finally Prissy murmured,

"No."

"Good-think about our conversation. I'll be back next weekend. Remember one thing-Mama and Papa are not the worst at understanding problems and another thing, I'll be right here with you. Remember no more of this self pity and thinking the world has come to an end. Promise?" Prissy nodded. "I have to go and help Mama now." Kate left the room quietly, absolutely exhausted with the burden of her sister's troubles. She felt useless, not knowing any answers, but realizing she had to try some way to help. Maybe Jeb Hawkins could come up with some answers. She'd talk with him when she returned to the fort. He did say he loved Prissy and wanted to marry her.

Prissy stared at the door after Kate closed it, wondering if what her sister said did make any sense. How could any man, though, ever look at a woman with an illegitimate child. Why! She didn't even know anyone in this awful situation, but one thing she did know, that bastard Keith Anderson would some day, some way pay for what he had done to her-he would pay! She grabbed a shoe, and flung it full force into the door smashing the lieutenant's imaginary face.

Temperatures took a frosty dip during the night, encouraging the Brandons to enjoy a second cup of coffee in front of the large stone fireplace rather than outside. John, having returned from a busy trip to Knoxville where he met with Colonel Roberts and Washington dignitaries for two days, explained the two day meeting to Mary and Kate. "It looks as though," he stood tapping his pipe against a stone, "within a year the fort will be closed. It's the only one in this area that is still in operation." He sat back down in the rocker, staring into the flames.

"But what about our home? Does that mean your job will be terminated here, John?" Mary wasn't smiling; she even seemed disturbed, Kate thought, as she watched her mother intently, feeling as though the breath had just been knocked out of her.

"It could be-" John observed his still lovely wife thinking how much he'd missed her those two days in Knoxville and how ridiculous this was for an old married man. He warmed her with a smile, realizing she didn't seem pleased with the idea of leaving their mountain home. Could this be true? He thought she'd be happy with the idea of leaving this remote area and possibly returning to Boston. "Of course, nothing has been finalized yet-and it could be postponed to a later date," he turned his attention to his daughter. "What do you think of the idea of leaving here, Katherine?" He sipped his coffee somehow knowing this girl's answer.

"Well, I-" Kate looked down, totally engrossed in the checkered pattern of her skirt while her heart slammed up into her chest. "I don't really want to leave here, Papa." Green eyes gazed into green eyes. "I know this is a remote area, especially compared to Boston, but somehow these mountains have reached out to me and," she glanced out of the window, drinking in the surrounding beauty, "I have become a part of them," she continued.

Mary observed this daughter, carefully seeing the pain etched on her face as she stared at the mountains; this mother also realized it was not only the mountains reaching out to this girl. Oh! Katherine, Katherine! What are you doing to yourself?

John nodded also glancing at the mountainous beauty surrounding them. "I certainly understand your feeling."

All thoughts and conversation were abruptly interrupted by galloping hooves coming to a skidding halt, and a large frame striding through the gate.

"Why, it's Jeb Hawkins," Kate rushed to the door, admitting the scout and sensing immediately something very wrong as the big scout rushed through the door, eyes darting from one to the other. He jerked his hat off, twisting it—

"Jeb, what's wrong?" John was at his side immediately.

He had trouble catching his breath, rushing and struggling with words, striding to the fireplace. John's concern was obvious as he watched this big man struggling for words. "They've got Wild Hawk."

"Who? Where?-calm down, Jeb-just sit for a moment and explain. Mary, get him some coffee."

Jeb paced, running his big hand through his hair. "At the fort-they have him in custody, that white bitch Evelyn Hollins accused him of molesting her." He ground his teeth continuing to pace.

"Oh! My God," Kate murmured, sinking into a chair as Mary shoved a cup of coffee into Jeb's hand.

"Words got out fast," he continued, setting his coffee on the table, "-ruffians, settlers 'n soldiers all over the place-I'm afraid they'll work into a mob threatenin' hanging. You know what it's like when a gang gets likkered up." He again walked to the fireplace. "And it's all a lie—a damn lie! I know that man-we've got to hurry-you will come and help?" Jeb pled.

"Of course," John didn't hesitate, picking up his pipe and tobacco, cramming them into his pocket. "When was this supposed to have happened?"

"Last night-after he left my place," he continued pacing, "we have to hurry-I ain't been able to talk to Hawk, but the Colonel will probably let you see him," he started for the door as John grabbed his coat and hat.

"I'm coming, too." Kate started for the stairs for her clothes.

"No," Mary interfered, placing a hand on her arm, "you must not get involved in something like this-no respectable girl would ever-"

"Mama, I'm going." Kate's green eyes steadily held her mother's. "Don't try to stop me." She marched up the stairs to collect her belongings, wanting to scream, cry, and yell his innocence, instead she asked the Dear Lord to please keep him safe.

"John," Mary couldn't understand why any man, any father would allow his daughter to become caught up in such a despicable thing, "can't you do something to stop her?" She was losing patience.

"Yes, I suppose I could-but I'm not going to. Hurry up, Katherine," he yelled, as he donned his jacket and crammed his hat on his head.

"Oh!" Mary ground out as she threw her chin out and marched from the room.

"Honey," John called, "I'll be back as soon as I can, but it will probably be after a hearing where a judgment and punishment is placed. What a hell of a mess this young man is in," he muttered, as though his thoughts took precedence over his conversation with his wife. "Mary, did you hear me?" he yelled.

"Yes, I heard you," she was standing in the doorway, "anyone down at the barn could have heard." He could tell she was angry at him, her chin was always elevated when she was out of sorts, as Kate bounced down the stairs and into the room with coat and valise.

"I'm ready to ride-and Mama, please don't be angry," Kate touched her mother's arm, pecking her on the cheek, "I simply feel I should be there; after all, he is one of my students." Kate avoided her mother's knowing gaze.

Before leaving, John strode to his wife's side, pulled her to him and kissed her. Her eyes and feelings warmed to his touch. "You can lower your chin now, dear, there won't be anyone here to see how angry you are."

"John Brandon, you are impossible." She couldn't keep from smiling at this man she loved so much and missed so very much when he was away.

"Yes, you've told me that," he patted her bottom, captivating her with his warm smile.

"Quit that," she smacked his hand as he followed the others outside, turning to wink at her before closing the door, enjoying her flushed face.

"Be careful, John, and watch out for Katherine." He nodded.

As she watched the three crest the near hill, Mary was more than a little disturbed over what might erupt at the fort. She couldn't believe John Brandon would be crazy enough to allow his daughter to be a part of such hostilities. When he returned home, she'd certainly give him a piece of her mind! Placing another log on the fire, she stared, watching the small flame flicker while she wondered if there could be any truth in the white girl's accusations about the Indian?

Chapter 18

The three rode at a grueling pace, reaching the fort around noon where ruffians, soldiers, and settlers milled around arguing, spittin', and raising voices in heated discussions as John and Kate faded into the background while Jeb joined Rusty near the blockhouse.

"Oh, say," an overweight buckskin clad bearded ruffian hauled a jug to his rounded shoulder, tipped it and pulled a long swig, "string 'em up-hell, any red savage touchin' a white gel ain't got no right t' live-Ah say kill em. Ain't that right, boys?" He squirted tobacco juice through his missing front tooth.

Several chorused an agreement, grabbing for their turn at the jug while cussing and bemoaning all Indians. "The only good Injun' is a dead 'un, ain't that right, Ned?" A scrawny weasel of a man, Nate Turner, scratched his sparse tobacco stained whiskers, only able to comment with the "boys" when he had a little liquor fortification under his belt. Those near grunted, nodded, spit and continued passing the jug.

Colonel Roberts strode purposefully through the crowd and up to the front of the blockhouse where Hawk was kept under guard, two soldiers placed themselves on either side, between the fired up riffraff and the entrance.

"All right-listen up-everybody." The disgruntled group kept mumbling, laughing and jeering when one stringy haired, long, lanky dirty ruffian yelled out, braver after indulging in his corn, "Naw, we ain't gonna' listen, 'cause we already know-"

"Yeah, that's right-You tell 'em, Haskel," comments were fired from several directions.

"We know what this red heathen done 'n you better listen t' us," he snickered, looking around, "cause we aim t' hang 'em," an abnormal flush colored Haskel Thornton's face as he thundered his final words. By this time Jeb and Rusty had eased up near the Colonel, rifles relaxed in the crook of their arms, but on the ready as several soldiers began surrounding the mob.

"No, Thornton, you will all listen carefully to me." His commanding tone demanded the hecklers to listen. "First, we will not tolerate a bunch of men getting likkered up to assume a false bravery in order to harm. You will stop this right now and go on home, or if you continue you'll be slapped in the guardhouse for disturbing the peace. Secondly, if anyone so much as makes a move toward this door he will find himself in the dirt. Now I have many well-trained armed soldiers who certainly wouldn't mind a little target practice." He stared steadily at the group. "I am the commander here, and any man, red or white, locked in the blockhouse will get a fair hearing with just punishment. Do I make myself clear?"

The mob had listened to this man who demanded respect and who stood his ground. They also observed the number of soldiers ready to do his bidding, which definitely had a cooling effect on their ire.

"Come on, Ned-ain't no sense hangin' round here waitin' to git our heads blowed off-'n ah ain't waitin' to be slapped in no cooler neither." Weasel scratched his whiskers, his bravery totally disappearing as his rat eyes shifted uneasily.

"Yeah-guess yore right-this ain't even no place to git drunk nor have no pleasurin' neither."

"Yep-let's git on over to Shorty's place," a squatty tobacco spitter whined, "Whar they's ready 'n waitin' wimmen over aire." He snickered, then straightened his face. "They ain't nuthin' here." He glanced around, "but them army dudes glarin' down them gunsights 'n a few 'uv them iceberg females decked in corset stays 'n 15 layers 'uv wrappins-why, hit'd take a body half a day t' find what he's lookin' fer," he hee hawed at this large joke, revealing big long yellow teeth as he poked the lean, lanky voice piece.

Kate stood with her father in the background, away from the turmoil but in hearing distance of the complete disturbance. John wondered at his own sanity of bringing her here and at the trembling hand on his arm before glancing at his daughter's paleness. "Are you all right, Katherine?"

She nodded, but wanted to scream out, of course I'm not all right! I'm worried sick over what these hell raisers might do to the man who means everything to me. It's horrible having to sneak around and hide feelings. "Papa, what do you think will happen?"

"You don't have to worry about this gang of riffraff. Colonel Roberts has the upper hand with soldiers to back him up, and I believe they're slowly beginning to depart. As soon as they leave I'm going to try and speak with Wild Hawk. Excuse me, honey, Lieutenant Phillips is standing behind us. I must speak with him-be right back." John moved three or four feet behind Kate and spoke to a tall dark haired lieutenant with a neatly trimmed mustache whose blue eyes were fastened on Kate.

The crowd was slow to disperse, mumbling continuing within the group of ruffians while they chawed, spit and protested, not wanting to reveal their yellow streak by leaving out too soon. Settlers in smaller groups seemed to be holding serious conversations, staying upwind of the smelly buckskin clad whiskey sluggers. Jackson Mayes, a tall slim gray haired settler in homespun and deerskin coat with a rifle hanging in the crook of his arm took a few steps toward the Colonel. "Roberts, we don't like none 'uv this 'n we ain't aimen' to jest run 'long when some Injun buck touched a white lady. We want something done-now!"

"Yeah" "That's ma' feelin'" "You tell 'em, Mayes," came from various directions.

Colonel Roberts' gaze held them steadily as he waited for the grumbling to quieten. "Mayes, you heard what I said earlier-the same goes for you and all the rest, "his gaze held the group. "The hearing will be in two days. Now go on home-all of you. There is nothing you will accomplish here but trouble for yourself if you remain." The Colonel stood his ground, obviously not thwarted by any remarks or behavior. "Now," he shifted his weight, "we have work to do in here and if any man is determined to stick around he will be escorted outside of the gate where he will remain until the hearing. Good day, gentleman." He waited while the soldiers encouraged the group to leave. Roberts was worn out. This mess had taken its toll and probably the worst was yet to come. With whiskey totin' filthy scalawags, hate filled settlers and many soldiers just itching to kill an Indian-well, his patience had worn mighty thin. It was doubtful Wild Hawk had touched that little feisty filly. He'd seen her in action around a few men, but hell, what chance did any Indian have against a white, especially a female.

The mob began to depart, many glaring at the Colonel while continuing to mutter and grumble their complaints, realizing though that they wouldn't buck the armed soldiers. One hefty ruffian caressing his jug as though it were a woman, yelled his farewell, "Yew kin 'spect us'uns back here day after next fer that there hearin' 'n you kin 'spect us to make shore thu right kind 'uv punishment is given to that varmint." His small close set black eyes squinted at the Colonel as he flung out a cud of tobacco.

John Brandon turned from Lieutenant Phillips in time to witness and hear a crude comment directed toward his daughter from the long haired one called Haskel. "Well, lookie thar' boys," he poked Ned, pointing to Kate, his yellow teeth revealed in his sneer. "She's a might purtier then ah thought-yesteddy ah seen her, yes sir ree, hit 'uz her all right, 'n that there Indian buck in aire ridin' mighty clost' together. I'd say she'z shore enjoyin' hit," he snickered, "I'm a wonderin' if'n that's all she enjoyed!"

The small groups scattered when a fist smashed into Haskel's face, sending him sprawling. "Get up, you disgusting whiskey soaked son of a bitch and apologize to my daughter, now!" John Brandon jerked the startled ruffian up by the greasy shirt front. This entire episode, trash milling around threatening a hanging, accusations that were probably all false and now this filthy creature insults his daughter-all of it was more than enough to cause his temper to explode. Haskel shook his head and rubbed his jaw, trying to get his bearings. His mouth opened and closed, accompanied by an active Adam's apple while John tightened his grip on a handful of shirt collar, making speaking difficult.

"I said, apologize before I beat the stinking pulp out of you," John hissed while his green eyes shot daggers at the man.

"I'm—a—tryin'," the ruffian croaked, as John's hand tightened, "Ah'm—sorry-missy," he struggled in his throat, "din'—aim'—no—harm—must 'uv mistook you fer somebody—else." The stench getting to him, John shoved the creature away, causing him to stumble as the man grabbed his neck, struggling with his breathing. Colonel Roberts strode into the midst while others gathered around.

"What's going on here, Brandon?" He eyed both John and Haskel, observing the cowering man pulling at his neck.

"A little lesson in behavior around a lady," he turned toward his daughter, observing his scratched knuckle.

"All right-let's all clear out," Colonel Roberts bellowed, seeing that the mob did just that before something else got out of hand. The soldiers escorted the group through the gate, while the Colonel walked toward Kate. "I'm awfully sorry, Miss Katherine. Did that scalawag harm you?" He gazed at her with a fatherly concern.

"No, not really," Kate smiled at her dad, never realizing before just how well he could swing his fist. "My father took very good care of him!"

"Well, young lady, this was not a good place for you to have been today-I'm surprised you brought her, John," he reprimanded, "anything could have happened with a group like that, and John, I would advise your daughter to remain behind doors the day of the hearing."

John replied, "I heartily agree," as Lieutenant Phillips approached the three.

"Mr. Brandon, I haven't had the pleasure of meeting your daughter, but if this could be arranged with the Colonel, I'd like nothing better than to offer my services as her escort until after the hearing," his blue eyes warmed to Kate's flushed face as her beautiful green eyes held him captive.

Not waiting for John to answer, "Lieutenant," the Colonel obviously grateful, straightening his one size too small coat over his tubby tummy, "that is a splendid idea. Miss Katherine Brandon, may I present Lieutenant Andrew Phillips-now that that's settled," he grabbed John's arm, pulling him toward the blockhouse, "I'm sure you agree, John."

"How can I disagree, since you seem to have settled all matters!" The others laughed, but Kate was in no laughing mood. Here they were making small talk, laughing and joking when a man's life was at stake. Did they have no feelings for anyone else?

"Colonel," John inserted as they strolled across the compound, "I'd like to speak with Wild Hawk with your permission. From what I've heard something doesn't seem to fit the person I know."

"Yes, I agree-come on. I'll write you out a pass." He ushered John along toward the blockhouse, throwing over his shoulder, "Lieutenant, see Miss Katherine to her lodging, then later escort her to the hall for the evening meal-we'll meet you there." He waved them off while John shook his head, smiling, overcome with Roberts maneuvering and arranging. What a character, but maybe that's what it took to command an Army post.

Handing John the signed pass, the Colonel confided quietly while they were still out of earshot of the guards, obvious concern written on his face, "I don't believe a word that Hollins girl is saying about this Indian, but unless we find some proof of her lying, it could go mighty hard for him." The Colonel looked down, shaking his head. "I'd certainly hate to be in his place. Well," clasping John's shoulder, "I'll see you at supper." He strode across the compound toward his office seemingly in deep thought while John gazed into the vividness of the late afternoon sun set, drinking in its beauty as it streamed its colorful shadows over this place, painting a rosy glow of peacefulness where only a short while ago vicious hatred glared its vivid colors. John started up the steps.

Lieutenant Phillips bowed slightly, "Miss Katherine, I can never remember when I have had a job as pleasant as this one." He smiled, revealing very white teeth in a tanned handsome face with blue eyes that bored into hers.

She faked a smile. "Thank you, but I can see myself to the Cooper residence." She was too upset to be decent to anyone. He noticed her smile didn't meet her eyes.

"Of course you can, but I won't let you defeat me in this most pleasant assignment." He picked up her valise with a rather impudent grin creasing his countenance, as Kate walked on, lost in her own thoughts, wondering if she'd ever see that lopsided smile again, the long black hair being caressed by a mountain breeze, hear the deep mellow voice. "I know John Brandon is your father," the lieutenant interrupted her thoughts, "but I haven't seen you before, Miss Katherine-I might add I was a little shocked to see you here today with all the hostility going on!"

"Wild Hawk is one of my students," she looked straight ahead, afraid she'd give away some emotion as she strolled on, pulling her cape closer against the very cool breeze.

"You teach Indians?" Disbelieving, the lieutenant's shocked expression was obvious as he stared at this attractive young lady with the captivating green eyes.

"Yes, five Cherokee braves who must learn to read and write our language before representing their clans in Washington." She turned and met his gaze. "Does that shock you?"

"Yes," he continued to smile, observing this very different but lovely young lady. Most females would flirt and flutter, but this one couldn't care whether he was here or some other place, and the girls he had known in the past would scream if an Indian came near. "Yes, a little shocked but thoroughly intrigued." He enjoyed her flushed countenance as they arrived at the Cooper residence where Kate rapped on the door. "I'll return to escort you to supper, Katherine, at 6:30." He was tired of this "Miss" business and his eyes twinkled as he observed her astonished expression. Turning, he whistled a lively tune, strolling over to a group of soldiers who milled around the compound.

"Philips," a stocky officer interjected chuckling, cuffing him on the arm, "you needn't think you can lasso that little filly, she's got a mind uv' her own," he elbowed another lieutenant, "ain't that right, Cason?"

"You got that right, she turned me off and even had that big scout Jeb Hawkins to do her bidding." He tossed a stick at his frustration, this slightly built officer continued to think about the luscious auburn hair and deep green eyes that had haunted him from the time he had first met her. He stuck his hands in his pockets and ambled toward his quarters. He wouldn't hang around here to discuss Kate Brandon wondering if he'd ever get up enough courage to approach her again. God, how he had fallen for her.

Phillips eyed the dejected officer, understanding why the strong-willed young lady wouldn't be excited over the mild-mannered Cason but his blue eyes suddenly filled with a spark. She'd sure be a challenge for him.

A bedraggled Janice Cooper opened the door to Kate's knock. "Kate, I didn't expect you back so soon." Her eyes were red and swollen, hair tousled and she was wrapped in an old blue robe. "Come on in-I was just lying down." She crept back to her bedroom while Kate followed, wondering what in the world was wrong with this girl.

"Janice what is wrong? Are you ill?" Kate questioned, revealing concern as she watched the girl light the lamp on the walnut table by the window before gazing out into the evening dusk.

"No," she walked back to her bed and sat. "Do sit down, Kate. Don't know where my manners are." She rubbed her head. "Please, just make yourself at home. I suppose I'm only tired. I slept very little last night."

Kate eased down into a rocker after removing her hat and wrap. Picking up one of her reading books from the table, she inquired, "What happened last night, Janice?"

The girl avoided eye contact, beginning to pluck and smooth the patchwork quilt. "All I know is what I was told-"

"-and what was that?" Kate probed, gazing intently at the girl while she rocked away waiting for an answer, thinking Janice was not herself. What was wrong with her?

"Just-just what Evelyn Hollins told-that Wild Hawk tried to molest her." She smoothed the sheet over the quilt, intently watching her hands.

"What time was this supposed to have happened?" Kate continued to probe.

"Around 10:00 or 10:30 last night."

"Seems strange Evelyn Hollins was out and about at that hour-don't you think, Jan?" Kate questioned.

"Well, I don't know anything about it," Janice irritably retorted. "There's been so much a to-do about it-that awful mess going on today. I really don't want to think about it," making a strong attempt to change the subject as she stretched out on the bed.

"I'm sure few people here wish to think about something so vile, especially the one man who is accused of the deed. You know that mob today was talking of a hanging, and if some one or something doesn't prove that the girl is lying then he might," she struggled with her voice as she croaked, "he—might—die." She covered her face with her hands. All day she had kept her feelings hidden when she was ready to explode. Now, it was too late-she was simply too tired.

Janice sat up, staring at her friend; for the first time aware that this girl had feelings for the Indian. Oh! My Lord-how terrible, she thought. How could any sensible white girl let herself care for a—a—savage. She continued to stare as she whispered, "You care about him, don't you?" astonishment written on her features.

Kate pulled a handkerchief from her pocket and wiped her eyes as she steadily stared into accusing ones. Lifting her chin she responded, "Yes, I do, but I can see you thoroughly disapprove."

"That's right," she again looked down smoothing the quilt. "I simply don't understand."

"I'm sure you don't, Janice." Kate stood, wishing she could lie down and rest, but there was not enough time. She wasn't even sure she was wanted here since she was contaminated by caring for an Indian. "I must freshen up." She strolled into the kitchen to heat water for the bath closet, wondering what was really wrong with Janice. She was acting so strange, unlike herself. Could it be that she knew something she wasn't revealing? All this was getting to her-this horrible turmoil and she had no answers with so little time left before the hearing. She had to see Wild Hawk tonight-just to see him and talk with him. Maybe she could persuade the Colonel if she took his reading book with an assignment. Oh! Dear Lord-all of this is so unfair. Tears filled her eyes as she searched for answers that weren't there.

The dinner was excellent with Lt. Phillips very attentive, but he had to excuse himself for a minor duty until Kate was ready to leave.

John filled the Colonel and her in on his visit to the block house as they finished their cherry cobbler with coffee. He had waited for the dining room to clear. "Colonel, that Indian is no more guilty than I am of molesting that girl. After he left Jeb Hawkins' checker game last night, he was walking between the Jackson and Cooper residences when he heard moaning coming from the back area."

"Did you say between the Jackson and Cooper residences?" Kate pointedly interrupted.

Her father nodded as he continued, "Well, Wild Hawk thought someone was hurt-the groaning became louder causing him to step back between the residences, thinking someone was hurt and he could help. Before he knew what was happening," John filled lit and puffed his pipe, "this Evelyn Hollins had thrown herself at him, arms around his neck, trying to seduce him, attempting to pull him toward the back of the Jackson residence. He pushed her away and said, "No", turning his back on her and walking away when she raised her voice slightly saying "You damn red heathen! How dare you turn away from me. I'll teach you a lesson you'll never forget!" He kept backing away when she began screaming, "That savage-he tried to molest me, rape me!" By that time she had torn her dress, scratched herself and mussed her hair." John looked at each one, puffing quietly.

"Oh! My God," the Colonel groaned, stretching his tired legs, "do you suppose there is anyone who could have heard or seen any of this?" He glared at his coffee cup in deep thought.

"There just might be." The kitchen crew came in to clear the tables, silencing Kate until they were out of earshot. She lowered her voice. "Something has happened to Janice Cooper-I didn't want to give this too much hope until Papa, you mentioned this horrible thing happened between the Jackson and Cooper residences. Well, Janice's bedroom is on that side and she usually opens the window unless it's freezing outside-wasn't there a full moon last night?" Both men nodded, looking at each other, "And since the Jacksons and Coopers are away from home, I imagine Evelyn Hollins picked that spot thinking Janice was away, too. What do you think?" Kate played with her napkin, her green eyes sparkled with excited hope as both men smiled, some of her hopefulness rubbing off on them.

"Let us hope," the Colonel responded.

"I think it's better if I try to reach her," Kate continued to toy with the napkin, "-and Colonel Roberts, I need to see Wild Hawk." She held up the reading book, "I have his reading book here with an assignment. Papa could see me by on the way to the Coopers and you could explain to Lieutenant Phillips," her green eyes pled, "I imagine he needs something to take his mind off the situation."

The Colonel shook his head, smiling. "You have a very persuasive daughter, John. Do you think it's all right for her to speak to that Indian?" He rubbed his aching leg, wishing he were at home with a hot toddy, and this whole mess were behind him.

John nodded. "She'll be all right." Kate's radiant smile was thank you.

On the way to the blockhouse Kate asked, "Where are the other Indians? I've wondered if you sent them back to their village?"

"Oh! Yes-they would have only gotten into trouble had they remained here. I also told them we would not continue studies here, there'll be too much animosity now. If and when we continue, it will have to be at our place." Kate was in agreement.

When the two entered the prison, Kate turned to her father as the guards looked on in astonishment that a girl would dare enter this place. "Let me talk to him alone, Papa, since you've already been here. I imagine he's in enough turmoil without being intimidated."

"You're probably right." John sat down in a straight chair by the door as Kate walked quietly through the dimly lit room to the figure sitting on the floor in the back corner near a cot. His head and arms rested on his drawn up knees, his long hair hanging on either side. He knew the footsteps approaching him.

"Wild Hawk," she whispered. He slowly raised his head, inner turmoil etched on his handsome countenance. He stood, his eyes never losing contact with hers.

"How in hell did you get in here, Katherine," he hissed. "Don't you know you have no business being here?" Searching the shadows for someone else, he spotted John Brandon sitting by the door. "It could cause you great trouble!" Those wonderful green eyes were ready to spill over tears, he observed, as he drank in her beauty. "I'm sorry," he murmured.

"Oh! Wild Hawk-I had to see you! The thought of what that evil girl is trying to do to you," She looked down, struggling for control, her eyes swimming with tears.

"Stop it, Green Eyes-this isn't helping either one of us and I cannot stand the tears. Please listen. I do not want you to come here again, no matter—what happens. You must promise me this." She nodded. "You must not drag yourself into this, not only for the harm it could cause you, but also your father and what he is trying to do for my people. He is our only hope right now. Go now, Green Eyes," he looked away for it was all he could do to control his emotions.

"I brought your reading book with your assignment marked." She handed the book to him, struggling with her tears and brushing his hand as their eyes met, speaking their emotions. "Don't give up hope," she whispered.

"I talked to my God Yowa-what ever happens will be up to him." He looked down at the book in his hand, wanting so to touch her-afraid he might never again hear her say she loved him. He kept staring at the book as she turned and walked to her father, glancing back while they waited for the guard to unlock the door.

Her salty tears saturated the pillow before Kate finished her prayers, asking the Dear Lord to please keep her Indian safe. Finally, a fitful sleep took over her exhausted body, accompanied by horribly disturbing dreams of Wild Hawk's magnificent lifeless body hanging with a rope around his neck. She awakened, struggling to get her breath, trying to become oriented to her surroundings while she listened to the moaning wind. She sat up, pulling her wrapper around her still tired body, afraid to lie back down for fear she would fall asleep and again see his lifeless body. As she moved to the rocker to place an afghan over her legs and read after lighting the lamp, but before she could pick up a book,

Janice let out a disturbing shudder in her sleep, followed by a loud agonized voice. "No—no—you can't punish him for something he didn't do! She's lying—I saw the whole thing."

Kate flew to Janice's bedside, her heart thumping wildly as she knelt beside the bed, questioning, "What did you see, Janice?"

"Through the—windows—she did it." Her voice came in snatches.

"Who should not be punished?"

"The—the—Indian." Janice seemed to relax somewhat in her sleep as she turned over onto her side, but Kate was urged to press for the truth now!

"Janice," she grasped the girl's shoulder, shaking it firmly. The girl bolted up in bed, wild eyed, grabbing the quilt firmly around her neck.

"What—what—is it? What—do you want?" Her fear evident.

"Janice, you talked in your sleep. You revealed what you saw last night through the window," Kate's eyes revealing her excitement, "and that Wild Hawk is innocent and—" Kate sat on the edge of the bed.

"I don't know what you're talking about." Janice picked at the covers with nervous fingers, her eyes darting back and forth, avoiding the green gaze.

Kate faced her challenge. "Don't you pull this on me, Janice. You know exactly what happened out there last night," she pointed to the window, "and if you don't come forth and tell the authorities, then you are contributing to Wild Hawk's death." Her voice raised, "Is that what you want?"

"No—no—," Janice sobbed into her hands, "I don't want any harm to come to anyone." She wiped her eyes with the edge of the sheet as she sat up, "but I can't go against white people, my family's best friends, Evelyn Hollins' parents," she sniffed. "It would destroy them, and I can't do that—I won't," she stated emphatically. "Don't look at me like that!" she yelled, turning her head away to avoid the staring eyes.

"Janice," Kate stood, watching the girls emotions playing over her facial features, keeping her voice calm but determined. "This is not speaking the thoughts or feelings of the girl I know. You are basically a good person, and regardless of who might be hurt you're not the type of individual who could, for the rest of your life, live with a lie, knowing you could have saved a man's life by telling the truth, but instead you avoided the truth and allowed an innocent man to die. This would not only destroy his life, but also your own. Can you do this? Can you live with it?"

"No—no—Stop it, now. Leave me alone. I can't stand any more," the girl screamed, sobbing as she jumped up, rushing to the bath closet where Kate could hear her retching.

Kate sat in the rocker, turned out the lamp, and listened to the early morning sounds of soldiers marching for the flag raising ceremony as the sun peeped it's beginning ray over the eastern mountain ranges. The normal activities of boots clicking along ground surface, soldiers changing guard, standing at attention for inspection, the normal early morning's happenings at this post; however, nothing involving her life was the least bit normal. It was insane, totally out of kilter. The sneering, smelly, whiskey drinking ruffians bellowing for hanging, Janice Cooper sobbing and running to throw up because she couldn't face the truth, all added to Kate's world that was insanely tilted. Katherine Brandon was not at all sure she could live in any world if something happened to her Indian.

The overcast day did little to dispel the somber atmosphere of a court hearing to pass judgment on a man's life. Circuit Judge Timothy Osborne, a rawboned gray-haired man in black from

Knoxville, entered the fort gate astride a large gray horse at 9:30 sharp, escorted by three soldiers. Already, many ruffians and settlers milled around outside the gate, which was not to be opened to them until ten o'clock, the scheduled hearing time. Much mumbling and grumbling were echoed around the compound when the Colonel's order of leaving all jugs outside the gate was enforced.

After dragging through yesterday, Kate was glad the hearing date had finally arrived. Nothing was quite as bad as the waiting. She was seated on the couch in the Cooper parlor, attempting to read but only managing to stare at the page while waiting for her father to escort her to the hearing. Lord, she was a wreck—so very tired from not having slept, swollen eyes, and her stomach so tied in knots, it had been impossible for her to eat anything! How could she stand the horror of the evil accusations that would be hurled at Wild Hawk today and the sentencing. She was aware of footsteps on the porch when Janice entered the room, opening the door for her father.

"Come in, Mr. Brandon, it's too cool and bleak to wait outside." He entered.

"Thank you, Miss Janice, but," he checked his pocket watch, "it's time we left. The hearing begins in fifteen minutes. Are you coming with us?" His eyes assessed this girl who looked as though she hadn't slept for a month.

She was nervous, her fingers busily pulling at a fringe binding her skirt pocket while her tired eyes shifted from John to Kate. "I— I don't know," she held on to the back of the walnut rocker. "I've been thinking about it for some time—" She looked down, toying with her thoughts then back at John. "I suppose I will, since you are escorting us, Mr. Brandon, but I might just get up and leave before it's over." He nodded. "I'll get my wrap," she exited the room.

"Thank God," Kate murmured as she donned her green cape with matching bonnet. Her fingers were shaking so, she could hardly tie the taffeta streamers.

The panelled room for the hearing was jammed with all types of male individuals, buckskin clad ruffians, settlers and soldiers as John escorted the ladies up the stairs where a separate area was roped off for females other than those testifying. There were six or seven ladies who dared to brave this masculine court room world; one, lo and behold, was Beatrice Roberts, the Colonel's wife, who had compassion for the Indian, especially this young man who quit a horse race that he was winning to help an injured white. She was here to see that he had a just trial. Besides, she had never liked that Evelyn Hollins-that snit was probably lying.

Sweat, tobacco juice and loud jargon permeated the stale atmosphere as the black clad judge strode down the aisle, gazing over his spectacles at the packed bunch of humanity, many disreputable. He thought, what a God awful day was in store for him, having to preside over some Indian-white thing with a bunch of illiterate riffraff interfering. Why he had to be chosen to deal with this problem in some out of the way hell hole he didn't know. The judge in Asheville was younger and just as near. Maybe he couldn't have handled it quite as well, he puffed up, but what difference did it make any way, as to what happened to some Indian! Besides, his rheumatism had acted up for the past week. He stalked on to the raised platform where he gratefully sank down behind a broad walnut desk, continuing to peer over his glasses. Not only did his joints ache from the jolting ride, but his bunions were killing him. It'd be a late day in June before he'd allow his wife to have another pair of shoes made for him!

He was jarred out of his miserable condition by a raspy voice belonging to a big obese box of a man clothed in greasy buckskin with a bald cranium adorned by a stringy brown fringe reaching his shoulders. "Now Judge," he looked around to note attention as his buddies poked each other, snickering, "whut do ya' think yore waitin' on? We 'uns is itchin' to git a goin'-hit's been 'u coon's age since we 'uns hed a rope 'round a red heathen. Hain't hit, boys?" He sneered at his cronies.

The "boys", crammed in around him, chorused, "Yep," "You said hit, Clem," "Too long—" sneering and hee hawing at some crude remark.

Crimson inched up from Judge Osborne's neck to his hairline as he slammed the gavel down and thundered, "Let me set you straight," he growled, "if you open your mouth for any reason, much less some inane remark like you just made and that goes for each of you," he stared them down, "I will have you escorted out of this," for his tolerance was low, "court room before you know what's happening and you will remain outside." He continued peering over his spectacles, "You better believe I have enough manpower to back up my decisions." He made his point clear as he squinted up at the soldiers surrounding the entire group.

The mouthpiece and his cronies stared at each other and the soldiers without uttering a sound as Jeb Hawkins escorted Wild Hawk down the aisle, followed by a soldier. Both the Indian and scout were clad in clean buckskin trimmed in long fringe, their moccasins making only a whisper of a sound while all eyes focused on the two fine male specimens. Judge Observe was shocked as he gazed intently at the magnificence of this Indian with the handsome and proud countenance. He wondered why one like this would have to molest any female, and Jeb Hawkins the scout he knew to be an honest and courageous man.

They took their seats in the front left across from Miss Evelyn Hollins who was lavishly guessed up in blue taffeta with matching bonnet that also matched her blue eyes. Next to her were her parents, Dolly and Eugene Hollins. Her mother, an older version of Evelyn Hollins, was overdressed in rose silk. Eugene, a tall emaciated mercantile supply store operator, spoiled his little blue eyed girl unmercifully. At present, he soothed her with his special endearments, hating that his baby had to be put through the horror of what that red animal had tried to do to her, by retelling the evil episode. As he thought of the horrifying ordeal his over enthusiastic Adam's apple jumped a double staccato.

Just as the gavel came down for the court procedure to begin, the outside door burst open for Lone Eagle in his finest regalia, accompanied by Rusty Poole. All eyes were glued on the proud chief as he gracefully walked the aisle, his long tunic fringe, turban fur piece and plume swaying with each step as he approached his son, stopped, placing a hand on his shoulder before seating himself by him. Rusty joined the trio. Judge Osborne cleared his throat, thoroughly impressed with the dignity and presence of the chief. The crowd murmured, pointing, some sneering.

The gavel rapped again as Osborne thundered, "This court will come to order and we will now hear from the commander of this post as to why this hearing was called and who it involves."

Colonel Roberts hauled his large tired frame from the chair and walked to the front of the gathering, explaining, "This hearing was called due to the accusation made by Miss Evelyn Hollins against Wild Hawk, a Cherokee from Lone Eagle's village. The accusation was that three nights ago around 10:30 p.m. this Cherokee man attempted to molest this young woman." The judge nodded for the Colonel to take a seat. Under current of mumbling could be heard throughout, followed by a loud rap.

"The proceedings are now under way," he eyed Wild Hawk over his glass' rim. "Now, are you guilty of these accusations made by Miss Hollins?"

Wild Hawk gazed steadily at this bigoted white Judge, knowing he had no feeling for the welfare of any Indian. He stood up, his large frame impressive in his fringed buckskin and in a calm deep voice spoke, "My name is Wild Hawk, son of Chief Lone Eagle. In this court, I think it would make little difference whether I am innocent or guilty. The truth is-the charges made against me by this white girl," he gazed at her steadily, "are false." He sat down while people murmured, astonished by his knowledge and use of the English tongue, including the judge whose mouth dropped open before he realized the barb thrown at him.

He sputtered, clearing his throat while rapping for silence. He continued to stare at this well versed Indian who also continued to hold his gaze. It was some what unnerving. "Is there anyone who wishes to speak for this man?" There probably wasn't, he thought; nevertheless, it was customary to ask. He shifted his gaze around the room while he took a drink of water. This place was getting stuffy and since the unwashed bodies had warmed up, well, the aroma was becoming disgusting. A couple of soldiers did his bidding and opened windows as John Brandon walked to the front of the room.

"I am John Brandon, Indian Consultant, who moved here from Washington this past January. I have known Wild Hawk since that time, finding in him," his gaze gathering the group to listen, they remembered this man who'd already shown his physical strength against a ruffian who had insulted his daughter two days ago, "integrity, honesty, and one who does not shirk responsibilities. He is at present studying to read and write the English language to represent his Cherokee clan in Washington." John looked at the young Indian, finding a "thank you" in the warmth of his dark gaze. "In this young Cherokee I have found qualities that many of us would love to own, but instead we tend to condemn." He turned and walked to his seat.

The judge squirmed, shifting papers on the desk wondering how many more of these back wooders were going to idolize this Indian. After all, he was only an Indian. Osborne again peered over his spectacles, scanning the room. "Anybody else have something to say about this man?" Jeb Hawkins stood, walking to the front. He stared at the group, demanding attention.

"I know many of you people, but I've known this man," he points to Wild Hawk," for many years, and a lot better. We hunted together, I've lived in his village, and I know if he says something is false, it's false. If he says it's true, it's true." He sat down, a mumbling spreading throughout.

Judge Osborne was miserable as he rapped loudly, reaching down with his left hand to untie his ill fitting shoes to ease his sore bunions. Surely there were no more to throw accolades at this Indian. He was already worn out with it, but before he could speak, the old scout Rusty Poole stood with a mouthful of disgusting tobacco cud.

"Jest thought I'd put ma word in 'n save ye askin', Judge," he grinned at Osborne. The crowd couldn't keep from laughing. "I'm a jest gonna'," he scratched his great shaggy head, "double everything Jeb Hawkins done said." He hauled off and let fly a stream of tobacco juice ringing the bell in a spittoon 10 ft. away. Rusty saluted Osborne. "Kin you do that, Judge?" He smiled before taking a seat.

"This court will come to order," Osborne roared, eyeing Rusty, obviously disliking the old man's outburst-so upset he forgot to slam the gavel. Rusty saluted him again, grinning, enjoying unruffling this important man while the crowd enjoyed it thoroughly.

"We will now hear from Miss Hollins," the judge had to get on with this or it could last through the night. He nodded toward the pretty young girl in blue, attempting a smile which was so unusual for him it looked more like a sneer.

Evelyn Hollins stood, taking her time enjoying the whispering, making sure she kept the innocence in her large blue eyes as she smiled at Osborne.

"Thank you, Your Honor," she strolled up near the judge, her blue taffeta swishing as she walked. "If you don't mind, I'd like to sit up here near you," she dimpled for him, "to talk about what happened is just so," she looked down shyly, "it's just so upsetting." She let her voice trail off.

"I understand, "he patted her shoulder while observing she did have the bluest eyes. "Oh! Bring a chair up here for the young lady," he ordered one of the soldiers standing near who complied immediately. Osborne was completely taken in by the beauty of this girl with the innocent face.

Evelyn sat staring wide-eyed at the group of people, making sure she had their undivided attention while she clutched her purse demurely, attempting to reveal her nervousness. "This is going to be very difficult for me," she looked down shyly, gripping her purse tightly, "to talk about what happened since it is so against my nature and beliefs." She looked at the judge for encouragement. He nodded. Several of the men mumbled, nodding. "Three nights ago," she kept her eyes downcast, "I couldn't sleep, the house was stuffy so I stepped out of the back door for a breath of air. It was cool, but I was so caught up in the beauty of the night," a weak smile touched her pretty mouth, "the full moon and all, I must have wandered a short distance from my home when suddenly this—this creature, "she hissed with venom and she pointed to Wild Hawk, "pounced on me like some sort of—animal." She covered her face with her hands. "Oh—h—h," she moaned, then uttered brokenly, "it's-too horrible to think about." She finally straightened, removing her hands, struggling to speak. "He put his mouth on mine-oh! It was—horrible. I pushed and pushed, beat his chest and kicked, but he was strong. When he pulled at my clothes," she shuddered as she opened her purse and took out a lace trimmed handkerchief, dabbing at her eyes, "and tried to get me on the ground, I turned my face enough to scream. That must have scared him for he turned loose and I kept screaming and screaming. Soon the soldiers were there." She dabbed at her teary eyes.

The court room became chaotic-men caught up under Evelyn Hollins' spell, yelling, "I say kill him before he tries it again-" "Hang the heathen." "Kill the bastard!"

The judge was thundering at the group, "Order in this court!" while rapping furiously with the gavel. "Escort Miss Hollins to her seat." A soldier stepped forward, taking her arm as she glanced at the Indian who had dared to ignore her advances. She was so pleased to see the anger in his dark flashing eyes and to think he'd probably die soon. She almost smiled, thinking she'd taught him the lesson of his life, for she did put on quite a performance. She sat meekly, staring at her lap while the judge bellowed at the group, finally getting them under control, threatening to toss them out if the noise didn't subside.

The hearing was finalized when two individuals spoke on behalf of Evelyn Hollins. One, a rather obese sergeant Mathias in a uniform he'd already outgrown, who pulled at a sparse beard covering his plump chin and went into detail on how this heathen, pointing to Wild Hawk, had viciously attacked him last summer at the fort for absolutely nothing.

"Pardon me, Your Honor," Jeb Hawkins jumped from his seat. "The sergeant's memory is failing him. Wild Hawk knocked Sergeant Mathias to the ground because he was beating on a small Indian boy, and it was the Indian boy who had done nothing." Jeb grinned at Mathias who was grinding his teeth. "Just thought I'd set the matter straight, Your Honor," he continued, smiling as he sat.

The judge stared at the big scout, not wanting a confrontation with him as a tall female stomped to the front.

"I'm Mrs. Gene Killingsworth, the wife of Major Killingsworth," the hawk nosed tall rawboned woman in navy stressed her impressive title. She peered from under a wide brimmed navy blue contraption doubling for a hat with a bright, plumed bird perched at the crown. The head gear swallowed her sharp pointed features as she expounded on this lovely girl's virtue, her innocence and honesty. "A beautiful girl like this should never have to be put through such a monstrous act, much less relive it. I say get on with the full punishment." She loped back to her seat, her thin mouth set in a firm line, emphasizing her fierce dislike for the Indian, any Indian.

The judge stood, worn out with the whole fracas, more than ready to finalize this mess by doling out the punishment. As he stepped from behind the desk, forgetting the untied shoe laces, he stepped on one and sprawled, glasses flying. Regardless of the seriousness of the situation, the spectacle was humorous to most. Glasses were retrieved, unbroken, by a soldier standing near as another attempted to assist the man scrambling from the floor. Osborne jerked his arm away, daring anyone to openly laugh as he tied his tight fitting shoes. He resented some dumb boy soldier acting as though he'z helpless. He resented this cramped court room with its sweaty unwashed body smell, and above all he resented having to be here!

"Ahem," he loudly cleared his throat as he pulled on the desk to stand, staring at the group over his wire rims before finally focusing on the Cherokee. It makes little difference, he thought, what happens to this Indian, no matter what two or three people think about him, he is still a heathen and they are all incapable of truthfulness, they are Godless savages. He rapped twice thinking it was time...

"Osborne," tall, slim Jackson Mayes jumped to his feet, "we're wore out with this damn messin' around," he spit, "everybody talkin! Ain't no use in takin' up no more time," he pointed his finger at the judge. "You heard the Hollins girl 'n it don't make no difference what that Indian said—we all know they don't know nothin' of the truth. Get on with it—we got the rope ready 'n you better do it right." He turned and eyed his companions as he sat.

The judge was livid. It took him a few seconds to control himself enough to speak, his Adam's apple jerking, thinking of this country jake ordering him around! "Take that man out!" he yelled to the soldiers while pointing to Mayes. Two armed men assisted the startled settler to his feet and through the room while he sputtered and verbally protested with stiff expletives. "What are you doing, you damn fools—what the hell's going on?" as they forcefully ushered him through the door.

"No one, but no one," his voice accelerated, "will again try to enlighten me on running a hearing - is that clear?" the judge thundered, glaring at the group, his face still a mottled red. "Now," he adjusted his spectacles lower on his nose, "I was just before pronouncing judgment when that voice-piece uttered his disgusting knowledge, as though it would make any difference!" He caught himself before he rambled on. The group was quiet, waiting— "Ahem," he loudly cleared his throat again. "I have followed these testimonies carefully," he walked back and forth, his hands clasped behind him, his gaze fastened on the ceiling, "and it is my opinion that this young girl," he stopped abruptly, pointing to Evelyn, "was a victim of a monstrous act, but one that she was fortunate didn't go further, thanks to her quick thinking." His arm pointed to the ceiling for emphasis. The judge fastened his lascivious gaze on the small luscious figure in blue, thinking how he would love being in that situation with this young beauty, rather than that filthy heathen. "Ahem!" he cleared his throat again, reluctantly pulling his mind and eyes from Evelyn Hollins bosom. "Therefore, it is my judgment that this Cherokee Indian is guilty and shall be hanged—" He didn't get to finish the statement due to the interruption of a strong soprano yelling

"No!" from the balcony as Janice Cooper grabbed Kate's hand for much needed support as they made their way down the stairs amid gavel rapping, loud talking, neck stretching and murmuring throughout the room. The two females made their way to the front despite the increasing turmoil, Janice holding onto her bravery through the girl beside her.

"What is the meaning of this, young lady, and who are you to cause such and interruption at this most important time?" He barked his anger at this uncalled for intrusion, his gray eyes cold as a winter's storm.

The young girl standing before him was obviously very nervous, but her honest countenance held the judge's stare while the many individuals in the room quieted in order to hear.

"I am Janice Cooper, daughter of Major Raymond Cooper," she pulled at the lace edging on her pocket, "and I've wanted to come down and speak throughout this hearing, but I've been so upset, torn between what I should and didn't want to do since I saw and heard what happened three nights ago," she shook her head, sighing. "I just couldn't think straight," she stared steadily at the judge through her pained expression.

He leaned closer, peering over his glasses. "You mean you actually saw and heard what happened between Miss Hollins and this Indian?" He peered intently at her.

"Yes, Your Honor—you see my bedroom window faces the Jackson residence and I had raised it because my bedroom was stuffy, and—" Janice jumped as a shrill voice penetrated.

"She's lying," the small blue clad figure exploded out of her chair, "Can't you see she's lying? Stop her, now!" Evelyn Hollings shrieked.

The judge wheeled. "Silence, and take your seat," he reprimanded sternly as Evelyn's blue eyes flashed daggers between him and the girl who was about to burst her bubble. "Continue, Miss Janice." He turned back to the girl in question.

She swallowed, taking a deep breath. "Well,—that night I guess it was around 10:00 or 10:30 -"

"Speak up, girl, so all can hear you!"

She nodded. "I couldn't sleep, the room was stuffy," she looked down, pulling at her handkerchief. "I had raised the window and was sitting there looking outside for there was a full moon when suddenly I saw a figure slipping around the back of the Jackson residence. I knew they were not home, neither were my parents. Soon I saw an Indian walking in front of the Jackson residence toward the gate where I believe four or five Indians were camped—anyway," she continued, twisting her handkerchief, "when he was between the residences I heard the one slipping at the back begin to moan as though in pain. This seemed to have caught the Indian's attention for he hesitated. As he did, the moaning became louder as though the individual were hurting. The Indian stopped than and started walking toward the sound—"

"That bitch is lying—stop her this minute!" Evelyn was out of her seat screaming—losing control, knowing she had been caught in her act!

"Sit down," the judge thundered, "you've had your say, and if you continue with these outbursts, Miss Evelyn, you'll force me to have you removed from this room." Evelyn's father soothed and coaxed his precious girl back into her seat.

Osborne wondered at these outbursts. Why was she afraid for this girl to speak if she were telling the truth, and such language from seemingly such an innocent! Could it be that things were not exactly as she had explained? He wondered as he nodded for Janice to continue.

"When Wild Hawk—by then I could see him clearly for he was even with my window," she looked down, so nervous she literally began shredding her handkerchief, "that's when I saw Evelyn Hollins throw herself at him, throwing her arms around his neck and kissing him—I watched as she attempted to pull him toward the back of the Jackson yard, but he pushed her away." Evelyn Hollins was by then making hissing sounds, her body jerking as Janice continued, "sternly telling her "no". He then turned his back on her and began walking away when Evelyn raised her voice, saying "You damn red heathen! How dare you turn away from me—I'll teach you a lesson you'll never forget!" Janice gazed at her torn handkerchief. "He kept walking away, and that's when Evelyn began screaming louder and louder and yelling "That savage tried to molest me—he tried to rape me!" By that time Evelyn had torn her own dress, scratched her self and mussed her own hair. The soldiers came while she screamed and while she kept repeating about his attempted rape."

Suddenly, Evelyn shot out of her chair, claws out ready to attack Janice as she hissed her venom, her face a mask of viciousness.

"Why you lying, mealy mouth, pale faced bitch—I'll claw your eyes out!" She rushed at this girl who was destroying her as Kate stepped between them, and from the judge's nod two soldiers grabbed either arm as they escorted the half crazed girl, followed by her solicitous father, crooning and soothing while mama sobbed into a lace handkerchief. As they came near Wild Hawk the girl shrieked with crazed eyes, trying her best to pull from the soldier's grasp, "How dare you spurn me you God Damn filthy red skin!" She leaned as close as she could to him and spit in his face. The whole courtroom was in chaotic turmoil as the Hollins girl, accompanied by her hovering parents, the mother chorusing her sobs, pitying herself, wondering what people would think.

"Hold up, Hollins," the judge fired at the retreating threesome. "The commander of this post will deliver just punishment to and for Evelyn Hollins, your daughter." He rapped, "Order! Order!" The judge bellowed, "If you don't stop this racket and settle down where I can finish this ridiculous fiasco, I'm going to slap a fine on each of you!" Some how this statement got through. He turned to where Janice and Kate had been seated.

"Miss Janice—just one question. Why did you wait so long to come forward and tell what happened?" He studied this girl, knowing what she had done was very difficult for her, while the crowd murmured and chorused their yeahs.

Janice steadily held his gaze. "Evelyn Hollin's parents and mine are good friends, and I hated to go against my people and hurt them. I was simply torn both ways, but I couldn't live with myself if I let that lie take an innocent man's life." She looked down at her lap before continuing. "She even tried to get me to go with her to Wild Hawk's village not too long ago." She heard people suck in breaths and murmur. "Today I was torn between both until you were ready to hang him—then, I simply couldn't let that happen."

She looked at Wild Hawk, trying to understand how Kate could care for him. He smiled, nodding a 'thank you.' He was a handsome man.

The judge turned again, clasping his hands behind him as he strolled forward. What a disgusting situation—here he was called into the middle of a so-called important hearing that turned out to be a nothing, a joke, lies made up from a little bitch who had the hots for an Indian. He'd like to kick her little ass all the way back to Knoxville, and wouldn't his cronies back there get a kick out of this! Well, he'd never let on what a fiasco it was. So what if he didn't hang an Indian! This one seems a cut above most of the rif raff jammed in here today, anyway. He glared at the filthy, illiterate misfits, crammed into this room and swore to himself never no never to be placed in another situation such as this if he had to plan a severe illness.

His eye brows reigned, eyes peering, over his spectacles as he barked, "This hearing is adjourned. I find the Cherokee Wild Hawk innocent of all charges. He rapped loudly. "This court is now dismissed!"

Many stared at the Indian wondering how any white girl could look at a red man much less touch one. The Hollins girl was crazy—that was all there was to it! The ruffians were totally disgruntled that they didn't get to hang a dirty savage. All in all it was one helluva day, they thought, as they glared and leered at the Indian while they shuffled on out the door, spittin' and cussin'.

Wild Hawk accompanied by Jeb stepped over to Kate and Janice. "I can never thank you enough, Miss Janice, for saving my life. I shall always be indebted to you."

Janice was touched by his sincerity and amazed at his use of the English language. "I guess you will have to thank Katherine, too," Janice touched her friend's arm, smiling, "she made me feel so so very guilty if I didn't go forward with the truth." She watched as the dark gaze shifted to her friend.

"Then I must thank Miss Katherine, too, for saving my life." Their gazes held, speaking many unsaid words, oblivious to others being in the room. The green eyes misted. She had been so tense for so long and now that it was over she was about to crumble. She grabbed her mouth, trying to cover her quivering chin.

"I'm afraid I'm going to cry," Jeb Hawkins thought he'd give most anything to have a woman look at him with such love in her eyes.

Kate dabbed at her eyes with a handkerchief as the Colonel and John moved beside them. Her father clasped Hawk's shoulder, smiling. "I always thought people had better things to do than eavesdrop, but we're all mighty grateful your curiosity got the best of you the other night, Miss Janice." He winked at her as her face flamed. All joined in laughter as Brandon's attempt at humor helped to ease some of the tenseness they all felt.

Both settlers and ruffians continued to stare at the Indian chief in all his finery and the younger Indian as they trailed out of the room, the ruffians definitely feeling they had been cheated.

"Wild Hawk, I never thought you were guilty," the Colonel steadily held the Indian's gaze.

"Thank you." Hawk was touched by the statement of this white man, shaking his hand and seeing the honesty in the man's eyes.

"John and I talked with Lone Eagle, and he agrees it would be wise for you two to remain here tonight. There were too many yahoos here today ready to participate in a hanging, and too many of those toughs left today feeling cheated out of it. That bunch will be liqoured up and ready to cause trouble in any direction." The Indian nodded his understanding.

Jeb cuffed his brother, smiling. "I suppose me and Rusty can put up with these two for one night!" As Hawk glanced at his friend, a tall lieutenant walked up, smiling at Katherine, his eyes warming as he moved to her side.

"Colonel, I hope I'm not interrupting, but I wanted to tell Miss Katherine that I'm waiting to escort her to her lodging or a stroll around the compound." Lt. Phillips smiled, his blue eyes fastened on Kate were like a dash of cold water thrown into Hawk's face. He knew she should find a white man, but it tore at him. Today had been more than enough, fearing he might lose his life because of a female's vicious lie and now—this. He turned for fear of revealing his emotions, walked to his father and Rusty. Sinking into a chair beside Lone Eagle, he rested his elbows on his knees, staring at the floor. The days of being cooped up, the tenseness of it all, especially today, had taken its toll—and then that lieutenant and the way he devoured Katherine with his eyes—Wild Hawk raised his head slowly, fastening his dark gaze on this girl who stirred such deep feeling within him. He must get out of this place, ride and feel the wind in his face. He again looked down, feeling her presence before she greeted Lone Eagle and Rusty warmly, then turning her attention to him.

"Wild Hawk."

He slowly lifted his head, holding her gaze with a countenance filled with sadness.

"I'd like to speak with you for a minute." He nodded slowly, rising following Kate to the nearest window where he leaned against the sill, staring outside at the crowd milling around, but actually seeing nothing.

"I just," she hesitated as she took in his handsome profile, fully aware of his clean manly scent, how near he had come to losing his life. "I just—ah—wanted to make sure you—ah—had the right study assignment to give to the others and I need to know when you plan to continue the lessons." Lord, what a mess she was making of this—omitting the things she really wanted to say.

He turned, looking steadily at this girl who was babbling on about studies which at this time didn't slightly interest him. He was aware of her flushed face, her nervousness, as she folded and unfolded a lacy handkerchief, her eyes looking as though they could spill over at any time.

"I will have the Cherokee at your home in two weeks to continue studies," he turned away from her, unable to watch her emotions and control himself.

I can't stand this, she thought. Again, he is so very cool to me—so factual, as though I mean nothing to him. How can I ever understand this man! "Oh! Why is it so difficult to talk with you sometimes? For the past two days I've wondered how I could go on if something happened to you!" She finally tore the lace from her handkerchief as Hawk watched, in turmoil, saying nothing until the tall lieutenant came into his vision and took a few steps toward them.

"Green Eyes, your lieutenant seems to be waiting for you," his eyes smoldered.

Upset that he had ignored her statement, she hissed, "He is not my lieutenant!"

Aware that he was hurting her, his jealousy pushed on, forbidding him to think clearly. "Maybe he would like to be!" his dark eyes snapped as green one flashed.

"Is that what you want?" she questioned raggedly, cramming the torn handkerchief into a pocket.

He couldn't answer, knowing it was the furtherest thing from what he wanted. All he had ever desired since first meeting this girl was to crush her in his arms and make her his, so life became more of a living hell since he could never have her. Maybe it would have been easier if he had been found guilty today.

She stared unbelieving, her eyes continuing to mist as she wondered why she had to love this man who ended up much of the time tormenting her! Well, so be it. She picked up her heart while uttering as she turned, "Maybe you are right!" Lifting her chin and pasting a frozen smile on her face, she walked to meet "her" lieutenant without a backward glance while smoldering features followed the two.

The handsome soldier smiled charmingly at Katherine, wanting to see some spark of encouragement in those lovely green eyes. "You know, Miss Katherine, some body down the line should have nicknamed you "Green Eyes"."

She spun around as though ready for combat, green eyes flashing fire as she hissed, "Don't you ever, ever call me that!" Her flushed face accentuated the fire in her eyes.

"Woah, girl!" He squeezed her arm as she pulled away and again began her trek. He frowned, wondering what the hell he had done to cause such an explosion as his long stride reached her. Staring at her, they walked through the soldiers and few remaining men who continued to grumble their discontent. "What's wrong with you? Here I pay you a compliment and you snap my head off!" He felt she owed him some explanation. He certainly wasn't used to females waging war on him! He stopped her again placing his hand on her forehead, "Are you sick?"

She looked at him, moving his hand away, ashamed of her fiery actions. A slight smile tugged at the corner of her mouth as she shook her head. "No, and I'm sorry for the outburst. Please forgive me."

"I'll think about it," his blue eyes twinkled as the two strolled on around the compound.

In explanation, she added, "Guess my lack of sleep and all of this turmoil for the last few days has had its effect." They walked on in silence amid stares from soldiers who wished they had been lucky enough to escort this auburn haired female around.

He couldn't stand this somber atmosphere any longer. He was a fun loving guy who wanted to know this very different girl, who had somehow taken over his thoughts of late.

"Katherine Brandon, there's a bench over there," he nodded toward one off the beaten path. She turned quickly toward him, intending to put him in his place for being so—so—brazen, but his pleading blue eyes were so like a little boy's, she could only smile which turned his bleak day to sunshine. He took her arm, guiding her toward the beckoning bench. As Kate watched the dashing handsome man by her side, her mind could only remember a brooding dark gaze as he spoke of "her lieutenant."

Chapter 19

The cold November morn breathed her chilly breath on the two scouts and Indians as they left the fort for Lone Eagle's village. Mounts pranced and cavorted to the morning chill, ready to run after having been cooped up with no exercise. The jibes of Rusty and the Eagle kept Jeb in total amusement. Morning mists clung tenaciously to blue mountain peaks and seemed reluctant to loosen fingers to the morning's brightness as the sun squinted her brilliance over the frosty countryside, creating a sheer blanket of sparkling wonderment.

Jeb sighed, feeling tuned with God's creation, glad to be leaving the man made structure, the total chaos of the last few days, and feeling very thankful that his Indian brother was alive and free. He studied the dark brooding countenance of this brother, realizing that his friend who should be happy to be alive, hadn't spoken a word. He didn't seem to be aware of anything. This sadness shouldn't belong to one who had just been given his life and freedom. What in hell was wrong? What else—? It had to be Katherine Brandon.

"Hey, you big brooding, black eyed moose!" Jeb pranced his big gelding beside Night Wind, who sidestepped his own rhythm. "Yore horse is gonna' step on yore chin if you don't git it off'n the ground." Jeb crinkled a half smile at this solemn friend. "Aw jest had the notion you'd sorta' be a might pleased seein' as yore ridin' free today!" Jeb ignored Hawk, who turned dark penetrating eyes his way. The big scout busied himself securing a tobacco plug from his pocket and plopping it into his mouth.

"Free—you say? Pleased?—That I am allowed to ride _my_ horse and return to _my_ village after some little white bitch has had my life suspended in evil turmoil for three days?" Hawk's black eyes snapped his anger, "—so—my brother, what you had in mind was all wrong. Free you say?" he smirked, "Be sure and explain the meaning of that word to an Indian!"

Jeb stared at this man he'd known most of his life and somehow felt the hurt that engulfed his friend.

"And," the black eyes snapped, "chewing tobacco is a disgusting habit!"

"Ain't it—though!" Jeb guffawed and spit as Hawk kneed his stallion into a run, leaving the three behind—feeling the much needed wind in his face and seeking time to be alone, to meditate, and to talk with his God, his Yawa.

Even though Andrew Jackson had been elected the big white father during the past week, causing this village of Cherokee along with many other tribes to be skeptical, some downright frightened about their future, the peacefulness of Lone Eagle's village seemed to ease the tensions of the past few days for the three who entered. The warmth and love revealed here added an extra touch to dispel the past turmoil at the fort.

Spotted Horse stepped forward. "Is our brother Hawk not with you?" Concern was etched on his dark countenance as he sought a response from his chief.

"No," the chief touched this faithful brave and friend on the shoulder, as a chubby Little Cub broke from his nearby mother's handclasp to grab Spotted Horse's leg, jerking and pulling the fringe. With his little chin quivering, the small brave squinted up at his big chief, struggling to ask, "Hawk? Hawk?"

"Hawk is fine, he'll be here later," Eagle leaned down, almost toppling from his horse, and patted Cub's head, clearing his throat feeling the emotion of this small boy as sunshine poured into the little face.

The horses pranced on through the village amid smiling faces, cheers, and questions while Cub unfastened himself from the brave's leg, scampering to his father who scooped him up, listening attentively as his son gathered each jaw firmly to focus eye contact while nodding vigorously amid strong laments of "Hawk—good—fine!" The father, smiling, nuzzled the tempting plump neck before his armful of bravery scooted to the ground. He looked around, not too sure a warrior such as himself should reveal such a display of affection before others.

Dancing Eyes' slamming heartbeat settled to an even rhythm after hearing that her Indian was all right, but—where was he? Her black eyes shot in all direction—he was nowhere! Could he be with that pale eyed Brandon she-dog again? She hissed under her breath. Her thoughts were interrupted as she listened to Old Crone's broken English with mixed Cherokee, jabbering a questionnaire at the chief and his reply.

"Hawk is fine—as I said before—he needed to be alone—and he will return here when he is ready." He waved the old woman toward his old friend. "Maybe Rusty Poole can explain better," he said as he kneed his roan toward his lodge, casting Rusty a backward twinkle as the old wrinkled crone zoomed in to waylay Rusty with a jerk on his horse's bridle.

"May-be Russey tell," she crinkled, her slit-eyed toothless grin waiting for the old scouts attention, which was slow in coming due to his mute cussing of the chief accompanied by a shaking fist.

"Ain't a thang ah kin tell ya thet ya' ain't already heered—now, if'n ye'll kindly unhitch them fingers offa' ma' bridle." She didn't understand half that he said, but she liked this little stub of a man with them sky eyes, and she cackled madly, sticking out her scrawny chest and attempting to push up her sagging, shriveled breasts while completing her flirtatious act by swishing her long stringy gray hair. Braves hooted and maidens giggled at the ridiculous display of the old woman, and thoroughly enjoyed the total discomfort of the old scout as they glanced at their chief whose body shook with quiet laughter.

"The dad-blamed, dog-nabbed old wrinkled she dog," Rusty muttered with face aflame while the braves hooted even louder at his misery. "Jest shet yore dad-burned mouths—you—you young coyotes," he yelled at the boisterous group while wheeling his horse to catch old chief Moose Dung, who had caused this whole fracas anyhow. Wail till ah give the mighty Moose a piece 'uv ma mind!—Siccing that old witch on me!

Dancing Eyes enjoyed seeing old crone whom she detested make a fool of herself, and the little old ugly scout's discomfort suited her greatly—he had no business even being here. Hearing that Wild Hawk was safe and alone made her heart warm. She would see him soon.

The Clip clop of shod hooves, creaking of leather, mingled with jingling harnesses dispelled the quietness as the small patrol of blue clad soldiers wormed its way around the wooded area near Lone Eagles' Indian territory. A tall lieutenant in charge signaled to halt. Spurring his horse to the leader's side, a sergeant waited a command, saluting.

"Yes, Sir."

"Have the men set up camp here, Sgt. Fraser," the leader commanded sharply, while glancing around the area, viewing the dense forest.

"Sir?" the sergeant questioned, not believing what he had heard. "Not disputin' yore word, Sir, but didn't you say this place is somewhat near some Indian village?" He shifted his bulk in the hard saddle, feeling he had grown calluses on his behind. The lieutenant glared at him while soldiers glanced at each other, wondering what the hell was goin' on with this fool placin' a campsite next to Indians.

"There is a village four or five miles northwest of here, but they are peaceful. I know them." Lieutenant Anderson's smoldering glance told the Sergeant what he thought of noncoms questioning their superiors. "—and sergeant, I'm not accustomed to having my decisions questioned—do you understand?" the lieutenant thundered.

"Yes, Sir," Sergeant Fraser answered, saluting as he wheeled his horse while barking orders to the soldiers who hastened to do the lieutenant's bidding, but still uneasy about being stuck in the lap of a bunch of savages. They didn't like this shave tail who they were forced to accompany on this patrol. Charlie Foley, a big ruddy-skinned private echoed their sentiments quietly to his longtime buddy.

"Les, there be somethin' wrong with this high 'n mighty lieutenant," he quickly glanced around making sure the guy in discussion wasn't in hearing distance. "He ain't been around that long, but even so's he thinks he's some kind 'uv big shot 'n all we got to do is jump when he opens his mouth. Aw kin understand our fort needs them arms 'n ammunition from this post that's supposed to close down, but they's some special reason behind him stoppin' here to camp close to savages." He shook his head as he placed extra firewood on a struggling flame. Les, a slightly built pimply-faced private glanced quickly at the lieutenant before studying the dense wooded area to their left. "Makes me plum jumpy, wondering whut could be skulking in them trees." He grabbed another stick to encourage the meager flame.

"Listen up." All eyes focused on the tall leader while he strutted around, spouting additional orders. "We rest here for a couple of days. There's a stream just inside that line of trees and I'm sure plenty of game if you could stir yourselves enough to bring some in. Continue with your work, men, while I scout around the area." He strode toward the trees as one lanky bearded corporal lolled back on an elbow, mocking him. "Continue your work, men, be sure to jump and squat when I say the word!" He released his frustration as he slammed a large stick across the compound. "Of all the damn fools in uniform 'n we had to end up with the biggest son of a bitch of all. Suit me just fine if one 'uv them red heathens busted his big ass with a flamin' arrow." He slapped his leg, guffawing as he visualized Anderson flying through the forest, screamin' with a flaming arrow stuck in his back end. The imaginary scene came alive to all as they joined in the laughter.

Keith Anderson hadn't been able to get the beautiful Dancing Eyes out of his mind since he had volunteered for this patrol duty, knowing his travel would be near Lone Eagle's village. Not that he was overjoyed to lead a bunch of misfits across country. God, but it had been worse than he had anticipated with the crude illiterates, their garbled broken English and their emission of disgusting body odors. Four weeks of this and his butt had to be laced with calluses. Each miserable day, though, brought him closer to the dark sensuous Cherokee maiden, and now, by God, he'd have her for his, one way or the other. He couldn't remember when some female had caused this much heated excitement to run through his veins. He crept on through trees and brush, keenly alert to any sign of Indians until he reached the river, where to his utter disbelief, two Cherokee youth were trying to hand fish. Neither was aware of his presence until the toe of his boot caught on a root, causing a stone to tumble down the bank near them. Both Indians froze in action, with fear etched on each countenance as the two quickly scrambled up the bank, attempting to run, but Keith was faster. He latched onto one of the two little mites, jerking him up as black eyes snapped in angry fear and the small brave squirmed and fought for his freedom, but to no avail. Keith roughly shook him. "Stop it—speak White tongue?" he asked. The Indian glared at him. "Look, I'm not going to harm you!" The black gaze flickered with some of the fear subsiding, telling the lieutenant this one did understand English. "Listen, I only want you to take a message to Dancing Eyes—do you know her?"

The black eyes stared at the man in uniform, afraid not to answer. He nodded, while the soldier continued holding him firmly.

"Tell her—to meet me at the falls," Keith pointed to the cascading water rushing into the river as the little Cherokee followed his hand movement, "in one moon as sun begins to sink. You will tell her—do you understand?" The big man squeezed the boy's shoulders.

The small Indian assessed the tall soldier with a dark penetrating gaze, wondering how he knew a Cherokee maiden—seeing in this man a nice face to look upon, but cold eyes. Little Gopher nodded, thinking it was the only way to free himself. Only then did Anderson loosen his hold and watch the little nit take to his heels, scampering through the brush, his long black hair flying as the small buckskin clad figure blended into the forest.

Dancing Eyes couldn't figure out who the soldier was who sent word to her. At first she thought Little Gopher was teasing her, but his pleading sincerity finally convinced her. Oh! She hoped Brown Wren and Smiling Girl could keep Swift Antelope occupied to give her time to slip away. He was becoming more and more demanding of her and always seemed to be around. She knew he cared for her, but he was a violent man filled with hate and jealousy of Wild Hawk.

She hadn't planned to meet the soldier, she didn't even know any soldier, only one who had moved away, but curiosity got the better of her. At least, she figured, she'd slip near enough to see who he was, then leave if she didn't wish to meet him. She smiled, covering her head and shoulders with an old faded shawl for disguise before slipping quietly behind the lodges when the afternoon sun began its descent for its evening rest. She kept her head down to avoid recognition, but no one seemed to be around at this hour.

The underbrush clawed at her doeskin tunic as she continued to creep stealthily through the forest, knowing she was nearing the rendezvous place. Soon the splash of the falls could be detected as it rushed over boulders, eagerly spewing its froth into the river below that swallowed it and snaked its way through the mountain valley.

Her heart thumped as she again spotted the handsome lieutenant she remembered from the fort visit. She peered around the trunk of a large elm, watching the well built man in the blue uniform who tossed stones into the water. She smiled, knowing she would meet this handsome one who stirred her blood, and who could make others jealous.

She stepped from her hiding place, removing her shawl as she slowly and sensuously strolled, the long fringe of her garment accompanying her movement toward Keith Anderson. The soldier, sensing a presence, turned to witness the breath taking beauty of the dark eyed, dark-skinned maiden who so seductively moved toward him, and who had occupied his thoughts so frequently. God, she was beautiful, he thought. Hardly able to breathe, he took a step toward her, charming her with his smile. She returned it, her eyes defining her name.

"Hello," his gaze caressed her face and traveled over her body before he pulled her to him, sinking into those dancing eyes. Somehow words were not necessary and she didn't seem to mind as he bent his head and captured her lips in a probing kiss, and to his astonishment she returned it as her arms crawled around his neck, leaving him tingling with yearning excitement.

"Dancing Eyes," he whispered huskily, drinking in her beauty.

"Yes," she nodded, smiling as she stared back at him, complimented by the smolder revealed in his hazel eyes.

"I have thought of nothing but you for so—long, and wanting you for so long," he searched her countenance seriously, wondering if she could understand him.

"Lootanan' like Dancing Eyes?" she teased him.

"Oh! Yes—yes," he nodded. "I want to make love to Dancing Eyes. I want her to be mine," he pointed to his chest. "Do you," pointing to her, "like lootanan'?

"Dancing Eyes can—no be yours. She her-selves'," pointing to self, her black eyes sparkling.

He nodded, smiling, "Please," his sincerity showed in his handsome face, as his hazel eyes pleaded.

She smiled, nodding, her eyes caressing him as she slowly took his hand. "Come." She led him a short distance from the falls to a secluded place near the old elms. Before she could sit he unbuttoned his jacket, placing it on the ground for her, thinking he certainly wouldn't need its warmth. He sank to the ground beside her, observing her beauty. Most females would lead a guy on, but then play coy, hard to get—but not this one; she was straight out. They wanted each other and there was no play acting here. He gently caressed her face, letting his fingers trail down her neck before slowly easing her back on the ground as he gently kissed her, brushing her lips with his before probing and plundering her mouth while exploring the curves of her body. She moaned in response as she pulled him closer, feeling on fire for this handsome white man.

Caught up in their love making and each other, they were unaware of anything or anyone else until and explosive figure jumped into their midst yelling, "Ai—e—e!" jerking the soldier from the girl and slamming a fist into his face before the lieutenant knew what was happening. The buckskin figure jumped him again, slamming fists into his face rapidly. The girl screamed in Cherokee, "No, Swift Antelope, stop it—stop it, you'll kill him!"

Keith vaguely heard her—he'd had the breath knocked out of him, he was bleeding profusely from the nose and a gash across the eyes which distorted his vision while this demon had him pinned totally helpless. As Anderson blinked the blood from his eyes, Dancing Eyes struggled with his captor who flung her off as he would a fly. He then drew a wicked looking knife that matched his savage countenance which was filled with hate and cruelty. His black eyes were wild as he hissed, "White—Dog—this day you—die!" With a cruel smirk he continued, "Sing your death chant, Dog," The knife was poised to plunge into the soldiers heart, the girl screamed, "NO!" while a brown clad figure grasped the attacker's wrist, knocking the knife away and throwing the attacker to the ground.

Wild Hawk furiously lashed out at Swift Antelope in Cherokee. "Are you insane? Don't you know if you killed a white - a soldier - Lone Eagle would be blamed. It'd give them the excuse they want to destroy the village." Hawk leaned down to help Antelope up, who jerked away, scrambling up on his own, his eyes filled with fiery hate.

"Don't you tell this brave what to do or not do and never put your hand on Antelope again. You, waiting to be big leader," he spat, "are a white lover. Stay away from me and stay away from Dancing Eyes," he wheeled around, glaring at the white soldier who had raised himself to his elbow, his face a puffy, bloodied mess. "White Dog, you come near Dancing Eyes again, Antelope kill you." He jerked the girl around, dragging her toward the forest.

Dancing Eyes turned frightened eyes, pleading with Hawk as he yelled, "Swift Antelope, if you harm that maiden in any way, I will put a hand on you, and plenty hard." Antelope ignored the comment while Hawk zoomed in on the lieutenant, his eyes blazing. "What are you doing here, Anderson? I am aware of what you were doing with Dancing Eyes, but what are you doing in this area?" Jeb watched and listened from a nearby shadow, seething over what this bastard, this snake had done to Priscilla, and what he had instigated against the Cherokee.

The swollen mouth interfered with Keith's speaking clearly. "I'm leading a patrol to the fort here for arms and ammunition to transfer back to the Arkansas."

"Where is the patrol?"

"Four or five miles east."

Hawk stooped down, glaring at this man who should be destroyed, but knowing this was not the time, for it would only bring additional suffering to Lone Eagle and the Cherokee. "And you thought you'd park them there, near Lone Eagle's village, so you could have a little fun with Dancing Eyes—after all, she is only an Indian, right?" The brave was having difficulty containing his anger, remembering what this no-good had done to the three young braves. Knowing he couldn't avenge their deaths—yet.

"Right," Keith sullenly echoed, "but it's not what is seems—we both felt something special for each other." He wiped his bloodied mouth with his shirt tail.

Hawk wasn't interested in anything this man had to say. "Listen, Anderson, and listen carefully—don't you *ever* bring your worthless hide near this village again—for if you do I will personally see that you never leave. I did not save your hide today for you, I did it for my chief. Now you take your sorry ass back where you came from—Now!" He tossed the soldier's jacket in his face.

The two friends watched as Keith Anderson struggled to stand and slowly drag himself off into the trees toward his patrol.

"Let us set up camp away from the roar of the falls. I need to talk to you." Jeb ambled on into the wooded area, securing stones, sticks and heavier wood for a fire. The task completed, Hawk joined his friend, easing his long frame to the ground while gazing into the meager flame that licked the dried wood. His mind reeled with the day's happening. How he had wanted to kill the traitorous white eyes, but could not harm his chief, nor could he allow Antelope to take the life. Swift Antelope had turned on him, he pondered—he knew they had never been close, but never had he guessed the depth of this Cherokee's feeling toward him. Was it jealousy over Dancing Eyes? Why, he had never pursued her or wanted to—pretty, yes, but vicious, and one who would take up with any man who appealed to her.

Jeb broke into Hawk's thoughts as he tossed another stick on the meager flame. "I know your feeling—I could have killed the worthless Dog myself. To add to his accomplishments, the s.o.b got Priscilla Brandon with child, promised to marry her after returning from a patrol which didn't exist—instead, he skipped the country, deserting her. Sorry, I got carried away." He looked down, poking the fire, readying the spit for the freshly cleaned rabbit. Hawk watched the emotions play on the big scout's countenance, knowing there was more.

After placing their supper over the fire, Jeb looked up, seriously gazing at his friend. "I'm going to marry Priscilla if she'll have me. I want to give that babe a name and I want you to stand up with me at the ceremony as my best man."

"Thank you," Hawk murmured, struggling with emotion, "I shall be honored."

"It's complicated, my friend," the scout stared into the night, "I love her—I have since I first laid eyes on her, but," he chuckled mirthlessly, "she thinks she still cares for that no good snake Anderson." He stood, slamming a heavy stick to the ground.

"Then my brother will just have to change her mind—yes?" Hawk flashed a smile as his friend echoed.

"Yes."

And, the Cherokee thought, you will need all Blessings you can get with that one who I don't believe ever had thoughts for anyone but herself.

"What about you and Kate, my friend?" Jeb questioned in concern.

The Indian gazed into the flame while murmuring, "Hawk has no future."

Chapter 20

Jeb approached the Brandon spread on a cold November morn while frosty crystals still blanketed the countryside, giving the entire area an ethereal quality. He was nervous, actually sweating as he secured his horse. How in the world would he get through the day? —A proposal, talking to parents? Hell, he'd been over the whole thing a thousand times in his mind, but it did no good. He was still like a bungling embarrassed school boy!

At the knock, Kate opened the door. "Jeb, what a nice surprise—come in—it's good to see you." She smiled a welcome after checking and hoping that there might be someone else with him, as the scout made his way to the inviting fireplace where a cheery blaze dispelled the morning chill. "Have a seat and let me take your coat and hat. Did you want to see my father?"

Handing her the fur lined jacket, he sank onto the nearest straight backed chair, keeping his leather hat, twirling it round and round.

"Uh!—no, not now. I'd like to speak with Priscilla, if you'd call her—uh, please."

"Sure, I'll get her." Kate left, smothering a smile at Jeb's nervousness.

"Oh! Jeb, thought I heard somebody talking with Katherine—good to see you." John shook his hand, then seated himself across from the scout, filling his pipe. "How have you been?"

"Fine—oh—uh—just fine!" Jeb was now sitting on the edge of his chair as he speeded up his hat twirling, thinking as Jess bounded through the door, my God, do I have to deal with the whole herd!

Legend of the Whispering Wind

"Jeb, you ain't visited us in a coon's age!" The imp squinted a grin while she sprawled in front of the fire. The scout barely managed a half smile as he cussed to himself.

Mary entered, wiping her hands on a dish towel. "Why, hello, Jeb," she smiled, "It's good to see you. How 'bout a cup of coffee?"

"Thank you, but uh no thank you." Damn, they were all staring at him as he wiped his sweaty face with his sleeve.

"Hey, Jeb," Tim made his debut along with the others, stuffing the last of a buttered biscuit into a mouth that was already too full, before flinging himself down by Jess.

Kate returned, halting abruptly as she assessed the situation before stalking into the midst. She eyed each one. "Are you by any chance having some sort of meeting?" They looked at each other. "I can't believe this," she continued, "Jeb came here to talk with Priscilla and you gather around him like chicks around a mother hen!"

Jeb could have kissed her as Mary glanced at John, both embarrassed by their stupidity. John muttered, standing, "Sorry, Jeb, didn't mean to close in on you—let's go, Tim, Jessica." Papa snapped his fingers.

"You all can go on—he can talk to her with me here, I don't mind," Jess squinted a grin at Jeb.

"Move—now!" Papa meant it, which more than encouraged the minx to hustle.

Kate sank onto the couch, sighing, "I'm sorry, Jeb—guess they just consider you one of the family."

"I know." After several seconds, he jumped up. "Damn it, what's keeping her?" He took a few steps toward the hall door as Prissy slowly crept into the room. Jeb was shocked at her appearance as his eyes roamed over her pale face, etched with dark circled eyes and the once lovely lady didn't fill out the blue cotton dress. He thought women gained weight when they carried a child, but this one must have dropped ten to fifteen pounds. His heart went out to this girl who needed help.

Sinking onto the couch, she murmured, "Hi, Jeb—what brings the scout out to the back woods?" Prissy's eyes were dull, he noticed, lacking the sparkle that had been so much a part of her beauty. He watched as her hands nervously played with the folds in her skirt, creasing and uncreasing.

Neither seemed aware when Kate left the room.

"Hello, Priscilla—I'm no good at speakin'—I've thought 'uv what I'd say to you fer hours 'n it ain't done no good." He stared at his hat as he carefully placed it on the table. He looked at the girl who was waiting for him to continue. The warmth and seriousness in his gaze should have spoken many words.

"I've come here to ask you to marry me." This seemed to give her eyes some life and her hands stopped their action as he continued, lowering his voice to a whisper, "I know you're with child, and I'd like to give the babe a name."

Prissy's mouth dropped open while she stared at the big man sitting across from her, dumbfounded. Who in the world would want to marry somebody who was carrying another man's child? She stared openly, not believing this.

"But why, Jeb? I don't understand—," she was breathless.

"It's simple," he looked into her eyes, never having been as serious, "I love you—since the first time I seen you." He stood, leaning against the mantle, staring into the fire.

"Jeb," she looked at her hands, "you are a very special friend, but I don't love you."

He walked over to her, and sat beside her, taking her hand. "You will, Priscilla, in time." She looked deeply into the serious blue eyes. She began her folding and unfolding of her skirt again.

"But, Jeb, how could you want to marry someone who carries another's child?"

"Well, a body don't turn love on and off—I care for you no matter what, and I'd like to care for the babe as my own."

Her dark eyes teared as she looked at this big man who warmed her heart with the love shining in his eyes. She had never known a man like this.

"Do your parents know about your condition?" He kept his voice down.

"No—I—I can't tell them—oh! Jeb," she stood, taking a few steps, "it's been so horrible." She turned, brushing her hair back, her eyes seeking his. "I've wanted to destroy the baby or myself." Her chin began to quiver while a tear slipped down her cheek.

He rushed to her, enfolding her in his strong arms, pressing her head against his shoulder, offering the strength she needed.

"Don't you ever utter such foolish statements again!" He rubbed her back as she sniffed, nodding.

"—and I can thank my thoughtful sister for sharing this blessed event with you!" she murmured.

"Don't come down on Kate, Priscilla. She had to talk to somebody and she knew I cared—and now we're telling your parents."

She jerked her head up. "No—oh! No—" her eyes filled with terror as she pushed against him, ready for flight, "Let me go!"

"No, Priscilla," holding her arms firmly, "You are telling them now. You can't keep hiding and destroying your health! You are telling them while I'm here."

Frantically, she pounded his chest. "No—no—I can't—I won't—damn you!" She began to sob. He called the parents to join them. As the two entered the room, casting glances at each other, wondering what this was all about, Jeb piled another log on the fire before joining the daughter on the couch. Both parents observed their daughter's flushed face and red eyes as Jeb took her hand.

"Priscilla has something to share with you," Jeb murmured while he gazed at the girl, squeezing her hand for support.

She raised her head, looking from one parent to the other, frantically searching each countenance as tears streamed down her face while she sobbed, "I'm pregnant." Her mother's mouth dropped open while she struggled to breathe.

"Why, you low down bastard!" John exploded out of his chair, grabbing Jeb by the collar, jerking him up and slamming a fist into his face. Jeb, table and lamp crashed to the floor before the others knew what was happening.

"No—John!" Mary screamed, jumping up as Prissy yelled, "Papa—no! Jeb didn't do it—" She grabbed her father's arm, yelling again, "Jeb didn't do it!" She finally broke into his anger as John looked at his daughter then the man on the floor, who rubbed his jaw. Finally understanding, and shocked at what he had done, he reached to help the scout up. "My God, Jeb, I'm sorry!"

Jeb smiled, working his jaw as he was assisted from the floor. "You throw quite a punch, John Brandon."

John jerked Prissy's arm. "It was that low down cur, Keith Anderson, wasn't it?" She nodded. He turned, running his hand through his hair as he strode to the fireplace, leaning against the mantle while the scout, with Prissy's help, straightened furniture and picked up shattered glass.

Glancing at her mother as she sat down, Prissy wanted to scream at her to say something, anything would be better than the sitting and staring into space as though she weren't here. My God! Other people had had babies when they weren't married—well, somewhere—she just knew it! And besides it wasn't totally hopeless—Jeb wanted to be its father.

Mary stared at nothing, remembering the morning sicknesses, the pallid features, the fainting, but she had refused to face any of it. She had told herself many times—not my daughter! But now they would all face it. She couldn't believe a daughter of hers would— she knew she should say something, but she couldn't. It was as though the breath had been totally knocked out of her. She glanced at this daughter who had everything but sense and watched Priscilla's hands as they kept a steady rhythm plucking and smoothing, plucking and smoothing a ruffle on her blue skirt. Why, the girl was a wreck! Some pity went out from the mother.

John shattered the silence. "Did Anderson know you were pregnant," Mary flinched at the word, "when he transferred?"

"Yes—Sir," Priscilla, staring at her hands, murmured meekly.

"You mean," his voice thundered as he wheeled around to face them, "he knew you carried his child and he left you?" He did not believe any human being could stoop so low.

"Yes—" she kept her eyes glued to her hands.

Jess screeched to a halt inside the door, totally out of breath. With hair flying and cheeks flushed she demanded, "What happened?" Prissy could have kissed the sweaty little imp for interrupting. "We heard yelling, then a crash—thought Stink Bear had come back and Mama wuz whuppin' up on him." She glared at each one, daring it to be true.

"Yeah," Tim panted, finally dragging through the door holding his side, since sprinting wasn't his best feat, "but what's goin' on?" he puffed.

"Nothing to be disturbed about," Papa couldn't think right off hand of an appropriate lie.

"Then why does Mama look like she'z seen a ghost?" Jess questioned.

"Oh! Don't be ridiculous," Mary finally came to and uttered something appropriate while pasting a smile across her face. A mother had to protect her young offspring. "Ha—Jeb caught his toe on the rug and landed into the table and lamp." She couldn't believe her glib lying tongue.

"Well! That ain't nothin' to be yellin' about," Jess retorted.

"You're right—but there is one thing I might yell about if I don't find that first stable cleaned up completely. You two left that job unfinished," Papa inserted.

"Stable?" Tim questioned. If there was anything he hated to do—he wished he'd never come in here in the first place. He eased toward the door.

"Stable?" Jess echoed, "I did my part."

John asked Tim, "And I suppose you did your part, too?"

"Oh! Yes Sir! I sure did!" The boy faced his father, expectantly.

"Well," Papa placed a hand on each shoulder, "since I am unable to figure out who the unfinished part belongs to, I'm sure you'll both be glad to finish the unfinished part together." He smiled as Tim sucked in his breath. Papa hauled out his pocket watch, "I'll check it in one hour."

"You silly nosy thing! This is what we get for comin' in here to see what happened," Tim hissed while giving Jess a shove as they reached the door.

"You lay a hand on me again, Fat Boy, and I'll flatten you!" Jess's best lady like manners were showing through again.

John waited until the two complainers slammed the back door in protest before turning to Priscilla. "Is there anything else you wish to share with us?" Was there a hint of mockery in his question? He studied this daughter who seemed at the moment rather pitiful. The fiery vitality that had been so much a part of her lovely countenance was no longer there. No one could have told this girl anything that would have lessened Anderson in her eyes. He had tried the night of the gathering when the lieutenant had escorted her outside, but John saw now it had made no impression on her. Do we dare to think maybe she has learned some lesson from her naiveté, her self-centered gullibility where she pays such a costly price?

Priscilla struggled with her emotions which seemed of late uncontrollable so much of the time she cried and cried. Jeb took Prissy's hand for encouragement, but after several moments of silence, both parents staring, he realized she was incapable of speaking.

"Sir—Mrs. Brandon—guess you're wonderin' what I'm a doin' here—just how I fit into any of this. Well," he smiled at Prissy, revealing his love, "uh! I want to marry Priscilla—I'd like to give the babe a name." He looked from mother to father who stared at him as though he'd suddenly grown horns. Finally, John found himself enough to speak, not understanding why any man would want Priscilla now.

"You really don't have to do this, Jeb. I realize you are trying to help out." He ran his hand through his hair.

"No, it ain't that a'tall—you see," he gazed at Prissy's bowed head, continuing to hold her hand, "I know I ain't much of a pick fer a gal, bein' a back woods scout 'n all, but from the first time I laid eyes on Priscilla I loved her and now I want to marry her, regardless of whose child she carries. I give you my word, I'll raise the babe as my own." The parents were both choked with emotion over the scout's proposal. they felt the uncomfortable situation for him, feeling their daughter didn't deserve such honesty and goodness in a man and the love that he held for her. They worried, too, for the uncertain and traumatic future facing this man with

Priscilla, fearing that their self-centered daughter could not nor would not change.

With the safety of Jeb's strength to lean on, Prissy smiled for the first time in ages, inserting, "Since it's my future you're deciding, I believe I should have a little say so in it." Tears had abated as she flashed her dark eyes at each of them, then back to the man sitting beside her.

"Jeb Hawkins, I accept your marriage proposal." She thought, if he just weren't so crude with all that broken English, but he is a good man and he's not too bad looking if he'd scrape the hair from his face and God knows, it's a way out for me.

Jeb leaned over and kissed her cheek as John bounded out of his chair, grabbing the scout's arm while shaking his hand. With emotion, he uttered, "I can't think of anyone I'd rather have for a son-in-law."

"Thank you." Jeb was touched with the emotion shown here as Mary placed a hand on his shoulder, smiling and murmuring, "John offered my sentiments exactly, Jeb."

"Well! Let's celebrate with a—a cup of coffee or something!" John was explosive as he rushed to the door, bellowing for Katherine, Jessica and Tim.

Laughter, hugs and seemingly happiness took the place of the previous morose atmosphere; however, the parents didn't excuse their daughter's immorality, but at the moment the upcoming nuptials should take precedence. Kate was overjoyed to see her sister smiling again and to hear the news, as Jess followed by Tim burst into the room.

She puffed, "What ever it is—we didn't do it!" Jessica boomed with Tim's accentuated head shake.

John gathered them into the group jovially explaining, "It's nothing like that—guess what?" They shook their heads dumbfounded at his happiness. "Priscilla and Jeb are getting married!" All were smiling at this happy announcement.

"Married?" Jesse's mouth flew open.

"How come?" Tim's freckled face searched the big scout's countenance, disbelieving any one in his right mind would tie up with Priscilla.

"Yeah—," Jess added, eyeing the couple intently, "cause Prissy was crazy over that lieutenant who left her—why, he'z the one she ran after all the time!" She shook her head, not understanding. Smiles faded into frowns as everyone stared at the mouthpiece who had never ever learned when to keep quiet.

Four days before the big event for Priscilla and Jeb, which was to be held at the Brandon household, everyone seemed to be in a dither. Dress fittings, cleaning, baking, the usual small wedding preparations kept growing into general chaos with Priscilla acting her usual temperamental self over Wild Hawk's being in "her" wedding, but Jeb held his ground and was adamant in the decision of his friend for Best Man. Of course, Timothy and Jessica added their billions of questions and both squawked loudly over their dress-up clothes, Tim swearing the collar would cut his breath off and Jess couldn't abide moving around in ruffles. Besides, they were both worn to a nub from all of their chores.

Mary took a few moments from the rest of the pack, knowing if she didn't sit for a few minutes, she'd drop. She sighed, sipping her coffee and eased her tired body into a kitchen chair before finding ingredients for her cake. With all the preparations to keep her mind busy, she continued to search her soul, asking herself time and time again how she had gone wrong with Priscilla. How could she have reared an immoral daughter, and did Priscilla feel as though she had done anything wrong? She sighed as John burst through the back door, stalked into the kitchen and tossed a letter in front of her, before sinking into a chair.

"What's wrong, John?" Mary stared at her husband, afraid to look at the folded paper, knowing he was very upset and thinking, no, I cannot handle anything else right now.

"Read it," he retorted.

"If it's something bad—," she took a sip of coffee, totally ignoring the missive, "well, I just don't want to know."

"Mary—read," he pointed to the letter, his voice commanding.

Mary picked up the folded paper, slowly unfolding it as though she'd catch a contagious disease, immediately recognizing Evangeline Brandon's, John's mother, sprawling handwriting. she read while her husband strode to the coffee pot for a little extra sustenance, wishing it were something stronger, but knowing Mary couldn't tolerate that, and she'd had enough to contend with lately.

"Oh! No!" Mary amused her husband with a most unladylike bellow.

"My sentiments exactly, Honey," he set his coffee down to massage his wife's tired shoulders.

"But, John, I only mentioned to your mother in my last letter that Priscilla was getting married, I didn't invite them. I even stressed that we were not having a big to-do," she sipped her coffee, splashing it as she set it down, "and here they're both coming, your mother and your Aunt Penelope. They must have had their bags packed, ready for any excuse!" She snatched up the letter again, staring at it. "Arriving in two days! Oh! Dear Lord, you know how critical they can be." She sighed as he continued with his back rub, letting her blow off her steam.

"I know, dear," he leaned down, pecking her cheek, "but we are not going to allow those two old gals to upset things—are we?" Stressing the last two words, he squeezed her shoulders and sat down to finish his coffee as Mary shook her head. She thought of John's mother and her garrulous mouth, butting in and trying to take over with everything. Of course, she loved her, but—not at this time—and—John's aunt, bless her heart, means well, but she's such a staid, complaining uncompromising old—old biddy. Maybe their stage will break down! At least, until after the wedding.

No such luck, though! The stage made it fine to Knoxville with no prayed-for mishaps, and of course, John was there to meet the vehicle and escort the two sisters in a rented carriage to their destination. Each woman was gussied and corseted to the fullest in their dark high necked woolen ensembles with matching hats. After jovial greetings, John caught himself thinking these two resembled two large blackbirds, ready for takeoff, their flapping capes resembling wings.

Climbing into the carriage, the two ladies eyed each other, realizing the contraption they were to ride in was rented, not believing John, who was practically reared into nobility, would not own his own carriage with a liveried driver.

"Son," Evangeline Brandon smoothed the fur lined rug around her ample hips, "I was under the impression that you owned your own carriage." She pulled on her already tight gloves, thinking he probably left his carriage at home for some reason, she was certainly not accustomed to riding in rented equipment.

"No, Mother, I do not—we have a spring board and buckboard for hauling. Seems to suffice around this rugged terrain." He smiled, noting the shocked expressions on both countenances; Aunt Penelope with her bird like features and thin mouth sucked in a big breath, with mother croaking her astonishment.

"For heaven's sake!"

John smothered a smile, knowing the day would certainly be a long one as he attempted to untangle his long legs amid hat boxes and valises.

The wedding day finally arrived on a cold bleak November 20th, which threatened to cast a downy blanket over the entire countryside. Excitement and nerves reached a high pitch as Evangeline and Penelope continued discussing and adjusting changes in the evergreen draping the fireplace. Candles were moved, table arrangement changed, rearranged and re-rearranged as the two Bostonians tramped from room to room inserting their vast knowledge of how a Tennessee farm house wedding should be held.

In the midst of the final pre-wedding hour of turmoil, with Jessica's lost slipper and Timothy's not breathing, Mary's nerves hit the highest pitch, her hand shook visibly as she stitched the last bit of lace to Priscilla's gown when a bloodcurdling scream penetrated the entire chaos. Mary, knowing some one had dropped dead or they were being raided, jabbed Priscilla with the needle causing another high-pitched scream, accompanied by "Damn it to hell!"

Voices yelled, "John, get your gun!" "They're coming after us!"

The rest of the family members clamored to the disturbance in the living area as John rushed from the hall with shot gun aimed. His mother was sprawled in the middle of the floor in a dead faint while Penelope's shaking finger pointed to the door as she croaked, "Indians!—Uprising."

"Oh! For God's sake!" John slammed the gun aside, gritting his teeth as he strode to the door, yelling, "They are part of the wedding party!"

"Oh, Dear Lord," Penelope grabbed her throat as she gasped, "bring my smelling salts, quickly Timothy—Katherine—someone before I faint." She swooned from the room. "Oh! Oh!"

The family members dissolved in rollicks of laughter as John greeted the guests Lone Eagle and Wild Hawk. "Welcome to the asylum—nut house—do come in out of the cold."

"Is someone injured?—I heard a scream," Eagle noticed the prone figure on the floor and questioned as he entered, a commanding figure in his finest regalia of plumed and fur turban accentuated by his long fur lined cape. Wild Hawk was magnificently attired in an intricately designed cream colored doeskin outfit with long swinging fringe and matching moccasins, a brown fur jacket hanging on a shoulder.

"No—no one's hurt." John bent down to assist his mother up, who now began fluttering her eye lids, moaning softly. "My mother and Aunt are visiting here from the north," he chided, "when they looked out and saw you two today," he couldn't keep from grinning, "they thought there was an Indian uprising and my mother fainted dead away." Wild Hawk threw his head back rumbling with deep laughter at the episode. He then stooped down, watching Evangeline Brandon, flashing a smile as Mother Brandon screeched, pointing to him, looking from John to Wild Hawk, her mouth moving without sound, grabbing her son's arm.

"Mother, ease off," he commanded. "This is Wild Hawk, a Cherokee friend who is Best Man in the wedding, and" before she could utter her astonishment, "his father, Chief Lone Eagle," he pointed in Lone Eagle's direction. The woman's eyes were like saucers, her mouth still working soundlessly as she stared openly at each while John finally assisted her up.

"I am very sorry we frightened you, Mrs. Brandon." Standing, Hawk smiled warmly at the rather pitifully frightened mother of

John. She stared in awe at this Indian, who was supposed to be an ugly vicious creature but he was handsome, and didn't seem a bit vicious. He was supposed to be a heathen, but spoke English so well. Why! John must have taught him, but did her son say this Indian was to be in the wedding? Oh—surely not! Surely her son had not stooped to that, for heaven's sake! "Thank you," she murmured, staring again at the regal chief in all his what-ever-he-had-on.

"Come, Mother, and sit." John winked at Hawk. "You're just a little tired." He placed her in a chair next to the wall as she glared from one Indian to the other, not believing they were actually in the same house with her—and such paraphernalia. She wished she had never come to this—this savage land—wedding or no wedding!

John visited with the Indians, laughing and talking, Mother Brandon seethed, conversing with herself, while green eyes, from the darkened hallway observed every movement and smile Hawk made causing her heart to thump madly. Kate swore, telling herself numerous times that she would not allow this Indian to affect her one way or the other. She'd ignore him the way he had ignored her in the past. Besides, she had a lieutenant who liked her! But continuing to stare, he was so handsome in his long fringed intricately designed outfit. She pulled herself away, wheeled, ignoring Jesse's plea to help find the lost slipper and bolted up the steps wishing she could run from this whole affair.

John welcomed the remainder of the guests, Colonel and Beatrice Roberts who brought Reverend Joseph Bridges, the tall emaciated circuit rider who seemed to have a nervous tick. Rusty arrived in a clean leather fringed outfit accompanied by a clean shaven groom, attired in a well tailored frock coat, a spotless cravat, and was apparently miserable in his wedding attire.

"Jeb, you couldn't have told me I was getting such a good looking son-in-law." John shook his hand as Beatrice glided to the pump organ, draping her royal blue clad ample bottom over and around the stool which completely disappeared. She reared back, eyes closed, the blue feather on her matching hat keeping time as she pumped out and fumbled through "Love's Old Sweet Song."

The host surveyed the situation after checking his watch for the second time—everyone seemed to be here. Of course, the music ensemble wouldn't begin until after the ceremony, for Beatrice Roberts must hold forth. John smiled as he watched the nervous circuit rider shifting his Bible from hand to hand while gazing repeatedly at the Indians. Jessica hobbled in without one shoe, zooming in on Wild Hawk as Tim followed, huffing and puffing while pulling at his collar. Mother? Where was she? As Beatrice clung to a high G the host thought, I've had it with this host bit...why doesn't Mary get the hell in here so we can get on with this thing? He checked his watch again, nodding to Rusty to see that everyone was in his place. Wild Hawk stood on the right of the fireplace with the nervous groom who pulled constantly at his cravat. While others were seated John dashed from the room, practically colliding with his wife.

"Oh! Mary—you look ravishing." His gaze devoured his wife whose rose taffeta and lace combination was more than becoming. He thought if the two of them could just leave with no one else. "You look so good I've almost forgotten to be angry over having to act the gracious host and the crowning blow having to put up with Beatrice Roberts' screeching over those love songs." He pulled his wife closer.

"Oh! John," she couldn't keep from smiling, leaning up to peck his cheek, "I think Beatrice does a—a—very well. Oh! I hear Katherine now which means Priscilla is ready, but before I go in there you've got to do something about your mother and aunt. They are in the dining room, rearranging everything and going at it about this wedding." Mary shook her head, almost tearing up under all the strain. "They won't," her voice broke slightly, "be in a home with Indians."

He squeezed her arm. "Is that right? Well, you just leave those two sisters to me." His green eyes flashed fire as he strode purposely through the dining room door. Shortly thereafter, John firmly escorted Mother and Aunt through the hallway amid their blustering vocal attempts

"Unhinge me, John, this minute!" and "I can't attend this uncivilized..." but his strong response and firm hand clasp silenced the two.

"Both of you came here to attend a wedding whether its to your liking or not and by God, that's what you will do. He forcefully ushered the ladies in as they cast startled glances at each other, not really understanding this rather brutal way of escorting them to seats where John placed them on either side of that little runt of a man in a leather suit. Of all thing! And here he was, grinning at her, Evangeline Brandon—how uncouth! Penelope pulled as far from him as possible, thrusting her chin into the air denoting her aristocracy. Mother Brandon practically swooned while thinking of the lavish Boston weddings she had attended, the magnificent grandeur. Ladies in gorgeous gowns and all men clad in the epitome of tailored frock coats. She could almost hear the beautifully orchestrated strings. Dabbing her forehead with her lace handkerchief, she was brought back to reality knowing she had never in her born days been placed in such a distasteful situation with so many uncivilized creatures.

Mary took her seat beside Tim, observing Jessica oogling and grinning at Wild Hawk while kicking her feet back and forth, one slipper missing. Dear Lord, she didn't know whether or not she'd make it through this day.

Beatrice took Mary's entrance as her cue to pump out the love refrain, prompting Katherine's entrance. Clad in a light green taffeta that squeezed her waist causing her full breasts to reveal an enticing cleavage that even the ecru lace gathered gracefully around the square neck line couldn't control, she was lovely. Kate's nervousness was evident as she crushed the nosegay to her waist and finally took her place across from the dark eyed man she had sworn to avoid. No longer could she resist as she lifted her gaze to meet his, feeling totally immersed in those obsidian eyes that seem to reach into her very soul, gathering her to him. This isn't fair, she thought, as she finally pulled away from those hypnotic eyes, turning to watch her sister approach, a radiant vision in pink and lace taffeta. The groom caught his breath for never had he witnessed such a beauty as the vision in pink and unbelieving his wife to be. His eyes misted.

For a few minutes, Prissy forgot the presence of Indians and a leather garbed scout as she became the center of attention. Oh! My gosh! She couldn't believe her husband to be was almost handsome. Her dark eyes danced at the thought of his taking her out of the mess she was in and as she looked at this man, she felt she could almost like him for that. Oh! The preacher was rattling on, but if he wasn't a sight in that ill fitting black attire covering his tall scrawny frame. She almost laughed 'cause he looked more like an undertaker. Jeb poked her, the preacher glared at this bride who didn't seem to have her mind on anything as he repeated her cue. Finally, the ceremony was over and the groom bent to kiss his bride as Beatrice all but throttled the organ.

The cake was cut, the couple toasted by an Indian, of all things, while guests became involved in the delicious food, cider and toe-tapping music by the small ensemble with Prissy and Jeb leading off the first swinging number.

Only the older Bostonians avoided the jovial atmosphere with raised eyebrows, leers and nods to each other as they pecked at their food, totally miserable.

Katherine was a bundle of nerves, dropping a glob of custard pudding on the lace tablecloth while attempting to serve Lone Eagle. The chief was aware of the girl's frustration, causing him to glance at his son who stood nearby leaning against a door frame with Jesse pounding his ears, but his undivided attention did not leave the serving girl. Eagle had watched this interchange between these two more than once. Oh! Yawa, he thought, this is no good! No one could miss the warmth in his son's eyes.

"Take your time, Miss Katherine—I am in no hurry." The chief smiled, trying to put the girl at ease as he held his plate for her to serve, but it made no difference. She did not hear or see him, much less the plate, for she was lost in gazing at his son.

"Katherine," Mary's strong whisper rocked her daughter back to the table situation as the mother moved to the daughter's side, "are you forgetting our guests?" Mary smiled at the chief.

"I'm sorry, Chief Lone Eagle. Please excuse me." Kate's flushed face was an apology in itself.

The Cherokee chief nodded, his plume sweeping with the motion before he strolled to his son. Not mincing words, knowing he had to say something, the chief stared at this handsome nephew who was a fine son and next in line to lead his Cherokee people. He had to try and put a stop to whatever was going on. "Am I incorrect in assuming that you and Katherine Brandon would like to be more than friends?"

The young man took his time in answering, suddenly becoming very interested in his food.

"No, you are not incorrect, my chief." there was pain in the young man's dark gaze, but he held his fathers steadily. The chief's feelings went out to this young man who had gotten himself into such an entanglement.

"This is bad." What an understatement—he could think of a thousand reasons to back his statement. He shook his head. "You know this can never be, especially with you to be leader of the people some day." The chief dipped into a delicious corn pudding before adding, "so you must put a stop to it."

Wild Hawk smiled sadly at his father, determined to put an end to this uncomfortable conversation. He placed his plate on a nearby table and thankfully welcomed John Brandon who appeared, ushering all into the parlor for a reel. This was a chance for Hawk to step outside and get his emotions under control. Damn, all I have to do, he thought, is just see her to know my feelings for her are stronger than ever. Who have I been kidding and of course, what my chief said is so true. He eased toward the door while the din of music, voices and people milling took all attention.

Rusty, having plied Evangeline Brandon with two full glasses of hard cider, escorted the tittering, giggling plump Mother Brandon to the dance room. Despite the disgusting protests, hissing and snorts emanating from Penelope, Mother Brandon clung tenaciously to the old scout's arm as she teased him with her fan.

As Wild Hawk eased through the door and took a couple of steps onto the front porch he sucked in this breath, halting immediately, for in arm's reach of him a lovely apparition stood with her back to him, the pristine moon finally winning a game of hide and seek with the clouds cast silvery lights over the green clad figure, caressing the cascading auburn mane.

He took his time drinking in her beauty. "Green Eyes," he struggled in his throat, while his heart thumped a beat to the lively music drifting from inside.

She had known who it was before he ever spoke. She would not turn and face him. She couldn't. Instead, she stared at the night's beauty cast over the serene countryside. Nor would she continue to be the aggressor around this man as she'd been in the past and been hurt more than once.

"Green Eyes," he eased up behind her, his whispered voice a broken caress while his warm breath on her neck caused a tingling sensation. "Please—say something," he continued, so close but not touching her. she shook her head slightly, clutching her shawl tightly which seemed to lessen her trembling. He took her shoulders, turning her around slowly to face him. When she wouldn't raise her eyes to meet his he tilted her chin while searching her countenance.

"Talk to me." He continued gazing into her eyes as she unraveled. "Green Eyes—all I had to do was look at you today…"

"Don't," she murmured, her misty eyes ready to spill over, "I won't put myself in a position to be turned off and on again—and," she was destroying the fringe on her shawl, "ignored—the last thing you told me—you told me," she looked down, "to go to my lieutenant. Well, he certainly wasn't mine, but he continues," she raised her eyes, "trying to be." How could she hurt this man who had been hurt so much during his lifetime and who meant so much to her? She watched the different emotions play across his features.

"I see," he murmured, disgusted with himself for revealing his feelings, angry with her for trying to make him jealous and succeeding or maybe she was speaking her true feelings. "And is this what you really wish, Green Eyes?" Dreading the answer.

"I am trying—after all, that's what you told me to do." He watched her for a few moments before turning and quietly retreating into the house. She strode to the porch edge, placing her forehead against an icy post, her heart breaking as tears streamed and she hated herself for hurting him and hurting herself.

Chapter 21

Thanksgiving was an almost festive affair with John and Tim bringing in a turkey on their first hunt. Of course, Tim was bursting with pride over his first kill, knowing full well his shot had missed the bird by a mile, but none the less, he took the credit. Mother Brandon kept the entire house hold in a turmoil over the making of her specialty, Plum Pudding, which was a must on anyone's Thanksgiving feast.

With Priscilla and Jeb's putting in an unexpected appearance, Rusty fiddling the old tunes while Beatrice pumped them out on the organ, everyone stayed in a jovial mood.

Later, Mary lay in her husband's arms—their bedroom the only peace and quiet she looked forward to since John's relatives had arrived. Her husband breathed evenly in a deep sleep, but she hadn't batted an eye. Her mind kept returning to the evening and her family. The dinner was a success and her jam cake was by far the best she had ever made. Everyone seemed to enjoy the entire evening, but something wasn't right with Priscilla and Jeb. Her daughter's eyes never warmed when she looked at her husband, and he was too quiet. Priscilla seemed excited only when she described what they saw or did in Knoxville, and she was more attentive to Lieutenant Phillips, Kate's friend, than to her own husband. Katherine didn't notice, though, her mind seemed to be elsewhere.

Dear Lord, why can't people be happy and love each other? How fortunate she was with her man. She yawned and smiled, scooting even closer as he nuzzled her neck contentedly.

Kate's adult Indian students arrived the day after Thanksgiving with the first covering of snow. The mounts pranced their friskiness as John directed them to the barn, out of the cold before escorting the Cherokee to the kitchen where Kate would hold her classes.

The teacher, waiting in the hall, pinched her cheeks gazing into the wall mirror before smoothing her full navy skirt. If her heart would quit thumping so loud. She opened the kitchen door just as John led four Indians inside, each wearing a dusting of snow, and each smiling his greeting as Raven's warm gaze traveled over his teacher.

Oh! No—where was he? Kate's face fell as she stared at the door thinking maybe he was finishing with his horse, but before she could inquire, Spotted Horse came to her rescue, explaining Hawk was not with them—he would come later.

"Oh! Well—ah—have seats while I hang your jackets in the hall. Raven, please pass out the reading books."

"Yes, Ma'am," he smiled warmly, thinking she was as lovely as ever, but something was bothering her.

Upon returning Kate passed on her father's information. "You may already know that this session of study for one week will complete our classes." She smiled at each one, then glanced at the door, disturbed over his not being here, wondering if she were the cause when she acted so cold the night of Prissy's wedding. Would he ever return? Gathering her thoughts back to the present, "We will just have to double up on our work, but I'm sure you can do it. Today we will read the last two stories in our third book, answering the questions at the end in writing, and there are three more books to complete this week."

"Hey, Teacher—lighten up! We are not trying to be scholars." Raven flashed his infectious smile.

Spotted Horse seconded this with, "Why I would never finish three more books—have concern, Miss Katherine." The Indians looked at each other.

"I am—that's why I'm pushing you, for time is running out. Soon you will make your trip to Washington, and my students must have knowledge of the white's written word." She began handing out slates at the same time Mother Brandon took this opportune moment to enter the kitchen and divest her treasure, a loaded tray of unearthed antique china. Upon entering, her babbling on about people hiding good china came to an abrupt halt as she spied four Indian men making themselves at home around John's kitchen table. Her screech rivaled that of a Banshee while she performed the flight of the china dance, flinging cups, saucers and plates into the air in all directions before they crashed to the floor. Another loud screech permeated the air as she crunched her way through the broken glass to the door, bellowing, "John! John! Come quick!"

Kate, holding a slate, simply stared at the mess of broken glass as the Indians eyed each other, twitching their lips, hardly able to control their laughter.

John and Mary rushed into the kitchen together, the father crunching broken china under his boot heel. "What in the world's going on here?"

"Why," Kate retorted sarcastically, "Grandmother Brandon left her calling card." She pointed to the mess. "Apparently she was nosing around in the dining room and decided we were not using enough china, so she piled it on a tray bringing it in here when she saw my students. I suppose she thought there was another uprising. Of course, you can imagine the rest."

"Oh dear," Mary stooped down, gently touching and cradling a broken rose design saucer. "This 'rambling rose' china belonged to my grandmother. I was saving it. I don't know why," she kept running her finger over the broken piece, "except that I was afraid it might get chipped if we used it." Her eyes misted as John pulled her up from the debris and into his arms, rubbing her back.

"Honey, I'm so sorry. I know how much your grandmother's china meant to you." He shook his head. "Those two will have to go. My mother and aunt have been here too long and they've kept this household in an uproar ever since they arrived." He bent down, trying to retrieve a piece or two that might be mended.

"No—no—you can't do that. You can't allow them to travel back North during winter weather."

John stared at his wife, smiling, thinking what a wonderful woman he was married to. Most would have jumped at the opportunity to rid themselves of two old busy bodies, but not his Mary. Suddenly, it dawned on him how rude they were being, interrupting Katherine's class when the Indians had traveled so far.

Mary dabbed at her eyes with her handkerchief as John glanced at Kate and her students while he ran his fingers over part of a rose design cup. "I'm sorry—please excuse this ridiculous intrusion. I'll clean this mess up later and," his voice rose, "I forbid anyone to even think of entering this kitchen. Do you hear me?" he bellowed as he ushered Mary from the room into the hall. "Anyone who sets foot in the kitchen will have the hide peeled from his or her behind—is that clear?" His explosive baritone could be heard, Kate was sure, a good mile away. Right now, all she felt like doing was escaping to her room and sprawling on her bed, certainly not dealing with students. Pasting a smile on her face, she listened with encouragement as the first Indian read aloud. Before the second one could take his turn, the back door opened slightly as two heads craned around the opening.

"What's goin' on?" Tim breathlessly puffed, while Jess exploded, "Whadda' mess! Who did it?" A book banged into the door frame not too far off target causing the two nosy imps to slam their retreat while chorusing the evils of a witch for a sister.

Kate was amazed at the progress and ability of these Cherokee. Upon finishing the session, she looked at each one smiling. "I can't believe the progress you have made. Your accomplishment in such a short while —why, it's like a miracle!" The Indians looked at each other with shining eyes while Kate gathered the slates, looking at the impressive writing.

Raven spoke softly, "The miracle was and is that you—a white woman—chose to teach us—to help us." His warm gaze and smile touched her as the others nodded, smiling in agreement. Kate busied herself pouring hot cider and passing cookies around, feeling choked up and ashamed at not wanting the Indians around today because one didn't show up. They were so very proud of their accomplishment, which touched her deeply.

Also, she should have been more understanding of her mother's tears over the broken china. Glancing at the shattered and splintered pieces on the floor, it tugged at her heart as she realized there, crushed on the floor, lay an era of long ago love and cherished memories.

Spotted Horse broke into her thoughts, "We will go and set up our camp now," he stood, nodding to the others. "I am sorry about your mother's broken dishes."

"Yes," she glanced again at the shattered mess, "I suppose if you had special arrows handed down through time, and someone destroyed them, it would be similar." She exited to gather their jackets as the Indians looked at each other rather sheepishly, feeling ashamed of their childish amusement over Mary Brandon's disaster.

After the Cherokee departed, Kate with her pent-up emotions stood gazing through the living room window at the winter's vivid sun set painting the mountainside with her red gold hue after the early morning's dusting of snow. Why didn't he come today—she kept asking herself. Was it because of her actions toward him at

Prissy's wedding? Is everything over or was there ever really anything there? Her mind was far away—a night at an Indian village, and evening in the moonlight, the brooding dark, sad countenance. Her thoughts were jerked to the present as a rapping on the front door drew her attention.

"Lieutenant—what a nice surprise! Do come in." Kate was pleased to see this soldier in blue, who usually made her laugh and today she felt she could use a little humor. After seating her guest she brought him a hot cup of cider. Sipping the hot liquid while stretching his long legs toward the flaming logs dispelled the chill that had penetrated his body.

"Oh, what bliss," he sighed, "a cozy room, warm fire, hot cider," grinning at Kate, "and a beautiful woman." He strode over to sit on the couch by her, taking her hand, kissing the finger tips. "Let's get married, Katherine." He watched her with a sparkle in his blue eyes. "What do you say?" He leaned closer, smiling.

"You couldn't be serious!" She laughed, caught up in his jovial mood while retrieving her hand.

"Well! I just thought it might be a good idea—we do have fun together—don't we?" His eyes sparkled as he sipped his cider wishing he could be serious.

"Oh! 'Course we do," she laughed, "but that certainly is no reason to marry—people marry for love!" She looked away, her mind drifting to another.

"Hey!" he grabbed her hand again, "No solemn thoughts from you—and anyway, we can work on that love part." She smiled at his pretended bewilderment. Pulling her up, he questioned, "Have you been closeted up in this house all day?" She nodded. "Then come on, pretty girl, grab a cloak, we're going for a brisk walk to put some roses in those cheeks." He gently ran a finger down her face, his smile fading as he took a step nearer. Sensing the serious moment, she quickly left to gather her cloak and bonnet.

They strolled toward the old large oak tree in the pasture, Andy amusing this girl with his humorous stories until her smile totally captivated him, and he realized how long he'd waited to hold her, to reveal to her something other than his wit. Suddenly, he stopped, pulling her around and crushing her to him, insistent upon kissing her.

"Don't," Kate pushed against his chest while turning her face away, half amused and half serious, which only spurred him on—he had bided his time long enough, he would not be put off as he held her tighter, holding her face still to receive his probing kiss. Without forewarning something landed into him, shoving Kate aside, knocking him to the ground, slamming well-aimed fists into his face while a knee slammed into his chest. My God, he struggled trying to block the barrage of vicious punches that split his mouth and crunched his nose. He realized he was no match for this savage who was trying to kill him.

Kate screamed, "Stop it, Wild Hawk—you'll kill him!" She pulled at the Indian, screaming again, "Stop it!" but nothing changed. Finally Tim ran up having heard the commotion.

"Get Papa—quick—hurry!" Yelling, she pulled at Hawk's arms, "You must stop this—now!" She screamed, but she was only a buzzing insect until John Brandon rushed up, throwing Wild Hawk from his target.

"What the hell is going on here?" John, out of breath, thundered as he viewed the bloody mass of the soldier's face, who only moaned. He knelt by the lieutenant feeling the pulse and quickly ordered Tim to have Mary prepare hot water, cloths and medicine, then return to help. "Quickly!" he yelled, then turned his gaze to the Indian. "I want an explanation now for this action—why?" he shouted at the Indian.

Hawk sat up, gazing at John steadily for several seconds before answering. "He was forcing himself upon your daughter."

John wheeled, facing the daughter. "Is that true?" Katherine seemed to be in a trance, working her mouth, but making no sound. Finally, she murmured, "He was insistent upon kissing me."

Staring from one to the other, John strode a few steps, running his hand through his hair before wheeling and yelling, "You half killed this man," pointing to the soldier, "for kissing my daughter?" His harsh question received no answer. "Wild Hawk, come inside—I wish to speak with you after patching up the soldier. Katherine," he turned a harsh face to his daughter, "be there." Hawk nodded as the soldier mumbled, "I'll kill the damn savage who did this to me," fumbling for a handkerchief. He pushed himself up as John and Tim assisted him slowly to stand, to get his balance, and then they slowly made their way toward the back door.

Kate, still in a daze, watched Hawk trailing after the others. Did she not understand or did she understand too well? Did he realize what a terrible thing he had done? Beating up a soldier—no telling what trouble he had brought upon himself. There she was thinking only of Wild Hawk when Andy Phillips was hurt. Oh, my Lord! She bit her knuckles to keep from crying as she watched and followed the parade toward the house.

John had forbidden any family member other than Tim from entering the kitchen, where he took his time cleaning and medicating facial cuts while Katherine sat through the ordeal, listening to the soldier spewing his venom at the Indian who had attacked him.

"Tim, get your mother—some of these must be stitched." He peered at an open gash where his mouth had split and a cut above the eye, thundering, "Quickly!"

"Yes, Sir," the boy feeling his importance, rushed to comply, returning shortly with his mother who came to an abrupt halt, her mouth dropping open as she observed the scene, but she refrained from asking questions. She would know in time.

"Get your sewing stuff, Honey. He needs stitches." She nodded. "And bring something to wrap a couple of ribs."

Returning shortly, Mary eased her husband out of the way where she could inspect the injured man and begin her work.

"Damn," the lieutenant swore as Mary quickly and efficiently finished her stitching, placing medication and a bandage over a head wound before wrapping his ribs.

"I'm sorry," she murmured.

"Mary, you and Tim can go on—and Tim, make sure no one, I mean no one enters the kitchen," John ordered. "I need to talk with Katherine."

"Yes, Sir," Tim dutifully responded.

"Honey," John ushered the soldier along with his wife toward the door, "make sure the lieutenant is comfortable near the fireplace—he might want to lie down—here is a cup of coffee if he can manage it. I'll talk with you later." John escorted them through the door.

"Thank you, Ma'am," the soldier muttered.

She nodded as she exited, hardly able to contain her questioning tongue. She didn't appreciate John Brandon's summoning her to do the work, then dismissing her as he might a hired hand without any explanation of what happened. "What happened, Tim?" Mary, grasping his arm, waylaid him in the hall, whispering.

"Papa will let you know when he is ready," the boy pulled from her clasp, moving down the hall with the lieutenant.

"Timothy!" she hissed, but suddenly his hearing seemed to be impaired.

In the kitchen, John glared at his daughter as though he could unravel this whole mess by staring at her, but she seemed only interested in her hands.

"Where is he?"

"He was sitting on the back step when I came in." She dreaded the confrontation which would follow.

Summoning the Indian who followed John into the kitchen and was or seemed to be totally composed after such an ordeal, the father stared at the Cherokee not sure he would find out the truth behind this mess. Kate's heart hammered as she stared at Hawk. How could he have done such a ridiculous thing? No telling what would happen to an Indian for beating up a soldier, and as those in judgment would believe for no apparent reason. Oh! Wild Hawk, her mind screamed, you certainly defined your name today! And why won't you look my way?

John kept staring at the Cherokee, a man he had respected since first meeting him. His remarks were blunt at times, but always honest. Why, oh why would he pull such a ridiculous stunt? Why, it could get all of them in trouble.

He poured three cups of coffee, placing them on the table as he eased his exhausted body into a chair, drumming his fingers on the table while staring. He probed again.

"Why did you beat up that soldier?"

Wild Hawk took his time in answering. Finally, black eyes met John's glare. "I told you before he was forcing himself upon your daughter!"

"—and it was your duty to put a stop to his trying to kiss her?" His voice raised, the father's anger was flaring as he struck a match to light his pipe, trying to calm himself while waiting for the real answer.

Obsidian eyes didn't waver as the Indian held the father's glare, while stating firmly but calmly, "John Brandon, I love your daughter." The black eyes shifted to Katherine with love and warmth reflected.

"You—what?" Screeching, John erupted from his chair, coffee cup and contents crashing and splattering over the floor as he began pacing. "My God, man—have you lost your mind?"

"Probably," the Cherokee responded, continuing to search Katherine's countenance for her reaction.

"Don't you know," John wheeled on his tormentor, "nothing, but nothing, can ever come of this? Who ever heard of such a thing—why, an Indian man and a white woman—how could you think of such a ridiculous," he wheeled on Kate, "and I'm sure you were not aware of any of this, Katherine, or you would have set him straight." He strode to the cupboard for another cup, pouring more coffee with a shaking hand. Love! An Indian!

Her emotional gaze never left the Indian as she struggled, "Papa, I've known of his feelings for me. You see, I love him, too." John's second cup of coffee splashed as he jerked around. "And Papa," she turned her steady gaze upon her father, "if he would agree I would go with him tonight and become his wife, or woman, or—uh—whatever."

"Katherine!" her father hissed as though his daughter had just committed an unpardonable sin. His gaze shooting daggers, "My sensible daughter revealing no sense at all—why, it's a disgrace!"

"To whom, Papa?" the green eyes locked, neither giving an inch—silence prevailed. "And we can't be together because this man who isn't good enough for me," she all but sneered at her father, "won't allow me to live the harsh Cherokee life with the fear that he foresees for his people's future. Now tell me—who is really thinking of my well being?" She jumped to her feet, anything to keep busy, to keep from crying as she cleaned up spilled coffee, picking up the long forgotten pipe and a broken cup while her father sank into the chair again with the weight of a mountain on his shoulder, neither knowing what to say or do about it. Never in his wildest dreams would he have believed Katherine, his sensible daughter, and Wild Hawk, a Cherokee—and yet, little things began to seep into his memory. When she didn't want Wild Hawk to bring the students—he bothered her—of course, he did and she seemed quite upset when Spotted Horse brought the children. The storm and Katherine's complete vigil when he was hurt by the bear. Her great interest in the trial, needing to see him. How could he, her father, have been so dense, so naive, so stupid! He looked from one to the other as they both patiently awaited another outburst.

"Wild Hawk," John's voice was almost normal, "I have great respect for you as a man, but not as a man for my daughter."

"I am aware of how you feel, John Brandon, and of how most Whites feel," the dark eyes flashed a spark. "Your daughter has already explained to you why I will not take her to wife."

"Yes, well—"John stood, running his hand through his hair as be began pacing again, stating profoundly, "You must stay away from each other."

The young couple looked at each other smiling sadly. Katherine, her green eyes so like her father's began tearing, thinking of her future without seeing this man sitting across from her. Goodness knows, she had tried to find someone else. Lt. Phillips was nice, amusing and she liked him until—until he was so aggressive in trying to kiss her—she then wanted to—slap his face.

Wild Hawk stood, gently pushing the chair back to the table. "Then I should leave now."

"No, you can't send him away now." Kate abruptly stood. "This week he must finish his studies along with the others. The Cherokee need him and he needs my teaching before representing his people in Washington." Her chin jutted out so like her Mother when proving a point. "You surely wouldn't deprive him or them of that. After all, this whole thing was your idea!" Kate drove her point home, flashing her misty eyes at her father.

"No—of course not." John Brandon was at a loss, not knowing what to do. Never in his life had he been confronted with such a personal dilemma, his daughter loving an Indian, of all things. Mary must never learn of this. "I'm sorry," he once again slumped into a chair, continuing as if an afterthought, "and Wild Hawk, you must stay clear of Lieutenant Phillips, who will have to remain here for a day or so—I'll try to help smooth this thing over some way, get him settled down if possible. Indians just don't go around beating up white soldiers for no reason if they have any sense."

Amusement spread into a crooked grin on Hawk's face. He felt no remorse for having beaten up a soldier that was forcing himself on the girl of his heart.

"Papa," she placed a hand on her father's shoulder, "I'll see Wild Hawk out."

"He knows the way through the door," John swiped at the spilled coffee with his sleeve.

"I would like to speak with him *alone*," Kate stressed the last word as she followed the Indian through the door before closing it.

Outside, as the moon cast its silvery light over them, Hawk turned toward her, observing the glistening moisture sliding down her cheeks. He gently wiped them away with his thumb while she stepped closer. "Green Eyes, we must not—" her arms gently encircled his waist, underneath his jacket. "Green Eyes," his breathing quickened while his heart thumped in rhythm.

"Hush," she tilted her face upward. "If we are not to see each other alone again, then we must make this parting—proper. Kiss me."

Smiling, he gathered her to him, practically crushing the breath from her while capturing her lips with a probing kiss. After releasing her lips he continued to hold her, rubbing cheek to cheek as their tears mingled.

"Good night—my love." She ran her fingers gently over his lips as she stepped from his embrace. "We will be together—someday, some way." She turned and walked back to the door, her eyes again beginning to spill over.

Kate's following week with her adult Indian students passed all too quickly. The students were wonderful with their progress, each in his own way very intelligent, grasping each lesson and study with full concentration. It was amazing and—here they were for their last day. Kate, trying to hold back time knowing she might not see her Indian again. Her heart was heavy for she had come to care for each one of them. "I'm so very proud of you in your great accomplishment during such a short period of time. She looked at each one who seemed to beam from her compliment with the exception of one who only looked at her with saddened eyes, throwing her train of thought completely out the window. Raven smiled watching the emotional play between Hawk and Kate, realizing the depth of feeling they had for each other and remembering his brief infatuation with this girl—the jealousy Hawk displayed—he feared for any future they might have.

Later while clearing books and supplies Kate found a pouch with a slate tilted against it with a written "Thank You" followed by all signatures. Inside the pouch were several hand made beaded items. She touched the beautiful designs reverently and wept.

Chapter 22

The Cherokee, a group from Georgia accompanied by an Echota spokesman Daniel Reed, the Tennessee group with John Brandon and Jeb Hawkins, were finally on their way to Washington. Having been delayed three weeks due to the death of Rachel Jackson, the President's wife which necessitated his remaining in Tennessee, the group was more than ready to be on their way and to soon find out where this new president stood in regard to the Cherokee future.

John was more than glad to leave the home chaos for a while. His mother and aunt unnecessarily in the way at every turn, pushing, commanding and transferring their innate knowledge of Tennessee festivities at Christmas. Being housed in due to bad weather, Tim and Jessica performed outrageous altercations daily. He knew Mary was ready to pull her hair—and never did he seem to have a moment alone with his wife anymore except at night when they fell into bed too exhausted to make love. He smiled thinking of the many hours she had slaved over this great fur jacket he now wore, his Christmas gift. Why, his relatives thought it was something heathen's wore, not Bostonian gentry. Oh, God, please send Spring soon so those two can travel home!

John looked around observing the ten Indians surrounding him, their fine horses cavorting and prancing to the afternoon's chill, but thank God the weather was now relenting some of its icy grasp, becoming relatively mild for January after the vicious cold they had experienced during December. He couldn't keep from wondering if this long trek to Washington, though, would prove anything positive for the Cherokee or just a pointless adventure, leaving them with only additional frustrations to fear for their future.

The jibes and banter between Jeb and Wild Hawk drew John's attention as the two seemed to amuse all the others, but John Brandon was not amused at anything this particular Indian did any more, for he continued to blame the Cherokee for Katherine's losing her senses, the ridiculous entanglement that continued to prey on his mind.

Four days out the travelers were more than ready for a rest after cutting through the rather difficult terrain of Virginia's mountain passes. It was agreed that they rest up for 2 or 3 days and find fresh meat before continuing their journey. By afternoon they arrived at a choice campsite nestled near a mountain stream surrounded by evergreens that supplied protection from severe winds. After erecting lean-tos Jeb and Hawk bet a beaded bag against a leather pouch with Horse and Raven that they would bring in the first deer.

"Moose, there's more on your mind than slaying a deer. You want to talk?" Hawk prodded Night Wind to Jeb's side as the two traveled the tree studded area west of the camp, but the scout only stared ahead, seemingly oblivious to the cold, the trees dusted with snow, or his friend's voice. Suddenly, the bridle of the big bay was griped tightly by the Indian.

"What the hell!" Jeb thundered at his friend.

"That is what I was wondering," the Cherokee retaliated, loosening his hold on the horse.

Jeb again stared into the forest, his hands resting on the pommel of the saddle. "I can't hunt today—I wouldn't see a deer if it jumped in front of my face."

"Hawk is aware of that," the Cherokee responded, sliding from Night Wind's back, patting the black beauty's neck as the animal nibbled his cheek.

"You don't need my problems. You've got enough of your own." Jeb shifted the reins to his left hand, not meeting his friend's gaze.

"You stupid Moose—how can you "help" us "savages" in Washington," his black eyes crinkled, "if your mind is hung up on you!"

Jeb couldn't help himself as he gazed at his friend chuckling. "You're right, my brother," he slid from the bay's back, snatching his fur cap from his head while rubbing the back of his neck. "You'll hear all my problems if I have to hold you down to do it!"

Having scouted around for firewood, and starting a small fire the two sat on a log, neither seeming to care whether they lost a bet or not. Jeb picked up a stick, drawing designs on the cold hard ground as he began to unload.

"I don't know what to do—I married her, but I have no wife. I wanted to be a father for the babe—here she is showing that she's with child, but she cavorts and flirts with the soldiers and she won't let me touch her." He turned his saddened countenance to his friend. Suddenly, he stood, slamming the stick down. "I can't live this way—I can't, but I love the bitch! Can you believe that?" He wheeled around, his laugh mirthless.

Hawk waited patiently for his friend to continue his miserable tirade, knowing no answer was necessary.

Jeb sat back down. "I've always been my own man—now, I seem to be nothing. I can't think, I can't sleep or eat," he leaned his arms on his knees. "I've let her possess me and yet, she don't give a damn about me." He rose as his voice rose, and began pacing again. Finally, as though totally enervated he stopped and pled, "Whadda I do, my friend?"

Hawk had never seen such sadness etched on a countenance. "Hawk can not believe you ask his advice since he knows nothing about helping himself with a woman—much less someone else's," the Indian smiled, "If such be in Hawk's life as you described, he would return wife to her home where she would remain, but this is something only you can decide. Priscilla should be most pleased and happy to have big Moose for her man." He stood, cuffing the scout's shoulder. "No woman or man is worth destroying another—so, my friend, talk with Yawa—it helps."

The scout stared at the Cherokee, feeling better by simply getting his feelings out in the open. No one is respected when allowing another to walk over him. Priscilla was at the Brandon's where she would stay until after the baby's birth. After that, who knew?

Jeb was so caught up in his own thoughts, bad memories and decisions that he wasn't aware the Indian had moved away until he heard the swoosh of an arrow, telling him there'd be fresh meat for supper.

Returning to the camp with their wild turkey, Hawk and Jeb took the guffaws and jibes from others. "I thought you knew deer didn't have feathers," Raven loved every minute of besting his good friend, "but Horse, maybe this is a new breed that we haven't heard of," he poked Spotted Horse as they both whooped, doubling in laughter while others joined in as Hawk threw the beaded bag, the lost bet at Raven's head which caused even more whoops.

Rusty pounded on the Brandon's front door, bellowing, "Anybody to home?" He hadn't seen a soul or heard a sound as he rode up. Surely nothing had happened to these good people—he'd promised John to look in on them and make sure everything was all right while he was away. He pounded again, ready to enter if somebody didn't open up soon. Finally, Mother Brandon eased the door open a few inches, seemingly quite startled that someone would be standing on the other side until she recognized the scout.

"Howdy, Ma'am—you remember me, don't you?" Rusty smiled, doffing his coon-skinned cap.

"Yes, of course, er—ah—Mr. Poole—do come in. Don't know where my manners are," she tittered. "Guess I was astonished that someone would be at our door." Rusty entered, fingering his cap as he headed for the fireplace's warmth.

"Well, I'm on my way to Lone Eagle's village 'n thought I'd drop by here; promised John I'd look in on his family 'n make sure everything was all right," he thrust his hands to the flames.

"Do sit down," she reached for his hat and coat, "I'll just take your coat and hat, Mr. Poole."

He turned to warm his backside. "I'z wondering where everybody wuz—'n jes call me Rusty—ah don't hold none with this Mr. Poole stuff—why, yuv' knowed me long 'nuff fer hit to be Rusty," he twinkled his blue eyes at the nervous and blushing Evangeline Brandon.

"Yes, well—ah, all right Mr.—ah—Rusty," she tittered as she left the room to fetch the others, and she did think this little bandy-legged scout was kinda cute, course she'd never divulge such to Penelope or even have anything to do with him, but he did have the bluest eyes.

Mary, the two young ones, Kate and Mother Brandon were all glad to see Rusty.

"Rusty, you will stay for lunch, which won't delay your travel all that much for we will eat in less than thirty minutes," Mary insisted as she handed the scout a cup of coffee.

"Wall, ah ain't much fer turnin' down good vittles—'n I've et 'nouf 'uv yore cookin' t' know how good them is—I'm appreciatin' the invite," Rusty smiled as he drank his coffee while warming his backside.

"Good, we're glad to have you with us," Mary liked this little man who destroyed the English language with every sentence, but a man she would trust with her life, and she had decided which was the more important long ago.

Rusty pushed his chair back from the table after consuming his second helping of tenderloin, turnips, yams, pickled peaches and cornbread. My, this woman could cook! And without being able to contain it, a mighty belch erupted. "Please excuse me—guess ah jes' overdone it with the food." Jesse snickered, covering her mouth. Tim giggled as Penelope jumped up, glaring at the rude man. She flung her napkin onto the table, elevated her nose and marched out, flinging over her shoulder, "Excuse me!"

Mother Brandon arranged and rearranged the silver by her plate, glaring at it as though she hadn't heard a sound or seen anything out of the ordinary, but she did know one thing, Penelope could belch with the best of them. She'd heard her many times.

Rusty chuckled, "Guess ah'v already wore my welcome out with some around here," he glanced at the door.

Jesse jumped in, "Oh! Don't pay no mind to Aunt Penny—nobody does 'cause she's always got her nose in a twitch about something or somebody!"

"You can say that again," Tim expounded, stuffing his mouth with the last bite of buttered cornbread, spewing a few crumbs with his exuberant comment.

"Thank you for the fine food, Miss Mary, and ye shore are one good cook. A body would think you wuz raised in thu' South," Rusty stood, smiling.

"Thank you, Rusty," Mary stood, knowing this was quite a compliment from the little scout.

They returned to the living room while Mary gathered Rusty's coat and hat.

"Thought maybe Tim'ud like to 'company me to the Eagle's village—only be gone couple of nights, I know them lil' Injun chillun' 'ud be mighty happy to see him," Rusty grinned, clasping the boy's shoulder.

"Oh! Mama, please," Tim blurted anxiously, "I ain't—I mean, I haven't been anywhere in so long, and I really need to see Little Acorn, you know."

"Aw, quit beggin' 'n puttin' on your good English," Jesse interrupted, "You ought to know by now, she'll either let you or she won't—'n what about me? Surely I'm invited, too!"

"No ma'am, Miss Jesse, ain't takin' no ladies this time. This here visit is jes fer thu' men." Rusty took his hat and coat from Mary, seated himself by the fire, waiting Mary's response as Jesse plopped on the floor without another word.

Tim expanded his chest. "Well, Mama?" Tim thought it was taking his mother forever to answer.

"He'll be in good care, Ma'am," Rusty assured her, stretching his legs toward the warmth of the fire.

"Oh! All right—I suppose you may go. Guess you do need a change from all the women, but mind your manners and do what Rusty and Lone Eagle tell you, wear your fur-lined jacket and boots and take those heavy blankets in your clothes press." Before Mary could finish speaking Tim was through the door and bounding up the steps for his clothing.

Boy was this going to be great, going to see his friends without Jess tagging along and the rest of his family, too. Boy!

By the time the entourage arrived at the Indian village in late afternoon, Tim felt if he had to bump in the saddle another step he would have no behind left—he was sure that part of his anatomy was already flattened out. Slowly he removed himself from his horse, giving himself ample time for the needles to quit pricking his legs before leading his mount into the village. Rusty was aware of the boy's misery, but kept quiet. Soon voices whooped with laughter as the youthful Cherokee gathered amid barking dogs around their friend. This joyful greeting helped to dispel Tim's distressful physical condition.

As the winter's sunset cast its deep rose ribbons across the sky and descended its brilliant head to its resting place, casting a warm glow over the village, Tim sat with other children around a large fire. He was totally enraptured by the deep voice of the old shaman. Was there ever really and truly a turtle so big a warrior could ride on it's back, Tim wondered. As he gazed around the circle he thought never in his whole life had he ever been so happy 'cause these were his friends. His attention was pulled back to the walnut colored wrinkled face encased in its gray wispy hair, the face with the piercing black eyes and deep voice. Tim grinned and the old Shaman crinkled a smile in return. Boy! Was he glad Jess wasn't here, trying to show off and tell everybody what to do!

The next morning dawned clear, but with icy fingers clutching tenaciously to twigs, bushes and the last clinging leaves. Mother Nature's frigid breath had spun diamond crystals to sparkle in the early sunshine. This beauty, however, was unheeded by Timothy Brandon who had to be poked three times before he began to move, and then it was slow.

"Hey, wait for me," Tim yelled as he crammed his plump feet into his boots. Flinging his fur-lined jacket on while exiting the door, he viewed the backs of his two friends with bows thrown over their shoulders. The two Indians stopped, turned, and smiled at each other knowingly.

"Hey, what's the big idea? You leaving me," Tim puffed, catching up with his friends, "you leaving me 'n we ain't even had breakfast! What's the hurry?"

Little Acorn's black eyes sparkled with humor. "Hurry? We wait very long time for a lazy one to move—think he not go—we go," His mouth twitched as he handed his white friend a cold corn cake, "Here is break-a-fast."

Tim took the unappetizing corn cake and trudged along with the Indians who headed for the woods. He thought about his mother's hot breakfast of milk gravy, biscuits, sausage and eggs while stuffing the cold morsel into his mouth. Heck, he knew he'd be starving before noon and he couldn't understand how people could live this way.

Watching a large blackbird squawk his protest at the intruding threesome, Tim bumped into Beaver who silenced his movement with a firm hand on his arm and a finger across his lips. What in the world? Silencing his movement, the three crept from the path and squatted behind thick bushes that hid them. All too soon the murmur of voices was heard as two braves and a maiden appeared, seemingly in serious conversation.

Swift Antelope, Dancing Eyes and another warrior that Little Acorn didn't know, but had seen before; the one with the scar running down his face. The braves and maiden left the path in the opposite direction, two of them finding seats on an old log while scar face squatted down, resting on his heels.

The voices carried but only part of the Cherokee conversation could be understood. The boys could tell, though, that Dancing Eyes was very excited for her eyes flashed, she smiled and jumped up with much hand movement as she explained something about after warm weather, judgment and both braves needed to take care of the bitch.

The boys didn't understand what the talk meant—and the bad word. Why were the two with scarface, and why were they planning something with him? They should report this thing to their chief.

Tim twitched his nose, sucked in his breath and pressed his finger hard above his upper lip, but nothing worked to stop his sneeze that erupted loud and clear. Both Indian boys jumped, glaring with flashing black eyes at their white friend who didn't know much. Suddenly, a large red-brown body parted the bushes, glared at the three and thundered in Cherokee while clasping Acorn's shoulder, "What is it you do, spying on braves and maiden?" Swift Antelope's scowl was threatening as Dancing Eyes and Scarface closed in on the boys, both scowling while waiting an answer.

Finally, Acorn found his tongue. "We not spying," he shuffled his feet, "only hunting." He offered his bow in proof. "We on path when we heard voices—we hid, not knowing who voices came from."

Apparently the little brave was believable even though it seemed an interminable time before the two braves and maiden made their decision.

Antelope snarled, "You go now and never snoop around this brave again or you be most sorry, and you, Pale Eyes," he poked Tim in the chest, causing the young white to gasp while backing up and blinking fear-filled eyes, knowing that any minute this evil looking warrior might draw his knife, "go back to other pale-eyes—this not your village!" The black eyes flashed.

Tim stared from one of the three to the other wondering why these Cherokee were so mean, always before, Lone Eagle's people had been so nice.

"You no understand, White Boy?" Dancing Eyes took a step closer, her black eyes flashing fire as she remembered this boy's scrawny sister who had tricked Wild Hawk into thinking he cared for her.

Tim's freckles seem to darken as his face paled when the glaring maiden clasped his shoulder. Speechless, he could only nod, hoping the clutching hand would remove itself.

"We go," Acorn pulled Tim away from the sneering maiden.

"Acorn, you heed words of this brave," Antelope snarled, "or you suffer."

Tim was visibly shaken as the three boys hurriedly entered the forest. "Don't believe I'll be able to do much hunting today." Still pale, he slumped down on a log to calm his thumping heart.

Placing a hand on his shoulder, Acorn helped to ease his friend's scare by explaining that there would be no hunting this day. They would go by another path, and soon return to the village where they would seek their chief and explain what had taken place with Antelope, Scarface and Dancing Eyes.

Chief Lone Eagle, accompanied by Rusty, met with the three young hunters in the warmth of the chief's lodge—where the glow from the fireplace warmed the chilled young boys and where Acorn, Beaver and Tim explained in detail the frightening encounter with Antelope, the Scar and Dancing Eyes.

As a detailed description unfolded of the meeting with the braves and maiden it was obvious Chief Lone Eagle was more than upset. With brow furrowed and black eyes squinted half closed, he continued to drill the boys on the conversation they had heard. He had forbid that Scarface entering his village for he was a bad one. He had also forbid his Cherokee from associating with him. The talk of judgment, bitch—he did not understand, it made no sense.

"Chief," Rusty interrupted the deep thinking, scowling Lone Eagle. The silence with only the crackling of the fire, the boys staring at the chief was getting to the scout. "Who is this warrior with the scar? Don't believe I've seen him."

"No," Eagle returned to his gazing into the fire, "he is an outcast from Chief Thunder Head's clan a great distance south of here; he killed a fellow Cherokee over a no good maiden who flaunted herself for all warriors. He roams and is not welcome in any village."

"Wall—what's he a doin' here?" Rusty continued, puzzled.

"That, my old friend, is what I would like to know and what I intend to find out," the Eagle stretched his long legs toward the fire, gazing into the flames as he tried to unravel the puzzle of the boys' encounter and his course of action with Antelope and Dancing Eyes. What were they plotting with the evil Scarface? He would not tolerate that evil one near his village, nor would he tolerate any guest in his village being mistreated.

The Indian delegation arrived in Washington amid the turmoil and excitement of Andrew Jackson's soon to be sworn in as the common man's President of the United States, and the common man was out in full force. Leather clad, tobacco spittin' back woodsmen crammed the streets caught up in the excitement of paying tribute to this next President who would be working for them.

The noise, turmoil and congestion dispelled any desire the Cherokee might have had of staying within the town itself. John explained, "You know there's housing already set up for the entire delegation, all of us at the block house which is in walking distance of the government buildings where we will hold our meetings."

The Indians looked to Wild Hawk who explained, "We thank those in charge," the others nodded, "you, John Brandon, and David Reed stay there, but we do not wish to do so. We will set up camp a short distance from this Washington where the noise is less. We go now to find campsite." Wild Hawk turned Night Wind southwest, retracing today's path. John Brandon shook his head, mounted up as all followed.

The Indian camp was set up a couple of miles out of Washington next to a small rippling stream against a tree lined hillside that broke the cold winds. It was ideal.

John took a letter from his saddlebag explaining the contents. "Didn't see any point in bringing this up sooner—there will be a get together function tomorrow evening at 6:00 pm and we are all invited. There will be food, music, dancing and such, which means this will be rather formal, so dress in your best. It would be an insult not to appear. If Jeb will bring you to the block house around 5:30, we'll leave from there together."

The Indians nodded. "I'll have them there," Jeb responded, "and I'm staying here with the Cherokee. I also agree with them. That town is too noisy for me."

John nodded as he and David Reed mounted up, retracing the road to Washington's Blockhouse and a real bed to sleep in. He couldn't wait for a full stomach of home cooked food and a feather mattress to ease his tired body into. How those Indians could sleep on the hard ground all the time and prefer it was a mystery to him. He was also glad they set up camp out of town, which gave him a break from Wild Hawk, too. Around him all of the time, he couldn't keep from thinking of him and Katherine together which tore at him.

The following evening the Indians, accompanied by Jeb, arrived at the Blockhouse shortly before 6:00 and were immediately escorted by John, David and Jeb to the night's festivities. The streets continued to be crammed with people oozing excitement, but eased off with some of their noise as they watched open mouthed the Cherokee, donned in all their finery. "Jesus," one drunk murmured, "them outfits 'nuff to cause a body to git dizzy watchin' all that there swingin' stuff," as he took another pull from his jug and staggered off.

The brilliance of the large reception room with its crystal chandelier, satin-backed walnut chairs, gilt framed mirrors over marble topped tables and beautifully draped serving tables was something to behold. Drinking this in, the Cherokee were ready to turn around and find their campsite. This place held too much glitter, too many people and too much noise.

Wild Hawk was thinking of signaling to his friend Horse to leave when a bass voice zoomed in on John Brandon and his troupe, erasing any thought of escape.

"Well, John, see you made it all right. Any problems?" John Calhoun pumped John Brandon's hand, smiling, "And glad your group could make it," as he took in the Cherokee and their elaborate dress.

"No problems, John—we just took our time," Brandon offered before introducing each Cherokee representative. "I believe you are already acquainted with Jeb Hawkins and Daniel Reed." Brandon gestured to the men.

"Why yes, how are you, gentlemen?" Calhoun shook hands around. He was impressed with this group, especially the Indians. "Do make yourselves at home, John. Afraid our President won't be able to make it this evening for he's been ill since losing his wife this past December. Several affairs he hasn't been able to attend, but he will attend the scheduled meeting with the Cherokee in two days." He lowered his voice as he moved closer to John Brandon. "By the way, do the Cherokee understand any English?"

Raven, standing near Brandon, not only heard but responded before John Brandon could speak. "Not only do we understand White tongue, we speak, read and write, too." He nodded, emphasizing this point as he glanced at the other Cherokee smiling.

"Well, I'll be—that's remarkable." Calhoun was genuinely surprised.

"Yes, it is," Raven continued, smiling broadly at the astonished man while Hawk wished he could cram something in the talkative mouth to shut him up.

"John, you know Martin Van Buren," Calhoun nodded toward a rather ordinary rotund individual with mutton chop who was in discussion around the food table with two ladies.

"Yes, we've met."

"Well, I suppose the two of us are considered in charge of this little shindig—so make yourselves at home. There's plenty of food, music and if any of you need anything just see Martin or me. Thank you for coming. Guess it's my job to mingle with the people and see that everything is all right." Calhoun took John's arm. "It is good to have you with us—I'll see you at the White House day after tomorrow." The Cherokee nodded.

While John Brandon was sidetracked speaking to acquaintances, Jeb nudged Hawk. "Come on, lets find the grub—I'm starved." The two walked toward the room where an abundance of food was lavishly displayed on a long table. There was a variety of everything from meats to sweets. Conversation died to a low hum as attention seemed to be riveted on the impressive Cherokee, other Indians joining them as they approached the serving table. Dressed in their finest regalia from light beaded doeskin with hanging fringe to turbaned head dresses, these Indians were a sight to behold.

"My God, Sarah—did you ever see anything like that?" Madeline Baker, beautifully coiffeured, her trim figure accentuating the latest fashion, whispered, nudging her friend as she stared at the Cherokee procession entering the room. What a sight; she had never seen such male virility, especially the tall broad shouldered one following the large man in buckskin. She wormed her way to the table pulling Sarah to assist. She wondered if these Indians could speak or understood a word of English.

"May I serve you?" Madeline questioned, pointing to the food then the plate, then her mouth directing the charming smile to Hawk.

Hawk nodded. "Thank you, Ma'am." Madeline almost dropped the plate when the Indian's bass voice answered in perfect English as he offered her a slight smile. She piled the plate with delicious food while dredging up some reason for further conversation with this handsome Indian.

Both ladies continued to serve the Cherokee and continued to be amazed at how verbal these Indians were. Most of these so called savages were handsome and used better manners than many whites. Shortly, the two women eased into a corner to plot a little strategy. Madeline was a very attractive, thirty year old blue eyed tall willowy blond ravishingly attired in blue velvet. Her life of wealth, which she pursued relentlessly before finally capturing the sixty year old widower, Robert Baker, a government official, seemed to be all her heart desired. After two years she found life boring with no excitement. Oh, she loved Robert like a father. He was good to her, bought her anything she wanted, but putting up with him in her bed was not what she bargained for. She cringed thinking of his bulk, pouch and groping pudgy hands.

Sarah Murphy, a plain Jane compared to her friend, was shorter but rather pretty in a sweet sort of way with dark eyes and hair, but definitely lacked the flair and aggressiveness of her friend. Sarah interrupted Madeline's thoughts, tittering behind her fan, "Heavens, some of those Indians, I overheard Van Buren say they are Cherokee, why they are plainly handsome! I thought they were supposed to be savages or heathens, but their English is as good as ours and they used manners. Why my James never thanks me for anything." Sarah glared at her rotund husband whose fat belly had already popped the bottom button on his elaborate satin vest.

"Sarah, listen—let's have some fun," Madeline squeezed her friend's arm, her blue eyes sparkling with excitement. "Some way, we'll get to know these Indians and some way," she smiled slyly, "spend a little time alone with them before they depart. Heaven knows, we deserve a little fun." She eyed her pudgy husband who was vociferously holding forth in a government official's face, attempting to amuse with a dull anecdote.

Sarah tittered, "My thoughts exactly," for she couldn't remember when James Murphy had noticed her in any way, not that she cared.

"Come on—let me handle this. We must be demure, sweet ladies whose only wish is to help make their visit to Washington more interesting and comfortable. Anything else might scare them away."

Madeline, followed by her friend, glided up to the group of Cherokee who stood near the outside dining room window with Jeb Hawkins. All conversation ceased as the ladies approached. Madeline broke the silence. "Please let us know if you would like any additional food. I am Madeline Baker, and this," she took Sarah's arm, "is Sarah Murphy—uh—ah—we are acting hostesses this evening so if there are any questions about Washington we'll try to answer."

"Thank you, Ma'am," Jeb observed the woman's glancing at Hawk. Oh no, he thought, not again. That's all we need here in Washington city.

"Mr.—er—ah," Madeline purred to Jeb, realizing he was the spokesman. She took a step closer, touching his sleeve.

"Jeb Hawkins, Ma'am," he responded, more than ready for this little confab to be over.

"I was just thinking," Madeline continued her cooing, "Sarah and I would be more than glad to show you gentlemen around the government buildings or for that matter Washington City itself," she flashed her charming smile at the big Indian.

Swallowing a bite of ham, Jeb stammered, "Well, that's mighty kind of you, Ma'am, but we are not exactly sure what meeting might be called or when, but thank you all the same." God forbid, he thought, that's all we need—some bored society wench wanting to get cozy with the savages. He smiled and took another bite. Raven quirked an eyebrow, speaking in Cherokee to Hawk, "See you have not lost your touch, Brother!" He couldn't resist Hawk's discomfort. The others grinned in agreement. Hawk hissed, "Back off!"

The ladies finally drifted back to the serving table, continuing to glance at the Cherokee. They both realized the gate had been closed in their face for the first round, but Madeline was not to be deterred. She'd think of something.

Finally, the Indians were ushered out of the noisy, smoke-filled room which seemingly continued to hold a multitude of people. Having met many dignitaries of whom names were not remembered, the only thing the Indians were concerned with was breathing fresh air instead of stale smoke and escaping the two society women. Nor were they aware of the two men who now walked behind them, who had also attended the reception and been most inquisitive about the Cherokee. Jake Taylor and Willie Mason, both work horses for the Georgia Militia, followed orders from the main source. Word came that a Georgia-Tennessee Cherokee group would be pleading their case with the President. It was up to Taylor, Mason and others to see that Jackson didn't soften his feelings toward the Indians even if drastic measures had to be taken.

Shortly, five additional leather clad ruffians materialized out of the darkness to join the two from Georgia. After conversing briefly they walked another block before crossing the congested muddied street and entering a plain wooden structure with a gas lighted sign above the doorway stating, "Hotel."

After climbing the rather dilapidated stairs Jake ushered the group into a second floor room that boasted a sagging bed, chifferobe, dresser, fireplace and three split bottomed chairs. Willie lit the fire while Jake commanded attention. He was not a large man, rather inconspicuously of average height, but the flashing black eyes and deep bass voice drew attention.

"This is the way I've got it planned, Boys," he strolled to the fireplace, leaning back against it. "We will have those Cherokee acting the savages they really are," he sneered. "I watched a couple of wenches making eyes at those heathens tonight at that reception—and that gave me the idea. Women—" every eye was glued on Jake as he paced back and forth so proud of his own brainstorm. "Now," he pointed at each one, "listen and listen carefully. The Cherokee meet with Jackson day after tomorrow at 9:00 am. When that meeting ends I'll make sure one of the cleaning women delays a couple of the Indians."

"Jake," Joe Thurman, a burly backwoodsman mumbled, "Ha don't get it, what good—"

"Damn it, Joe, you won't get anything unless you shut your trap and listen!" Joe nodded sheepishly when the boss came down on him, but listen he did along with each one as Jake went into detail explaining the action that would take place in two days and what he expected from each one of them.

Back slapping, nodding, guffawing, followed as they all agreed with Jake's brilliant strategy to defeat the Indians. The outbursts grew even louder as the leader retrieved a jug from under the bed and passed it around.

The following day the Cherokee refused John Brandon's invitation to tour Washington. They had had enough mingling, noise, congested streets and crowds which made their campsite the most enticing place to be.

Outrageous stories were exchanged after arm and body wrestling. While Lone Wolf and Straight Arrow cleaned the young buck they brought in, Raven made it clear to them never to include Wild Hawk or Jeb Hawkins on any hunt, for neither knew the difference between a deer and a turkey. Swoosh—as he finished the last word a wet, soggy moccasin caught him full in the face which encouraged whooping laughter to fill the camp. This camaraderie, along with fresh roasted meat helped to dispel some of the uneasiness the Cherokee felt over their upcoming meeting with Jackson.

Later that night, Wild Hawk, snoozing in his fur robe smiled as he thought of the day's activities, but soon, as usual, his thoughts were of a green eyed girl who crinkled a tiny dimple so prettily, and wondered if she thought of him. Not to ever see her again—he almost moaned aloud. Surely life could not be that cruel.

All too soon the Cherokee, Jeb, Daniel Reed and John Brandon climbed the steps to the President's house, or as some termed it, the "White House" in Washington. All seemed to be awestruck by the magnificence of the structure, the columns, the grandeur—yet, there was a simplicity in its beauty. The group was ushered down a hallway that boasted several closed doors. Finally approaching one on the left, they entered a rather spacious room where book cases lined with many leather bounds surrounded a fireplace. A view of the lawn could be seen from any one of the four long windows that were encased in deep wine-colored drapes reaching the floor. Three men sought the warmth of the fireplace while others sat at a rectangular mahogany table. Conversation ceased and those seated stood when the group entered, led by John Brandon and Daniel Reed.

"John and Mr. Reed, gentlemen," John Calhoun stepped forward, shaking hands and nodding to the Cherokee. "I'm sorry our President has been delayed, but he should be here shortly." He made introductions. Brandon followed with Cherokee introductions.

"Have seats, gentlemen," Calhoun pointed to the table and chairs, "while I pour us some coffee or tea while we wait." John and Daniel were grateful for a good cup of coffee; however, the Indians refused both.

Conversation seemed to be a might strained. The Cherokee sat stoically while Brandon, Calhoun, Reed and Van Buren conversed about upcoming affairs. The other members of Jackson's cabinet were rather shocked at the appearance of the red men. They thought the Cherokee had adopted or tried to emulate the white man's dress and ways, but certainly not these. Why, their native attire was tremendous, beautifully inscripted on soft doeskin and each with a commanding appearance. As the whites and Indians scrutinized each other, the door slowly opened to reveal the President of the United States.

He slowly made his way across the room as all stood. A tall, erect slender man with a shock of white hair and deep sadness etched on his countenance. He came forth and shook hands with each one, calling their names during introductions.

The Cherokee appreciated the warm, firm handshake of welcome; however, Wild Hawk felt their timing was bad. How could anyone so filled with grief concentrate on or be concerned properly with their Indian affairs? He disliked this man from all he had heard and knew he had turned his back on the Indians after using them, but there was something about him that reached out to people.

"Have a seat, gentleman," Jackson urged as they all took seats with eyes glued on this white-haired leader. "I apologize for keeping you waiting," he shifted through papers in front of him before sipping coffee placed on the table. "I understand, Mr. Brandon and Mr. Reed that you are spokesmen for the Cherokee here." He eyed the two men carefully.

"No, Mr. President," John Brandon leaned toward the rather gaunt leader, "I am Indian Consultant for the Southern Cherokee and at Fort Hamilton, but as far as spokesman, Sir, they speak for themselves." John eased back into his chair as Jackson stared at him, clearing his throat.

"I see—and you, Mr. Reed, do you speak for this group?" Jackson eyed Daniel Reed carefully.

"No, Sir, I represent the Echota Cherokee as Consultant, but they, too, speak for themselves."

"Well, am I to believe that each man appearing here today will be speaking?" He was losing patience with this bunch. "That would take the entire day and what about their speaking English?"

"President Jackson," Wild Hawk's resonant bass voice drew attention from everyone as he stood. "My name is Wild Hawk, nephew of Chief Lone Eagle of the Cherokee village in Southern Tennessee, a part of the big mountains. There are five from my village present. Each of us not only speaks the white tongue, we also understand the written word and write in your language." He sat down while mumbling and whispering passed among the white representatives, all impressed with the man and what they had heard.

"Well," Jackson smiled, "I suppose that clarifies everything."

"No, Sir," Hawk responded. "We just did not want to be spoken of as they, them and their when we are present and can speak for ourselves."

"I see—and I am glad you straightened things out, Wild Hawk." Jackson was irritated along with being impressed and amazed with this young Indian. The white representatives looked at each other, surprised and also thoroughly amazed at the astuteness of this Cherokee. If all of these Indians were this intelligent and verbal, this might turn out to be a very long day.

John Brandon sighed, thinking they might as well pack up and leave now—Wild Hawk should have had sense enough not to irritate the President of the United States. Jeb Hawkins and the Cherokee all smiled inwardly.

"Wild Hawk," Jackson glared at the Indian, "why are you here?" He was direct and expected a direct answer.

"President Jackson, there are others who would like to speak— then I will reply," Hawk nodded to the Cherokee as Van Buren leaned over to whisper to the President who shook his head, putting his hand up for conversation with Van Buren to cease. Jackson nodded to the Indian.

Lone Wolf of the Echota Cherokee stood. "President Jackson, my name is Lone Wolf of the Echota in Georgia. Our Cherokee nation is being overrun by Georgia Militia and others who are destroying our property, killing innocent people. We need your help—" his voice trembling, he sat down. Straight Arrow touched his friend's shoulder, knowing how hard this was for Lone Wolf's wife had been killed by the Militia. Wolf sat up straight, ashamed of having shown such emotion.

Raven stood, another commanding figure. "President Jackson, I am Raven of the Big Bear Cherokee Clan, south of the big water in Tennessee. You have just been elected the big chief of this big country." He waved his arms to indicate vastness. "Surely you do not want people who have lived here before the white man ever came to be destroyed out of hate and greed. I have heard you are a fair man. We need those treaties that were signed to be enforced." Jackson's representatives whispered among themselves as Van Buren again pled with the President who again waved him off as Jeb Hawkins stood.

"Mr. President, I am Jeb Hawkins, Army Scout, and friend of the Cherokee. What they speak is the truth. They are fine citizens for I've knowed and lived with them. They take nothin' that ain't theirs." His voice raised—even with his broken English the group realized he was quite an orator. "But to allow a bunch of rabble to destroy, kill and take what belongs to the Cherokee ain't right and somethin' must be done!" Jeb took his seat as he glared at the President looking for some understanding and concern on Jackson's countenance.

Hawk stood, waiting until every eye in the room was focused on him. "When I was eleven years old I watched white men kill my father, rape and kill my mother. I could do nothing, I was only an Indian boy so I ran from this North Georgia area where we lived; hiding, crying, starving, and scared until I finally reached my uncle Lone Eagle's village. I never knew my father to be a violent man or to hurt anyone—certainly my mother never did." He struggled with the memories. "I know first hand what this hate is and what it can do." He stared at the President. "It's been going on far too long that a man is judged on the color of his skin rather that what he is made of inside." John Eaton stared at this Cherokee with misty eyes, wanting to shout how right he was. Martin Van Buren looked at his hands, John Calhoun watched the President as Hawk continued, "Too much of our land already belongs to the white man—now, we must keep what is ours and President Chief Andrew Jackson, it's up to you to see that we do." He sat down, spent, as the others stood applauding.

Jackson waved them for silence and to be seated. He was shaken by these comments that he knew to be true, but what could he do? How could he go against State's Rights? At this time, he knew he was in no condition to have this burden dumped on him. He wasn't eating, he wasn't sleeping, and he didn't hate the Indians.

"Gentlemen," he finally responded, lifting his eyes to meet those around, "I and my colleagues appreciate your coming here," each nodded his agreement as Jackson again sifted through the papers in front of him, wanting so to end this meeting for he did feel for these Indians, "and expressing your feelings over the Cherokee situation. Believe me, I do understand your concern, but at the present I'm not at liberty to make any hasty decision; however, I will study these concerns and think about every point you've made, carefully." He began gathering his papers as members stood, taking Jackson's action as the meeting being dismissed.

"President Jackson," Straight Arrow stood. "I am Straight Arrow of the Echota Cherokee," Jackson waved for his members to sit. "When you were General and led your men into battle against the Creeks you needed additional warriors to help you win the battle. The Cherokee came to fight with you. We did not say we will study about this—we came and fought by your side. Have you forgotten it was the Cherokee who stood by you when you needed help?" He sat, glaring at the man who could make a difference in their lives.

Jackson hesitated in his reply, continuing to stare at the papers in his hand. Finally his eyes lifted and locked with the flashing black ones that waited in desperation.

"No, Straight Arrow," he uttered, sighing, "I haven't forgotten." Jackson's brow was furrowed; he was miserable.

"And," Wild Hawk added, leaning toward Jackson, "unless we are wrong in our history, it was a Cherokee who saved your life from the hand of a Creek to give you this chance to be President, Big White Father. Now, the Cherokee asks for your help."

John Brandon and Daniel Reed both stood, feeling impelled before this meeting ended to speak.

Jackson acknowledged them. "Mr. Brandon and Mr. Reed. I wondered if you came here just to listen." He smiled, glad for any change from looking into those desperate dark eyes.

"Mr. President," John Brandon addressed Jackson, not particularly pleased with the man's last comment nor the way things were shaping up with no commitment from Jackson of any help, "These people have traveled a long way to speak to you about their lives, their future as a nation, things I'm sure you are aware of. They deserve your immediate attention to help enforce those treaties that have been overlooked. What is our government if the laws voted on are not enforced?" He eased back into his chair, staring at Jackson, beginning to wonder if this were simply a wasted visit, but how could anyone who had authority allow these fine people—he gazed around the table—who had hurt no one, who only wanted their land and their lives—how could anyone who had power to help—turn his back on them.

Daniel Reed placed a hand on John's shoulder. "Mr. President, John Brandon and the Cherokee have shared my thinking and feelings very well. They deserve your backing, your help to live peacefully within their nation without any interference from the Georgia Militia, who has done nothing but kill and steal." He sat.

Andrew Jackson rose, making eye contact with each Cherokee, Jeb Hawkins, Daniel Reed and John Brandon. "Gentlemen, I thank you for your visit and as I stated before, I'm not at liberty to make a hasty decision, but will think carefully about your comments." Feeling so exhausted and confused over this entire affair, the President knew he had to put a stop to this meeting. He didn't dislike the Indians—he felt for them, but how could he go against a state? "This meeting is now adjourned. If you will excuse me, gentlemen, I do have a commitment." He stalked very erectly from the room without another word.

John Calhoun and Van Buren shook hands with Brandon, Jeb Hawkins and Reed, a final friendly jester to cover Jackson's rudeness, before walking the group to the door. Brandon whispered to Daniel, "It looks as though we've been dismissed."

Jeb and the Cherokee followed, each with his own thoughts about the rather abrupt dismissal and each feeling that nothing had been gained with all the pushing to learn the white man's reading and writing.

As the group filed out of the room led by the dignitaries, Spotted Horse tapped his friend on the shoulder to wait up. "Hawk, do you think anything will be done to help our people?" Worry etched his features.

"No—Jackson is not going to turn his back on the State of Georgia. The Cherokee gains nothing this day," Hawk hissed through gritted teeth. Both with thoughts in turmoil over the meeting's outcome, neither noticed the cleaning lady standing in an opened doorway, struggling with a piece of furniture until she finally dropped to her knees as the two Indians came near.

"Ma'am," Horse stooped near her, "can we help you?" The woman gazed at the dark handsome man who had a kind face.

"Why, yes," she struggled to stand. "Please help me up." He took her arm, pulling her to her feet. Dusting off her skirt, she explained, "The man who was to move the furniture became ill suddenly. There was no one else to do it but," she looked at her hands, shaking her head, "I can't seem to manage and I hate to ask you to help me."

Horse smiled, answering, "We don't mind—Hawk, tell the others to go on—we will soon catch up." After complying, Wild Hawk returned to assist with the furniture.

"Now, Ma'am, what do we move and where?" Horse questioned, noting this small woman didn't look strong enough to move much of anything.

She stared at the Indian wondering why she was paid to lie and slow these Indians down. "Yes, I'm sorry—that piece," she pointed to a chest of drawers she had struggled with, "and a desk is to be moved two doors down the hall." She pointed to the room. Following her direction the Cherokee quickly moved the furniture.

"Thank you so much. I don't know what I would have done without your help." She watched the two Indians exit the building wondering what she was involved in, for the two men seemed very nice. Shrugging her shoulders and rushing to get out of this place she snatched a threadbare shawl from a wall hook near a back door and exited through it.

Upon exiting the building, Horse and Hawk were consumed with thoughts of Jackson and today's meeting. Each was in such deep thought over the outcome that neither had a second thought to why one scrawny white woman was attempting to lift furniture in the White House when no one else was around. Lost in thoughts, seemingly in no rush to join the rest of their group and hash over what they were all feeling.

Jeb turned, thinking he would wait up for his friends. As he did he heard a scream and watched spellbound as Hawk and Horse sprinted into an alleyway. Knowing the two were probably jumping into some bunch of trouble, Jeb rushed to the scene, followed by John Brandon, who had also heard the distressing ruckus. Both men were in time to witness two unsavory characters assaulting two women. By the time the men had wallowed the women to the ground to have their way with them, the two Cherokee swooped down on the scene, grabbing the males and with solid punches flattened one while the other ran for his life with blood streaming from his face. The Indians then bent over the ladies attempting to assist them up when screams erupted from each female.

"Help—help! Get your dirty hands off me you dirty filthy savages!" The blond, hard featured, yelled and screamed as she tore her blouse. The other dark headed woman kept screaming and yelling, "Help! Get the police—these Indians attacked us!"

Wild Hawk and Spotted Horse were shocked beyond belief. They couldn't understand why and what this was all about. It then dawned on them when they saw Jeb motioning for them to leave quickly—the women continued to scream, but before the Indians could exit the alleyway, the law arrived.

"What's goin' on here?" A middle aged big bellied figure in a uniform made his way to the middle of the fracas, pressing his authority by spitting tobacco juice between the two Indians.

The women rushed to the officer's side. The blond, big eyed and teary, sniffed, "Oh, Officer!" She wiped her eyes then batted her lashes. "Me and Mable," she smiled, pulling her friend closer, "wuz on our way home when these two savages, these Injuns," she cringed, "pulled us into this alleyway and well," she sniffed, "well, you know," she broke down into a sob. "To think—think, a body can't even walk down a street—"

"Well, what about you?" the officer asked the other woman, totally ignoring the Indians.

"That's right—Ruby done told you jes like it was, jes like it happened," she kept nodding, emphasizing her point. "See her blouse—it's all tore and my skirt," she jerked at her skirt making sure the law saw the rip and her legs.

"Who else was a witness to this mess?" the officer bellowed, dispelling a large tobacco cud.

Two men approached, disreputable in appearance. "Cap'n," a scrawny bewhiskered individual with nervous hand movements and small eyes that batted constantly. "Ha seen it 'n hit wuz like them girls done told you—me 'n Joe here," he pointed to his bleary eyed buddy, "well, we'z comin' in the back way down 'aire." He pointed to the back alley entrance while Joe amened everything his buddy said.

"'At's right—zackly right," he kept nodding.

"All right, all right." The law man was becoming weary of this whole thing. He rubbed the back of his neck before pulling out a note pad. Hell, what a mess. He would bet these two "ladies" were whores and two bums for witnesses, but God he hated Injuns. Look at 'em standing there like stones.

"All right," he spit tobacco juice from his fresh cud near Hawk's moccasins.

"Officer," Jeb Hawkins spoke up, "Ain't you gonna question the Indians or let some body speak who really saw what happened?"

"You got something to say, Mountain Man?" he squinted his eyes at Jeb and John Brandon. The officer was ticked off and worn out.

"That I have," Jeb's commanding size make the rotund officer take a step back. The scout pointed at the women and the two men who lied. "These people are lying."

"Why, how—dare you," the blond sputtered.

"Now, see here," bewhiskered muttered.

Jeb ignored both of these minor interruptions and continued persuasively, "Looks like this was all planned, a put up job to harm these Indians. I saw all of it and so did Mr. Brandon here," he took John's arm and related the entire happening.

"Is zat so?" The officer squinted his eyes at the two whores and bums knowing the big man probably told the truth.

"That's exactly what happened, Officer. I, too, saw all of it just as Jeb Hawkins here explained," John backed up the scout.

Oh! Ah real educated 'un, a cool one. The officer squinted, rolling his cud around. This high 'n mighty could probably talk the socks off'n all of um put together if he had a mind to. Well, he was sick of this whole stinkin' mess! "Is that yore story, Injun?" The law man didn't care whether the stones grunted or not. They acknowledged with a nod. "You come back here." The two bums were easing toward the exit when the lawman bellowed. Reluctantly, they shuffled back to the group.

"Well, Injuns, you'll have to come with me—do you understand?" He began motioning with his hand.

"We understand perfectly," Wild Hawk responded, gazing intently at the plump law man who practically swallowed his cud upon hearing the perfect English. My God, he thought, what is this—savages speaking parlor talk? What is this world coming to?

Educated heathens! He eyed both savages, their fine clothes, their arrogance and hated them even more.

"Injuns, you'll have to come with me as I done said—can't make no decision here."

"What do you mean?" Jeb burst forth, "you've got the facts from two reliable sources—US!" He eyed the whores and bums with a sneer.

"All's the same, the sheriff will want to talk to them Injuns." The officer wrote names and addresses of the two women and men who first described the happening. "'Now you best be where ah kin reach you if need be." He turned, spit, and motioned for the Indians to move.

John Brandon stopped him. "Where are you taking the Cherokee, Officer?" The law man swung around, scowling.

"To the court house 'n jail." He strutted off feeling his importance, following the Indians as they approached a contraption pulled by horses.

"Mr. Hawkins and I will be there tomorrow morning for the Indian's release." Brandon raised his voice to make sure all heard clearly. The officer turned, glared at Brandon, spit and shoved the Indians into a double back door of a black hearse like carriage, locked the door, crawled up by the driver before the two overworked horses took off with a start.

After a pacing, sleepless night in the dank filthy, rat and vermin infested cell, Hawk and Horse finally drifted into fitful sleep, sitting leaning against the wall with arms draped over their knees.

The loud jingle of keys penetrated the light slumber, causing a fat rat to scamper for his escape route and causing the inmates to abruptly stand.

"All right, Injuns, you're out 'uv here—let's go," a fat bellied, tobacco chewing pleasant voice ushered the two where Jeb and

John Brandon awaited them in the outer room in conversation with the sheriff.

"I asked you a question," John Brandon's temper was showing, his face flushed as he stared at the big burly sheriff who sat behind a desk, savagely chewing on his cigar while shifting it from side to side in his mouth and glaring at this man who was sticking his nose into his business.

"Now you listen to me," the big law man stood, wheeled himself around his desk, poking John in the chest, "I'v done give them Injuns their freedom, now you take 'em and git."

"Just a damn minute," John's voice was loud, "and don't ever put your hand on me again." He shook the morning's newspaper in the sheriff's face. "Have you read this or should I read it to you?"

"I ain't no time to fool with papers," was the lawman's reply.

"Well, you'd better listen up then—this rag," John thumped the newspaper, "and I quote, "Two Cherokee Indians assault and attempt molestation of two ladies."

The Indians glanced at each other, wanting only to leave this place rather than get involved in another altercation. They glared at Jeb like 'do something', but the big scout only smiled, shrugging his shoulders for he was rather enjoying John Brandon in action.

"Well, Jeb here and I followed your so-called witnesses, street bums or beggars," John smirked, "and as you might guess, this big scout," again pointing to Jeb, who crossed his arms while glaring at the law man, "can be a might persuasive." The red-faced sheriff was having trouble breathing. "Anyway, the bum witnesses, after only a few seconds, were more than glad to relate the whole story and the so-called ladies," John poked the paper again, "are street whores, witnesses all hired by the Georgia Militia, a bunch of rabble who put on this little street drama to help destroy these Cherokee Indians in the eyes of the new President and the public!"

The Indians stared at Jeb who nodded while John continued his oration. "These men," his voice lowered as he pointed to the Cherokee and Jeb, "had just visited the White House in conference with the President of the United States." The sheriff paled under his splotched red face. "Now you cram this in that cigar and chew on it! This town and the President will know the truth and this newspaper will retract these lies," his finger went through the paper, "and they will print the truth. In this truth Washington City will know what a bunch of inept or inadequate law enforcement they really have—now—chew on that!"

The four exited; the two Cherokee smiling while Jeb escorted the still smoldering John Brandon out the door.

The splotched, pale-faced sheriff eased himself into a chair behind his desk, his breathing harsh, and mulled over this botched up mess—street whores and bums! He glared at his deputy, who was leisurely leaning against the door facing chewing his cud, watching him.

"Well, don't you have nothing to do—and what are you glaring at?" the boss bellowed at the lazy deputy, who jumped and moved quickly to the back of the room for one carrying his overstuffed bulk. He snatched up a few papers from a dilapidated oak desk with great concentration even though his comprehension was less than adequate.

Outside, John explained he and Jeb would be detained since they had a trip to make to the news office and they would also be sending a message to the President.

"Your horses are out back," Jeb added before they left. "We thought you might need to rest up before leaving this place—I'll meet you at the camp."

Hawk stuck out his hand. "Thank you, John Brandon, and you too, Moose." Horse did the same.

Making no comment after shaking hands, John nodded and strode off as Jeb followed, his thoughts in turmoil. These two Cherokee were good, honest people except, of course, Hawk's romantic feelings toward his daughter, which would come to nothing—he'd see to that. Other than that, both were intelligent and only wanted to live in peace, but rabble—ignorant trash who were the savages—seemed to rule supreme. Without a doubt the person who could do something about the atrocities inflicted upon the Indian, the President of the United States, is not committing himself to help.

As the Indians were nearing the city limits on the way to their campsite, a beautifully decorated carriage emblazoned with a crest and pulled by a pair of high stepping black horses careened in on them.

"Madeline, don't do this," her friend Sarah hissed, pulling on her arm. "These Indians are the ones who tried to molest—it's here in the paper—you saw it—here." She shook the paper at her friend.

"Shut up," Madeline knocked the paper from Sarah's hand, patting her navy and sky blue bonnet into place before leaning into the window as Night Wind cavorted and danced at the too-near contraption. "Hi, there," she smiled her charm. Wild Hawk glanced at Horse. "You remember me—we met at the reception—I'm Madeline and this is my friend Sarah—you met her, too." She pointed to Sarah, who was making noises. Madeline continued with her ravishing smile that had enraptured many a male.

The Indians nodded. "Yes, we remember," Hawk responded without smiling.

Madeline was not to be deterred. "As we are taking our afternoon outing," she heard a loud hiss beside her, "we thought you might want to follow us—the nearby park is only a mile from here and it is the beauty spot of Washington, and," she moistened her lips, "we could explain some of the city's history. How about it?"

"For God's sake, Mad—they might try to—"

"Well, yes," Madeline murmured to Sarah, placing a little more of her body in the window, revealing the low décolletage and more, "they might."

"No, Ma'am, thank you, but we have important business to attend to. We will not follow you or join you." Hawk kneed Night Wind and the two Indians sped away, hoping they could put distance between them and the carriage before these hot blooded females knew what was happening. What else could happen to them while they were in this place? Yawa, please let us leave soon.

"Well, of all the rude—the nerve of those Indians! I can't believe this." Madeline was not used to any man spurning her, especially some crude Indian—she moved back in the seat, her eyes flashing. "Oh, of course," she adjusted her blue gloves, "I would never have anything to do with a *savage*—I was only trying to be nice!"

"Of course," Sarah turned her head, making a face. Madeline would have been nice enough to lift her skirt, but thank goodness the Indians had sense enough not to succumb to Miss Charm. She picked up the Washington paper and again drank in every word about the Cherokee heathens molesting white ladies.

It took Brandon and Jeb along with Daniel Reed a couple of days to clarify and change the news article to the truth along with a message to President Andrew Jackson, awaiting his signature that he had received and read the message, also, the President had inscribed a brief note expressing his sorrow to all involved over the unfortunate happenings.

Finally, the group was in high spirits to be leaving Washington City and hoping not to return. The trip back would be long and tedious, but spirits were up, the weather was warming, birds were singing and they were heading home.

It was late March when the weary travelers entered the fort in time for a hearty noon time meal, make their Washington report, receive the latest news and eagerly head for home. The Indians all left for Lone Eagle's village. Daniel Reed would remain at the fort for a couple of days before meeting the Echota Cherokee for their return to Georgia. John was approaching his horse assuming Jeb was as eager as he to be with his woman. About time, he thought, when he saw the big scout approaching.

"Let's ride," John swung up on his mount.

"I need to talk to you." This was going to be harder than Jeb thought to explain.

"Where's your horse?" John was having trouble figuring out what was going on.

"I'm not going with you," Jeb couldn't look John Brandon in the eye. Instead he fumbled with his knife, cutting a plug of tobacco. John simply stared, waiting. "I'm not going back to Priscilla. The whole thing was a mistake." Jeb struggled in his throat as he raised his eyes to meet John Brandon's steady gaze. "Priscilla don't want me around—she's never let me touch her," he hesitated, looking at his hands, "we've never been man and wife," he looked away with angry embarrassment. Rubbing the back of his neck, he struggled to continue. "God, I loved her and wanted to father the babe," he kicked a loose stone. "I'm sorry, John Brandon."

Several seconds passed, John gazing into the distance before he could respond, knowing what the scout said was true, knowing what a simpleton and bitch Priscilla could be. Leaning on the saddle pommel he murmured, "I'm sorry, too, Jeb—but maybe this is what Miss Priscilla needs to come to her senses—," he hesitated, knowing how difficult this was for Jeb. "Will you be staying around this area?"

"No—I'll rest up here for a while, help the colonel with stuff for closing the fort. Visit Lone Eagle's village." He gazed around this place that had been home for several years—a loneliness touched his heart. "Then I'll move on to the Arkansas territory—a scout can always find a job." He again struggled to tell this man good-bye. He stepped closer, rubbing the horse's neck. John Brandon was a friend, someone he would probably never see again, and the father of the girl he still loved.

"Take care, John Brandon." Jeb reached up and shook hands.

"I'll do that—you do the same." The two men stared deeply into each other's eyes feeling a bond through their handshake. The scout watched his friend sitting straight and tall in the saddle as he exited the gate. He whispered to himself—take care of her, John Brandon.

"Papa," Jess screeched and Tim yelled as the two bounded down the porch steps flinging themselves at their father who barely had time to remove his boot from the stirrup. The three laughing and hugging, Tim even forgot men didn't act this way.

Jess excitedly yelled, "Prissy has a baby!"

"Yeah, Papa," Tim chimed in proudly, "and it's a baby boy."

"You don't say—and when did this happen?" John questioned, smiling, feeling proud to be a grandpap and so very happy to be home with his exuberant family.

"He's two weeks old!" both children chorused.

He looked—where was Mary? His thoughts were answered as he heard the screen door close. There she stood—still so beautiful. God, he'd missed her so much. Untangling himself from four arms and hands, he took a few steps toward his wife, whispering her name. With a radiant smile and misty eyes she flew into his outstretched arms. He crushed her to him, inhaling her spring flower scent, just breathing in his Mary before kissing her with a youth-filled passion.

The two children were in total shock at the way their parents were acting. "Ga—a," Tim sucked in a big breath, "I didn't know old people acted like that!"

John stopped kissing his wife long enough to breathe and tell her how much he'd missed her and loved her. Completely oblivious of his audience he captured his wife's lips again and repeated the same kissing procedure.

"Papa, stop that—if you don't you're gonna hurt Mama." Jesse bellowed in exasperation, pulling her father's sleeve.

The two broke apart, laughing, finally aware of their audience. Ruffling Jesse's hair, "Oh, honey," John sighed, smiling at his wife, "It's so good to be home." He leaned toward Mary, whispering, "Please get the entire gang to bed early—I've been too long away from my woman."

"Oh, John!" Mary looked down, blushing.

"Well, don't you agree, woman?" He bent down, looking into her face.

"Yes," Mary's face deepened in color while he squeezed her waist, chuckling and shaking his head—still the blushing bride after four children.

"Hey, I hear I'm a granddad—it's about time I saw that boy."

"It's so good to have you home," Mary's eyes radiated her love for this man as she squeezed his arm, starting for the porch.

"Tim and Jesse," John called over his shoulder, "please take care of my horse, and when you come in bring my saddle bags—there might be something in them—I'm simply too tired to do anything right now," John admitted while draping his arm around his wife's shoulder and continuing toward the porch. He stopped, pulling his wife against him, drinking in the countryside beauty. "Honey, I've missed this—it's still the most beautiful spot anywhere."

"Yes, Sir," Tim responded, then lowered his voice, "He sure didn't seem all that tired a few minutes ago—come on, Jess." They headed for the barn.

"How *is* Priscilla?" John was almost afraid to inquire.

"Well," Mary smiled, shaking her head, "I can't believe the change in her—maybe it's because of the baby, I don't know, but she certainly isn't like the old Priscilla."

"Thank God for all blessings," John muttered, "and how's Katherine?" He brushed a leaf from his wife's shoulder.

"I really don't know," Mary glanced into the distance. "Her mind seems to be elsewhere so much of the time. Oh, she continues to help me, she's considerate and seems crazy about the baby, but there's something I can't put my finger on." Mary hesitated. "She's quiet; takes walks alone often."

"Ummm—do I dare inquire about my mother and aunt," he pushed a strand of auburn hair from his wife's face as he again drank in her loveliness, smiling. "Since the house was still standing, I assumed they might be ailing!"

"Oh, John!" Mary couldn't keep from laughing, "You are terrible! Your mother and aunt are resting now. They are well—sometimes," she stooped and picked up a twig, "I wish they were ailing, nothing serious of course, but I would so love to run my household without all of the interference. I know that's awful to say—"

"No, honey, it isn't," he pulled her into his arms. "My poor Mary," he rubbed her back, "having to put up with those two for so long." He pulled back. "Haven't they mentioned going home?"

"No, and we can't mention it either," she commented.

"Well, my dear, you watch me—within a month if they haven't decided to travel home, I will decide for them. The weather will be fine and I won't be patient any longer."

Mary smiled, "Come on—it's time you met your grandson. Priscilla was nursing him, but he should be finished by now," his wife hurried up the steps.

"Priscilla—nursing a baby? Will miracles never cease?" John was amazed as he followed his wife into the house. Mary nodded toward Priscilla, sitting in a rocker by the fire, then eased on out of the room to give the two some time together.

Priscilla sat neat the fireplace, rocking her baby, humming a tune softly while smiling at the beautiful bundle in her arms. "Papa—it's about time you made it home to meet your grandson, the most beautiful boy in the world. Come and see." John couldn't believe the radiance from his daughter as she peeled back the blanket, proudly revealing her son who slept peacefully. The granddad stepped forward, stooped down and traced the plump little cheek with his finger.

"You are right—he is some boy and you seem to be a very contented and happy mother." John looked steadily at his beautiful daughter who seemed to be at peace with the world.

"Yes, I am," she pulled the blanket up. "I had no idea what it would mean to be a parent. I love my baby so much and I've never been this happy. I feel very blessed—and thinking back on the way I was before the baby came," she looked at her father steadily, "that is a person I no longer wish to know." She looked down, bringing her son's tiny hand to her mouth and placing a soft kiss on each small finger. "Papa, where is Jeb? Why isn't he here with you?"

John stood, walked to the mantel, leaning against it, avoiding her eyes. "Honey, he isn't coming." The silence lasted too long, he turned to observe the tear-filled eyes.

"Oh, Papa, I've missed him so! I didn't treat him right when we were together. Now, what I care about is the baby and Jeb's coming home. I didn't realize how I felt about him until he was gone. Oh! This is all my fault, and he doesn't even know he's a father," with this thought she broke down and sobbed.

John knelt, putting his arm around her shoulder. "Honey, don't cry. This is not the end of the world, and who knows the future. Your son does not need a disturbed, crying mother." She wiped a tear from her face.

"I know," she found a handkerchief, wiped her face and blew her nose, "and you haven't even asked my son's name. It's John Jebediah Hawkins," she proudly explained.

John flinched. What a handle! Poor little tyke, having to live with such a name. "I'll see you and my grandson later. Keep your chin up for I have a feeling things might work out for you. Now I'd better round up the family I haven't seen." Priscilla stared into space in deep thought.

Chapter 23

At the fort, Jeb was keeping busy helping Colonel Roberts with paper work, anything to keep his mind off Priscilla. Being this near the Brandons, it was hard not to go to her. He wondered if she'd had her baby.

A couple of nights after returning, he and Col. Roberts were in the Colonel's office relaxing for a few minutes after a busy session with inventory. As they were ready to call it a night, a young private rapped on the door.

"Colonel," the nervous soldier called.

"Yes, come in," Colonel Roberts barked.

The wide eyed private entered, out of breath, attempting to stand at attention. "Relax, Private—what's going on that's so important at this hour?" He looked at his watch.

"Sir," the soldier had to stop to get his breath, "Rusty Poole sent me—he is with Sergeant Mathias over at the hall 'n the Sergeant is drunk as all get out 'n Rusty said for you and Jeb Hawkins to come now 'cause it's important, Sir," the private shuffled and saluted.

"Let's go," the three exited quickly and within minutes were entering the hall where they found soldiers playing cards at two tables, several standing around the bar and Rusty with Mathias near the entrance. Fortunately, Rusty had maneuvered the sergeant with his back to the entrance and our of earshot of the other soldiers. Jeb and the Colonel slipped into chairs behind the two where they could hear the entire conversation.

"Wall, now, Sergeant Mathias, let's jes have one more before we call hit quits." The sergeant was leaning his head on his fist as Rusty poured another shot.

"Coursched 'nuther 'un then 'nuther, 'un 'n nuther 'un," the robust drunk giggled, grabbing the drink and sloshing it down.

"Why—ah thought you'n Lieutenant Anderson wuz the best 'uv buddies," Rusty prodded as he sipped his drink.

"Hell, no, man. How many times I gotta' tell 'ya—he wuz a big ashe, chicken shit. Ah done his dirty work, ah done it all right—Mr. Big Ashe—he come to me, he shays "Math-i-as I's gotta job fo' you—you my friend, but ah'm a payin' ye in gold—lotsa gold—" The sergeant stopped. "Pour me nuther, Rush."

Rusty picked up the bottle, taking his time. He certainly didn't want this one passing out before exposing everything. The scout looked over to a group of soldiers playing cards—he nodded toward the table. "Ain't that soldier over air playing cards the Dittmore boy?" Mathias, bleary eyed, had trouble focusing while Rusty filled the drink with water and a slight amount of liquor.

"Yesh," the drunk replied, "another horse's ashe with a mind no bigger than a rabbit turd." Rusty could hardly keep a straight face as the sergeant picked up his drink.

"I knowed you and the lieutenant wuz friends, but why wuz he a payin' 'n fer what?" Rusty urged.

"Wall, jush gimme time—a damn minute. He'z gonna pay me in gold thet he had stashed—hell, he'z had no gold, jesh a fat lyin' mouth—'n ah kilt thet scrawny bastard witness fer them Injun killins—" He shook his head.

"Oh, ye are joshin' me—" Rusty pushed on.

"Joshin', hell, 'n thet damn likker's lash its taste," he looked at his glass. "Ah know whut ah done fer thet big ashe thet paid me nuthin'—then when he come back ah wuz dirt 't him—dirt," the sergeant sneered, looking glassy eyed.

"Aw—you're jes puttin' me on with this stuff—he's your friend," Rusty egged him on.

"Hell—don' tale ye—he ain't nobody's friend. He set up them Injun killins 'n plotted how ah could kill the only witness fer plenty 'uv money 't live on resh 'uv my life," he hesitated, "but only thing ah got wuz the dirty work so's his big ashe got off free—no money fer doin' his dirt!" Mathias was now whining.

"What did you do with thet witness?" the scout pushed on.

"Wall, whadda ye think? Wha' does anybody do with a dead body? Bury it, you dumb or somethin' Rush," the sergeant snickered.

"Man, ah don't know—thet seems like yore sorta' kiddin' me. Where in the sam hell could a person bury a body on this army post with all them soldiers running around all over thu' place. Why, hits impossible." Rusty kept pushing.

"Wall, ah done it," Mathias pushed his glass over for another drink. "Ah'm a gittin' dry lesh have one more, Rush, 'n ah'm tellin' ye," he gazed bleary eyed at the scout, lowering his voice, "ah buried him over to the horse stables behind 'em with no body a seein' me. Ah done it, but," he hesitated, "but now ah get the shivers ever' time ah go by there 'n fer what'd ah do it," he began to sniffle. Putting his head down on his arms, he sobbed, "Fer that lying low down dirty bastard." He pounded the table with his fist.

The Colonel nodded for Jeb to go for the military security who arrived shortly, arresting and practically carrying Mathis out to the guard house where he was placed under heavy security.

After giving the military security orders to organize a work detail to dig behind the stables for a buried body, the Colonel and Jeb joined Rusty at the table. Anyone listening would have thought he had accomplished the feat of the year, shaking his hand, slapping him on the back and extolling his accomplishment.

"Aw, git on now—cut this out. Ah ain't done nothin' more 'n anybody else would 'uv." Rusty shook his head, pouring himself a much needed drink. "But Colonel, what's you gonna do now with thet there body?"

Roberts explained that after the body was found, he, Jeb, the prisoner with the body would travel to Lone Eagle's village where he knew the Chief, Wild Hawk, and Spotted Horse would join them on the journey to the Arkansas Territory where Anderson was stationed, and where the death of three innocent Indian boys and the killing of a witness would at last be avenged.

"Colonel and Rusty," Jeb commanded their attention, "ah might as well clear this now," somehow it was beginning to be difficult to keep relating—he leaned his elbows on the table—"when I travel with thu' group you mentioned to the Arkansas Territory, well—I'm stayin' there. This fort is closing soon, anyway." He looked down at his hands while the other two stared at him before Rusty burst forth.

"But what 'bout yore wife?"

Knowing this was coming, it was still hard to explain. Jeb wiped up a water spill with his sleeve, concentrating on the effort. "That didn't work out." He stood, changing the subject. "You know, Rusty," he placed his hand on the old scout's shoulder, "Lone Eagle can never thank you enough for avenging the death of three little innocent Indian boys." He strode out of the hall and into the night.

By early morning the work detail had uncovered the body of the missing witness. Wrapping and securing what was left of the decomposed body, packing food and gear and readying themselves for a long journey, the two men along with the prisoner and dead body took off for Eagle's village early the following morning, the sooner the better to rid themselves of this distasteful mission.

John was just finishing his second cup of coffee, enjoying the warmth of the early spring morn, the birds chirping their jubilee, and the peacefulness of the Tennessee hills. Ah! He didn't want to leave this place. He'd learned to love it. Granted, there were conveniences in city life—he knew Mary had missed regular church services—but also social pretenses that he couldn't handle anymore. When the fort closes, he thought, I'm resigning my job as Indian consultant. I can not nor will not work for a government that mistreats any group of people. His thoughts were interrupted as his eldest daughter descended the porch steps to sit with her father. He noticed her paleness and dark circles under her eyes.

He patted her shoulder. "How's my girl?" She smiled, but it didn't seem to reach her eyes as she smoothed her green cotton skirt.

"Oh, I'm all right, Papa, but you've said so little about your Washington trip. Did the reading and writing help the Cherokee?" She gazed steadily at her father, needing to hear any news relating to her Indian.

He gazed into the mountains. "Nothing seems to help the Cherokee, certainly not the new President, who would not commit himself, and I don't believe he will go against the state of Georgia." He pulled out his pipe, lit it and puffed away.

"Oh, Papa!" Deep concern was etched on her face. "What will happen to the Cherokee?"

"Who knows? Guess only time will tell." He had to change the subject. "Katherine, you don't look as though you feel well," he caught a lock of auburn hair, removing it from her collar, "honey, the weight loss and dark circles around your eyes. Are you not eating and sleeping well?"

She looked down at her hands which were busy with skirt folds. "I don't seem to be very hungry, and at night when everyone else is asleep I come out here and walk, sometimes just sit for it's so peaceful," she sighed, looking into the distance.

He stared at his lovely sad-eyed Katherine, wishing things were different. "It's Wild Hawk, isn't it?" he murmured.

"Yes," she raised her misty eyes to look steadily into his. "Papa, I've tried so hard to forget him, but I can't." She shifted her gaze to the mountains. "If he were to come here today and ask me to go with him, I would, but he adheres to your demands and he will not jeopardize my life for the harsh and uncertain Cherokee existence and future." A tear slipped down her face.

"Oh, Katherine!" he gathered her into his arms, feeling deeply for this daughter's misery, while stroking her hair and pressing her head to his shoulder. "I'm so sorry," he murmured while her tears flowed.

Horse's hooves helped to diminish the emotional situation as Kate wiped her eyes with her skirt, and John stood, walking toward the gate.

"Why, come in here, Rusty Poole, and welcome. Missed you at the fort on our return from Washington." The little scout entered, greeted Kate, noting her red sad eyes.

"Wall, thought I'd git over here to see if'n youse still kickin' or if thet high society in Washington don' wore ye to a nub," he chuckled, slapping John on the back.

"Oh! We all made it, as you know, but don't believe much if anything was accomplished," John commented. "Have a seat, Rusty, and I'll tell you some good news—I'm a granddad," John puffed out his chest, "and he's about the finest looking young man anywhere," he proudly related as he sat by Kate.

"Wall, I'll be a suck egg mule—ain't thet mighty fine 'n how's Miss Priscilly a doin'?" Rusty seemed much concerned as he sat.

"She's fine," tuning to Kate, "Honey, get Rusty a cup of coffee and tell the family to come out—Rusty has news—know he didn't come here to inquire of my health, and tell Tim and Jess to bring chairs." John smiled, puffed his pipe and waited.

Mary, followed by the youngest two, greeted the scout. "Rusty, it's about time you paid us a visit—it's certainly good to see you." She smiled, placing a hand on his arm while taking a seat by him. Kate followed, handing Rusty his coffee.

"Thank ye, Ma'am—" he looked around, "Whar is that baby boy? Ain't I gonna' git 't see him?" Gazing at the porch, "Where is Miss Priscilly?"

"She's on her way." The screen door closed, "Here she is now with our new baby," Mary proudly explained the obvious.

"Well," Rusty stood, "bring thet young 'un over here. John's about 't bust thu' buttons clean off'n his shirt, he's so proud, but do hope this babe don't take after him in looks." Rusty peered at the plump pink-cheeked baby who crinkled a tiny smile.

"Wall, I'll be dadburned if'n he don't know ole Rusty already," a gnarled finger gently slid down the baby's soft cheek. "He shore is a pretty one, Miss Priscilly." He clapped John on the back who had moved up with the others to again view his namesake.

"Let's all sit down. I'm sure if our baby needs us he'll let us know." He felt the scout might be wearing down with all the family stuff. "Believe Rusty has some news for us."

"Wall, I do—guess ah should have come over 'fore this, but got busy at the Fort." He took his knife out, cut a plug and plopped it in his mouth. With a contented smile on his face he gazed at Mary. "Hope you don't mind, Ma'am." She shook her head.

"I thought you had something to tell us, Rusty, but you sure don't act like it," Jesse chimed in as she sprawled on the ground.

"Jessica, that will be enough!" John glared at the mouth, "Rusty does not need any assistance from you."

"Yes, Sir," she murmured, sticking her tongue out at Tim who had poked her in the ribs with his foot.

"Wall, couple 'uv weeks ago I wuz in the hall over at the fort one night jes' millin' around when I noticed Sergeant Mathias wuz drinkin' right steady like. You 'member him, John, Lieutenant Anderson's side kick. The one always doin' chores fer him." John nodded. "Any how, ah set down with him 'n fore ah knowed hit he wuz shore wantin' t' talk. Course, I egged him on thinking he might give some kind of information on thet missin' witness, so's I sent for Jeb and the Colonel, 'n shore 'nuff he told hit all 'n they heard hit all. Wall, to shortin' hit—he told how Anderson set it all up to kill the three Indian boys," Mary gasped, "'n how the lieutenant had hired him to kill the only witness. Wal, the body wuz where Mathias had buried hit." Rusty took time out to spit a tobacco stream.

"Oh, my goodness!" Jessica was breathless. "Do you mean a real, honest t' goodness dead body?" Her eyes were as big as saucers.

"Yes, Ma'am, that's zackly right—anyhow, the Colonel, Jeb, the prisoner Mathias with the body went to Lone Eagle's village to pick up the chief, Wild Hawk and Spotted Horse. The whole bunch left couple of weeks ago for the Arkansas Territory to nail Anderson with all the necessary proof." Rusty stretched his legs while eyeing his audience, especially Priscilla.

"Thank God," John murmured, "but Rusty, if you had told me sooner, I could have gone with them." He ran his hand through his hair, wondering why he wasn't notified.

"Thet's zackly why ah didn't tell you—yore needed to be here, not trapsin' around the country again so soon!" The old scout twinkled as he spit his juice.

Mary clapped her hands. "You tell him, Rusty!" John chuckled.

"Ga—" Tim added, "who'd want to go anywhere with a dead body?" He shuddered.

"How long will they be gone, Rusty?" Kate had to know something. She hadn't seen her Indian in three to four months.

"Why, I'd say—two or three more weeks. They should be back by then, Miss Kate." Rusty was aware of the girl's eyes that looked so sad and were surrounded by dark circles.

"Rusty," Priscilla hesitated, gently stroking the baby's cheek, "did Jeb say anything before he left—ah—about me or us?" She looked down, for her eyes were misting.

Oh, my, the old scout thought, this was what he was dreading, and he simply couldn't lie to her. Damnation—he'd rather not to know anything than git hisself in the middle of all thes. He leaned up, resting his arms on his knees, looking at the ground. "Yes, Ma'am—he said he wuz a stayin' in the Arkansas Territory—that things didn't work out for you two." He cleared his throat fer thangs wuz stayin' too quiet fer too long.

"Thank you," Priscilla murmured as she stood and started for the porch before the tears spilled. She quickly went to her room where she placed the sleeping child in his cradle before slumping down on her bed thinking she had to do something to keep her husband. She simply could not nor would not lose him now. She loved him. It was strange, she thought, hearing about Keith Anderson for she had no feeling whatsoever other than she wanted him to get just punishment.

Kate excused herself to see about Priscilla.

"I'm sorry, Miss Mary and John—ah didn't know what to do, but tell her thu' truth," he shook his shaggy head, "She was bound to know it soon." He looked at the parents for forgiveness.

Mary tried to ease the scout's mind for his honesty, but as a mother would, she felt for her daughter who was being such a good mother and seemed to have changed so much for the better.

John and Mary insisted Rusty stay for their noon meal. Of course, he complied, chuckling to himself knowing he always planned to visit just at meal time so he could enjoy Miss Mary's cookin' fer she wuz shore a good 'un! He also enjoyed seein' John's mother who wuz a mite plump, but still a purty woman 'n he believed she kinda liked him. Guess he'd jes haf to come 'round oftener. He chuckled again, shifted his cud to the other side of his mouth and waved good-bye to everyone.

Before he mounted up, Priscilla had walked around the outside fence. "Rusty, I have to talk with you." She seemed excited. Her eyes flashed and he thought he'd done thu' wrong thing telling her what Jeb had said. He removed his foot from the stirrup and followed her through the pasture to the old oak tree where there was a bench. They sat down and the scout waited until the fidgety girl began. "Rusty, I have to go to the Arkansas Territory." She turned pleading eyes to him.

"You—whut!" Rusty wheezed as he jumped up glaring at her.

"I have to go and you'll have to take me."

"Ye've lost yore mind, teetotally! Ye cain't go sashaying 'round the country 'n ah shore won't be no part—" he threw up his hands.

"Rusty, you must." He sat back down while she continued, "I can't let him go. I didn't know how much I loved him until he was gone." She wiped a tear from her face. "I need him—my baby needs him." She broke down sobbing. "Please—" Rusty cussed inwardly—how in hell could he get tied into every terrible thing that happened? He patted her shoulder awkwardly.

"Now hush them tears—you can't do this. Whut 'bout the baby?" He felt that would stop such ridiculous thinking.

"My baby will go with me. He's fine and healthy." She was emphatic.

"Ye've done lost ever bit 'uv sense ye ever had," he slapped his old leather hat against his leg. "Ah ain't a gonna do hit."

She looked at him long and hard. "Then, I'll have to go alone." She stood.

"If'n ye ain't the dad burnest, doggonnest stubbornest, senseless female I've ever saw—" He stood, pacing back and forth running his fingers through his shaggy gray hair. Stopping, he sighed. "Ah cain't let ye go alone. No tellin' whut could happen to you and thu' babe, but you know John Brandon will have yore hide and mine too, don't 'chu?"

Wheeling around, she smiled and hugged him. "Oh, thank you, thank you Rusty. I'll never forget this—"

"Ah probably won't neither after yore Pa tends to us both! Anyhow, when is this jaunt to be?" he questioned.

"Day after tomorrow—I'll be ready at first light." Her eyes flashed her excitement and determination.

"I'll be here, 'gainst ma better judgement," he slammed his hat on his head as she collared him for another hug and kissed his leathery cheek.

"Thank you so much," she whispered.

"We'll take several of Lone Eagle's braves with us for protection." Oh, I must be losing my mind to do a gol-darn thing like this, he thought.

She nodded, thanking God, and watched as Rusty shook his head, mumbling to himself before mounting up.

Priscilla confided in Kate before leaving on her journey west, and left a note for her parents trying to explain the reasoning behind this venture, the people escorting her, and that her husband would be returning home with her.

After an uneventful trip west, Priscilla and escorts arrived at the Arkansas Territory Army Post within two weeks due to good weather, with efficient and protective Indian guides. Little Johnny was a dream baby on the journey and had no trouble walking right into the heart of each traveler. The braves and Rusty took turns sparing Priscilla with the child's care. For entertainment the Indians chanted their Cherokee songs while baby Johnny cooed and smiled his thanks.

On an early sunny afternoon, the rather strange entourage arrived at the busy army post causing quite a stir. Most groups arriving at this place did not consist of a lovely white lady with a baby, four Indians and an old scout.

A neat well built young man in uniform approached the group, introducing himself and inquiring, "I'm Sergeant Jacobs—Is there something I can do for you?" His blue eyes traveled to the young lady carrying the baby while several soldiers looked on and listened.

"Yeah—ye might say so," Rusty replied, easing back in the saddle trying to eliminate some of the numbness in his back end. "We'll be a visitin' some 'uv the people here for thu' Anderson court case—these here," pointing to the Cherokee, "is Chief Lone Eagle's braves, and the young lady is Miz Hawkins, Jeb Hawkins' woman 'n ah'm Rusty Poole, army scout." The Sergeant stared at Priscilla wondering how the big scout Hawkins could ever wind up with a beauty like this. Those gathered around, listening, were wondering the same and mumbled the same to each other.

"Sergeant, if'n ye'd show us to Jeb Hawkins' quarters we'd be much obliged. The little lady is a might weary from travelin'."

"Yes, Sir—Williams, show the lady to her husband's quarters," he commanded a young private.

"Yes, Sir." A dark eyed, slightly built young soldier appeared by their side.

"Oh, Sergeant, we'd appreciate you keepin' it quiet 'bout us bein' here, if'n ye don't mind. She'd sorta like to surprise her husband—ah!—you know," Rusty twinkled and smiled knowingly to the amusement of the listening soldiers as they poked each other wishing something like this gal would surprise them.

The Indians were shown to Lone Eagle's campsite while Private Williams directed Priscilla and Rusty to Jeb's quarters where Rusty stuck around until Prissy had settled in and making sure the baby had everything he needed. He then took his leave to find the Indian camp and tend to the horses. The old scout shook his head, amazed that Priscilla had not complained once during the entire journey and thinking this young woman had certainly changed from the bitchy person she used to be.

After changing and feeding the baby, Prissy laid her sleeping son on one of the two army cots and stretched out by him, not realizing how exhausted she really was until she lay down to rest, but soon fell sound asleep.

The sound of a door opening and closing rather loudly awakened her. Disoriented, she leaned up on an elbow and stared at her husband who leaned against the door, his eyes and mouth wide open.

"Priscilla,—what in hell are you doing here?" he thundered. She was so beautiful lying there, it almost took his breath away. Neither moved.

"I've come to get my husband," she calmly replied causing his heart to thump wildly as they stared at each other, neither moving.

"You've what?" He continued to thunder at her, not believing her, not daring to hope.

"You heard me, Jeb, I came to get, to fetch, to find my husband." She sat up on the side of the bed not taking her eyes from him, her tumbled hair enhancing her beauty.

He looked distraught and viciously rubbed his arm while stating firmly as he continued leaning against the door, "You have no husband except on paper—as you well know. We've never been man and wife to consummate those vows." He frowned miserably, hurting inside.

"I know," she whispered as she stood and walked slowly toward him until she came within a foot of him, her hands touching his chest causing a trembling in his body. Her eyes were pleading as she repeated, "I know." She hesitated before continuing, "I made a mess of everything and I'm asking forgiveness." Her eyes misted. "I didn't know how much you meant to me until you were gone." He was having trouble breathing with her so near. 'Course, she was saying what he wanted to hear, but could he believe her? "Then," she pled, "you didn't come back to me and it broke my heart—for you see," she looked into his eyes, "I love you, Jeb Hawkins. I love my husband and I want to be his wife." She inched closer as Jeb removed her hands and stepped around her with his back to her. He struggled with his voice as he uttered.

"Priscilla, don't trifle with me—I can't take any more of it." She turned around viewing his stiff back and clinched fists which only encouraged her to take the necessary step to reach him. She put her arms around his waist and buried her face against his back while she stifled a sob.

"Please don't shut me out, Jeb, for I need you so. I'm not the same person you knew. Please believe me. It's only you I want."

He didn't pull away and had to struggle with himself to keep from turning and crushing her in his arms. "How the hell did you get here, Prissy?" He turned toward her, gazing steadily into her eyes, hoping beyond hope she was telling the truth. Her hands slipped to his waist while tears bathed her face. She wiped at them before responding.

"Rusty and four of Lone Eagle's braves brought me. I told the old scout if he didn't I'd make the trip by myself." Her beautiful eyes were hypnotizing him.

"You what?" he bellowed, "why you little idiot!" He finally smiled.

"—and I would have, too, I wanted my husband. Please, can't you just hold me in your arms?" She stepped closer.

"Oh! Priscilla," he reached for her, enfolding her in his strong embrace. "Do I dare believe you?"

"Yes, my husband," she sighed, "but right now let's not talk—just kiss me."

He gazed into her beautiful teary eyes believing or maybe wanting to believe that he did see love there. He bent his head, capturing those lips that he'd only dreamed of for so long. The kiss deepened and she responded fully while her arms crept around his neck and her body molded to his.

Needing to breathe, Jeb looked into those hypnotic eyes. "Woman, do you know what you're doin'?"

"Yes," she replied, her eyes twinkling mischievously, "I know exactly what I'm doing, but before we finalize those marriage vows, I have a surprise for you." She took his hand, leading him across the floor to the bed. Turning back the coverlet, the sleeping baby was exposed. "Darling, meet your son."

Jeb stared at the beautiful child, awed by the fact that he was a father and she had brought his son to him. "I don't know what to say," he touched the baby's cheek gently and struggled within his throat. "He is so beautiful and he is my son. Oh, Priscilla, thank you," his own eyes were misting. She stooped down putting her arms around her big gentle man, and proudly explained, "He's named after his father."

"Oh! My God, Priscilla," he murmured, "how could you?"

"His name is John Jebediah Hawkins."

"Woman, how could you tag such a damnable handle onto this innocent child," he shook his head.

"We call him Johnny," she all but whispered. "And now that you've met your son—oh! Jeb, please—just love me." He pulled her up, wrapping her softness in his arms and kissing her soundly.

"Woman," he teased as he began unbuttoning her dress, "Meet your husband."

The following day the court case of one Lieutenant Keith Anderson and one Sergeant Brody McThias was finalized with the following judgment. Each man would be stripped of any and all army insignia and classification and given a dishonorable discharge where he could never again be a part of the U.S. Military service. They were both to be escorted to Washington City where they would remain imprisoned or be put to death, whichever the higher military court decided.

The Cherokee felt justice had been reached in the White man's court, but the whole thing had been trying, renewing the death of three innocent Indian boys. Each Cherokee was more than ready to return home, including Wild Hawk who had done a lot of thinking about his own life these past few weeks. Knowing he could not be with Katherine Green Eyes, and knowing he could not be as near as his Indian village to the Brandon home without seeing her, his decision was made. He would leave Lone Eagle's village, travel to the Echota Cherokee in Georgia and live there for the time being. He knew they could use another brave to help fight the Militia. He felt, too, that John Brandon would leave this area when the fort closed and return to Boston, which meant he would never see his

Katherine Green Eyes again. Oh! My God—these thoughts tore his heart out. He wanted to weep and yell at the injustice of mankind. Instead he leaned his head back against the old gnarled oak, closed his eyes and relived the times he had been with Katherine which were too few. He had to see her one more time and explain his plans.

When Jeb returned to his quarters after the final court verdict and dismissal of the trial, he was met by an exuberant wife who threw her welcoming arms around his neck.

"Well," he smiled, "I might go out and come back in for such a reception," he teased. "Did you miss me these three hours?"

"Yes," she whispered, her eyes caressing his face, "I hope it's all over so we can go home."

"Home?" he questioned.

She nodded as he pulled her to the bed, sat down and placed her onto his lap.

"Now what is this home bit?"

"Well, I thought we could return home until the fort closes and by that time," she straightened his shirt collar, "you would have made up your mind what you want to do and where you want to be, and whatever you decide will be fine with me." He nibbled her neck, causing goose bumps.

"You figured all this out?"

"Uh huh!" He smiled, brushing her lips with a feather kiss.

"I'll think on it," he rocked her back and forth. "You know, Priss, when I first saw you here what came to my mind?" She shook her head. "Ah was wondering if you had come to try to help Anderson in that trial."

She eased up, staring into his face, frowning. "Oh, Jeb—how could you?" She looked distressed.

"Well, why wouldn't I?" he smoothed the hair from her face, still holding her in his lap.

"It's strange, I guess." She gazed steadily into his eyes. "At one time I thought I really cared for him, but apparently it was infatuation for when Rusty described where you were and for what reason, I felt nothing for Keith Anderson other than wanting him to receive his just punishment." She rubbed the short fringe that decorated his shirt front. "I suppose, Jeb Hawkins, when you walked into my heart there wasn't room for anything else." She reached up and kissed his lips as he pulled her to him.

"Oh! Priscilla—tell me this is all for real—that it's no dream."

She snuggled in and whispered, "It's no dream, believe me."

In two days on a bright sunny April morn, the entire group of Indians, scouts, Priscilla and little Johnny were heading home from the Arkansas Territory. Even though a trifle weary from the emotional turmoil renewed, loss of sleep and being 'out of pocket', the travelers were in good spirits to be heading home.

Jeb, cradling his son in his arms, burst forth in his not-so-melodious baritone voice, with a dirty ditty, "and she jumped in bed and covered up her head—wuz shore I'd never find her," Little Johnny smiled and cooed at his dad.

"Jeb Hawkins—" Priscilla could hardly keep a straight face, "don't you dare teach your son those bawdy songs!"

"Hush, Woman—ah ain't finished this 'un yet 'n sides, my son's enjoying every word of it.—'but damn it t' hell, I gotta tell—I jumped in right behind her—and saw her sausage grinder—'"

The whole troop burst into laughter along with Jeb as he rolled his eyes at his wife who was doing everything possible to keep from joining their fun.

Wild Hawk rode Night Wind near Jeb's horse. "Hand Johnny to me, Moose. He needs soothing after having to put up with your screeching dirty words in his ears." Smiling at his friend, Jeb handed over his son, knowing Wild Hawk just wanted to hold the baby.

"Sleep, Little One, sleep," Hawk crooned in his mellow bass voice,

"The Wind whispers your name,"

"Mother Earth calls the same,"

"Sleep, Little One, sleep,"

The Indian lullaby seemed, along with the voice, to have had an effect on the child. Before the baby's eyes closed in sleep, he reached up and touched the Indian's face. Hawk gathered the tiny hand in his and kissed it. The thought that he would never hold his own son or be able to sing to him brought tears to his eyes which he did everything in his power to hide. Finally, he kneed his horse into a little faster pace to be in front of the others.

Jeb knew what his friend was feeling and he hurt for him.

The return trip couldn't have been better. The weather cooperated beautifully with no storms. Priscilla, in her glory, slept in her husband's arms each night and the Indians again contributed to the care of baby Johnny. Wild Hawk kept the baby with him the early part of the night to give his mother and father some privacy before the child awakened for his feeding. He couldn't believe how much he enjoyed having the little tyke with him.

After two weeks, the travelers arrived home. The Indians were a little sad to tell 'their baby' good-bye, especially Wild Hawk; however, none would miss the sometimes off-key baritone that kept producing daily alehouse ballads, with Rusty's screeching protests.

Chapter 24

Three Indian ponies were tied a distance away as Dancing Eyes, Swift Antelope and the Scarface crept near the Brandon's home in the middle of the night. Dancing Eyes shushed the other two as they all stooped down behind some bushes to watch the porch and lawn.

Shortly thereafter, Kate wandered onto the porch, clad only in her long nightgown, seemingly drinking in the peacefulness of the night. She looked to the hills as she descended the porch steps, but saw only shadows cast by the silvery moon, which were the usual. She sat on a bench wondering if he would ever come back, and wondering if he even thought of her. It had been so long, more than four months. Prissy and Jeb had returned three days ago from Arkansas, and she knew Wild Hawk had returned with them for Prissy had shared how he had become so attached to the baby.

The three Indians watched the white girl as she walked slowly around and around the yard, over and over again, occasionally glancing into the hills. Finally, after a good hour had passed, she ascended the steps, sighed heavily, looked again at the hills and went inside.

Scar Face grabbed Dancing Eyes' arm, pointing to the white girl, frowned, then pointed to his head as though the pale face were crazy. The Indian girl smiled malevolently, nodded as she placed a finger to her lips for silence. The three waited several minutes before creeping silently on moccasined feet to their mounts, leading the horses a distance before mounting up.

It was in the wee hours of the morn before the three Cherokee reached the entrance of Lone Eagle's village. Behind a clump of evergreens they dismounted, staked their horses, and made final detailed plans for their adventure to save their tribe from evil white forces. These plans would take place in four moons. Before departing, the three made a brotherhood pact through hand signs accompanied with Cherokee mumblings. Upon departure each went his separate direction, but not one of the three was aware that a young Indian boy had been close enough to hear their plotting.

Little Acorn had awakened very early needing to relieve himself. He had exited his lodge, and finding himself wide awake he strolled on to the edge of the village, enjoying the early morning bird sounds and the shadows cast by the moon that hadn't put her head to rest. He stood enjoying the peacefulness when he heard horses approaching. Scampering behind a leafy bush, he hid, thinking an enemy might be approaching. There were three and when they halted their mounts Acorn was within a few feet of Dancing Eyes, Swift Antelope and Scar Face. The three stooped down behind the trees but he was near enough to hear everything they said. After they left he thought about their talk, but some of it didn't make much sense. Judgment and they didn't use names. He didn't know Lone Eagle's Cherokee had more white enemies that wanted to do harm. He yawned, again feeling sleepy as he started toward his lodge, knowing he'd think a lot about their talk before mentioning it to anyone.

The following night Kate again found herself wide awake around 11:30. She'd just heard the clock in the hall strike the half-hour. The house was all quiet and the moon was again shining its glory, making everything seem peaceful. To be outside, to be a part of this peacefulness made her feel closer to him, some way. She slipped out of bed, snatched up an old shawl for the wind seemed to have picked up, and tiptoed down the stairs. She exited the screen door, immediately searching the hills. Oh! Dear Lord, he was there! The wind seemed to be stronger, to almost whisper.

Grabbing the porch post to steady herself, she shut her eyes, thinking she was dreaming. Upon opening them—he was still there! Dropping the shawl, she bounded down the steps. Oh! Dear Lord, please don't let this be a dream. She was practically sobbing as she fled across the pasture and into his waiting arms. "Oh! Wild Hawk," she sobbed her tears onto his chest as he held her tightly against him. Neither seemed able to speak. Tears were filling his eyes as he smoothed her long auburn hair with one gentle hand. She raised her head, searching his beloved face that she had dreamed of so often, but now his eyes were filled with tears. He wiped away her tears before she wrapped her arms around his neck while he captured her lips with a hungry kiss that told of his pent-up passion and deep love.

"Oh! My Katherine, my love, my Green Eyes. How can I ever explain what I have to tell you?" He nuzzled her neck, continuing to hold her as she pulled her arms from his neck, searching his eyes that seemed to be so sad.

"What is it?" She only whispered, knowing something was wrong.

He took her hand, pulling her along with him for a few feet. Finding a soft grassy spot he sat, pulling her into his lap and for the first time the moon was bright enough to reveal the circles around her eyes, her paleness, and cradling her, he was aware of her thinness.

"What is this—the circles around your eyes," he stroked her cheek, "the paleness, and you are thinner. What is wrong?" His worry was evident.

She looked into those sad and worry filled eyes with the too-long lashes, gently touching the handsome face and smiling. "It's you—do you realize how long it's been since we have seen each other? Over four months and then we were alone together for a minute or two." She nestled her head against his chest as he held her with both arms. "I don't seem to be hungry anymore, and I have trouble sleeping."

She raised her head and smiled as he crushed her to him, kissing her beautiful trembling mouth, trying to tell her what was in his heart.

She leaned her head back against his arm, looking up at him. "Now tell me what's wrong."

"Green Eyes, you know you have been with me every day since we last saw each other. In Washington City where I stayed busy, having to attend functions, meetings, dealing with the Georgia militia, but I could close my eyes and you were with me. At night I dreamed of you, holding you in my arms. I have been so torn between wanting to be with you and staying away, knowing we can not be together that I have finally made a decision." He sighed. "I have to leave this area. I am not strong enough to live in Lone Eagle's village, this near you, and not be with you." He looked into the distance, struggling within himself as he cradled her tightly in his arms. "I am leaving this area to live with the Echota Cherokee in Georgia. They need all of the help they can get to fight the militia. There, I will not be able to come to you."

She leaned up, looking him straight in the eye. "I'm going with you."

"No, you are not!" He was emphatic. "I can not nor will not destroy you. I love you too much," he smoothed her hair from her face. "Don't you know if you were with me, living in the chaotic life of the Cherokee, this love that is so deep between us would also be destroyed?" He pulled her close to him, not able to look at the pain in her face.

She whispered in his ear. "Please don't leave me. I'm not sure I can make it or that I even want to if I can never see you or be with you again."

He was so choked up with her statement he couldn't answer. He could only press her head against his chest and hold her.

Finally, he continued with what he had come to say. "My Green Eyes, it is only time before the Cherokee nation in Georgia and here will be destroyed. I felt it even more so when we were in Washington, and it seems there is nothing we can do to stop it. There are too many whites willing to let it happen and now," he stood, pulling her up with him, "and now, my love, we must say our good-byes—prolonging this is killing both of us." He took her face in his hands and gazed into the lovely tear-filled eyes. "Know that wherever I am, my heart will always be with you. Know, too, that if you can not be my woman, my wife, there will never be anther. I love you more than life, my beautiful Katherine Green Eyes." He then pulled her to him, kissing her deeply before abruptly letting her go and turning quickly, but before he could walk to his horse she grabbed his arm.

Her chin quivered as she raised her voice. "Is this it, then? You arrive, tell me you love me, you kiss me good-bye and that's it—and I have no say in anything? Well, I'm going to have a say, so you will know, for you haven't the slightest idea what it's been like for me or what it will be like." Her green eyes flashed their fire. "It's been hell—" she took a few steps away and wheeled around—he only stared, startled at her response. "I happened to have fallen in love with an Indian, apparently that was and is the greatest crime of the century. I saw him for a minute or two four months ago and I've been housed here with my family, eating my heart out, not knowing whether I'll ever see him again or whether he really cares for me."

"Oh! Green Eyes—please," he reached toward her and she slapped his hand.

"I haven't finished—while I'm sitting here," her eyes filled with tears, "with all my doubts, loneliness, and heartache, he's ripping over the country doing what he wishes, where he wishes with his buddies, and now," a tear slipped down her cheek, "he drops by after four months to kiss me and tell me good-bye, that he's leaving and we won't see each other again. Well, damn you, I can't live on dreams, and you're saying you'll always be with me. Hah! That's a lie. If you loved me enough you couldn't leave me like this! Run on and live your life to the fullest." She lowered her voice, walking a few steps, then turning, "You've never known this Katherine Green Eyes. Maybe you don't care to," she wiped at a tear, "we've had no time together—well, know this, I'm not some fragile ornament. I'm a woman who loves and needs to be loved by a real flesh and blood man, not a dream that runs over the country for other causes. And I don't care what others say, my father, your chief, any others. This is not their life. I'd rather die than be miserable and wither away on some farm." She raised her voice again. "Go on—run!" She wheeled around sobbing, and started running for the house.

"Katherine!" he called. She didn't slow up, but with a few strides he soon caught her, tumbling her to the ground, holding her tightly in spite of the flaying arms. "Please don't cry like this, my love. It breaks my heart," he soothed.

"Well, something needs to," she struggled, wiping at her tears.

"Green Eyes, we can not part this way," he murmured, gently smoothing her hair.

"I'm not parting—you are," she thrust at him.

He hesitated. "Right now, I do not know any thing or what I am doing. Guess I have been selfish, thinking of myself and what I had to do without considering your feelings." He brushed her hair back. "When I came here tonight, I knew all the answers, I thought, but right now, I am not sure I know anything." She stared deeply into his eyes.

"Let me up, Hawk—we can't lie here all night." She could hardly keep from putting her arm around him.

"Oh, I don't know," he murmured as he drew her to him and brushed her lips with his. He smiled. "I do know, my little cussing spitfire, that I became better acquainted with you tonight," he teased, running his finger down her cheek, but seriously adding, "I do know, too, that I love you with all my heart. Never doubt, and I promise I will do nothing before I see you again and soon."

She put her arms around his neck. "Promise?"

"I promise." He pulled her up and gathered her to him. "Another thing, Green Eyes, you should not be running around at any hour, day or night, in only a night gown."

"Well," her eyes were large and innocent, "I knew if I saw anyone it would be you."

"But after all, my Green Eyes, I am but a man of flesh and blood," he teased. She smiled devilishly, wrapped her arms around his neck and kissed him, while murmuring, "Good night, my handsome brave—not good-bye." She quickly ran toward the house, stopping once to blow him a kiss. He sighed, watching the slip of a girl as she fled across the pasture. She might look like a young girl, but she was quite a woman, his woman. Oh! Yawa, please show me the way for the future. I seem to be right back where I was, not knowing what to do. He watched her until she reached the porch where she turned and waved.

Kate continued her nightly vigil from her front yard seat. It had become a habit during her late hours of sleeplessness. It was her peaceful time without family interference. Here she was in her night gown again, and he had told her not to run around in it day or night. Sitting on the bench, smoothing her soft cotton gown over her knees, she stuck her legs out wiggling her bare toes. She giggled to herself for she was happy, having seen her man and she did love him so and he would be back. He promised—and some way, some how she would not let him leave for any Georgia. They could fight their own battles down there. Thinking of the other night when she had seen him and of her outburst, she was ashamed. Such cussing—no lady would ever do such a thing, but she was angry. Course, she couldn't stay angry with him for very long, but he had everything figured out without considering her feelings or desires.

A sound penetrated her thoughts—a movement—she smiled, whispering, "Wild Hawk," but before she could turn around a brown muscular arm snaked tightly around her waist, a hand covered her mouth to muffle any sound, before she glimpsed a terribly scarred savage face. Her feeble attempt to ward off her attacker only brought a snarl and a rather vicious rapping on her head which sent her into black oblivion.

The limp body collapsed against the attacker before being thrown roughly over a muscular shoulder and carried soundlessly through the gate.

Dancing Eyes, excitement shining in her dark eyes, and Swift Antelope met Scar Face outside the entrance. Both clasped his shoulders indicating their congratulations for a job well done. Not speaking, the threesome with their bounty still slung over Scar's shoulder made their way carefully back to their horses, that were ground tied a quarter of a mile away from the home.

When they reached their mounts, Swift Antelope and Dancing Eyes took over with the girl, gagging and tying the mouth to make sure there was no sound when she did awaken. Afterwards Antelope placed her none too gently in front of him on his swift moving bay. The three then took off rather hurriedly for Judgment Rock, the highest peak in the entire area, and one that had devoured several staked out bodies during past years. Even if one were able to loosen his bonds, there was no way a person could descend that rock alone. The trip would take two to three hours, and Dancing Eyes laughed to herself as her pony kept the fast pace with the others. This is one time that the pale eyed scrawny bitch couldn't win. She'd lose Wild Hawk, that she'd always tricked, and her life. Dancing Eyes sneered in her evil enjoyment, and she was proud of herself for planning it all. She had convinced Swift Antelope that with this pale face Kate out of the way, Wild Hawk would leave and return to his home in Georgia, giving Swift Antelope the title of chief, even if they had to remove Chief Lone Eagle with some accidental death. Then Dancing Eyes would be Chief Swift Antelope's woman. Antelope was the nearest distant relative to Lone Eagle with Hawk away. Little did Antelope suspect that when the pale eyes Kate's body was found, Dancing Eyes would be the innocent, convincing all others that she had overheard Antelope and the Scar plotting the entire horrible act. That it was their idea to rid themselves of Wild Hawk, make Antelope Chief and establish Scar in this village as a prominent brave. This way, she would rid herself of Swift Antelope and she would have her Wild Hawk. She giggled to herself at her cleverness.

    Before taking the pale bitch to her final place on the rock, which would be quite a struggle for two strong braves to get her up there, Dancing Eyes would make sure she was quiet with no knowledge of anything. Before leaving her village, the Indian maiden stole a sleeping potion from the old Shaman's lodge which would be poured down the pale eyes' throat before the two braves began the final climb. This would also keep this white one from fighting the elements. Course, there would be no one to hear her cries. The Indian maiden smiled wickedly. Proud that she had thought of everything.

Sunshine took over late the next morning after an early morning shower that was badly needed. Priscilla burst through the porch door to find Mary, John and Jeb enjoying their second cup of coffee along with the beauty of the warm spring morn.

"Kate's gone—she's nowhere in the house!" She was breathless as she descended the steps.

"Oh," Mary waved her silent, "she's probably walking, which she often does." She sipped her coffee, watching squirrels frolic around the oak.

"Listen to me," Prissy's voice raised, "her bed wasn't slept in last night."

John jumped up, thinking oh my God, if Wild Hawk came for her, she'd go with him. "She may have slept in the living room, on the couch, "he paced back and forth, running his hand through his hair. "Send Tim out to check near the barn, the pasture—"

"I've already done that—Kate is not here—would you please listen to me!" Jeb stood, and walked to her. "Jeb, I'm worried." She lowered her voice, "Do you think Wild Hawk could have done this? She cares for him."

"No," Jeb defended his friend, "he wouldn't do anything underhanded. I know him too well."

Mary and John were speaking in lowered tones, both with worried expressions. Finally, Mary pled, "Surely, John, this isn't true. Surely she can't be missing. People just don't disappear—do they? Surely she is around here somewhere." She shook her head, but had no answers.

By mid-afternoon, the family was frantic, but sane enough to keep Kate's disappearance from Mother Brandon and Penelope, who were persuaded to take their afternoon rests. Jeb had returned from scouting around the near area to report finding unshod hoof prints of three horses and horse droppings, not more than eight to ten hours old. He had ridden on, but the early morning rain had washed away any trail.

"Oh! Dear Lord," Mary sobbed into her hands, "they are Indian horse prints, aren't they?"

"Yes," John rubbed her shoulders. Jeb and Prissy looked at each other at the sound of a horse skidding to a halt near the entrance and shortly thereafter Rusty rushed through the gate.

"Sorry to barge in like this." It was quite evident the situation was strained. "What's wrong, John?" He knew something was not right here before he ever arrived.

John answered as he again began pacing. "Katherine is missing—since last night. She didn't sleep in her bed." He kept walking, pulling his pipe out with shaking fingers and stuffed it.

"Strange," Rusty commented, "Ah've had a naggin' feelin' all morn that something' wasn't zackly right over here—thet's why I had to come over. Have ye saw any signs 'uv anything?"

Jeb related finding the unshod hoof prints and droppings, which prompted Rusty's leaving for Lone Eagle's village to see what he could find out while Jeb remained with the family to continue scouting a larger area.

John persuaded Mary to go inside with him where he made her sit and rest while he fixed something cool to drink. He knew his Mary and by all signs she was almost ready to crack. The damnable part was they were just here waiting, knowing nothing to do when their daughter might be hurting or dying. Why would anyone want to hurt Katherine? Please, God—keep her safe.

Mary's eyes were filled with tears as she pulled on her husband's sleeve. "John, I can't stand this—I'm going crazy with worry—and here we sit, doing nothing when she could be lying somewhere—John, can't you do something?" She broke down, tears streaming down her face as she pled with her husband.

"Stop it, Mary," he gathered her into his arms. "This doesn't help anything, and I feel Rusty or Jeb will find out something. For the children's sake you must be strong."

She nodded. "Of course, you are right," she wiped her tears with her handkerchief. "Where are they?" She took the glass of cider.

"I've tried to keep them busy with chores. I'll check on them soon." He smiled, "They must be very disturbed, too, for they haven't complained once about their chores." He tilted her chin up. "Honey, we must have faith that God will bring our daughter back to us."

She nodded with a weak smile.

Priscilla burst into the kitchen. "I found this near the bench out front. It's a button with a piece of material attached. It's from Kate's night gown. Looks as though it was torn off, possibly in a struggle." She put her arm around her mother as she handed the find to her father. The three immediately went to the area, where the button was found and with keen inspection, John was able to find grass disturbed and mashed by activity other than walking. It seemed Katherine had put up a fight.

Rusty approached Lone Eagle's village at dusk. Usually, the old scout drank in the beauty of the place and relaxed in its peacefulness, but today this was overlooked; however, the children and dogs met him with their chattering and yelping. Finding out that Eagle was at his lodge, he hurriedly bypassed his usual chatting and candy tossing with the little ones.

As he approached the chief's lodge, his old friend greeted him smiling. "What brings this famous scout to my humble village?"

He stood as Rusty dismounted. Quickly, Lone Eagle sensed something was badly wrong as Rusty shook his head.

"Let's go inside," the scout's voice lowered, "this is only fer yore ears." The chief snapped his fingers and a young Indian boy came to tend Rusty's horse.

Upon entering the lodge and closing the door, Rusty turned to his friend. "Katherine Brandon has been kidnapped. She must 'uv been walking or sitting outside in her yard late last night which is a usual thing for her since she don't sleep good. Anyhow, Jeb found three unshod hoof prints and droppings not over 8 to 10 hours old this 'evin bout quarter mile from the home, but the trail had been washed clean by the rain." The chief looked thoroughly distraught. "Eagle, is there anybody here that might know something—anything? We cain't let nothin' bad happen to thet girl." He sighed, watching his friend hopefully.

"Oh! My—this is terrible." Walking away, the chief shook his head, hesitating, then wheeling around. "Wait a minute—" he pointed his finger at his friend, "something triggered my mind that two of my little braves heard. I will send for them immediately." He quickly exited the door to send a small Indian boy to bring Acorn and Beaver. Within minutes the two young Cherokee rapped on the door of the lodge and entered, not having any idea why their chief would send for them.

"Sit," the Chief commanded, pointing to the floor. Complying, the two boys stared at each other and stared at their chief, waiting to be reprimanded for something.

"What I am telling you today must not go beyond these walls. Do you understand?" The chief questioned in Cherokee. Both boys nodded. "Katherine Brandon, your teacher, has been kidnapped. This happened last night. Think back to the time Tim Brandon was here and you three overheard the conversation between Antelope, Dancing Eyes, and the Scar—"

Little Acorn jumped up yelling, "No—oh! No!" with tears welling in his eyes. "I heard more, my chief," his chin quivered as he lowered his head.

"When? Where?" Grabbing the boy's shoulder, Lone Eagle prodded—both he and Rusty leaning toward the boy, hanging onto every word as the little Indian quickly revealed what he had heard four nights ago. A tear slipped down the boy's face that was quickly wiped away.

"Why did you not tell this to me?" Lone Eagle questioned angrily. "Do you know it might be too late now!" The Chief's tone reprimanded the little Indian as he walked back and forth in deep thought.

"I am so very sorry—never would I harm Miss Kate." The young boy put his head in his hands as he cried.

"Hit's Judgment Rock, ain't hit? 'N they've staked her out to die?" questioned Rusty as he shook his shaggy head.

"Yes—I am afraid so," the Chief paced back and forth. "We must waste no more time. Wild Hawk is the only man I have known to climb that peak alone, and, of course, he is not in the village, but hunting in some special place that he and Jeb know about." The evil ones planned this act well if they wanted to kill the girl for that peak is not accessible, but maybe Yawa will keep her safe, Lone Eagle thought to himself. "Go—take Acorn with you, explain to Brandons and tell them my prayers are with Katherine and them. Rest assured the evil ones will be dealt with severely, but they must not know we have found out about their evil act until the girl is safe. Jeb will know where to find Wild Hawk." The Chief waved the two on.

Rusty and Acorn made a nonstop trip to the Brandons', resting their horses only once. Knowing every minute counted, they skidded their horses at the Brandon gate around 10 pm. John invited them in where the family was gathered around the outside table awaiting news. Thankfully, Mother Brandon and Penelope had retired.

"Rusty—do you have any news?" John blurted, strongly ushering the two in and grabbing the old scout's arm. Rusty and Acorn sat with the family at the table.

"We have news, but it ain't all that good." The old scout took a glass of cider.

"Well, for God's sake, man, tell us—this waiting is killing us!" John thundered, plopping down with the others.

"Kate's been taken to Judgment Rock, the highest peak around, and staked out—" Jeb sucked in his breath.

"Oh my Lord," Mary moaned, putting her head in her hands, "Why would anyone do this to Katherine?"

Rusty continued as John stood, rubbing his wife's back and shoulders while his green eyes flashed deadly fire. The children looked at each other while Prissy latched onto her husband's arm with both hands.

"The Chief said Wild Hawk was the onliest man to 'uv climbed that peak alone, but he's out huntin' in some special place that you know 'uv, Jeb." He turned to the scout.

Jeb nodded. "I know the special hunting ground where he is and I'll leave now to find him." He stood. "It'll take three to four hours to reach him." He stalked around the yard while thinking. "Then it'll be around noon tomorrow probably before we can reach the rock." John, Tim and Acorn rushed toward the barn while the others stood, drinking in every word. Priscilla, with her arm around her mother. Jeb continued his thinking and pacing. "I'd say we'd be back here tomorrow night—sometime with Katherine." He turned to Priscilla. "Honey, fix me some food. Be sure and pack enough for both of us and keep the prayers goin'." She nodded, hurriedly ascending the porch.

Rusty walked up to Jeb. "This was done by Dancing Eyes, Swift Antelope and the Scar." Jeb shook his head—not believing the stupidity. "Seems it wuz' thought up'n done through Dancing Eyes evilness. 'Course, you know every minute counts," he slapped the big scout on the shoulder. "Be careful, and God go with you."

As Priscilla handed the food and water to her husband, John brought a sturdy rope and strips of leather. "Take care and God's speed." John clapped him on the back and Mary hugged his neck, her eyes misting, her voice quivering. "Thank you, Jeb."

"Darling," Prissy eased up close, "Please be careful. I couldn't make it if something happened to you." He gathered her to him and kissed her. As he exited the gate Tim handed him the reins. His horse was saddled and ready to ride with food and water skin attached.

"Thanks, Tim," he cuffed the boy's shoulder.

"Take care, Jeb." The boy watched as the big scout moved rapidly into the night.

With Rusty's encouragement, Acorn and Tim relayed the conversation they had overheard between Dancing Eyes, Antelope and the Scar when Tim and Rusty visited Lone Eagle's village. The family gave their undivided attention, not understanding any of the whys behind this plotting as they all grouped around the table, sipping their cider. Prissy excused herself upon hearing her son demanding his night feeding, and Acorn continued explaining what he had overheard from the three, five moons ago. He almost broke down, "I am the most sorry—they did not say Miss Kate's name. Acorn would never ever hurt her. Please forgive for Acorn not telling Chief. I did the wrong—I tried to think on it." A tear slipped down his cheek which he quickly wiped away.

"Oh, Acorn," Mary walked to him, putting her arms around him. "We don't blame you for anything. We're just glad you could help us. Now you and Rusty will stay here tonight and I'm sure you are both very hungry. Jessica, would you help me prepare some food and drink for Rusty and Acorn?"

"Mama," Jesse jumped up, "I can fix it by myself." Rusty flinched at that. She started for the porch.

"Well, I'll just come and help you. Being busy is what I seem to need right now." She joined her daughter as John stuffed and lit his pipe, smiling.

"I'd sure hate to think I had to eat something Jesse fixed." He puffed his pipe. The two boys giggled as Rusty's eyes twinkled, wanting to amen the statement.

The following day, lie upon lie leaped from the Brandon's mouths as they unraveled the mystery of Katherine's non-appearance to Mother Brandon and Aunt Penny. She was ill, not wanting any visitors, afraid what she had might be contagious. The latter word put the clamp on the sister's continuing to pry and visit. Never in a million years would they go near anything contagious.

Other than the lies, the Brandon household was relatively quiet, each trying to do his own thing to keep out of each others way with his own thoughts and prayers. Mary measured ingredients twice for her biscuit dough, remembered just in time to dump it and start again. Prissy diapered and rediapered Little Johnny again without thinking. John went through all of the harness, the second time in five days, checking to make sure everything was intact. The three young ones were riding horses after cleaning two stables, and Rusty, seemingly the only sane one, was entertaining twittering Evangeline Brandon over a cup of coffee.

"'N ah tell ye that there black bear rose up on them hind legs, why 'hit must'uv been eight or nine feet tall 'n 'hit wuz a comin' fer me." He leaned nearer Evangeline.

"Oh, my goodness!" She gasped, putting her hand to her chest, her eyes as big as saucers. "What in the world did you do?"

"Wall, ah looked him in the eye, pointed ma finger at him 'n said, 'Git—go on, now!'—'n he done hit!" He chuckled, his eyes twinkling as John rounded the corner of the house.

"Oh, John," his mother fluttered, "Mr. er—ah—Rusty was just telling me about his bear tale." She smiled sweetly at the old scout.

"Oh?" John retorted, "that must have been more than interesting. I've always enjoyed bare tails, especially Mary's." He sat, puffing his pipe as Mother Brandon finally caught on to her mistake. Her face flaming, she stood.

"Excuse me," she trotted for the porch, stumbled up the steps, mumbling to herself.

The afternoon hours dragged on forever. If Mary checked the hall clock once, she did ten times, to find the hour hand had only moved twice. Each family member had done a good job staying clear of each other when finally Mary gave up. She could no longer stand herself or her thoughts. Thinking it might help to walk, she persuaded her husband to join her, but she was too immersed in this kidnapping to let go. Strolling through the pasture, she stooped and picked a white twinkle flower. "John, what if he can't climb that peak?" She stopped, sniffing the flower. "Even if he can, what if he can't get her down?" She smashed the flower in her hand. "Oh, John," she turned to him, sobbing, trying to find solace in his arms. "Oh!" She flung her arms around his waist. "I can't lose a child!" She sobbed against his chest.

"Mary—Mary—please, you are making this twice as hard for yourself and others." He rubbed her back. "Don't you know this is just as hard on the rest of us. Tim and Jesse are suffering, too. No matter how they complain about wicked older sisters, they love them, and neither of us has paid any attention to the younger ones in two days. We are too caught up in our own worry." He brushed hair back that had fallen over her eyes. "Please, we must have faith that God will help Wild Hawk in bringing our Katherine home to us. We must, Mary." He pulled her head back, holding to either side of her face, looking deeply into her eyes.

"Yes," she wiped her eyes, "we must." She reached up and kissed his cheek. "No matter what, my husband, you always make things seem better, and I'm ashamed I've been selfish with my own thoughts causing me to neglect my other children." They returned hand in hand.

Finally, the soft evening shadows cast a quietness over the Brandon family as they kept their vigil while seated around the table with Rusty and Acorn there. The birds even seemed to know something was wrong for they kept up a chorus of cheer. Having plied Mother Brandon and Aunt Penny with two glasses of cider, John made sure the two nodded off at an early hour. In fact, both needed a little assistance in climbing the porch steps and the stairs after Evangeline swore, "These steps are moving."

The moon climbed her nightly path, casting a silvery glow over the countryside as numerous stars winked and twinkled their brightness, but this nightly beauty was unobserved by the Brandons as they kept their silent vigil.

"Papa," Jess blurted out, "I can't stand this—nobody sayin' anything—we just sit here. Mama, with her back all stiff, jumping at every little sound then drummin' her fingers on the table. You puffin' so hard on that pipe it's a wonder it ain't broke 'n the rest of us just sittin' not sayin' a word. I'm sure Kate wouldn't want us actin' like this!" She jumped up from the table and John drew her to him.

"Honey, I think you are right." He pulled her down on his knee.

"What time is it, Papa? It seems awfully late," Jess continued, rubbing her eyes as the father pulled out his pocket watch and was able to see the time by the moon and lantern light.

Gazing at his watch, "It is exactly 10:23 o'clock," but before the watch was returned to its resting place, horses hooves could be heard. Mary went rigid, grabbing her husband's arm.

Tim ran to the gate, and with exuberance yelled, "They're here, and Wild Hawk has Kate!"

"Oh thank God!" Mary slumped against her husband. "Thank you, dear Lord," while a tear crept down her face.

Acorn reacted quickly, exiting the gate to help Tim with the horses as they were instructed to bring any medication from Hawk's parfleche. Prissy flew to her husband before they could enter the gate, hugging him and watching Hawk as he gently removed Kate and himself.

"Thank you, my husband, and thank you so much, Wild Hawk. How is she?" She studied the greased face and swollen, cracked lips.

He shook his head. "Not good."

Jeb and Priscilla led the way through the gate. Wild Hawk followed, carrying the slight form of Kate, who was clothed in a fringed Indian shirt with arms and feet wrapped in bandages. Her face glistened in the lantern light from an ointment smeared over all facial features. She clutched tenaciously to the Indian with one arm around his back, the other around his neck.

"Oh! Dear Lord," Mary took a few steps toward them. "My Katherine—I can't thank you enough, Wild Hawk, for what you've done." She rushed on toward them as Wild Hawk nodded and sat down on a bench continuing to hold Kate. "How is she?" Mary noted Katherine's closed eyes, smeared face and swollen lips. She also stared at the way the Indian kept holding her daughter.

"Not good," Hawk murmured as John stepped up and grasped the Indian's shoulder, struggling to speak.

"We will never be able to thank you enough."

"No thanks are needed."

Mary could not understand why the Indian continued to hold Katherine like that, and what in the world was she dressed in? Why?—And bandages. Well, she would take over now. She stepped up, putting her hand on her daughter's shoulder. "Wild Hawk, I'll take care of her now." She attempted to move Katherine.

"Don't touch her." Hawk's eyes flashed as Kate's arm grasped tighter around his neck.

"What? John—did you hear that?" she sputtered, backing up a step as she raised her voice. "I'll take care of my own daughter if she's ill. I'm her mother. Katherine, honey, it's Mama. I'll help you now." She took a step closer as Hawk gazed steadily at this mother who was being so persistent. The Indian looked at John for help.

"Papa," Kate struggled to speak, her voice little above a scratchy whisper, "make her go away. I only want Wild Hawk to care for me." Her eyes stayed closed as she snuggled even closer into the Indian's arms.

"Some one please fix some broth for her—she must have nourishment." Wild Hawk stated firmly.

"John," Mary started, staring at her husband for help.

"Please, Mary," John took her arm, leading her toward the porch, "do as he says, for he knows her condition and remember, if it were not for him Katherine would not be here at all."

"Well," Mary's eyes flashed as she again checked the way that Indian was holding her daughter in his lap, and that Indian garb—with half of her thighs showing. "Why does he continue to hold her like that? It's not decent," she whispered, jerking her arm from his grasp.

"Apparently, he's holding her like that because it is what your daughter wishes," John retorted. "Now, would you please fix the broth or should I ask Priscilla?"

"Oh!" Mary seethed as she marched up the steps and into the house. She wondered if John Brandon had a lick of sense in his head, and whoever heard of an Indian coming in here giving orders, telling me what and how to do for my own daughter!

Prissy walked up to Hawk, questioning, "Is there anything I can do to help?"

"Not unless you help your mother who, I believe, is fixing broth. She does not like an Indian helping her daughter, but I will continue to do for Katherine until she is better. Right now she must have nourishment." He looked down, smoothing hair back that had blown across her face. Pissy noted the gentleness of his large brown hand, the warmth in his eyes, and she sensed the love this man had for her sister.

Jesse sauntered up, having waited as long as possible to approach the two. She took a seat. "Wild Hawk, why are your arms and hands all scratched up. They almost look like they're bleeding in places." The Indian looked at his arms and hands the best he could without disturbing Katherine.

"It is nothing. I had not noticed this, but I guess it happened when I brought your sister down the rocky cliff." He smiled at his friend Jesse.

"You have done the thing that nobody else could do, climbing that rock to bring Kate home. Will she die?" she questioned seriously with misty eyes. She did think Kate acted like a witch sometimes, but she sure didn't want her to die.

"No, we will not let that happen." He looked at the girl in his arms, thinking how close he had come to losing her to the rock. Had she been there another day she would not have had enough strength to make it.

"Papa said that God would help you to bring her home and he did." She jumped up and kissed his cheek before bounding off to find Tim and Acorn to tell them Kate would be all right. As Jess scampered away, Rusty moseyed up squeezing Hawk's shoulder and nodding to him. No words were needed.

Mary exited the house with a tray. As John met her at the steps smiling, it was all she could do to keep from crowning him over the head with the tray, broth and all. She side stepped him and placed the tray on the table without a word, then sat. John eased in beside her, thinking what a damn thunderhead she was being to this man who had just risked his life to bring their daughter safely to them.

Wild Hawk murmured, "Katherine, we are going to the table now—I am going to shift you—"

"No—no—" she squeaked, "don't put me down—hold me. Just hold me," her voice scratched.

"I am holding you, but I must move you to my other arm. This one is wanting to sleep." He took her arm from around his neck, placing it around his body as he shifted her to his left side. She placed her other arm around his neck, smiling contentedly while he sat down with her at the table.

"Katherine," he murmured softly while Mother and Father sat near watching every move and drinking in every word.

"Huh," she squeaked.

"You are going to drink some broth, now," he continued.

"No—I'm not hungry, just want to stay here with you," her voice squeaked.

"Katherine, you will drink the broth for me, or—someone else can help you."

"No—no—no one else, you help me—I'll drink," she whispered. Mary ladled the venison broth into a mug, handing it to Wild Hawk who placed it to her cracked lips.

"Green Eyes," he murmured, "drink the broth." She drank several sips before he saw blood on the cup from her lips. Mary handed him a clean cloth to blot the blood. Nodding his thanks, he continued his ministrations. "Katherine, we will finish the broth with a spoon. You are doing so very well." She smiled, pleased that he was pleased. Mary, despite her feelings toward this man taking over with her daughter as though he owned her, couldn't overlook the gentle care he gave Katherine.

Having finished feeding her, Hawk stated to the parents, "The wrapped legs, feet and hands are from a deep sunburn. Underneath, she wears ointment to take the burn away, which is also on her face. I am sure you wonder about the shirt she wears. It was necessary to destroy the filthy nightgown she wore, bathe her and wash her hair at the falls then dress her in the only garment I had, my shirt."

"You what?" Mary exploded out of her chair, drawing all eyes and attention to her as she glared at this savage who had seen and touched Katherine's naked body.

"You mean, young man, you actually took it upon yourself to see and touch my daughter's naked body?" Her eyes were wild, she was screaming.

Stirring, "Papa, make her hush," Katherine croaked.

"Yes, Ma'am, I did that not to see and touch her, but to clean the bodily filth that was all over her. Jeb was helping." Hawk summoned assistance from Jeb with a glance as the big scout started to the table. This mother was acting with little sense.

Hawk stood with Katherine in his arms. "I am taking her to her room. She must rest—"

"No," she squeaked, "not unless you stay with me—Wild Hawk, I need you with me." She opened her eyes, looking at him and smiled weakly with her cracked and swollen lips, which grabbed at his heart. He smiled down at her with love in his eyes.

"I will stay with you," he looked at both parents, "and Katherine's parents, if you wish to be there with us, that will be fine, but," he looked steadily at Mary, "I will be with your daughter as long as she needs me." He started for the porch, carrying Kate with John accompanying him. Mary was too distraught to move or even be around this Indian who was taking her place and who was being entirely too familiar with her daughter. Whoever heard of such a thing, and to think her husband was going right along with everything as though this was an every day occurrence. Well, John Brandon would do something to change it or by Heaven, she would. This was her home and her daughter.

As they entered the bedroom, John lit a bedside lamp which cast a warm glow over the neatly arranged blue and white room. Hawk sat on the edge of the bed, continuing to hold Kate. "I am very sorry your wife does not want my help. She does not want an Indian to help or touch her daughter. I know this, but I will take care of Katherine's wishes until she is better, not what your wife wishes."

I understand and I am sorry for my wife's actions." John smiled at this big gentle man who was so honest, who had saved his daughter's life, who loved her, but who had no right to happiness with her. What a sad thing, and Katherine couldn't stand to be away from him.

"Some one should put a clean night gown on her and help her with bodily functions before I put her in bed." Wild Hawk gazed at the father. "And she needs a pitcher of water."

John nodded, "I'll get Priscilla," and started for the door.

Shortly, Prissy entered with water, helped with the night gown and necessary functions while Hawk waited in the hall. It was difficult to detach himself from Green Eyes, but with an understanding that he was near and would be back when she was readied for bed, it was finally accomplished.

Tucking Katherine under the cover, nothing would satisfy her until Wild Hawk was stretched out by her side with his arm around her as she nestled into his shoulder. He couldn't keep from smiling, knowing how badly he was spoiling her, doing exactly as she wanted, but it happened to be what he wanted, too; however, this night had been and would be most difficult for him. To have held her so long in his arms, on his lap and now stretched out by her, other arrangements would have to be made. He prided himself on being able to restrict his emotions, but after all he was a normal man. Of course, he wanted nothing more in life than to care for and spoil this beautiful Katherine forever, which would never be possible. He felt her hand reach up and come to rest on his chest as she sighed and drifted into an even breathing sleep. Waiting several minutes for deep sleep to settle in, Hawk very gently moved her head from his shoulder to the pillows and eased from the bed. Finding a cushioned chair, he moved it next to the bed, took her hand and there sat for his nightly vigil.

Down on the lawn, Priscilla gathered the family around her mother who remained seated at the table, her face drawn tightly. "Come on, everybody. Jeb will tell us about Kate's rescue—that way he won't have to repeat himself a dozen times." She was thinking maybe this could unravel some of her mother's anger.

Mary glanced around as everyone took seats at the table. Jeb leaned on his elbows, Prissy holding his arm with both hands while he began, "Well…"

Mary burst in. "You mean that Indian is in Katherine's bedroom alone with her?" She jumped up trembling, glaring at her husband. She screamed, "Well, do something!"

"I am," John said calmly. He was more than tired of hearing and seeing his wife as a shrew. He'd had enough.

"I'm telling you to damn well back off!" His green eyes flashed. "You are acting like a shrew without a heart." Mary couldn't believe what she was hearing as she sank into her chair. John stood and began pacing, running his hand through his hair. He wheeled around, "Here is a man who risked his life to save your daughter and bring her home, and what have you done? You've ripped him apart with stinging accusations and spewing your venom. Well, that's enough, woman."

The people gathered around the table only looked at each other, feeling very uncomfortable. Making no sound or movement, they only hoped the storm would soon abate.

Mary stared at her hands, not really seeing them, but wanting to break down and cry. Never had her husband talked to her like that. Was it true what he said? Was she really that bad? Seeing Katherine and the Indian together, the way he held her and her daughter wanting no one else seemed to trigger something deep within her.

"And Mary," her husband's anger was subsiding, "before you ask another question I'm going to clarify it, which will rock you to your toes." Mary's tear-filled eyes stared at her husband. "The reason Wild Hawk remains here is because Katherine wants that—she is in love with him and he with her. They also know that being together permanently is impossible."

"Oh dear Lord," Mary practically choked on her words. That was it—that was what she had feared, the feelings that had been triggered deep inside.

"Come on, folks," John urged, "it's too late to continue hashing over anything else tonight." He walked near his wife. "We all need rest and sleep. Excuse the turmoil between my old lady and me. The storm's over and I do hope we can forget it, and be forgiven." He placed his hand on her shoulder, stared at his wife, smiling 'please', he pled with his eyes.

"Priscilla, will you and Jeb take turns tonight helping Wild Hawk with Katherine?" John pulled Mary up as the others filed into the house.

Jeb answered, "We'd be glad to—come on, Pretty Gal," he prodded Prissy. "Let's go check on those two and you know that son of ours is gonna' be ready to eat soon." He took her hand, pulling her up the steps.

As John turned out the lantern, he thought of the altercation with Mary that might be hanging on, but face it he must as he approached the steps.

The night passed rather smoothly. Each time Prissy and Jeb checked on the twosome, each was asleep, Wild Hawk in a chair by the bed, always holding Kate's hand, and apparently that touch plus sheer exhaustion kept her asleep.

The next morning while birds were outdoing each other with their chorusing, the sun making its debut peeping over the mountain crest, John opened the door to Kate's bedroom. His entrance was greeted by Katherine bounding from the bed into Hawk's lap, throwing her arms around his neck and planting a soft kiss on his lips. A crooked smile and a murmuring of, "What a beautiful way to wake up," from Hawk also greeted John. Neither aware of his presence until he cleared his throat.

"Papa, look—I'm much better." She smiled brilliantly, continuing sitting in Hawk's lap.

"Why, yes," her father's matching green eyes smiled, "It's quite obvious." He cleared his throat again.

"Oh," her face flushed. She removed herself from the lap, grabbed her robe which was spread at the foot of the bed, donned it and sat on the bedside, trying to change the subject. "It's so good just to sit up, and if you two will excuse me, leave the room please." She waved them out. "But don't call Prissy, I'll take care of myself."

The two men left the room and descended the steps. "There's water in the pitcher on the back porch, and by the time you finish up your needs, help me and we'll take breakfast upstairs. Know you're hungry as a bear, and let's hope Katherine can eat something 'cause everything's ready." John opened the oven door to check the biscuits.

"Thank you, John Brandon, for your understanding and help." The Indian exited the back door.

John shook his head, thinking, he thanks me for sticking up for him, for cooking a measly breakfast, when he risked his life for my daughter.

The two men entered the bedroom with trays, silver covered dishes of scrambled eggs, bacon, biscuits with jelly, a pot of coffee and a pitcher of milk.

"Oh! Papa, thank you so much. Did you cook this yourself?" He nodded, rather proud of his accomplishment. "Where's Mama?"

"Well, as a matter of fact, your mother is still in bed. I reprimanded her rather severely last night and in front of others. So-o-o—I suppose she continues to sulk. Let's eat. I don't want my endeavor to turn cold." They dug in including Kate who took small bites slowly, but food had never tasted so good and to her amazement she was hungry.

Legend of the Whispering Wind

She looked at Wild Hawk filling his breakfast plate, clad in a fringed vest that revealed his lean muscular frame to perfection. He was so handsome with his long black hair, black eyes that were so expressive, outlined with those long lashes that would be the envy of most females. He caught her warm appraisal and smiled that crooked smile that always touched her heart for she did love her Indian, who had saved her life from whatever horrible place that was. She had avoided thinking about or asking about the kidnapping or where they had placed her—somehow she didn't think she was ready to hear about it. Now, she was home and he was here, too, eating breakfast with her. She was happy and her mother could pout or do whatever she was doing.

By afternoon Prissy had helped bathe and dress Kate in a green cotton dress with matching green sash, accented with a green ribbon in her hair. Totally exhausted from the ordeal, she was forced to lie down and rest.

Mary, having seen Wild Hawk and John walking toward the barn, took this time to visit her daughter. She rapped on the door, "It's Mama," and before waiting for an answer Mama entered. She smiled at her daughter, a tight smile that failed to reach her eyes.

"Mama, I thought you would have come to see me before this." Kate pushed herself to a sitting position.

"How are you feeling, Katherine?" No hug—Mary sat in the chair by the bed, looking at her daughter steadily, revealing little warmth.

"Oh! I'm better, Mama. I ate a regular breakfast this morning. It was so good, but after Prissy helped me bathe and dress this afternoon, I was totally exhausted and had to lie down." Kate busied herself straightening the coverlet while realizing what a strained conversation this was. She looked up, watching her mother's hand nervously playing with a shirt button. The mother staring at the button, seemingly in disturbing thoughts.

"Mama," Kate blurted out, not being able to stand the strained conversation and silence. "What's wrong? I know I wasn't at all sociable last night. Seems I was so tired, coming to and passing out over and over—and I just didn't want to move or do anything. I'm sorry." Her voice faded as she stared at her mother. "It's Wild Hawk, isn't it?" Kate swung her legs over the side of the bed where she pushed herself to a sitting position.

Mary stared at her daughter, the daughter that had always seemed so sensible and dependable, that had never been at all flighty like Priscilla, and now this ridiculous, unbelievable—"Your father said you cared for that Indian." Mary's mouth was a drawn line as though she smelled something bad.

Kate was aware of her mother's tension—the way she grasped the arms of the chair. "Yes, I care for him—I love him and he loves me. Oh! Mama," Kate slipped from the bed, kneeling at her mother's feet, taking her mother's hand. Her eyes teared. "I've tried very hard not to love him, knowing this was not the accepted thing. I tried to care for others, but it somehow didn't work." Her eyes pled with her mother. "We've stayed apart and that didn't work either. Please, Mama," she squeezed her mother's hand harder, "I know it's too much to ask you to understand, for I don't even understand, but please don't dislike your daughter." Kate's eyes filled with tears as she stared at the cold countenance of her mother. Her chin quivered, "And please don't dislike him, for he has done nothing wrong."

Mary stood, taking her hand from Kate and moved toward the door, too upset, too distraught to respond while her daughter continued to kneel where she was, her head bowed, the green ribbon askew while tears streamed down her face. Kate was not aware of the door opening and closing.

Shortly, there was a rap on the door. Kate didn't notice nor did she hear the door opening for she continued in her kneeling position with tears streaming, remembering and not believing her mother's coldness. Wild Hawk reached her in three strides, scooped her up and held her tightly in his arms as he sat down in a rocker and let her sob into his chest. It had to have been Mary Brandon. He had seen her mother leaving the room. Katherine couldn't stand such treatment from a mother, not now, not when she was so frail, so weak. Smoothing her hair, rocking her as he would a small child, he quietly sang a Cherokee lullaby. Kate pushed against his chest, raising her head, listening to his mellow voice as he continued singing and smiling. She wiped her tears on her sleeve.

"Oh, that's beautiful! I didn't know you could sing. You've never sung to me before."

"Of course I can sing—we have never had time together to think of singing." A muscle twitched in his jaw, but he had accomplished what he had tried to do, stop her crying. "That was a Cherokee lullaby."

"Wild Hawk." Kate touched the fringe on his vest, smoothing it. "My mother was terrible when she visited me today. Seems my father had told her we love each other, and I verified it, but she won't accept that. To her, that's unbelievable for she's filled with prejudices, as though she is full of hate." She hesitated, continuing to smooth the fringe. "I always thought she was a loving, understanding, giving person and mother, but the woman who was here today—I don't know her." She looked at her Indian who seemed so concerned and slowly traced his jaw line with her finger.

"I love you," she whispered as he pulled her face to his and gently kissed her puffy lips.

"I know, and I love you so much that it tears at my insides to think you are going through so much stress and heartache because of me." He held her to him, smoothing the rich auburn mane, loving the feel of her against him knowing this would cease soon. He would have to leave this home the next day for Katherine was now eating with his encouragement, and sleeping with only one nightmare. He would stay another night. After that, what would he do? Where would he go? How could he live miles away from her and how could he stay near and not be with her? Please, Yawa, show me the way for I have never been this helpless in my life.

"Green Eyes." She sat back, looking into his eyes knowing something serious was beginning. "I am leaving tomorrow."

"No." Her countenance clouded.

"I can not stay here—you know that. Your mother wishes I had never stayed." He stared through the window, a muscle twitching in his jaw. "She wishes that I had brought you home and left immediately." He caressed her face with a gentle hand, "but I couldn't do that. I had to be with you to see that you were all right. Now, you are eating, you are stronger and you will be all right."

"Not without you," she interrupted.

"Yes, you will, and your mother needs the chance to be herself again. She can't do that with me here."

Kate pushed herself up from his lap, stood and walked to the window, pushing the curtain back, looking outside. Even though the sun shone brightly, her day had clouded over. "Where will you go?"

"Right now, to Lone Eagle's village to spend time with him and Spotted Horse. I must know the punishment brought against those evil ones who tried to take your life. I promise I won't travel any distance without first seeing you." He stood, taking a step toward her when she faced him, her eyes brimming with tears.

"It seems we're right back at the beginning, doesn't it? You'll go to your village, decide your future and let me know your decision." She hesitated, clenching her hands into fists and began walking around him. She stopped, turned abruptly, "And since you are always concerned about what others want and think, I'm sure I won't be a part of your decision." She turned her back to him, looking at her hands which were clasped tightly. "Just go on—go on today if that's what you want."

He strode to her, wheeled her around, grabbing her arms. "Stop this! You know more than anything in the world, I want to be with you," his black eyes flashed, "to love you, to make you mine, to be with you forever. You also know, Green Eyes," he crushed her to him, "I can not have you!" He raised his voice on these final words.

He moved her back, dropping his hands to his side, murmuring, "I am sorry—I did not mean to yell." She stared at him, beginning to understand some of the frustration, the turmoil he was going through. "Are you going to be all right?" His concern was evident.

"I'll try, but I won't promise anything."

He pulled her to him. "I will stay the night, and leave at first light. It's best I sleep outside."

"No," she was emphatic, "best for whom? My family? I'm the one who needs you near. It's what is best for me right now." She gave him a saucy nod of the head.

He grinned, flashing those whit teeth. "I will be with you this night. Now, lie down and rest before it is time to eat. I must go and speak with your parents."

She nodded, "Yes, sir," as she pulled his face down and kissed him gently, murmuring, "Pray for us." He looked deeply into her beautiful green eyes before heading for the door.

Seated on the front lawn, oblivious to the sweet trilling of the birds and scampering of squirrels, John and Mary were attempting a much needed and difficult conversation to try and unravel the entanglement of the night before. In John's estimation Mary was still acting like a sore tailed cat, and to Mary John was still the sergeant giving orders.

"John, John."

"Oh, good Lord," he erupted, "Now, of all times we're blessed with my mother's presence."

Evangeline Brandon burst through the screened door, excitement with fear etched her plump face. She all but stumbled down the steps as she pointed to the house. "There's an Indian in there," she puffed as Wild Hawk made his entrance.

"For crying out loud!" John's disturbance with his wife spilled into his outburst.

"Oh, no," Mama Brandon pointed to Hawk, "That one wouldn't make anyone cry—he's too pretty," she tittered, covering her mouth as she stopped at the bottom step, turned, charmed by Hawk's smile with very white teeth against his bronze skin, "but young man, why are you half-dressed with no shirt on?" She shook her head.

"Mrs. Brandon," Hawk's black eyes looked her up and down as he stopped at Evangeline's side, "I bet I am more in comfort than you are. It is my guess you wear ten petticoats."

"No," she tittered, poking him on the arm, "Only nine—the other one is on the line, drying." Evangeline was enjoying herself exchanging quips with the handsome young man. Looking around, spying Mary's sour expression, Mother Brandon immediately cleared her throat and marched to a seat. "Oh! What a lovely day, don't you think, Mary?"

John could hardly keep a straight face noting his mother's antics with Wild Hawk and the tight squeeze of her fat fanny, her overly plump hips as she squeezed and wiggled by the hardest to fit into Mary's small antique rocker. His wife cringed, afraid the antique piece of furniture might split with the overload.

"Yes, Mother Brandon, this is a beautiful day." Mary was engrossed in her hands as she peeled potatoes, groaning inwardly as she glanced at her mother-in-law.

"Mother, you do remember Wild Hawk. He was in Priscilla's wedding. Have a seat," John motioned to Hawk who eased onto a bench.

"Oh! Uh—yes, Mr. Hawk—uh, are you here to help John with work?" Evangeline was only trying to make conversation, so why would John be making faces and gritting his teeth?

"No, Ma'am." Hawk charmed Evangeline again with his smile.

"And son," Evangeline continued to push, on turning to John as the rocker squeaked its protest, "don't you have a shirt you could loan him? He's extremely bare." She pointed to Hawk, smiling.

"Mother, if you will please excuse us there is something Wild Hawk wishes to discuss—ah—isn't there?" he questioned the Indian hoping to remove his mother.

"Yes." Mary stood, gathering up her potatoes and peels to leave, not wanting any conversation with this Indian. "I wish to speak to both you and your wife, John Brandon." Hawk steadily gazed at both, while Mary sank back into her seat, glaring at the Cherokee who seemed to be calling the shots.

"I suppose that means I'm to leave." Mother Brandon rather huffily pushed on the arms of the small chair to release the loaves that were stuffed underneath. Hopefully, she could make it without the rocker clinging to her bottom when she stood. No, but nothing that simple for Evangeline. She stood halfway, her back bent, the chair clinging, squealing frantically.

"John, John—unhinge me. Why would anyone have a chair around only large enough for a child—!"

John stood, doing his best to stifle his laughter as he pulled on the chair, but Mother came with it. "Wild Hawk, I need your help. Pull the chair in your direction while I hold my mother and pull her in the opposite direction." Hawk nodded, his lips twitching, as the heave-ho began. Finally, the loaves gave way with mother and son sprawling one way, Hawk and rocker tumbling the other. The two men exploded in laughter while Mother Brandon scrambled on hands and knees to erect herself. Finding no humor in any of this, Mother Brandon, with red splotched face and trembling, burning hips, babbled incessantly about foolish people as she trotted for the porch. Even Mary found it hard to keep a straight face.

Laughter finally abated, the two men stood, both feeling better that there had been something to laugh about. "Honey," John turned to Mary, mopping his face with a handkerchief, "we'd better hide this rocker—who knows, my mother might try it again." He shook his head while throwing himself into a chair. "Can't believe anybody'd bring an old thing like that outside."

"Priscilla was rocking the baby—guess she forgot to have Jeb take it back inside," Mary clarified. "Don't believe that old chair could stand another battle like the one it's just been through." She shook her head, her lips twitching.

"You did wish to talk to us," John questioned the Indian, motioning for him to sit.

"Yes." Hawk hesitated, disliking to return to the somber and sad situation of Katherine and her family, but it had to be done. He sat at the table. "Today, when I returned to Katherine's room her mother had just paid her a visit. This visit, Mrs. Brandon, left your daughter sobbing." Mary stared at this Indian who was taking it upon himself to explain her daughter.

"Young man," Mary's coolness was obvious, "are you attempting to tell me what I should and shouldn't do with my own daughter?" Her voice rose as she stared at this irritating man.

"Yes, Ma'am, I am." The mother's mouth dropped open at the Indian's asinine statement. "You see, I love your daughter, and all I care about right now is what is best for her. She is very weak, lack of food, lack of sleep and the terrifying ordeal—had that lasted another twenty-four or thirty-six hours," his voice broke with the memory, "she wouldn't be here at all." He stared at both parents. "She must not be stressed or hurt in any way."

"Are you saying I hurt my daughter today? Now see here—" the mother's harshness vibrated, but before she could continue—

"Yes, Ma'am, I am." His dark eyes held hers steadily. "You turned your daughter off today because she told you she loves an Indian. Prejudice and hatred are strong emotions, but the love you have for your daughter must be stronger than those vile emotions that eat and destroy a person's insides. We did not plan this love for each other," he shook his head, fingering a napkin, "we tried to blot it out, but," he smiled sadly, "it didn't work. If you, Mary Brandon, can not give this daughter the love and care she so badly needs now, then I can always ask her to leave with me and she would." His black eyes flashed. "More than anything I want to make Katherine mine, but I cannot do that because of you," his gaze steadily held Mary's, "and people like you who have hate in their hearts and the uncertain future of the Cherokee. I love your daughter enough to want what is best for her. I am leaving at first light tomorrow—if you cannot care for Katherine's needs I need to know before leaving. Tonight I will spend sitting by your daughter's bedside, holding her hand. If anyone wishes to chaperone us that is fine. Thank you for my food while I have been here." He stood, tuning to leave.

"Wild Hawk." Standing and taking a step toward the Indian, John struggled with his voice. "How can we ever repay you for what you have done in bringing our daughter home?"

"Repay?" Hawk looked at him steadily. "How could you ever think Hawk would not want to do this for Katherine? You owe me nothing." He turned to leave, but hesitated at Mary's voice.

"Wild Hawk—I—uh—I'm sorry." Mary stared at her hands, not able to look the Indian eye to eye as Hawk nodded and walked up the steps. She wanted to say more, but somehow she didn't know what to say. Was what he said true? Was she so prejudiced and hate filled? Dear Lord—

The birds were chorusing their early morning happiness while the light of dawn began to gradually diminish the nightly dark cloak that was draped over the mountains. A rooster crowed as Hawk stirred, gently replacing Kate's hand by her side. He drank in the glorious mass of thick auburn hair, the long dark lashes that dusted her cheeks, the sleep induced flushed face that even though thinner now, was still beautiful to him. How could life be so cruel to have brought them together, to have had them fall in love and then torn them apart to live in misery. He leaned over and gently brushed a kiss across her lips. She murmured softly, turned over and continued sleeping as he quietly left the room.

Descending the stairs, Hawk was aware of the rich aroma of bacon and coffee that permeated the air. He smiled upon entering the kitchen watching John in the final throes of preparing a hearty breakfast. Removing biscuits from the oven and pouring coffee, John filled two plates with an abundance of bacon and eggs which hit the spot for two hungry males.

After filling the water pouch and packing the remaining biscuits with bacon, despite Hawk's protests, John fixed a good lunch and would take no argument from the Indian.

Hawk stood to leave, shaking hands with John. "Thank you, John Brandon, for the food and," he hesitated, "everything else. May God bless you and yours." His black eyes revealed the warmth that he felt for this man who not only had helped his people, but had backed him, despite his disapproval of his daughter's caring for an Indian.

"I've done so little for you to be thanking me." John shook his head. "Without you, our daughter wouldn't even be alive. We will never be able to thank you enough, but right now I wish to apologize to you for the things I said when first learning that you and Katherine cared for each other." The father ran his hand through his hair. "It was just like you explained to my wife—" he paced a few steps, turned and steadily looked into the black eyes. "I was prejudiced—caring what society thought. I never felt hatred, though. Forgive me," he pled, "for expressing such 'white beliefs'." He sincerely needed forgiveness from this Indian who was more of a man than most whites he knew.

"There is nothing to forgive. Feelings are bred into us." Hawk watched this man who needed to get this apology behind him. "You are a good man, John Brandon, but I will ask a favor—please take good care of your special—Katherine."

John nodded. "May God go with you, Wild Hawk." Their eyes held as they shook hands, both realizing there was a special bond between them, one green eyed girl.

Chapter 25

Here it was only three days since he had left, the longest three Katherine could remember spending, and she could still see him everywhere, eating breakfast with her, sitting by the bed, holding her in his arms, smiling that crooked smile. Dear Lord, was this the extent of her life—dreams? And he didn't even bother to tell her good-bye. Sadness and depression seemed to wrap her in a heavy cloak constantly. She did try to converse with her family, for her mother was being especially nice. Kate also tried to eat her food for one look in the mirror had frightened her; the thinness, paleness, the dark circles surrounding her eyes. What was really happening to her? The kidnapping, that's what they said. Maybe it was just as well she hadn't been lucid enough to know what went on. Of course, Wild Hawk brought her home—and was here for a day or two, but what of her life now? Would it ever be any different or would she simply sit here and wait for him to drop by to tell her a final good-bye—always good-bye—always. She sobbed while sitting at her dressing table attempting to brush her unruly hair that had lost much of its luster. Kate quickly deposited the brush, wiped her tearstained cheeks and attempted a cheery "come in" upon hearing a rap at the door.

Jesse bounded in, sweaty and wind blown, followed by Prissy and Little Johnny who looked squeaky clean from his bath.

"This must be a special occasion, a visit from both sisters and my beautiful nephew." Kate reached for the baby, cuddled the plump armful while planting a kiss on a rosy cheek. "You know," she continued to the delightful bundle, "you'll break all the hearts when you grow up, young man." In agreement, Little Johnny cooed and crinkled a big smile while plunging his hands into his aunt's hair and giving it a firm yank.

Jesse, oblivious to the conversation, made her way to the dressing table where she reached for the perfume bottle, applying an ample amount behind her ears and upon her sweaty wrists.

"Jessica," Prissy intervened, "you know sweat and perfume do not mingle—besides, that belongs to Kate —ask before helping yourself!"

"Oh! She don't care. 'Sides, who would she wear it for? Wild Hawk's done gone and probably won't ever be coming back since Kate looks so bad 'n skinny." Jess picked up the hair brush attempting to untangle her mass of unruly hair as Kate handed Johnny back to his mother. Chin quivering, eyes misting, Kate realized she was a mess with emotions ready to erupt at anything. She must do something to control herself.

Prissy, realizing the situation, took over. "Run on, Jesse and tell Mama we'll be down shortly for Kate to get some sun. Tell Papa to come to help Kate in about 15 minutes. Sure don't want her slipping on the stairs and knocking Johnny and me on our faces." She smiled, attempting to lighten her sister's mood. "Run on, Jess."

"No, I'm busy—you run." Jesse was now powdering her sweaty face, billowing the white stuff throughout the room.

"Jessica Ruth," Prissy's elevated coughing voice firmly reached her target, "Now!"

Jesse slammed the powder puff down while mocking her sister. "Jessica Ruth, Jesse, now you run on and do what ever your older sisters want!" She slammed her way out the door.

Kate smiled at her sister. "Prissy, I'm so sorry—" She stared out the window. "Seems I'm ready to crack if anyone says anything—I'm so miserable, Prissy." Her green eyes tear filled, reached for comfort and understanding from her sister.

"I know that," Prissy took her hand, "but sometimes when things seem so hopeless and we can do nothing to change anything," she rubbed the back of Kate's hand, "we have to turn things over to a higher power. Believe me, I know." She looked down at her son, lovingly. "It hasn't been too long since I was ready to destroy my own life or that of my beautiful son. Oh! Kate," she shuddered, "it frightens me so to think of the person I was and what I might have done." She grabbed her son up close, hugging him while he protested and tears slid down her face. "But for you my dear sister Kate, who gave me hope and encouraged my prayers that God did answer, I might have completed my destructive path. Now, I don't for a minute believe the good Lord helped Wild Hawk save you so you could live in misery for the rest of your life. Think on it, dear sister." She stood, having soothed her son back to sleep, smiling her encouragement.

John rapped on the door before entering. "Come on, lovely ladies. It's high time you drank in that beautiful sunshine out there." He bent and brushed a kiss across the baby's rosy cheek. "My, he's a handsome lad! Looks exactly like his grandpa." Their father grinned and raised his arm for Kate to hold as they exited. Both girls laughed, enjoying their father's quips.

"Be right down after putting Johnny to bed," Prissy retreated to her room, worried about her sister. Kate was always the strong one. She could never remember her giving up on anything, but love could do strange things to people. So what if Wild Hawk is Indian! 'Course, she hadn't felt this way a year ago, but if Kate loves him and he loves her, what else really matters?

They were all enjoying the beautiful early peaceful afternoon sitting in the yard after partaking of a delicious lunch. Even Kate's spirits seemed to have improved after having eaten two pieces of fried chicken and a piece of apple pie still warm from the oven.

Legend of the Whispering Wind

"I declare, Katherine—it's good you are beginning to eat something, you're as skinny as a rail," Aunt Penelope leered with her usual biting and insensitive comment.

Kate looked at her hands, toying with her handkerchief as tears filled her eyes.

"Aunt Penny," Prissy came to the rescue as she strolled over and sat on the bench by Kate while scrutinizing her great aunt. "You don't look all that laden with flesh yourself. In fact," she peered closer in the great aunt's face, "you look a little gaunt. Haven't you been eating well?" She showered Penelope with a dazzling smile as John choked on a puff of smoke with his sustained laughter.

"Guess she told you, Aunt Penny—that's sorta like my mother's saying something about a black pot calling a kettle—" Jesse giggled while plopping on the grass most unladylike.

"Well, of all the rude—Mary, you should teach this daughter some manners." Penelope threw her nose into the air as horses hooves came to an abrupt stop at the gate, interfering with the less than comfortable conversation.

John stood, walking to the gate to receive the guests. "Well, do come in Chief and Rusty, it's good to see you."

"Thank you," Chief Lone Eagle entered, regally attired in a long fringed tunic with matching leggings and moccasins. Rusty wore the same as usual, but clean.

"We 'uns tried to git here sooner to eat some 'uv thet there apple pie we done been smelling a mile down thu' trail, but guess John's already gobbled 'hit all up." Rusty waved at everyone. "Glad to see you about, Miss Kate, 'n Miss Vangie, you're lookin' mighty 'phert in thet blue dress."

Mother Brandon tittered, wiggling her frame while smoothing her lace collar. "Thank you."

Penelope jumped up clearing her throat. "Excuse me." She would not sit here and listen to the crudeness of that tobacco spitting bantam of a man nor listen to anything that savage had to say. It was difficult to believe her relatives had stooped so low. Without another word she marched up the steps and into the house. The sooner she left this place the better.

"Lone Eagle and Rusty, have seats. It's nice to see you again." Mary graciously welcomed the guests, hoping to conceal the rudeness of the aunt. "You know, I just might find two more pieces of apple pie in the warming oven." She smiled as she headed for the porch, motioning for Jesse to follow.

Lone Eagle watched the girl who was so pale, so thin. This was not just from being on the rock—this girl was pining her heart away. "How are you feeling, Miss Katherine?" His deep voice soothed.

"I suppose I'm some better, but still weak." The sad green eyes steadily looked into the warm black gaze of the chief. His heart went out to this girl who loved his nephew. Wild Hawk had met with him and revealed everything including his thoughts of leaving for the Echota Georgia.

"And how is that fine son of yours, Miss Priscilla?" The Eagle turned his attention to Kate's sister, but before she could answer, Jeb rounded the corner of the house, answering.

"Well, he happens to be the handsomest, most intelligent son a man ever had," laughing, "guess that sums it up don't it, honey?" He smiled at his wife, the family answering in agreement.

"If you say so," Priscilla's warm smile spoke words of love to her husband.

"Now folks, it is time to listen up. Chief Eagle here had a special reason for coming here today." Rusty gathered all attention as he strutted over to take a seat by John's mother who blushed, smiled and made room for him.

"Jesse, before the Chief begins, go and find Tim—believe he's at the pond fishing. Know he won't want to miss any news Chief Eagle brings us," John mentioned as he puffed his pipe.

The chief leaned his elbows on the table, looked at the family gathered around before beginning. "I felt I owed you an explanation of the wrong done to Miss Katherine. Explain the guilty ones and the punishment handed to them. Three people, two from my village, planned and executed the kidnapping."

"Kidnapping?" Mother Brandon whispered loudly.

"Dancing Eyes, a maiden who has always desired Wild Hawk even though he has never given her cause to do so, did the planning. She tricked Swift Antelope, also from my village, and Scar Face, an Indian that has no home into believing with Miss Katherine out of the way, Wild Hawk would then return to his home in the Georgia. She also planned killing me, if necessary, so Swift Antelope could become chief. Little did the two braves know when Katherine's body was found—"

Mother Brandon grabbed her mouth with the loud exclamation, "Oh! No!"

"—Dancing Eyes would lie and place the blame on them, that way ridding herself of Swift Antelope and having Wild Hawk for herself."

He leveled his gaze on each. "The punishment for the three, they are total outcasts and may not be a part of any village, ever. They are not allowed to be within a large area of your family or home, John, or my village. If seen anywhere around these areas they will be killed, and I have many braves helping to secure this."

"Oh! My—oh! My—" Evangeline screeched, throwing up her hands. "I said there'd be an uprising—what about kidnapping?" She wheeled around for information.

"Mother," John replied firmly, "Katherine was not ill, she was kidnapped as Chief Eagle just explained—"

"She was what?" Mother Brandon exploded.

"Listen and do calm down. We tried to save you and Aunt Penny from worry and questions we couldn't answer." John was losing patience.

"Well, I declare." She drew her mouth up. "I've never heard anything so ridiculous—the nerve—"she blustered, shaking her finger at her son. "Why—I—"

"Mother, please—I'm sure these others are not interested in our confab." He shook his head, running his hand through his hair, then turned to the others as Rusty leaned over to whisper in Evangeline's ear, causing her to titter and poke him in the arm, murmuring, "Go on, now!"

"Jeb," John turned to his son-in-law, "you've never explained the rescue. I believe this is the right time since Lone Eagle is here." The Indian nodded. "And we could all do with something cool to drink."

"I'll get it, Papa. Come on, Jess, you can help." Prissy stood, motioning for Jesse to follow.

Jeb moved to sit at the table with the chief. "As most of you know after Rusty and Acorn came here and explained where the evil ones had taken Katherine, guess I left here around 10:30 that night and finally found Wild Hawk around 2 or 3 am. Upon hearing what had happened to you, Katherine," he smiled at her, "he was like a mad man—wild—he fit his name. I thought he would absolutely come apart. Not taking time to eat, we chewed on beef jerky that he had brought." The Indian nodded while every eye remained glued to Jeb, making no sound. "The trip to Judgment Rock took us a good six to seven hours because of resting the horses. It of course took time for him to map out how and where he could best climb the severe cliff. Remembering," Jeb shook his head, "watching him climb, barefoot, clinging, clutching and struggling—" he stared into the distance as though reliving the entire treacherous climb, he rubbed his forehead and continued, "It was terrible to watch. He was laden with water bag, rope, leather strips and moccasins thrown over his shoulder." Jeb was definitely reliving the nightmare. "To know he could plunge to his death at anytime." Jeb stared at Kate and the other family members, especially Mary as she lowered her eyes, looking at her hands. He continued, "He had to move as quickly as possible knowing it was a matter of life and death with you staked out in the sun, Katherine, and all I could do was simply watch while he risked his life inching his way up the side of the treacherous rock."

"Finally, his Yawa brought him to the top. The climb he made was the steepest, most difficult, but the shortest way for every minute counted. He found you severely sunburned, Katherine, from being staked out in the sun, lips cracked, and covered in your body fluids. He ministered to you the best he could, cooling your feverish body with water, getting you to sip water in your unconscious state and as quickly as possible he strapped you very securely around his body, then secured the rope double around both of you. After connecting the rope securely around a boulder and testing it for strength, he then began the slow descent, protecting your body, Katherine, from being scraped on jagged edges with his own." He looked at the girl spoken to, seeing her eyes filled with tears. He continued—

"After reaching the ground there was a prayer offered and quickly you were unstrapped, given more water, placed with Hawk on Night Wind and headed for the Hawasee Falls which was near. The filthy gown was ripped from your body, Katherine, you were soaped, scrubbed and rinsed, including your hair. Wild Hawk and I took turns covering your nakedness with a piece of doeskin. The cleansing of your body seemed to have revived you somewhat. You opened your eyes, tried to smile and whispered Hawk's name. The rest you know." He stared at Kate before glancing down at his hands as though still remembering the rescue nightmare.

Mary looked at her lap, fumbling with a handkerchief, feeling so very ashamed of the way she had acted toward Wild Hawk. What a dreadful and dangerous responsibility he had taken upon himself to save Katherine. How could she have been so callous and unfeeling? No wonder John had said those harsh things to her. Could she ever be forgiven for the cold and ungrateful way she had acted.

For a short time the entire group seemed too stunned to speak, having been totally involved with Jeb's vivid description of the horrifying rescue mission.

John finally probed, "What distance was the climb Wild Hawk took?" He frowned, shaking his head, as though the whole thing was unbelievable.

"Around a half mile—give or take," the scout responded.

"Jeeze! How did he even do it?" John stood, taking a few steps and running his hand through his hair.

"By strength, love, determination and seeking God's help. The easier way to reach the top, which we wuz sure the evil ones took to get her there was between three fourths and a mile. Hawk didn't feel he could take that extra time, every minute counted in saving her life." Jeb explained this before some one else asked.

"Lone Eagle, we can never thank Wild Hawk enough." John was deeply touched by the young man's accomplishment and the risking of his life to save his daughter. "He is quite a man. Not many would risk his life that way." He shook his head, remembering his wife's treatment to Wild Hawk. Frowning, he gazed at her.

"Yes, he certainly is," Lone Eagle smiled, "I could not ask for a finer son." He looked at Katherine who was listening to Prissy whispering in her ear.

Mother Brandon's mouth worked, but no sound came out. She was totally beside herself that these two men had bathed Katherine's naked body. Oh! Dear Lord, what ever was this world coming to? The life and death situation was not the important factor to Evangeline.

Jesse couldn't hold in any longer. She gazed at her mother as she stood. "I don't understand why you don't like Wild Hawk. Why you treated him bad, when he saved Kate's life 'n he could have been killed," her lips trembled, "I don't think I like you anymore." Her voice raised, she wheeled, ran up the steps and into the house, slamming the screen door. The door immediately opened again as Jesse stuck her head out and bellowed, "Guess I'll just leave with Chief Lone Eagle and live in his village." Bam! The door slammed.

"Jessica!" John jumped up, striding toward the porch.

"Leave her be, John," Mary stopped him. "We will take care of her later." She gazed at her lap where she folded and unfolded the lace on her handkerchief, understanding why Jesse felt the way she did, but also knowing the child must be reprimanded.

The quietness was overbearing. Rusty took out a plug, popped it into his mouth, and tried to lighten and change the subject.

"Chief, I heard Wild Hawk is leaving the Echota in Georgia—maybe he's already gone. Ain't that right?"

Kate interrupted, eyes flashing at Rusty while her hands clenched her skirt tightly. "What did you say?"

"Ah said—hit wuz told Wild Hawk is leaving or gonna' leave fer thu' Echota in Georgia." He frowned, wondering why this girl wuz so upset.

Katherine stood abruptly, made her way to the porch, struggled up the steps as Prissy caught up and assisted her into the house.

"Did I say something wrong? Jes' repeatin' what 'ah heard." Rusty spit his tobacco juice, not knowing what the devil wuz goin' on here, but guess he'd done gone 'n put his foot in his mouth again.

"Rusty, you said nothing wrong. It just seems," John stood, stuffing his pipe, "we've all been on edge since this kidnapping—we jump and seem to take offense easily. We need to just settle down and be a family again." He looked at his wife. "Katherine is safely back home." He bit his pipe, puffing away as he stared into the distance. "—and Wild Hawk didn't lose his life. Believe we could do more with thanking the good Lord than complaining to each other." He walked over to the fence puffing away and drank in the mountain's beauty that had become such a part of him.

Prissy helped Kate to undress, put on a clean night gown and crawl into bed where she sobbed her heart out.

"He's leaving, Prissy, and," she sniffed, "I doubt he'll even tell me good-bye because he feels it upsets both of us so much." She caught her breath, wiping her tears on the sheet hem. "Of course it upsets me," she all but yelled, "and if he cared enough he couldn't leave me!" She broke down again while Prissy folded her clothes and let her rave on until she got some of it out of her system. Kate hiccuped and started again. "But I won't beg and I won't seek him, I'll just take care of me." She turned onto her side, closed her eyes while commenting, "Prissy, don't bring any food or water up here and don't let anyone else do it." Her sister stared at the figure on the bed, not liking the statement she had just heard, not liking it one bit—afraid of what Kate had in mind.

Prissy stood at the window looking at the mountains that were cast in twilight's magnificent lavender to deep rose hues. With a sigh she thought of the peacefulness these hills evoked. People just didn't stop to embrace the beauty and peacefulness. They rather stayed in a turmoil, and a few months ago, she was the worst. She let the white curtain slide back in place, looked at the bed and walked to the door.

Following a delicious meal of country ham, the guests departed for Lone Eagle's village. With dishes washed, put away and Johnny tucked in for the night, Prissy and Jeb visited Kate to see if she needed anything. She was in the same position as before, eyes closed. A complete tray of food was sitting on the bedside table, untouched.

"Kate," Prissy shook her sister's shoulder as Jeb eased into the rocker.

"Huh," Kate murmured.

"You haven't eaten a bite. Here's your plate of country ham, biscuit and everything that goes with it. Sit up now and eat something." Kate opened her eyes, turning.

"I don't want to eat and I'm not going to—so, take it back or let someone else eat it, please. Just let me be." She closed her eyes.

Prissy shook her head and looked at her husband who shrugged his shoulders before placing a piece of ham in a biscuit and polishing it off dreamily.

"Would you like some company, Kate? Just to talk." Prissy tried for any response.

"No." Kate emphatically responded.

Perturbed over her sister's action, Prissy and Jeb left the room. Something had to be done. She couldn't watch her sister take her own life through starvation and it looked as though that's where she was headed.

After two more days of begging, pleading, coaxing and sterness, Katherine continued to travel her starvation road. Mama, Papa and Prissy tried everything they knew but nothing mattered. Kate did not want to live. She was now too weak to sit up, even on the chamber pot if someone lifted her to it. They now had to place thick padding under her. Finally, at wit's end, John made one more try while Prissy did her best to console her mother.

"Honey," John pled, "how about drinking a little water and eating a biscuit with honey on it?" He struggled in his throat.

She shook her head as she tried to focus her eyes. "Papa," her voice was a horse whisper, "I had the strangest dream." She reached to touch her father, hesitating as though gathering her thoughts. "I was sitting on a bench outside in our front yard when I heard a loud whirring noise." She had to stop to get her breath. "When I looked up a large dark hawk hovered over me, then flew to me and took me by the hand." Her trembling hand grasped her father's while she continued in her whispered hoarseness. "Holding my hand he led me to a beautiful black horse." She attempted to smile. "He then dropped my hand and flew to land on the horse's back. When the horse turned his head toward me it was Night Wind and he nudged my shoulder. I looked back to the hawk." She seemed excited, her glassy eyes misting. "Papa, the hawk had turned into Wild Hawk." Tears streamed down her face, also her father's. "He reached for me smiling, pulling me up in front of him on Night Wind, held me close and we rode away." John gathered his emaciated daughter into his arms as her tears soaked into his shirt front while his dampened her night gown. He eased her back into her bed and left immediately, too choked up to speak. He had to talk with Priscilla and Mary now.

"Priscilla," John found them in the yard. "Go and sit with your sister while Jeb goes with me to Lone Eagle's village. Please find your husband first and send him to me." His eyes misted as he stared at his daughter. "Your sister is dying, Priscilla. She doesn't want to live without Wild Hawk and I'm going for him." He walked over to his wife and knelt down beside her, taking her hand in his. "Mary, I can't sit here, do nothing and watch her die because of prejudice." His green eyes pled, "I can't let her destroy herself. I'm going to ask Wild Hawk to marry her whether you go along with this or not, I have to do it." He pled with misting eyes as she put her arms around his neck with tears streaking her face.

"Go ahead," she murmured. "I know what she is doing to herself, I can't stand it either and I can't let her destroy herself." He pulled her up, hugging her tightly as Jeb rounded the house, leading the horses already saddled.

"Priscilla told me, and we're ready to ride." Jeb swung up on his bay while John mounted up, nodding a thank you.

The two arrived at Lone Eagle's village around 7:00 PM amid the usual noisy dogs barking and children excitedly laughing and skipping along with them. Hard candy was tossed to the little happy ones.

Lone Eagle met them in front of his lodge. "Welcome, John Brandon and Jeb. Somehow I don't think this is a social call." Eagle was a sensitive man.

"You're right, Lone Eagle." John attempted a half-smile as he dismounted, stretching his tired muscles. "We are here to see Wild Hawk. Is he around?"

"Yes, he is with Spotted Horse at his lodge. They brought in deer meat today and should be finished with dressing it out. Come on, I will walk with you." The erect chief strolled through the village with his friends, fringe swinging, little ones skipping along until he shooed them off to play. As they reached Spotted Horse's lodge, Wild Hawk burst through the door, immediately assuming something was wrong. His eyes flashing, his breathing labored as he gazed from one man to the other, "What's wrong—is—is—it Katherine?" He felt as though a fist had slammed into his middle. "Is that why you are here?"

"Slow down, Wild Hawk, with the questions," John responded, "Is there some place you and I can go and talk?"

He nodded, "Come." Even though it was a short distance to his special rock, it seemed to take forever to reach the area. He was having trouble breathing with his stomach in his throat. Finally they reached their destination.

Hawk glared at the white man, willing him to get to the point. John met the expressive black eyes.

"Katherine is dying."

Before thinking, Wild Hawk grabbed John by the shoulders, shaking him. "Don't you say that! She can't die!" Hawk's eyes filled with tears while he stared deeply into John's eyes that had begun misting. "She was doing much better before I left." The big Indian dropped his hands from John's shoulders as a tear streaked down his face.

"That's what I'm talking about. Three days ago Rusty and Lone Eagle visited us for Eagle to explain the kidnapping and punishment." Hawk nodded. "Jeb also explained your climb, rescue and descent. Katherine heard all of this when Rusty piped up afterward and said you were leaving for the Echota."

Wild Hawk turned, staring into the mountains. "I had thought of living with the Echota, but somehow I couldn't leave knowing I would not see my Katherine again." He wiped at his eyes.

John lit and puffed his pipe. "Since Rusty's statement, Katherine hasn't eaten a bite of food or had a drink of water or any liquid. She is now too weak to sit up or even be placed on the chamber pot."

Wild Hawk wheeled around, staring in misery at this man who brought such devastating news. Something must be done.

John looked steadily at the big handsome Indian whose pain was etched on his countenance. "If she can't be with you, Wild Hawk, she doesn't want to live. That's why I'm here, to ask you to come and take my daughter for your wife. She doesn't know I'm here, she would forbid it. She told her sister she would not beg for anything."

The Indian stared at this white man, hoping but not believing what he had just heard. Of course, he would give anything to be with his Green Eyes. Staring at John, he knew this man had taken the biggest step of his life. How many men would ask an Indian to marry his white daughter?

"You do love her, don't you?"

"More than my own life," Hawk gazed into the distant mountains as the late twilight painted its glorious hues. "What about her mother?"

"Her mother gave her consent before I left. We would both feel responsible if we sat back and allowed our daughter to die. Oh! Almost forgot—" John sat on the flat rock, suddenly feeling exhausted. Stretching his long legs he began, "I must tell you of Katherine's dream which she told to me right before I left to come here." Hawk sat next to John, still not believing what was happening. Could it be true after all of the months trying to stay away from his Katherine? Knowing they could not be together as man and wife, could this really be happening that Green Eyes would be his woman?

John told Katherine's dream in detail, for it had effected him deeply. After the vivid dream description as his daughter related it to him, Wild Hawk jumped up, his eye flashing with excitement.

"Come, John Brandon, let us visit the Shaman. He must hear this dream the same way you told it to me." John followed as Hawk led him again through the village until he rapped on the door of a lodge set apart from the others.

"Enter." They stepped inside of the dark interior with only a fire for light. The smell of sage permeated the air while the old shaman sat in the middle of the floor, cross legged. He looked up as the two men drew closer, squatting near. The black piercing eyes were sharp with intelligence, the face creased in wrinkles while wisps of gray hair fell in strings over the bony shoulders. "Old man know why you here," he grinned, revealing only a few teeth, "the girl." Wild Hawk nodded, quickly speaking in Cherokee. The old Shaman nodded.

"Please explain the dream, John Brandon." John's attention was drawn from viewing the many skins, bones, pipes and dream catchers. "Don't speak too fast, for I will interpret in Cherokee." John nodded and began giving a vivid description of Katherine's dream as it was told to him. When he had completed, the old Shaman leaned back, mumbled, clasped his hands and spoke in Cherokee to Wild Hawk. He smiled, waving Hawk on as the Indian explained the meaning of the Shaman's words.

"He is saying her dream is again the same as mine which happened many moons ago. He is saying that this is the vision of our future. He believes through our union a bridge will be formed that will help the relationship between Indian and White. He is also saying we must leave immediately for Katherine is very ill. No time to smoke pipe."

Hawk very seriously made his answer to the white man. "I accept this, John Brandon, to marry with Katherine if it be your wish."

John smiled, shook his hand and the Shaman's. "It certainly is my wish—let us speak to the chief and be on our way." They left hurriedly, finding Jeb with the chief at his lodge.

It was difficult for Wild Hawk to contain his excitement, his happiness, how his life had turned around. It seemed a miracle—it *was* a miracle. He thanked his Yawa as he prayed for Katherine to be well.

Jeb picked up his friend's excitement by simply looking at him. If a man's face could be radiant, this one was. It was difficult for Wild Hawk to explain to his chief the entirety of what was happening. At times, he choked up, but he explained firmly that Katherine Brandon was more important to him than anything in the world. The chief did understand. He had deeply loved one woman in his life, and gave his nephew his blessings.

After explaining Katherine's illness which demanded them to leave immediately, and since Katherine's improvement depended on Wild Hawk's being there, the three left. The young Indian made a commitment to return after he and Katherine had made their wedding plans.

The chief waved them on their way. His sad heart was not revealed in his countenance. This would not be an easy life for either of these two, a white woman and an Indian man, but if this were Yawa's wish, it would be his.

The three riders arrived at the Brandons' home around 10:30 that night, only stopping once to rest the horses. They knew each minute counted due to Katherine's already weakened condition. Prissy and Mary awaited them on the lawn while all others had retired. Prissy had just finished bathing, caring for and changing Kate's bedding and gown assuming Wild Hawk would arrive soon.

"Thank God you're back," Mary exclaimed, both women meeting their husbands as they entered the gate, "and Wild Hawk, thank you so much for coming." Mary's eyes spoke her sincerity and gratefulness.

"Thank you for allowing me to come." He was aware of the mother's deep concern. "Is there any change? Has she eaten anything?"

"No, Mary sighed, "no change, and she seems to be getting weaker by the moment. I have made hot broth if you can get any of it down her." Mary's comments were desperate. She seemed to struggle to keep the grief from her voice.

"Don't worry," he smiled at the mother, touching her arm, "she will eat and drink for me. I must go to her now for the sooner we get nourishment into her, the sooner she recovers."

"Yes, go—someone will bring the broth and water up soon. Go on to her." Mary was asking him to be with Katherine. This woman had changed, thank goodness.

He started for the steps, tuned, eyeing the parents solemnly. "Thank you for bringing me here and know that I will do everything in my power to make her well and happy." They both nodded as he turned and strode through the door to his Katherine.

He opened the bedroom door. The soft bedside lamp revealed the frail figure lying quietly with eyes closed, seemingly not aware of anyone's entrance. He eased down on the bed beside her.

"Katherine," he murmured, gently touching her face.

"No, go away," she croaked, "I'm not eating."

"Oh, yes, you are, my Green Eyes." He ran a finger down her cheek.

"Wild Hawk," she struggled in a hoarse whisper, "I'm dreaming of Wild Hawk. In my dream he's with me." She attempted to smile as she clutched the cover.

"It is not a dream, Green Eyes." Tears filled his eyes. "I am here with you." He gently placed a kiss on her cheek.

"What a beautiful dream," she sighed, touched her cheek and struggling with the words as Hawk grasped her shoulders, pulling her up and shaking her slightly.

"Open your eyes, Katherine—now." She struggled and finally with half opened eyes, frowning, she saw the dark handsome face that she knew so well.

"Wild Hawk," she murmured softly as she reached slowly with shaking hand to touch his face. "I'm dreaming."

"No, you are not dreaming, my Green Eyes. I am with you and never never will I leave you again." Tears filled his eyes as he held the frail body to him. Running her shaky hand through his hair, she pushed back, drinking in the beautiful countenance of her Indian.

"Am I really alive and are you really here?" Tears slid down her cheeks.

"Oh! Yes, you are alive and I am really here, but know this, woman. I will not wed a sickly, skinny one." His pretense at firmness was beginning to crack as he drank in the pathetically thin, pale features.

"Wed?" Her eyes became saucers. "Did you say 'wed'?"

"I said wed," he said lovingly, "as in my wife, my woman." He smiled, then laughed as a light spread across her features. With as much strength as she could muster, she threw herself at him, encircling his neck with thin arms.

"Tell me I'm not dreaming, that you are here, that you didn't leave for Echota, that we are to be married." She untangled her arms and pushed back. "Tell me—tell me!" Her voice became stronger.

"Yes, it is all true." He held her to him and kissed her gently. Looking deeply into her eyes, "I could not leave you, my Green Eyes, but now we have things to accomplish before we can make plans." Her eyes were big as she listened. "First, as I mentioned, but I do not believe you heard me, your eating and drinking begin now." He tweaked her nose. "You are to be fatted up for this brave does not wish to crawl under the sleeping robe with his woman whose bones are so sharp they pierce his side." He twinkled a smile as a rap sounded at the door.

"Enter," Wild Hawk called, not caring that he might be caught in a compromising position.

Prissy marched in with the chicken broth as Jeb followed with a pitcher of water, mug and glass. Both noticing a sparkle in Kate's pale face, a liveliness they hadn't seen in days Glory be!

Kate smiled, continuing to stay in Hawk's arms. "I'm ready to eat, I have to get fat so I can get married." She pulled Hawk's earlobe.

"That's certainly a great reason for marriage," Jeb sarcastically threw in. They all laughed, but Prissy added seriously, "We are very happy for you both, and where there's love," she smiled at her husband revealing her love, "there will be happiness despite the hardships." Jeb put his arm around his wife and pulled her to him. After a few moments nestled in her husband's arms she remembered why she was here and poured the chicken broth into the mug.

"Here," Prissy handed the mug to Wild Hawk who held it for Kate to sip. Never in her life had she tasted anything so good. To herself she murmured, Thank you dear Lord for sending him back to me.

She continued sipping slowly until she finished all of the broth. "May I have some more and do we have any biscuits left from supper?" The three eyed each other, smiling as Wild Hawk responded.

"Maybe one biscuit, but we will not over do it too quickly."

Prissy left to fetch the biscuit and relay the joyful message to the parents of Kate's change in eating habits and the happiness that radiated from her. "He is certainly the best doctor she could ever have," Prissy laughed as she climbed the porch steps.

After Jeb left, Hawk explained to his future bride if she couldn't manage the chamber pot by herself, he could place her on it. There would be no more disturbing Priscilla to do 'clean up'. "After all," he smiled, "I have seen you without clothes, I have scrubbed you down and I am fully aware of bodily functions." His eyes twinkled at her.

"Yes, sir," she saluted him, her cheeks flushed from the topic of conversation.

The night passed with Wild Hawk sprawled in a chair near the bed holding Kate's hand while she slept peacefully. She awakened with birds chirping their usual wake up chorus to watch her Indian as he stood at the Eastern window. He seemed to be totally enraptured by the panoramic beauty of the sun gradually peeping over the large hillside. As he turned, he looked into those beautiful green eyes that possessed him.

"Good morning," she murmured smiling, pushing herself into a sitting position. Even though a little dizzy, she managed to swing her legs over the side of the bed.

He walked to her, brushing a strand of hair from her face. "Good morning, my wife to be." He knelt down beside the bed taking her hands, looking deeply into her eyes. "It is still so hard for me to believe that with all our mishaps, all our trying to stay apart which made us both miserable, that Yawa, God, placed us together. He tells us, "That misery is enough, you belong together." He squeezed her hands tightly, almost too tightly. "You don't know this, Green Eyes, but many moons ago when I was in Echota at the great Cherokee gathering, I had a vision dream that was almost the same as yours. We rode away together on Night Wind into the future."

"Oh, that's incredible!" Her eyes were big and brimming. "Do you think it was Yawa or God talking to us?"

"It seems to be. Oh Katherine, I am so full of joy I am ready to burst." He stood, pulling her up and crushed her frail figure to him. "It is time for me to go outside for morning prayers. Do you need help before I leave?"

"No, I will manage for I feel stronger this morning."

"Of course, you do. You have me." He kissed her lightly.

She smiled, "I know, but make yourself useful. I need hot water for bathing and I'm thirsty. Also, if it's not asking too much, I'd like to have breakfast at the table on the lawn." Her eyes grew big as she smiled, so needing to be outside. "I'll dress in my robe and you can carry me. Lord knows, you've had enough experience with that."

He grinned, "Anything else, your majesty?"

"Not that I can think of right now." She could hardly keep a straight face.

He retorted as though angry. "Here she is giving me orders and we are not even wed." He shook his head.

"You love it." She heard his chuckle as he headed for the stairs.

Mary and Prissy were finishing up breakfast as Wild Hawk started through the kitchen. "Good morning," Mary was stirring gravy when she looked up and saw the Indian. "How is your patient this morning."

"Oh! She's much better—she's making demands—hot water for bathing, drinking water and she would like to have breakfast at the outside table." He smiled, loving it because she felt well enough to want breakfast.

"Isn't it wonderful she's demanding all of these things." Mary smiled at Hawk. "That certainly means she's better." She stopped stirring and turned. "Thank you so much, Wild Hawk. Without you she did not want to make it." She gazed at him steadily.

"I know. Without her, I would not want to make it either." He turned and started for the door. "After my prayers I will take the water to her."

Prissy yelled to him, "Don't rush—I'll take the water to her."

As he exited the house he wondered if Katherine's mother would ever change toward him because of the man he was, not because Katherine made it so.

By the time Wild Hawk had scooped up his bundle and was bringing her down the stairs everyone was seated at the breakfast table. As John sipped his coffee he saw them through the doorway. "Come on in, you two, and have some breakfast." All eyes turned to the two who now stood in the doorway.

"What's he doing with Katherine?" Penelope screeched, jumping up—eyes flashing from the Indian to John.

"Why, he's carrying her, can't you see?" Evangeline put in, "but," she hesitated, looking at her son, "why *is* he carrying her?" she sputtered.

In a conspiratorial whispered tone, leaning up, John murmured, "He's kidnapping her. I told him to come and get her." Mary could hardly keep a straight face. He continued, "You know she hasn't been good for anything lately."

"Yes, I know—but, but," Mother Brandon babbled, "You, what?" His comment finally seeped in while Penelope leered at the Indian.

"Oh! Papa—" Kate broke in, laughing, poking Wild Hawk to keep him from bursting forth. She immediately changed the subject. "Mama, I want to eat outside at the table. It's so inviting." She rested her head on Hawk's shoulder.

Hawk broke in, "I will take her there and come back for her food." Her breathing against his neck was driving him crazy.

"No," Prissy inserted, jumping up from the table. "Jeb and I will join you and we'll bring your food."

Kate called over his shoulder. "I want milk gravy, biscuits, eggs 'n that good salty side country bacon. Oh! It's so good and I'm *so* happy." She grabbed Hawk's face, turned it, and planted a kiss on his lips. Sighing, she murmured, "It's such a beautiful day." He chuckled and agreed thoroughly. Descending the porch steps, he carried her to the fence and put her down where she was standing.

"If you become too weak or dizzy I will not let you fall." His arm was around her waist as he pulled her against him. She nodded while drinking in the mountainous beauty and thanking God that he had placed them together.

Pretty soon the entire troop had left the kitchen to finish breakfast at the outside table. That is, all except Penelope who finished her breakfast and took to her room. She wanted no part of people who had Indians running around all over their house. And Katherine yelling about country salty side! Who ever heard of such! Well, she paced her room as her thoughts continued to race. She was not going to be a part of this sloven Southern situation. Indian men holding white women—why, it was indecent! Whether Evangeline joined her or not, she was leaving this place. She was returning home to Boston where there was genuine culture—civilized people. Why, Jeb Hawkins marrying into this family was bad enough, but Indian savages running around and that crude bantam of a scout slaying the English language with every breath. Oh! No, she could stand no more of this place. She would pack her valise today.

Outside at the table Kate called for attention. "Everyone please listen. I have something very important to tell you." Kate looked at her husband to be lovingly. "Wild Hawk and I are going to be married." She smiled, looking at each one.

Jesse, who was scrunched up next to Hawk dropped her fork, screeching "You're what? I thought he was just helping you out!" She stared at Hawk. "I thought you wuz' gonna wait and marry me!" All eyes turned to Jesse whose face wore a vicious frown. The family was rather enjoying the ridiculous situation.

"You see, Jesse," Wild Hawk turned, facing her, touching her arm, "Katherine just couldn't live without me." At this, Kate almost choked on a bite of biscuit, recovering after a back thumping from Hawk.

She looked at her Indian and stated, "Jesse, he is exactly right."

Jesse eyed them both. "Do you love her?"

"More than anything in the world."

"Do you love him?" she questioned Kate.

"With all my heart," was her sister's reply as she smiled at her husband to be.

"Geez, guess I'll have to go along with it then," the imp replied, "but somebody should'uv told me so I wouldn't 'uv wasted my time." Everybody laughed.

"'Scuse me," Tim jumped up, "I gotta get out of here. This is all gettin' too gooey for me, all this love stuff." He stalked off carrrying his plate and glass, "but I'm glad about the marriage."

"We haven't set a date yet. First, we need to find out when the circuit rider will be in this area. Anyone planning to go to the fort?" Kate questioned, looking around the table.

"I need to check with the Colonel on work. I promised him I'd help close the fort," Jeb offered. "No reason why I can't run on over there today—should be back before supper time." He looked at Prissy, who nodded.

"Thank you, Jeb, that certainly helps, and as soon as you return we'll set a date." She smiled at Hawk, her eyes filled with love.

"Did someone mention marriage?" As usual, Mother Brandon was a few minutes on the back side.

"Yes," Kate laughed. "I did—we are." She held up her hand, clasped in Wild Hawk's.

Mother Brandon sputtered, working her mouth. "Oh! My—Oh! My—don't you think?" She played with her silver, arranging and rearranging it around her plate. "Or, don't you think—uh—for you two that that is a bit unusual?" Not waiting for an answer, she jumped up, "I must go and rest." She started for the porch, holding her chest. Oh! My goodness, she thought, no one, but no one in Boston must ever hear of this. It's unbelievable for people don't marry Indians.

Jeb returned in late afternoon to inform Kate and Hawk the circuit rider would be at the fort in one week which meant the wedding would take place May 14th. If weather permitted, it would be held outside near the old oak in mid afternoon.

After breakfast the next morning Hawk took Kate aside to speak to her alone. He held her hand as they sat on the bench in the front yard. "Green Eyes, I am going to leave in a short while." At these words a frown creased her brow as her eyes questioned. He smiled, squeezing her hand, "I am only going to my village to be with Lone Eagle for this next week. Hawk can not be a part of women discussing some dress color, hem lines, how many steps someone takes. I do not care what anyone wears or does. I only want you for my woman." He was so sincere she couldn't keep from laughing.

"I understand and I don't blame you. It will definitely be a mad house around here for the next week, but promise me you will return the 13th, a week from today." He squeezed her hand again.

"You know I will, but regardless of the mad house, you must promise me you will eat three meals a day, and anything else in between.

"Yes, sir, I promise. Oh! I almost forgot, I want Little Cub to be our ring bearer. Rings?" She covered her mouth. "I forgot."

"Do not worry, I have rings." She looked at him in astonishment.

"You do?" He smiled, nodding. She jumped up, hugged him, and began pacing. "Of course, Lone Eagle, your Shaman are invited—what about my students? Oh! Just ask any and everyone who wishes to attend. What about Spotted Horse?"

He smiled, pulling her down beside him. "I have been so excited about our being wed, I forgot to tell you, he is now on his way to the Echota for his own wedding. You remember Raven? Of course you do, for he had eyes for you." Wild Hawk's black eyes flashed with jealousy. "Spotted Horse will wed Little Sparrow, Raven's sister. He left a gift for us in my lodge."

"Oh! How thoughtful, and you know I remember Raven." She smiled as his eyes flashed again. "Why, Wild Hawk, I believe you are jealous!"

"Thinking back, the way he looked at you and arranged to be around you—it tore me up for you were mine, even if we could never be together." He leaned closer, running the back of his hand down her cheek, his eyes softening with love.

She took his hand holding it against her face. "You know I've cared for only you. There's never been anyone else."

He smiled, leaned closer and placed a kiss on the tip of her nose. "I certainly hope this next week passes quickly. Now, if you wll get my parfleche, I will find Night Wind and meet you outside the gate for I intend to tell my woman good-bye most properly." He flashed a teasing smile while heading for the pasture.

Wild Hawk traveled at a leisurely pace, happier than he could ever remember being or ever thought he could be. He still couldn't believe that this woman he loved so dearly would be his. He was thoroughly enjoying the peacefulness and warmth of the spring day, listening to the birds chattering and singing their joy accompanied by the rushing stream making its path over the stones. He chuckled to himself—so glad he wasn't around that stitching and carrying on at the Brandons. Halfway to his village, he stopped for a few minutes to rest and water his horse, with his back to the path he stood watching the tumbling stream when he sensed a presence. Whether or not there was some sound he wasn't sure, but he half turned and ducked at the same time an arrow whirred by him.

Swift Antelope and Scar Face approached from behind trees, assured they could finish this Cherokee off who had interfered with their plans, causing them to be outcasts.

"You lover of the white dogs, sing your death chant for today you die." Swift Antelope crouched as Scar circled around to the left, all three with knives drawn. Before Scar knew what was happening, Hawk landed a vicious kick to his jaw sending him flying backward into a large bolder where he hit his head hard, crumpled to the ground and didn't move.

"Come on, Swift Antelope. Come and fight a man. You usually hide behind a woman's skirt." Hawk belittled him in the Cherokee tongue. "You will receive Hawk's knife for harming his woman." Enraged, Antelope lunged for his hated enemy, but not quick enough as Wild Hawk sidestepped, only receiving a scratch on his arm. Whirling, his own blade penetrated deeply into the stocky brave's heart causing a startled expression on Antelope's face. With blood seeping from his mouth, Swift Antelope breathed his last before sinking to the ground.

Hawk turned in time to witness Scar Face reaching for his knife. The Scar crouched, attempting to kill. "Come on, old woman, let us see how rough you are with a man after trying to kill my woman." Hawk pealed forth in Cherokee, again taunting the Scar, who took the bait. The evil one was no match for Wild Hawk's lean, muscular body that was in perfect condition. Struggling, the Scar was never able to harm the evasive Cherokee who was only toying with him. As Hawk tired of the game, he allowed his opponent to try for the kill, but side stepped, whirled and plunged his knife into the second heart.

He felt no remorse when he tied the two bodies onto their horses which were grazing nearby with a third horse. Oh! Yes, Queen Bitch would appear soon. He patted the horse's rump thinking had their wish been accomplished, Green Eyes would be dead and probably his chief, too.

Dancing Eyes peered around a bush knowing what had happened and pleased that those two were finally out of the way. She had viewed the entire scene from a distance. With heart hammering, she watched Wild Hawk in action. What a great warrior and what a superb muscular body, she thought. Having watched Hawk gracefully maneuver the other two to their deaths, she felt it was high time she claimed that body for hers. After watching him tie the bodies to the horses, she sidled up to him, purring her want while brushing up against him.

"Now we can be together, my handsome warrior, with those evil ones out of the way." She rubbed his arm. He shoved her away, causing her to stumble backward.

"Stop it, don't say another word." His temper was exploding as he grabbed her quickly and bound her hands in front of her.

"But, my warrior," she sensuously strolled to him again.

"Not another word—and do not come one more step toward me or I might slit your throat for the evil bitch that you are." Her malevolent black eyes became slits as she realized she was getting nowhere with this Cherokee she had idolized for so long.

"But, Wild Hawk," she made another attempt when he grabbed her, stuffed a cloth into her mouth, tied it securely, and dragged her to her horse. Throwing her upon its back, tying her feet together beneath the horse, he whistled for Night Wind. Sighing, he thought—so much for the beautiful, peaceful day as he mounted up dragging two dead bodies and a bound female to his village.

The entourage entered the village: the children's usual joyful reception died in midair when they viewed the dead bodies, the gagged woman, and Hawk's stern features.

"Where is your chief?" Hawk questioned.

In answer, a small brave pointed to the chief's lodge.

Dragging his booty to the Chief's door, Hawk summoned his leader as he dismounted. Lone Eagle was not surprised at what he saw when he exited his lodge. He stared at his nephew awaiting the explanation.

"I was on my way here, stopped to water my horse when I sensed or heard a presence. I ducked as an arrow whirred by me and it was then Antelope and Scar Face make an appearance, drawing their knives. They had been following me, but with my newfound happiness, life so beautiful," he chuckled, "I was not as alert as I should have been."

The chief nodded and smiled in understanding while Hawk continued. "This evil female," pointing to Dancing Eyes, whose eyes flashed fire, "deserves to die, but I have never stooped to killing females. Do with her whatever you wish as long as she is out of my sight."

Chief nodded, calling Little Calf to fetch his mother. Two braves were summoned to dispose of the two bodies.

Strong Woman appeared shortly, dragging Dancing Eyes from her horse. Listening to the chief explaining that the women of his clan should decide what manner of punishment they want for this evil one. Strong Woman nodded, dragging Dancing Eyes away despite her mighty protests of kicking and screeching. Even though the gag prevented loud voice noise, Strong Woman had had enough. Hauling off, she slammed a meaty paw across Dancing Eye's face, causing the noise and kicking to cease. She also explained to the maiden she was removing the gag, but if she gave any trouble or made noise the gag would go back.

Dancing Eyes was then thrown into a small security lodge that was bolted up and held under tight security until the women made their decision. First they would meet, make their decision and meet with their Shaman before anything could be done.

As the sun cast its pastel ribbons across the western sky, Wild Hawk sat on the front step of his uncle's lodge, leaning against the wall, his long legs stretched out in front of him. The chief sat near, whittling a horse for Jeb's baby. It was peaceful being here with this man who had been a father and chief to him since he could remember.

"You know, my chief, I can not fulfill the position of Chief to this clan after you are gone." He gazed at this man warmly who had and always would mean so much to him. "First in my life will be to take care and protect Katherine. I am sure you know our life will not be easy. The prejudice that abounds in her society and mine too, will make life," he stood, walked to the porch edge, sat leaning, his arms on his knees, staring over the village, "very difficult at times. Hawk hopes our love is strong enough to overcome this." He turned toward his uncle shaking his head. "I am sorry, I should not bother you with such as this." He looked down, picked up a stick and made designs in the dirt.

"There will always be things to worry about. That is life, but it is best if we wait for them to come, and meet them the best that we can." He smiled at his nephew who was his son. "This is a time for your happiness and nothing else."

Wild Hawk nodded, smiling. "You are so right."

Lone Eagle stood. "I have a gift for you to give to Katherine. It is something I have saved for your bride." He reached inside and brought forth something wrapped in soft doeskin. Upon unwrapping, he held up the most beautiful white doeskin dress, moccasins and matching head band that Hawk had ever seen. The intricate and colorful beadwork was amazing. Eagle caressed the softness of the dress. "This was your aunt's wedding dress, and I might add," as he gently touched the beadwork, "she was the most beautiful maiden anywhere. She has always been my only love." He kept running his hand over the soft dress. "Even though she has been gone ten years." He looked at the dress lovingly, as though he could see the girl when she wore it. His eyes misted. "Little Dove would want Katherine to have this dress whether she wears it on her wedding day or not."

Wild Hawk took the gift, touched by the cherished present. "Thank you so much." He touched the beautiful beadwork. "I am sure Katherine will be more than pleased with such a fine and lovely gift." Hawk re-wrapped the dress to leave with Lone Eagle until he departed.

"I need help, my chief," Hawk smiled. "You know a wedding ceremony does not have a great meaning for me. All I really care about is making Katherine my woman, my wife, but it has a big meaning to her." He smiled, thinking how he missed his Green Eyes. Quickly he returned to the conversation. "The people from our village who should be at the wedding, please invite them." Lone Eagle twinkled a smile at his nephew, nodding, knowing the young man's thoughts. "I will talk to my cousin about Little Cub handing the rings…"

"Rings?" Lone Eagle jumped up. "I knew there was something else! I told you years ago I had rings that were worn by your great-grandfather and mother. Those were passed down to grandfather and mother then to me, and now to you." He went inside and brought out intricately designed silver bands with turquoise strips woven into each that were unique and quite beautiful in their simplicity. Hawk's heart was touched by the priceless gifts of his heritage.

"Thank you so much, my uncle, for such wonderful gifts from my past, which I have done nothing to deserve." Running his finger over the rings, "and to think Katherine and I will be wearing these that once belonged to my great-grandparents." He looked up with misty eyes, stood up and hugged his uncle who coughed, moved away and was rather shocked at this unusual display of affection, but nevertheless warmed by it.

"I hope," Eagle cleared his throat, "that someday your son and his wife will wear these same rings."

Hawk nodded, entered the lodge to place these precious gifts in safe keeping until he left for the Brandons, and to quiet his struggling emotions. He thought being here in this village for a week would be restful, just what he needed, but it was not. Of course, he enjoyed being with his uncle, but other than that he didn't know what to do with himself. Knowing he and Green Eyes would wed soon, he wanted her now. He missed her, didn't want to be away from her. He chuckled, reminding himself of Night Wind after a young filly. He wanted to be with her all of the time. She had absolutely ruined him, but what a wonderful way to be ruined.

Dancing Eyes met her evil end four days after she was placed in security. Two lines of village women with sticks and clubs faced each other four to five feet apart while the evil one attempted to make it through the hundred yard path. Instead of using her strength to run the gauntlet, she cursed, kicked, and fought which slowed travel and caused her to be clubbed to death before reaching the finish line. Without any one village woman feeling responsible for the death, they were glad of the result for she was nothing but evil.

All of the necessary things were taken care of, and packed for travel. Having been hunting the day before, Wild Hawk brought in two deer, one for the Brandons and one for his village. They were already dressed out and distributed for the women to roast. The village women under the eagle eye of old Crooked Toe would also take care of readying Hawk's lodge for his bride. Life was beautiful, which reminded him in the evening to seek his special place, the rock outcropping for his meditation.

The moon was climbing its silvery path into the heavens when he ascended the rock. Standing with outstretched arms he murmured, "If it be your will, keep my village safe, happy, and may they have abundant life in their Tennessee land." The cool night's breeze caressed him while he continued. "Yawa, God, this humble Indian does not have words to thank you for all the blessings you have heaped upon his life. He does not know the future path his life will bring, but he knows you will be there with him. You made it safe for him to rescue his woman, and you now gave this woman to him. Others say it is wrong for a white and Indian to wed, but you must not agree for you make it possible that we do so. Hawk may not find the words to thank you for all of your great blessings, but you know his heart is overfull of these feelings." He sat down on the flat rock that he had rested on many other times during his life. This was his place when he was sad, happy, lonely, and now— so very thankful. He sighed, leaned back and watched the moon stream her brilliant path over the mountainous countryside accompanied by a multitude of diamond studded stars.

Wild Hawk arrived at the Brandon's in early afternoon, May 13th, astride Night Wind laden with food and gifts. Kate, having watched for him the past three hours was the first to hear the horse's hooves. She flew through the gate and flew into his arms as soon as he could slide down from Night Wind's back. Gathering her to him, he kissed her deeply while her arms encircled his neck. "Oh, my Green Eyes." He smiled that crooked smile, looking deeply into the beautiful green depths. "I have not known what to do with myself this past week. All I wanted was to be with you." He hugged her tightly and kissed her again.

"I know." She touched his face. "I've been the same way. I really didn't care about dresses or what the plans were." She reached up and lightly brushed his lips with hers.

"Katherine," he struggled with his breathing, "we will have to stop this now." He retrieved her arms from his neck, stepping back. "Our kissing and hugging will have to wait until after we are wed." She frowned: he took her hands in his, smiling. "My Green Eyes, there are things you probably don't understand about a man—about me." He looked down then back to those green eyes that had grown large in wonder.

"Yes?" she murmured.

Squeezing her hands too tightly, wanting to crush her to him, but knowing he shouldn't he abruptly burst forth, "Every time we have been together Hawk has had to hold his emotions in tight. This has been going on so long I can not do it any longer. I want you too much." He gazed deeply into her eyes.

"Oh," she stammered, blushing, "I guess I understand."

Anything to change the uncomfortable conversation, he turned to his horse, unstrapping the load of food. "Here, help me unload Night Wind. I have gifts and food." She went to the gate, summoning Tim and Jess, still confused over Hawk's statement about kissing.

"Take all of these to the outside table there." Kate opened the gate as the two, laden with bundles, entered depositing their bounty onto the table.

Tim eagerly offered, "Go on in, Wild Hawk, I'll take care of Night Wind. Do you think he'll let me ride him to the pasture?"

"Come," Hawk took Tim to the horse's head, had him breathe into the animal's nostrils then pet him. "Now, crawl up on his back." Tim had to be given a hand up for he was still a might pudgy to crawl up on anything.

"You may summon the family if you wish. I have a few things for them." Kate went to do his bidding, returning shortly with the entire troop with one exception—Penelope.

After all were seated, Wild Hawk began by handing the roasted deer meat to John while Tim and Jess unwrapped another. They took a sizable roast to Mary to see if it met with her approval. "Oh! Wild Hawk, it looks wonderful and smells delicious. You are tempting me. Thank you so much for your thoughtfulness." She smiled sincerely. He nodded, returning the smile.

"Did you kill the deer, Wild Hawk?" Tim questioned.

"I brought in two yesterday, one for my village and one for here since there would be several attending the wedding." He smiled at Kate. He then handed a beautiful intricately designed beaded bag for Mary and a fringed soft leather vest for John. Both individuals were overcome with Wild Hawk's graciousness. Mary swallowed, her mind drifting back to how rude she had been to him. Her eyes misted.

"This is absolutely beautiful, Wild Hawk. Thank you so very much." She smiled, rubbing her hand over the lovely beadwork. John was choked up as he tried the vest on, which fit perfectly. "Thank you my friend—my son." He clasped Hawk's shoulder as the Indian smiled, warmed by the term, 'son'.

Hawk then held up the beautiful Indian wedding dress, moccasins and head band for Katherine. The oohs and ahs echoed around the yard, each so very impressed with the beauty of the garment. "This dress, moccasins and head band were the wedding garments of my aunt, Chief Lone Eagle's wife, Little Dove, who passed away ten years ago. The chief wishes you to have them, Katherine, as his gift to you, but you do not have to wear them when we wed." Kate jumped up, ready to hug Hawk, but remembering his conversation she caressed the lovely dress instead.

Kate gently ran her hand over the intricate beading, whispering, "It's the most beautiful dress I have ever seen. Thank you so much and thank Chief Lone Eagle. She rubbed the soft doeskin against her face, almost bursting into tears she was so happy.

To Priscilla he handed soft moccasins, "and these are for Little Johnny." He handed two tiny moccasins designed totally. "Oh! Thank you, Wild Hawk." Prissy jumped up and hugged his neck.

"That'll be enough of that," Jeb inserted as they all laughed.

Tim was handed a beaded belt with his name woven into the beading. "Boy!" he bellowed, "Look at this and with my name, too—thank you Wild Hawk." Tim smiled, cuffing Hawk on the arm.

He handed Jesse beaded moccasins. As she was ready to stuff her dirty feet into them, Mary intervened. "Don't you dare put those filthy feet into those beautiful moccasins, Jessica." She eyed her mother then eyed her feet.

"Yessum—thanks Wild Hawk. I've always wanted a pair of moccasins." She also jumped up and hugged him.

Hawk then walked over to Mother Evangeline Brandon, knelt before her and began unbuttoning her high top shoes. "Young man," she jerked her skirt and petticoats around after he had pushed them out of the way. "What in the world do you think you are doing?"

"Why, I am releasing your feet from these terrible pointed toed shoes that cause pain in your feet." By this time he was removing her shoes and slipping a pair of soft moccasins on her feet.

"Oh—oh," she sighed joyfully. What heaven sent pleasure to have her bunions and corns released from their terrible terrible captivity. "Never have I ever had anything on my feet that felt so—so—wonderful. Oh! It's heaven. Now, come here young man." Still kneeling, he leaned up to her as she hugged him, stating, "Now you behave."

Smiling, he retorted, "You had better behave, woman." He squeezed her hand as he stood while all joined in laughter.

Evangeline stuck her feet out in front of her, looking at her new moccasin shoes, wiggling her happy toes.

Wild Hawk sat next to Kate. "I should bring more gifts to receive the many hugs, but I did not receive one from my wife to be." He looked deeply into her eyes as she turned and hugged his neck. She murmured, "After our conversation I was afraid to."

"Oh! No, "he took her hands, "my Green Eyes, I love your kisses, your hugs and Hawk wants them always," he whispered, "but until we are wed, I don't trust my emotions around you." He planted a kiss on her cheek.

"My gift to Katherine is at my village," Hawk raised his voice for all to hear, "I could not bring it." She nudged him.

"What is it? Tell me."

"No, you will have to wait." He was amused at her childish insistence.

John stood, continuing to wear his new Cherokee vest. "It is difficult, Wild Hawk, to thank you for all of your generous gifts, the food which will last many days and all of the individual gifts. All of the things are very much appreciated. Now, our wedding gift to you and Katherine." He puffed his pipe while walking to the fence. "You may select any plot of ground you wish on this farmland and build your own home on it if that be your wish. This will be deeded." John's green eyes drinking in this beautiful acreage.

"As long as you don't pick out our plot," Prissy interrupted. "Papa and Mama gave Jeb and me a plot for our wedding gift, too," Prissy chirped as she swung onto her husband's arm.

"Thank you so much for such a special gift. If or when this property is deeded maybe you should put it in Katherine's name." He looked into the distance. "Seems that an Indian is not allowed to own land." John was shocked at the astuteness of the Cherokee. "Thank you for such a fine gift." He shook hands with both John and Mary before Kate hugged them both.

Hawk took Kate's hand, drawing her away from the others. "If it is all right, I wish to be excused from other activities today, tonight and tomorrow until our wedding time." He continued holding her hand, not caring what the others thought.

"Is something wrong?" Kate frowned, stepping closer to him.

He smiled, looking deeply into her eyes. "No, my Green Eyes," he murmured, "everything is so right. I need to be alone with the elements, and I will also check for our special plot of ground. Before you ask, I have food and will fix my meals."

"I guess it will have to be all right. Remember tomorrow we can't see each other before the ceremony. So—if you need anything you'd better tell me now." Her eyes shone with love.

"All I need is you," he whispered in her ear, his breath sending chills through her. She giggled while the family tried to ignore them.

"There are things we must go over about the ceremony." Kate took his hand. "Come on, everyone listen. All of you who are in the wedding move over toward the fence. We must run through the ceremony before Wild Hawk leaves to spend the night somewhere on the farm." She smiled at him.

"Kin I go with you?" Tim burst forth.

"No, not today. Hawk will be alone, but soon the two of us, maybe we will let Moose tag along, will hunt and camp." He eyed Jeb who was holding his son and slipping the new moccasins on his feet.

Tim took this time to strap on his new beaded belt which barely fastened in the last hole. "Oh, boy, this is great! I'm sure lookin' forward to our hunting, Wild Hawk." He gave the Indian a toothy grin.

No one interrupted as Kate explained the do's and don'ts, how's and why's of the wedding ceremony. Finally, it was time for Wild Hawk to seek his camp site for the night.

"Well, don't you want me to walk with you to find your camping place?" Kate's big green eyes were almost angry wondering why he hadn't mentioned it.

"Of course, I want you to. Hawk thought you might have many things to do." He smiled down at her, grabbed his parfleche, and took her hand.

"I don't want to do many things," she murmured as they walked hand in hand through the pasture.

Mother Evangeline watched them. Her eyes were old, but she could see how those two felt about each other. She shook her head. Indeed, he was a handsome one, and she could understand how he could turn Katherine's head, but marriage? Oh! No. A few years ago she might have given him a passing glance, she cleared her throat, and he seemed to be a nice man. She looked at her moccasins, but people didn't marry Indians.

Hawk's and her wedding day! Could it really be true? Kate wanted to yell for joy. Instead, she kicked the coverlet off, bounded from bed and ran to the window. As the sun began its peeping over the mountain, she saw him in the distance, arms stretching to heaven for morning prayers.

Dear God, she looked into the heavens, thank you for giving me my Indian. I know life won't be easy, but I also know whether it be harsh or easy, you'll be there with us for you gave us to each other. Thank you, Dear Lord, and may I be a good wife and as we grow in life may we grow in You.

Kate threw on a robe and bounded down the steps still barefoot, yelling, "This glorious day is my wedding day!" She twirled around the room, throwing kisses, causing Mother Brandon to almost fall from her chair. Evangeline blabbing about, "An uprising might be easier to handle than this—this—" She glared at Katherine while sloshing coffee down the front of Penelope's dress causing her to erupt and bolt from the room.

Tim added his biscuit chomping blessing. "If Wild Hawk could see this mess and how crazy Kate is today, why he'd run the other way. Geez, look at her." He nodded to his exuberant sister as she pulled her father out of his chair, wheeling him around the floor in some dance routine. Papa seemed to enjoy it, catching her up, hugging her and both laughing.

"It's your turn, Mama," as Kate and her mother did a turn or two and laughing.

"I'm gettin' out of here before she starts on me." Jess crammed a sausage and biscuit into her mouth while exploding from the table, and rushed for the back door.

"Me, too." Tim moved faster than anyone could imagine and managed his escape about the same time Jesse did, munching, "Believe I liked Kate better when she was just sick."

"Mama, were you this excited on your wedding day?" Kate smiled at her mother as she squeezed her shoulder.

"You bet she was," her father intervened, smiling lovingly at Mary, "and we have four replicas to prove it."

"John!" Mary turned a rosy pink as she smiled at her husband, remembering her wedding day so long ago. Her John was the most handsome man in the world in his long frock coat, and she in her lace gown. Their vows said at the altar of the beautiful cathedral—so very different from today and this one.

Papa walked to his Mary, aware of her thoughts. Pulling her into his arms and gazing deeply into her eyes, he murmured, "She's still the most beautiful woman in the world to me."

Jess and Tim were thinking of returning for more food since all seemed quiet. As Tim took a step into the kitchen and witnessed his parent's embrace, he backtracked.

"Gol—it's still goin' on! Even our Mama and Papa! They all seem to be crazy today."

The crazy excitement continued until Prissy finally shoved her sister into bed in early afternoon demanding she nap. "If you don't get some rest, you won't make it through your wedding night!" Prissy realized too late that she had made the wrong statement. She could kick herself.

Kate flipped the cover back, jumped out of bed and walked to the window, pulling the curtains back. "Prissy," she questioned, "What do I need to know about my wedding night? Ah—as you know I've never been with a man." She turned, facing her sister awaiting an answer.

Prissy groaned, straightening a couple of chairs before answering. "Kate," she gazed out the window as in deep thought—remembering. "If you love someone and that someone loves you—then—," she looked at her sister, "joining your lives is a beautiful union. Just follow your heart!" Prissy was out the door before another question could follow.

"But," Kate yelled to the door, "You didn't tell me anything I didn't already know!"

Kate was slipping into her lovely doeskin dress when she heard the drum. Rusty followed and struck up a tune on the fiddle while Beatrice held forth on the organ. Oh! My—the guests were here! Her heart skipped a beat. As she placed the beaded head band on her head, she studied her reflection in the mirror. With her long hanging hair and Cherokee dress, she looked like an Indian maiden.

Prissy entered dressed in a plain but elegant rose taffeta dress, stating, "It's time—oh! Kate, you are absolutely beautiful." She twirled her sister around. "Simply radiant," she murmured as she stepped closer and hugged her sister. "Here, Wild Hawk picked these wildflowers for you. Jeb brought them a few minutes ago."

Kate's eyes filled as she drank in the lovely white twinkles and wild roses laced with green fern. How thoughtful he was.

"They're beautiful." She gently took the nosegay and exited the door followed by Prissy.

They descended the stairs where Papa waited, dressed in his new fringed vest and wearing a loving smile for his beautiful daughters. Whispering to Katherine, "You certainly make a lovely Indian bride." She smiled, kissing his cheek.

Prissy recognized her musical cue to take her place as her sister's attendant. While she traveled to her destination, Kate caught her breath and stared at the most handsome man in the world, her Indian. He was wearing a new all white fringed doeskin outfit with intricate design that matched her own dress. He was magnificent.

The chord sounded for the bride to appear. As father and daughter traveled the short distance to the arched lattice work filled with greenery and wild flowers, the bride and groom only had eyes for each other. Wild Hawk was awestruck, for never in his life had he ever viewed a maiden as lovely as his Katherine, his Green Eyes. Whether proper or not, he took her hand and held it as both continued to look deeply into each other's eyes. Neither was aware of the Adam's apple doing double time in the circuit rider's neck, his ill-fitting black suit, nor his overall state of nerves. They made their vows with love and sincerity only to each other as Little Cub approached, dressed in a white outfit similar to Hawk's.

Searching diligently for the rings in his new matching parfleche, Cub first retrieved two stones, a piece of leather and his special live frog that jumped from his hand to Mother Brandon's feet, causing brief hysterics. Rusty soothed the situation before Evangeline's swishing skirts revealed not only her new moccasin shoes, but even more than her plump knees.

Cub gave out a whoop as his sought after treasure was rescued. With a toothy smile he handed the rings. "Here Kate—here Hawk." With twitching smile they were received before Cub slung his parfleche into the crowd, dropped down, crawling on all fours in search of his toad.

The preacher shifted his Bible, cleared his throat, and attempted to continue the ceremony when the wind picked up as though whispering through the trees. This wind was accompanied by a whirring noise. Hawk squeezed Kate's hand, nodding as he looked above where a large Hawk circled, screeched his amen before settling on a branch in the old oak tree. This is where their feathered friend witnessed the final vows and tender kiss between a Cherokee Indian and his Katherine.

"Legend of The Whispering Wind"

"Legend of Whispering Wind" was first written and directed as a drama in 1975 by the author, Wanda Lee Jones, a creative writing, high school English and drama teacher.

After the first, presentation, Highland Rim Historical Society of Tennessee requested this drama be presented as a Bicentennial production.

Successfully presented again in 1976 at Volunteer State Community College, the play cast and director were asked to tour with this production. Due to the involvement of eighty high school students, touring was an impossibility. During the next two years, the author was contacted through Western Kentucky University Speech department to review this drama. "Legend of the Whispering Wind" was then selected as the amphitheatre production to be presented at a site in Wondering Woods, Kentucky, near Mammoth Cave. After site and cast selection, unforeseen financial circumstances prevented the amphitheatre production's completion.

Years later, after retiring from teaching and many requests from earlier drama viewers, "Legend of the Whispering Wind" is now in novel form.